DEVIL YOU KNOW

A LOST BOYS NOVEL

L.A. FIORE

DEVIL YOU KNOW

A LOST BOYS NOVEL

L.A. FIORE

Rosa,
Thank you for your support
for your support books
with my books
and promotion. It
was so awesome
to finally begin
JD Fiore
~ Liz

This is a work of fiction. Names, characters, organizations, places, events, and incidents are either products of the author's imagination or are used fictitiously.

Text copyright © 2016, L.A. Fiore
All rights reserved

ISBN-13: 978-1541345751
ISBN-10: 1541345754

Cover design © Hang Le, byhangle.com
Editing by Editor in Heels, Trish Bacher
eBook formatting by Erica Smith
Typeset graphics, title page art and paperback formatting by Melissa Stevens, The Illustrated Author, www.theillustratedauthor.net

To Princess Leia,
my first hero,
you are now one with the Force

PLAY LIST

Work Song...Hozier
F**kin' Perfect...Pink
The Glory of Love...Bette Midler
Say You Won't Let Go...James Arthur
You and Me...Lifehouse
Jealous Again...Black Crowes
Please Don't Leave Me...Pink
I'm Still Here...Jem and the Holograms
I Can't Live Without You...Bad Company
Piece By Piece...Kelly Clarkson
What If You...Joshua Radin
Trouble...Pink

Still Into You…Paramore
Perfect Memory…Remy Zero
Baby Mine…Bette Midler
The Sound of Silence…Disturbed
Shake It Off…Taylor Swift
Lost Stars…Adam Levine
Run…Snow Patrol

PROLOGUE

My horsey was brown with a white spot on his head. The ride went around and around and Mommy waved every time we went by. Daddy's big hands were on my back so I didn't fall off and he lifted me from the horse when the ride was over.

Mommy was waiting for us. "Did you see us, Mommy?"

She was looking at Daddy and smiling. She always smiled at Daddy and hugged him and kissed him. I was glad she didn't do that to me because it was gross.

"How about some ice cream, pal?" Daddy asked.

"Chocolate chip!"

"You got it."

Mommy wrapped her arm around Daddy, resting her head on his arm.

"Mommy, are you getting ice cream too?"

She didn't answer me. She never did. She was too busy staring at Daddy and smiling.

Mommy was crying again. She was crying a lot lately, and shouting at Daddy. She used to be so happy with Daddy. I wished it were like how it used to be.

"Hey, buddy." Daddy walked into my room. He was big. I had to look all the way up to see his face. "You okay?"

"Mommy is crying again."

He sat next to me on my bed. "I'm going away, pal."

A trip! I loved riding in the car. "Can I come?"

"No. I tried, I really did. Thing is, both Mommy and Daddy want you, but Mommy is sad. You can make Mommy happy again, right?"

I missed Mommy's smile. She always smiled when Daddy was around, and I looked just like him. Maybe I could make her happy again. "I think so."

"That's my boy."

"Where are you going?"

He stood and looked down at me. Mommy wasn't the only one who was sad. "Just away."

"When will you be back?"

"I'm not coming back. It's going to be you and Mommy from now on."

I didn't understand. Why was Daddy leaving? Was that why Mommy was crying so much? Why couldn't I go with him? My lower lip started to shake, but I didn't want to cry. Not in front of my daddy.

"You're the man of the house now, Damian." He leaned over and kissed my head, his big hand stayed on my cheek for a second before he turned and walked out. I wanted to be the man of the house for him, but he was the one who played with me, who talked to me, who tucked me in at bedtime. Mommy didn't, Mommy never had. I jumped from my bed and ran after him.

"Take me with you. Daddy, take me with you."

"I'm sorry, son. I'm so sorry."

"Daddy, please take me with you."

Mommy wailed as Daddy reached the front door, but I just stood in the hall and watched as he walked out. Mommy dropped to the floor, and I was scared at how sad she was, but I was the man of the house now. I walked over and kneeled down next to her.

"It'll be okay, Mommy. I'll take care of you."

"Go away." She pushed me and I fell back on my butt. "Just go away."

Daddy had been gone for almost a whole year. He used to call every week at the same time and I would sit in the chair in the kitchen and wait for his call. After a few weeks he started calling every other week and then every month and now he didn't call at all. I asked Mommy for his address so I could write to him, we were learning how to write letters in school, but she wouldn't give it to me. When she wasn't crying she was mean, saying things to me I didn't understand but knew were bad. And then there were times when she was nice and she would talk to me like she cared. One time she even touched my cheek like Daddy used to do. I was so happy that she was happy I drew her a picture in art class and couldn't wait to bring it home to show her. That day she was in her room; she stayed in her room a lot after Daddy left.

"Mommy?"

She smiled at me and I felt full inside. "What do you have there?"

I walked to her bed. "I made this for you." I had spent days on it. It was the merry-go-round, the last really good memory I had of my daddy and mommy and me.

She touched the paper and her eyes got all wet. "It's beautiful."

She looked at me and touched my cheek again. "You look just like him."

I puffed up my chest because I wanted to be just like my daddy. "Thank you, Damian. I love your picture."

"Do you want to watch TV with me?"

"Maybe later. I need to sleep."

"Okay."

I walked to the living room, but for the first time since Daddy left I felt like the man of the house because I had made my mommy smile.

Two days later I found my painting in the trash can. She threw away my picture. It was the first time I felt a pain in my tummy that hurt and it was the first time I cried myself to sleep, but it wouldn't be the last.

3 YEARS LATER

Mom was shouting again. I didn't know what set her off this time, but she was tossing things and swearing at the top of her lungs. Her rants were usually about Dad and always turned on me because I was there to take it.

She grabbed my head and forced my face to the mirror. "Look at yourself. You'll never be anything. You're nothing. Do you hear me? Nothing." Her lips curled up like I had seen in my cartoons, but I didn't laugh because when she did it, it scared me.

"He took the best years of my life and left me with you. He's a monster, a fucking devil, and you are just like him. His evil little spawn."

My body started to shake as the tears fell. I didn't want to cry, I was nine, but sometimes I couldn't stop them. Dad never came back; he had moved on and married someone else. He said he wanted me, but I knew that wasn't true. He left me just like he left Mom. And Mom hated Dad, hated him as much as she had once loved him. And I hated both of them. There were times I even thought terrible things, wanted to hurt them, wanted to make them feel what I felt every day since Dad left. I knew it was wrong. You were supposed to have kindness in your heart, love and understanding, but I felt hate and anger and rage. When she hit me, I wanted to hit her back. When she screamed curses at me, I wanted to scream them back. I had even thought a time or two how easy it would be to smother her with a pillow when she passed out from drinking too much.

"No fucking good," she said as she grabbed her glass and headed out of the room. "He should have fucking taken you with him, but he didn't want you either."

I *wasn't* any fucking good. The ugliness that burned inside me was wrong. Maybe that's why they didn't want me; because they knew I was fundamentally bad. Maybe I really was the devil.

CHAPTER 1

Only eight months, I only had eight months and I was out of here. The events of September 11, 2001 put things into perspective…as shitty as my life was it could always be worse. And watching the first responders, running into hell to help others…I wanted to be a part of something that made a difference. I couldn't lie. I wanted to get away from the hell I lived in too. I had met with an army recruiter and had taken the aptitude test. I was enlisting. All I had to do was complete high school.

My home life had gone from bad to a nightmare. My mother was a drunk and the more she drank the nastier she got. I took to staying out late, coming home only when I knew she was passed out for the night. I often hung out near a garage in the neighborhood because I liked cars and working on them. After a couple of months of coming around, the owner offered me a job. I had only been sixteen at the time and didn't have working papers, but he paid me under the table. I never told him about my mother, but he knew. He even opened a bank account for me in his name so she couldn't touch my money. And she had tried. Screaming and raging that I had stolen it and that I was no good and then she took it and spent it on vodka. I had gotten into the habit of not carrying much money and often went without food since there was never anything to eat at home.

It was lunchtime and I had forgotten to hit the ATM, so I was going without lunch again. I'd stop later to get something to eat on my way to work. I took a long drink from the fountain and didn't realize anyone was behind me until I turned to see Cam Ahern. He was in some of my classes. I usually avoided people, but he had the kind of personality that made it hard not to respond to him when he set his mind on talking to you.

"Have you got money for lunch?"

He was also one of a few who knew the situation at home. He had somehow gotten me to talk about it during one of the conversations he had instigated.

"I'm good."

"No you're not. I've never heard a stomach growl like that. When was the last time you ate?"

I didn't like pity or charity. "I'm good."

"Bullshit. You can treat next time." He pulled out his wallet and I was about to object when my eyes landed on a picture that caused my chest to grow tight and my pulse to pound. She had to be his sister, they had the same eyes, but where his hair was blond, hers was brown and wild with curls, and she was smiling so big it took up her whole face. I couldn't look away, just stared because I had never seen such unabashed joy before or someone so beautiful.

"Crazy hair, isn't it? That's Thea, my twin sister."

His words jarred me from the moment and I wiped my expression because no way would he want a guy like me sniffing around his sister.

"It fits her personality because she's a goof." He handed me a few bills. "Let's eat, I'm starving."

I hesitated in taking the money, but I was hungry. "I'll buy lunch tomorrow."

"Good deal."

We did have lunch the next day and every day after. And Thea. I couldn't get her out of my head. I wanted to know the girl with the crazy hair and beautiful smile. Then one day Cam invited me home for dinner. I didn't know at the time that by saying yes I would be forever changed.

THEA

"Boys, dinner. Thea!"

I stood in the hall out of sight as Cam came running down the stairs. He was only older than me by two minutes, but he played the older sibling card all the time. As far as 'big' brothers went, he was cool. He didn't tease me, he didn't mother me, he let me hang with him and his friends and he always had a shoulder for me to cry on. I loved Cam, even when I thought he was being a dork. But it wasn't my brother that had me hiding in the shadows; it was the lone figure that followed after him. Damian Tate. I had seen Damian at school, but I never imagined he would be having dinner at my house. He just seemed so removed from everything, like he was a celestial being who had come to Earth to checkup on his charges. My brother knew him, and well enough to invite him home for dinner. I might have to rethink Cam's dork status. I had watched Damian earlier in the kitchen as he stood in the corner while Cam whipped them up an after school snack. He didn't talk very much, he watched like someone used to being on the outside looking in. And his eyes, a pale green that hid so much—a sadness that was too heavy a burden for someone so young to carry. As he had done earlier in the kitchen, he turned those eyes on me and

16

it was the feeling that accompanied his silent stare, like he was as aware of me as I was of him, that I liked…a lot.

"You coming to dinner, kiddo?" I jumped out of my skin.

"Dad!"

"You're skulking again.'"

"I'm not skulking. I was observing."

"You were checking out Cam's friend."

"I was…" I thought to wiggle out of it, but what was the point. "Oh all right. I was checking out Damian. He's cute, but he looks… sad."

Dad looked past me to where the guys were settling at the table before brown eyes that I shared looked back at me. "Have you ever thought about following in your old man's footsteps? You have a knack for reading people."

"Becoming a cop? There are a couple of problems with that idea. First, you know my feelings about running, so chasing down a suspect is not going to happen. And blue is not a good color on me."

Dad chuckled. "Come with me. I have something for you," he said.

"For me? Why?"

"Why not?"

"But it's not my birthday."

"So."

He took me to his study and reached for the little chest he had on top of his bookcase—a chest that was usually locked. He opened it and pulled out a small package.

"For me!"

"Open it."

My hands shook with excitement as I tore off the paper to discover an MP3 player. "Oh my God. How did you know I wanted one of these?"

Dad gave me a look. "You're asking this of the man taking the detective test next week."

"Good point." I threw my arms around him and hugged him

hard. "Thank you."

He held me close for a few minutes, long enough that I said, "Geez, Dad."

He released me, but the look in his eyes had my next comment dying on my tongue. "Dad?"

"Edward, Thea, dinner is getting cold."

"We better hurry or Mom will have us doing KP duty instead of Cam."

I wondered what had brought on that look, but the moment had passed. "Thank you for the music player."

"Maybe I'll surprise you with something else. We can make it our little thing," he said.

"Can I surprise you too?"

He pulled me close as we walked to the dining room. "Absolutely."

Dad took his place at the head of the table and the only other open seat was the one next to Damian. Normally, I had an appetite that put Dad and Cam to shame, but not that night. Every part of my body felt on edge, like I was next in line for the rollercoaster... excitement and fear waging an internal war. Damian was the same age as Cam and I, but even at seventeen he was a big kid. The space between our bodies was only inches and I felt him, my entire left side burned from the proximity. He hadn't yet spoken to me, but I didn't need words because he was such a big presence, even being a quiet one—and he was beautiful, even more so because there was just so much hidden behind those eyes. I was pulled from my thoughts when I heard Cam laughing.

"He can cut his own food, Thea."

It was only then that I realized I had been cutting Damian's meatball. Mom had made her mega meatballs; they were the size of a cat's head. A quarter pound of her deliciously seasoned ground beef and I was leaning over his plate cutting his like he was four. My cheeks instantly warmed as I not so gracefully removed my offending limbs from his personal space.

Glancing at him, those pale eyes were looking back. "Sorry. I...

they're just so big." I wanted to fade into the wallpaper. Cutting his meatball? What was wrong with me?

He didn't say anything, but his lips tilted up just slightly and in response my heart pounded so hard it should have cracked my ribs. His beautiful lips parted and he spoke his first words to me. "Thank you, Thea."

Three words and I was a goner. I didn't understand what I felt for this boy nor did I appreciate the uniqueness of it at the time, but I did know that little smile and those three words was all it took for Damian Tate to claim a piece of me that I would never get back.

I was pretty sure when Dad put me in self-defense class, the intent was not to use my newfound skills on catty bitches. However, I was very close to doing just that. Brittany and Taylor, the banes of my existence, ate mean girls for breakfast. I understood the psychology behind why they were horrid little douchebags. They liked Cam, but I had encouraged him to stay at arm's-length because with the amount of action they saw it was anyone's guess what was growing in them or on them. Apparently, they didn't have a problem with being sluts, but they didn't like people calling them that. Their relentless passive-aggressive shit had started at the end of last year. I would have much preferred them punching me in the face. Sure it would hurt like hell, I might even suffer a broken nose, but the stories I could tell. More importantly, they'd get over their vendetta. Instead, I got smiles from one side of their mouths and sneers from the other. Cat scratches from manicured nails. Today was no different. Taylor's locker was just a few down from mine; how was that for crappy luck. It was daily that I was subjected to their particular brand of torture.

"Are you using a new hair product, Thea? I don't know that I've ever seen hair quite that *full* before," Taylor called from her locker, loud enough a few kids passing by snickered.

"Full enough for small animals to get lost in." Brittany was a sidekick. She never had an original thought. Her only skill was to parrot off others.

Yes, my hair was a bit unruly with spiral curls but I liked it. It wasn't frizzy, except during times of high humidity where it morphed into a terrifying sight, it was just curly. I ignored them and continued to swap out my books.

"I'd suggest you cut it, but then it'll stick out all over your head. Maybe you should wear a hat."

Taylor used a flat iron on her blonde tresses. Every strand was in perfect place. I'd like a minute alone with her flat iron and her perfect blonde hair.

"I don't know that they make hats big enough for all that." Brittany's laugh sounded more like a cackle. Her dig wasn't even funny; it was an observation and a stupid one at that. I wasn't even getting bullied by clever repartee.

I sensed the change in the air before I heard Taylor's sharp inhale. Seconds later my entire body grew warm, and since there was only one person who could get a reaction like that from me, I knew Damian was close. I didn't realize how close until I closed my locker and saw him leaning against them. He didn't say anything, just stared, and that was okay with me because I couldn't form a thought even if I wanted to. He then reached for a curl and rubbed the strands between his fingers. It took me longer than it should have to realize what he was doing and my heart just melted in my chest. He was defending me, without speaking a word he was calling out my tormentors. I fell just a little bit in love with him in that moment.

The bell rang. Damian playfully tugged on the strand he still held, then winked and walked off. How I wanted to walk off with him, find an empty classroom or closet, I wasn't picky. When I managed to pull my gaze from his departing form, I saw that Taylor and Brittany stood there with dropped jaws; staring at me in disbelief.

I purposely fluffed my hair—*Pantene* would be calling to get me into one of their commercials—before I said, "Yeah…" I let my eyes wander down the hall in the direction Damian had gone. "I'm thinking no on the hat." Then I walked away, whistling as I did.

The movie was terrifying as I curled myself up on the end of the sofa. I wanted a blanket, but I didn't want the others to know I was scared.

Damian sat on the other side of the sofa and every nerve in my body was tuned into him. After his silent rescue at school the other day, I couldn't stop thinking about him. He was quiet, but what he did that day…I wanted to know the boy behind the silence. The urge to slide across the distance between us and cuddle up next to him was strong. I wanted his arm around my shoulders, his body pressed to mine. I wanted to bury my face in his chest when I was really scared. Part of the reason for the need to be close to him was fear of the movie, but that was a very small part.

He stood and I had to bite my lip to keep from protesting. He had been coming around for a month, practically every day, and still he was so very quiet, often leaving without so much as a good-bye. I wasn't ready for him to leave, just having him close made me ridiculously happy.

It was tempting to twist my head to see where he was going, but I managed to keep my eyes on the television and the woman who was not centered in the frame of the video camera she held. I felt him before he walked in front of me and in his hands was a blanket. Wordlessly he handed it to me and then he settled back on the sofa, but instead of being on the opposite side, he sat right next to me…his body touching mine. I looked up at him and those pale eyes studied me right before a little grin pulled at his mouth. He rested his arm on the back of the sofa, the invitation clear. I didn't hesitate, shifting into his body to press right up against him. He smelled good, not cologne or aftershave, just his natural scent. He was over six feet and surprisingly muscled for a seventeen-year-old.

I felt a bit light-headed being so close to him even wishing I could be closer. I wanted to run my hand over his stomach and around his side, wanted my cheek on his shoulder or buried in the crook of his neck. I wanted him to shift us, pulling me under him so he could kiss me...my first real kiss. Instead I curled into him, savored his quiet strength and wished the same wish I had since he came into my life...that I could call him mine.

DAMIAN

I woke when my mother slammed open my bedroom door. I had been in the middle of a great dream featuring Thea. She felt so good pressed against me during that movie, which I hadn't paid a damn bit of attention to because all I wanted was to pull her under me and kiss her. I wanted to do a hell of a lot more than kiss her, but I had to control that shit.

The last remnants of the dream faded as I became fully awake. I jumped from my bed because I didn't want to give my mother the more advantageous position.

"Where have you been spending all of your time? There is shit that needs to be done around here."

She didn't work, had managed to work the system for a nice monthly payout. As far as I was concerned she could clean the fucking house, especially since it was all her shit littering it.

"Answer me you little fuck."

There was no way I was telling her about the Aherns, although there had been a few times I almost confessed everything to Mr. Ahern. He was a cop, he could make her stop, but he was also Thea's father and if he knew what my home life was like, he might not let me hang with Thea or Cam anymore.

"Do you have a girlfriend? Is that where you're spending your time? You have responsibilities here, to me. I come first, not some cunt." She tilted her head as a sneer curved her lips. "Who am I kidding? Your own mother can't stand the sight of you, what am I worried about. You're trash, anyone can see that."

She slammed the door closed behind her. Not even the memory of the dream made the knot in my stomach fade or the doubt that wormed in to taunt me. She was my mother and she thought I was trash. It was hard not to believe that there was some truth in her words.

I dressed and grabbed my keys. My mother was on the sofa, passed out. I fisted my hands and had to force myself to walk past her. It would be so easy to stop her shit, so fucking easy. Instead I climbed into my car. The lights were off when I reached the gym, but I had a key. After a year of coming in almost daily, the owner trusted me with a key. I suspected he knew more about my home life than I'd shared. I parked in the back and headed inside, flipping on the light over the punching bags. Sometimes this was enough to calm the beast and sometimes it wasn't.

THEA

After school I stepped outside and saw the circle that had formed, heard the cheering and yelling. Fights happened often at school. I was never a bystander, but for some reason I was drawn to this one. I pushed through the crowd to find Damian in the center of it all, beating the crap out of another kid. It wasn't just that he was fighting at school, but the cold look in his eyes that made my breath catch. I had never seen him look as he did then. As I watched, his body tensed seconds before his head lifted, his fist froze, and those eyes locked on mine. For a moment, I entertained the notion that he knew I was there before he'd even seen me. He then dropped the kid, grabbed his backpack and walked off—the circle separating for him to pass. Sure I crushed on Damian, but we had also grown into friends and he needed one then. I had to run to catch up and even after I settled in next to him, I didn't immediately speak because I wasn't sure what to say. Asking why he was fighting wasn't really my business, so instead I decided to try to take his mind from whatever had brought on that ugly scene.

"My friends and I are taking a poll on what mystery meat was served today. I think it was chicken but the color seemed off. It was pinker than chicken ought to be. Maybe it was something concocted in the biolab, an experiment to lower costs by creating a new meat-like substance that's a fraction of the cost of real meat. Either way, covered in the flavorless gravy and runny mashed potatoes, it was a culinary disaster. Bright side, now I have room for seconds at dinner. I wonder what Mom is making tonight? And will there be dessert? I love dessert; a meal is not a meal without dessert. Don't you agree?"

I looked up at him, but his expression gave nothing away.

"You should have seen my floor exercise in gymnastics today. The Olympic committee will be calling. I nailed it. No one can do a forward roll like me, my skill and artistry left my gym teacher speechless."

I got no reaction at all from Damian. My shoulders slumped as I stared down at the ground and muttered what I really wanted to say. "If you ever want to talk, I'm a great listener."

Silence followed for a beat or two before Damian said, "I didn't get the mystery meat for lunch. I've made it a rule that if I can't identify the substance, I don't eat it."

My head jerked up to find him looking at me. "And it has been a long time since I watched skill and artistry that left me speechless. I'm sorry I missed your floor routine."

"You'll see it when I claim the gold."

He gave me a little smile in reply.

My smile wasn't little, it went from ear to ear because the coldness of his expression was gone and I had been the one to make it go.

I was in my room working on a sketch for art class. It was supposed to depict some church in Florence, but I had sketched Damian from the other day in that fight, the coldness of his eyes and the harsh lines of his face. I didn't know much about his home life except that he lived with his mother and we never went to his house to hang out. I didn't want to step over the line and invade his privacy, but I worried about him and suspected he had no one in his life looking out for him. I went in search of Dad. He was working from home today.

He was behind his desk when I entered his study. "Do you have a minute?"

"Sure."

I settled across from him.

"What's on your mind, kiddo?"

"Can we keep this between us?"

He leaned back in his chair, but he was giving me the serious Dad face. "Okay."

"Damian was in a fight the other day and I know kids fight, but this was different. And the fact that Cam and I have never been to his house..."

"You think there's abuse at home."

My eyes burned thinking about it. "He is too big and strong so it's not likely he is physically abused now, but as a little boy. And you know there are other forms of abuse. You should have seen him at that fight. He was so cold Dad, so angry, but you've seen him here. He's quiet, but he is polite and respectful; he's kind."

"I have seen that. He's a good kid." He rubbed the back of his neck but I saw the anger. "Damian isn't the kind of guy who wants people messing in his business."

"I know, but I think it would mean a lot to him to know he has more than just Cam and me."

"What are you asking me to do?"

"Talk to him. He doesn't have a father figure and I'm guessing he doesn't even have a mother figure even with her living under the same roof."

"Why do you say that?"

"Because if Cam or I spent as much time at a friend's house

as Damian does here, you and Mom would have introduced your-selves to his or her parents. If for no other reason than to know where we were spending our time."

"Good point."

"Cam and I take it for granted how awesome you and Mom are. Damian doesn't have that."

He studied me for a minute. "Okay." Then he smiled. "You're a good person, Thea, and a good friend. Your old man is damn proud of you."

DAMIAN

Thea was baking something, but the puff of smoke that came out of the oven was not a good sign.

"Oh, come on." She pulled the tray of burnt cookies from the oven and dropped it on the stove. That action, combined with her wild hair looking even more unruly, made it hard to keep from laughing out loud.

"We can't eat them. I incinerated them." Thea was adorable when upset.

"How the hell high do you have the oven? Are you trying to cremate something?"

"You in a minute. I always wanted to be an only child." Thea shot back at Cam.

Before the two broke out into a fight amongst the ruins of the cookies Thea had spent the better part of an hour making, Mr. Ahern walked into the kitchen with a fire extinguisher. Thea huffed and leveled narrowed eyes on her dad.

"It's not that bad."

"I was asphyxiating on smoke in my study and that is on the other side of the house."

"That's it. I'm not baking for you again, ever. Even when I become a master chef and make the most mouthwatering treats, none of you get any." Her eyes turned to me and softened causing my chest to tighten. "I'll bake for Damian because he is a gentleman and kept his comments to himself."

"Sorry, man. You should have said something." Cam's comment earned him a pot holder to the head.

Mr. Ahern turned his attention on me. "Damian, do you have a minute?"

Shit. My muscles tensed even as I rose and followed Mr. Ahern to his study. I knew it couldn't last, but I really liked coming here. I didn't want to take a seat, it would be faster to walk out if I was already standing, so I stood by his door.

"Won't you sit?"

"I'm good here."

He moved around his desk and sat on the corner.

"I don't usually involve myself in other people's business, not a big fan of people doing it to me, but I wanted to tell you that you are always welcome here. And if you ever need anything, even just someone to talk to, I'm here. We all are."

This was not the conversation I thought we would be having. My chest was tight again but in a good way.

"You're seventeen, almost an adult, but still figuring it out. I've been there and if you need help with anything…finding a job, applications for college, finding an apartment, please don't hesitate to pick my brain."

I pushed my hands into the pockets of my jeans to hide that they were shaking. I hadn't felt emotion this strongly since I was little and my dad walked out. But unlike then, this felt good, really fucking good.

"Do you know what you want to do after high school?"

"I want to join the army. I've already taken the test and have spoken with a recruiter."

"I won't lie, that scares me a little given the state of the world. You've thought about that, right?"

"Yeah, but I want to be a part of something that makes a difference."

"You're a good man, Damian."

I actually wanted to cry. I lowered my head until I got a handle on it.

"I won't keep you, but my offer stands. You need anything, let me know."

I turned for the door because my eyes were bright, but I did say loud enough for him to hear, "Thank you, Mr. Ahern."

I walked right out the front door and went for a walk around the block to pull myself together. Never in my life would I have thought a man like Mr. Ahern would talk to me like he had. I had thought I didn't need anyone, I had done well going it alone, but I hated being alone.

"Hey."

My head snapped to Thea. I hadn't heard her approach.

"I thought you were staying for dinner. We won't have dessert because I burned the damn cookies, but..."

She drew her lower lip between her teeth and her big brown eyes glanced down. Understanding nearly knocked me over. She was nervous talking to me. This beauty was nervous around me?

"I was just going for a walk."

"I'm sorry." She pulled a hand through her hair and she looked back at her house before her focus came back on me. "I asked him to talk to you. I just...I don't pretend to understand your home life, but I wanted you to know that we're here. We are all here for you."

I thought Mr. Ahern's words rocked me. Hearing that from Thea nearly brought me to my knees. And still I had to ask, "Why?"

She worked her lower lip again, her focus shifting away from me. "You've got the prettiest eyes I've ever seen even with the sadness that lurks behind them. I'm kind of hoping that pain will fade if you hang with my crazy family." Her eyes found mine. "If you hang with me."

She irrevocably marked me in that moment, like a brand. I'd never been so fucking happy to be burned. I had to actually work at not falling all over myself for this girl, though I suspected she'd catch me if I did. "I'd like that." She exhaled, as if in relief, and I wanted to pull her into my arms and kiss her. Instead, I teased her,

"Even without the cookies."

She flashed me a smile. "I'd be willing to try the cookies again."

"Maybe Cam should be the taster."

Her smile turned wicked. "Good idea."

I stuffed the last of my things in a bag. I had made several trips already. I was moving out. As soon as I turned eighteen, I called Mr. Ahern and he helped me find an apartment. It wasn't much to look at, but it was mine. The Ahern family was even now at my new place. Mrs. Ahern was determined to turn the shit apartment into a comfortable and welcoming home...her words.

The plan had always been to enlist after graduating, but I could admit I wasn't in so much of a hurry and the reason was the beauty with the wild hair. I was addicted to her goodness, to her smile and laugh. She had gone to her dad. She knew me well enough to know I needed help. Nothing could come of it. I wasn't in the same league as her, but for the first time in my life I felt connected to someone and that was a heady fucking feeling and not one I was ready to walk away from.

It would be stupid to not consider how my moving out was going to affect my mother. And there was always the chance of her doing something to fuck up my world, but I was done with living in fear.

It felt good walking out of that house and leaving all that shit behind. A car pulled up behind my piece of a shit. The driver climbed out.

"You're finally doing it."

Anton Scalene. I met him when I was fifteen. He stepped in when I found myself in a situation. Later, he started to bring his car in for service at the garage where I worked. He came from a place even worse than the bullshit I grew up with. I used my fists to channel my anger, but he had channeled his anger another way, making money and building a reputation for himself. And he was doing it. He could be scary as fuck when he wanted to be, but he was a friend…the first I'd ever had.

"It's about time," he added. "Is that girl part of the reason? Thea, was it?"

"Yeah."

He studied me as I loaded my bags into my trunk. "You like her."

"Hard not to."

"Good for you." His focus shifted to my mother's house. "And the bitch?"

"She's not home, hasn't been for a few days."

He muttered something but moved on when he said, "I stopped by your new place but it was crowded."

"Yeah. Rosalie is determined to make my place a home."

Something moved across Anton's expression, longing maybe. He'd never had a mother either. "Why don't you come back with me?"

"Their dad's a cop."

"Yeah, so." Anton was on the wrong side of the law. He was smart, fucking business savvy, but a guy like him, coming from where he had and being as young as he was, didn't have all he had without bending the rules…a lot. "They're different."

He seemed to weigh my words before he agreed when he said, "I'd like to meet this Thea."

THEA

Damian had his own place. It wasn't much, but Mom would fix that. I was a little miffed with Damian because he had turned eighteen but never told us. Birthdays were clearly not to him what they were to me, but still there should be some acknowledgment of the day that he was born. My family had invaded and though he didn't say one way or the other, I think he liked having us there.

"Thank you for helping Damian get this apartment."

Dad was checking the appliances in the kitchen for their 'soundness' as he called it. "He hasn't had it easy. His mother is a real piece of work. I won't go into detail; that's for Damian to share, but him having his own space…it's the right thing."

"You co-signed the lease, didn't you?"

"They wouldn't have given him the apartment without it. He has no equity and he's young. I would have done the same for you and Cam."

I hugged him hard. "And this is why I love you so much. You've got a big heart, Dad."

He inhaled funny, like he was holding back tears.

We were pulled from the moment when Cam said, "Mom, he's a dude…seriously."

We turned to see Cam holding up a throw blanket.

"It's cold in here. He'll appreciate that blanket when he's watching television."

"He's a dude. He'll freeze rather than wrap himself up in this. Dad, come on, back me up here."

"What color is that?" Dad asked.

"Taupe."

"It looks pink."

"It's taupe," Mom huffed and snatched the blanket from Cam. "Fine, I'll put it in the closet."

"And the flowers? My man parts are shrinking the longer I'm here."

The door opened on the tail end of Cam's comment. Damian clearly heard it because he grinned. He carried several bags and I walked over to help, but I came up short at the guy following Damian in. He wasn't much older than us, but he carried himself like someone who was.

Mom walked in from the bedroom. "Where's the washer?" Her attention shifted to the door. "Damian. You're back. I was just getting your laundry sorted."

Oh my God. Mom was sorting Damian's laundry. I blushed; Damian didn't have a reaction at all.

"Sorting his laundry?" Cam threw his hands up in the air. "She's losing it."

Mom ignored Cam and walked to Damian's friend. "Hello. I'm Rosalie Ahern."

"Anton Scalene."

Dad tensed at my side pulling my attention from Anton to him. It was the way Dad was looking, his cop face that piqued my interest at the same time it made me nervous. I understood because there was something about Anton, the way he carried himself. He dressed really nicely too, but I didn't think it was family money. He wasn't a pampered rich kid, no way. However he earned his money, he had worked for it and I'd bet money whatever he did wasn't legal.

"It's nice to meet you, Anton. That's my husband Edward, Cam and Thea."

Anton's gaze settled on me and I swear I saw the corners of his mouth tip up. Weird.

"We were just helping Damian get settled and then we're heading out for pizza. Would you like to join us?"

Mom was the Tasmanian devil. She swept everyone up into her world. She didn't judge. Everyone was good until they proved her otherwise. My focus was on Anton though because he had that same hesitancy that Damian had when he first started coming around...a sign that he wasn't used to kindness or being included. That made me sad.

Dad had come to the same conclusion when he said, "Maybe you two could help me move this back. I'm getting too old." Dad could move the oven back, but he was trying to include Anton. He and my mom were the same in that people were good until they proved him wrong.

Cam walked over to Anton and held out his hand. "Hey. I'm Cam. Why don't you and I help Dad and let Damian save his laundry from my mother."

Mom rolled her eyes. "What's the big deal? I sort your laundry every week."

Cam called from over his shoulder, "Let's stop talking about laundry."

Mom glanced over at me. "Boys are so weird."

"Pepperoni and mushrooms...that is a damn fine combination," Dad said as we sat around a large table at the pizzeria.

Damian liked pepperoni and mushrooms on his pizza. I'd have to remember that.

"How did you and Damian meet?" Mom asked Anton.

Anton looked over at Damian who jerked his head, like he was giving Anton permission to answer.

"Damian was in a fight, five against one. I didn't like the odds so I stepped in. Turns out, I didn't need to get involved."

Mom wasn't the kind of mom to get upset about a fight, but she did study Damian and Anton for several long minutes before she said, "It was good of you to have his back."

"We've been looking out for each other ever since."

I was coming back from the restroom when Anton appeared, blocking my way. The man was ridiculously sexy, not as sexy as Damian, but he definitely turned heads. It was the danger that radiated off him that stirred fear, which was why what he said didn't at first compute for me.

"Thank you for helping Damian get his own place."

"Ah...well it was my dad."

"But you went to your dad, right?"

"Yeah."

"Why?"

"Why did I go to my dad?"

He nodded.

"He's happier than he was when we first met, but there's still sadness there. I suspect it's his mom causing it and whenever I need help, it's my dad and mom I turn to. Since he can't turn to his, I offered mine."

His reaction was very strange. He rolled back on his heels and smiled. "I get it now."

"Get what?"

"I'm glad I got to meet you."

I had the sense I had just passed a test, but I hadn't a clue on what. I felt his comment needed a reply so I simply said, "Yeah, me too."

Dad, Mom and Cam headed home after the pizzeria. Anton also left. I liked him, liked that Damian had a friend like him. I was going back to Damian's because I had something for him there, something I didn't want to give him in front of everyone else.

He'd been quiet for most of the night, something I was learning was just his way, but he had engaged a little…laughed, even smiled. And now that he was no longer forced to be near his mother, my hope was he would laugh and smile more.

Once in his apartment, I walked to the kitchen and took from the cupboard a cupcake with white icing and a candle. I'd baked a bunch, this one turned out the best. Damian's expression caused an ache in my chest when I turned toward him, his focus going from the cupcake to my face.

"I baked it, so fair warning."

I lit the candle and slid the plate in front of him and then I sang happy birthday. Tears burned the back of my eyes because his expression was one I would never forget. Heartbreaking. It was why I didn't include my parents or Cam because I knew how the gesture was going to hit Damian…hard. His eyes were bright when he blew out the candle.

"Happy birthday, Damian."

He responded by pulling me into his arms and holding me

there for a long, long time.

"What was it supposed to be?" Cam asked of the concrete-like substance in the baking pan.

"Brownies."

"A door stop would be a better application."

We were at Damian's. We usually stopped at his place first after school, hung out for a bit, did homework before going home for dinner. I didn't have much homework so I thought I'd make us a treat, but something went horribly wrong.

"It smelled good until it didn't." Cam wasn't helping with his observations.

"I think I need a jackhammer to get this out of here." I should just toss the pan and buy Damian a new one.

Damian was of a similar mindset when he grabbed the pan, opened the trash can and tossed it in.

"That was easy enough, but now you've got me in the mood for something sweet." Cam started rummaging through Damian's fridge.

"I'll go to the market," I offered because I wanted something sweet too.

"I'll take you."

The bakery section of the market and Damian, it was like I was living in a dream.

"What are you in the mood for?" I asked Damian a little while later as I hunched down in front of the bakery case and eyed the donuts.

"Pie."

"Pie." I stood. "You're on to something."

The kid working the counter called our number. "What can I get you?"

"What kind of pie do you have today?"

"Pecan, cherry, apple and chocolate silk."

"Give us a second," I said as I turned to Damian who stood with his hands in his pockets, grinning at me.

"Which one do you want?"

"Chocolate or pecan."

"Agreed. My choices too. So which of those?"

"You pick."

I huffed out a breath because that didn't help. I could be here for days. I turned back to the kid and leaned against the case. "Which would you get, pecan or chocolate?"

"They're both good."

"But if you had to buy one, which would it be?"

"Probably the pecan."

"It's not too sweet?"

"No."

"And the nuts aren't soggy? I don't like soggy nuts."

"No."

I glanced back at Damian. "Pecan?"

His eyes were bright with laughter but to me he simply said, "Okay."

"Pecan it is."

"We should do whipped cream. I can whip it up. Cinnamon or nutmeg?"

Damian glanced at his wrist, even though he wasn't wearing a watch. "We should make both or we'll be late for dinner."

We left his apartment a little after three and dinner wasn't until half past six. "Are you teasing me? Is Damian Tate teasing me?"

He brushed the hair from my shoulder and my legs went weak. "Maybe a little."

I had always been addicted to sugar, but I was developing a new addiction, one that was so much sweeter. I didn't realize I was staring at his mouth until his tongue touched his lower lip…sexiest thing I'd ever seen. That was until I looked into his eyes to see a heat so hot it threatened to incinerate me where I stood. Whatever was going on between us, I wasn't alone in feeling it.

CHAPTER 2

We were graduating high school soon. Cam and I were starting college in the fall. I wanted NYU, but I wanted Damian too. Ever since the night of our private birthday celebration, something was growing between us. What had been a simple attraction in the beginning had morphed into something so much bigger. I wanted to know him, every facet that made up Damian Tate, and I was running out of time.

He was joining us for dinner like he did most nights. Even Anton was becoming a regular around the table. He wasn't here tonight, though I suspected he wasn't because Uncle Tim and Uncle Guy were joining us too. Uncle Tim was a defense attorney and a friend of Dad's since they were kids. Uncle Guy was Dad's former partner at the NYPD when Dad was a beat cop before he got his detective shield. The three of them were a riot when together since Dad and Uncle Guy often teased Uncle Tim for his choice of profession.

We were clearing the table while Uncle Tim and Uncle Guy debated a case that was in the headlines. "It doesn't matter if he is guilty. The search was unconstitutional. It can't be admissible."

Uncle Guy made a sound in the back of his throat before he countered Uncle Tim's comment. "He practically confessed."

"The law is the law. We start bending it, it is a slippery slope."

"I don't know how you do it? Defending people you know are guilty." I was of a similar mindset as Uncle Guy. I couldn't do it.

"I don't focus on the client, I focus on the law."

"I'm glad you can. I'd make a horrible defense attorney," Dad added. And he would. He was too passionate, too black and white. There was right and wrong. No gray areas.

"Thea."

My head snapped up from the dishes I was collecting.

"I have something for you."

Our exchanges. After that first time, we exchanged gifts every month. One of the gifts I had given him was a picture I had drawn of him. He had been in his study working and I sat outside his office and sketched him. He had been so consumed by what he was doing he hadn't known I was there.

I put the plates down and followed him. I didn't know Uncle Tim had joined us until he said. "Ah, the coveted box."

Dad had received the box from his mom, right before she died. Grandma and I had been very close. I was even named after her. One of my fondest memories was of watching her make cookies at Christmas time. She was a petite woman who only ever wore dress-es. And every Christmas her counters were covered with cookie ingredients…flour, sugar, spices, crushed nuts, chocolate chips. It was a sign the Christmas season was in full swing seeing her deli-cate hands that were only ever adorned with her wedding ring, a three-stone band, rolling out the sugar cookie dough. Uncle Tim was right; it was a coveted box because Dad only put his most precious things in it. And every gift he gave me, the ones that fit, were always stored there. Uncle Tim went to the bar to pour himself, Dad and Uncle Guy a drink as Dad took the key from his ring and opened the box to pull out the small wrapped present…a ring pop in cherry.

"I love it."

Dad grinned and Uncle Tim just shook his head, but he was smiling. Uncle Guy walked in a few minutes later.

"Do you like my new ring?"

"I do. I would like it even more if it was grape."

I didn't stick around because they often closed themselves off in Dad's study to debate cases and sometimes it even got heated, but they always ended the discussions amicably. Cam and Damian were cleaning the dishes and Mom was sitting at the kitchen table with her feet up.

"I could get used to this," Mom said.

I joined her. "What? Having the guys doing the cleaning? Me too."

"I need to get them to do the cooking as well," Mom said as she winked.

"I like this plan. Do you hear that Cam and Damian? Mom is going to teach you to cook so you can feed us for a change."

"You could benefit from lessons, Thea. Your cooking isn't all that great," Cam teased as he looked at me from over his shoulder and winked.

I stuck my tongue out at him. Sure I cooked poorly, but that kept me from getting roped into feeding people. It was all part of my diabolical plan to rule the world.

"Are you staying for dessert, Damian?" Mom asked.

"No, ma'am. I have plans tonight."

I was curious about these plans because lately he seemed to have 'plans' often.

"And you, Cam?"

"I'm going to a movie with Shelly."

Shelly was Cam's girlfriend du jour. She was okay for an airhead.

"That's more dessert for us, Thea."

Curious about Damian's plans, I wasn't as enthusiastic as I

usually would be when I said, "Works for me."

I lingered in the hall after saying my goodbyes to Damian—Dad would say I was skulking again—and heard he and Cam making plans to meet up later. Cam had said he was seeing Shelly, so why was he making plans to hang with Damian? What was even stranger, I recognized the address they were discussing. The place was close to home, but there were no clubs or bars or hangouts there. I was much like a cat, curious to a fault, so that night when Cam left the house I did too. I gave him a head start because he would drag me back home if he saw me.

The destination was a brick building not far from our house that used to be a deli but had shut down years ago. As far as I knew it was abandoned. Inside, voices came from the lower level. I didn't immediately go in, waited for a group of people so I could tuck in with them. The place was crowded—a good thing so I could stay hidden—and at first I thought it was illegal gambling and wasn't sure how I felt about Cam and Damian getting messed up in that, particularly with Dad being a cop. And then I saw Damian. He stood in the middle of a circle of people that had formed around him. He wasn't alone, another guy stood with him. The fight at school flashed through my head and yet somehow I knew this was going to be so much worse.

"Now for the fight you've all been waiting for. Damian isn't one for pageantry so let's just get on with it."

"Damian is so hot. I'm going after that."

My head snapped around to the skanky chick who was eyeing my boy. He wasn't really mine, but I definitely saw him first.

"Me too, let's make it a party," her equally slutty friend purred as they high-fived each other while I battled the overwhelming need to yank their hair, hard. My heart pounded even as jealousy burned through me and my stomach clenched when Damian and the kid started to fight, bare knuckle, no holds barred. The kid moved around a lot, he was tall and lanky and had fast hands that repeatedly nailed Damian in the face and gut, but it was Damian I couldn't pull my eyes from. He took the hits, like someone manning up to take his punishment, and yet the brutal attack didn't seem to have any effect on him. He moved with deliberateness and control that made him look almost possessed. I had the sense that who he fought wasn't what he fought. And when he struck, he was fast with so much behind his punches the other guy stumbled backwards from the bone-jarring hits. His opponent got in a double punch, one that halted Damian's forward momentum and jerked his head back. He wiped at his nose and looked at the blood before turning his focus back on the one he fought. If I'd been that dude, I would have run away because Damian looked positively lethal—the sight of his blood only fired him up more. The fight lasted no more than ten minutes before Damian caught the guy under the jaw with a punch so vicious he was airborne before landing in a heap on the dirty cement floor. Damian stood in the center of the circle as his fans cheered his victory and he looked totally and completely alone. Cam and Anton appeared. Not alone, I liked that...a lot. They talked for a few minutes before shaking hands. Cam and Anton left together and when I turned my focus back on Damian he was gone. Before I could scan the crowd for him, a hand wrapped around mine...one with cuts and blood on the knuckles. It was Damian and he looked pissed.

"What the fuck are you doing here?"

My heart hurt seeing his face—a cut near his left eye, blood smeared down his cheek and a blooming bruise on his jaw. "I heard you and Cam talking. I was curious."

He had been walking me toward the exit but those words stopped him. His feet sort of rooted themselves to the concrete floor as his head turned in my direction. "So you walked here alone?"

"It wasn't far."

That wasn't the right answer apparently because he hissed between his teeth. It wasn't an actual word, just a release of frustration.

He started toward the exit again. "What are you fighting when you are out there?"

We had just reached the stairs when he pulled me behind them and pressed me up against the wall. "Come again?"

"When you fight, what are you fighting?"

"Not who am I fighting?"

"No, your opponent isn't what you're fighting."

He leaned in and lowered his head to look me right in the eyes. "How do you know that?"

I gently wiped the blood from his face. "I know you."

He had the strangest reaction to that. He closed his eyes, like he was in pain, and lowered his forehead to my shoulder. "This can't happen."

Those words caused a chill to move right down my spine. He was wrong. It totally could and should happen. "Why not?"

He lifted his head and for the first time I saw so much more in those eyes. "Cam is a good friend and your parents are like my own."

"And?"

His lips brushed along my jaw and I had to lock my knees to keep from sliding down the wall. "And if I did to you all the things I wanted, I couldn't sit at their table without them knowing that I claimed every part of you."

I didn't know what these things were, but I really, really wanted him to show me. "I'm still not seeing how this is a bad thing." I had never had anyone look at me the way he was. Like I was a hot fudge sundae. I bit my lip because I was very close to begging him to kiss me. His eyes went to my mouth just as a sound rolled up his throat.

"One taste." The words were more a growl as his fingers threaded through my hair and he palmed the back of my head seconds before his mouth claimed mine. I had never kissed a boy before; closed mouth kisses sure, but not open-mouth, tongue tying, halleluiah-inspiring kisses. I pressed into his body and I fit like I was made for him. His arm wrapped around my waist as he pulled me even closer to take the kiss deeper and all I wanted was for the world to stop so I could live in this perfect moment forever. My lips were sore and I was breathless and light-headed when he ended it.

"I need to get you home."

I didn't want to go home. Not yet. "I don't want to go home."

"I need to take you home."

"Why?"

He touched my chin to hold my gaze on his. "Because I want you, every part of you, and I'm feeling reckless enough to not care about the consequences."

Heat pooled between my legs and I felt both embarrassed by my body's reaction and reckless too. "I want you. Be my first." *And my last.*

"Don't offer me that, Thea."

He reached for my hand and led me out of the abandoned building and down the street to his car. We didn't speak during the ride home. He told me not to offer him my virginity, but I already had. He pulled up to the curb in front of my house. Uncle Tim and Uncle Guy were still over and likely out back with Mom and Dad.

"Thanks for the ride." I reached for the handle, but his next words stopped me.

"Being your first is special and you should only offer that to someone you love."

I couldn't look at him or he'd see my tears. "I just did." Then I climbed from the car and ran up the steps and right to my room. Only then did I let the tears fall from the pain of his rejection.

DAMIAN

I held the steering wheel so tightly I was surprised the thing didn't break into pieces. Every instinct in me said to get out of the damn car, to follow her, to claim her. To hold her close and never let her go. But she was beauty and I was sin.

I just did. Those three words should not have the power to render me weak, and yet that was exactly how I felt when those words came from her and in the context they were given. I shouldn't have watched, I should have driven away, but I couldn't. I watched her run from me, and the words I felt but didn't say. I shouldn't have kissed her and yet I would take countless punches to the face and listen to the never-ending rhetoric spewed from my mother's vile mouth just to kiss her again. Imagining what she tasted and felt like had driven me to the edge of madness and now knowing, I had happily slipped over that edge. Our kiss would haunt me, would become one of the many ghosts I fought to keep at bay.

I went home and right to the punching bag I had setup in the living room, a move in gift from Anton. I pounded on that bag until my body was too exhausted to feel anything else and still I ached for her.

THEA

I was pulled from my homework when something hit my bedroom window. Once, twice…on the third tap, I looked outside to see Damian. It had been a week since we kissed and I knew after badgering Cam that Damian was fighting every night. He never came here after a fight and fear that something was wrong had me running down the stairs and out the back door. He hadn't moved, just stood there with his hands in the pockets of his jeans.

"Damian."

"I can't stop thinking about you."

My legs went weak and I had to make a conscious effort to keep them under me. I studied his face, the bruises at his jaw and the swollen eye. My heart hurt.

"Why do you have to?"

"I'm not good enough for you."

"That's bullshit."

"No, that's a fact. And even knowing these hands have no business touching you, it's all I want. I'd fucking sell my soul to have you for just a night."

"You don't have to sell your soul, not when I want you just as badly."

"Give me Saturday."

Nerves had me shaking from my head right down to my toes. "Yes."

The pad of his thumb rubbed along my lower lip. "I'll pick you up around noon."

"I'll be standing at the curb."

"Sweet dreams." He turned from me but not before I saw him taste the thumb he'd used to touch my lips. There was something so very erotic about that gesture, but moving at the same time. I stood in the yard long after he walked away. I was having sex for the first time on Saturday, and with Damian. The smile was slow to form but lasted for the rest of the night.

Damian and I often hung out, so Mom hadn't even questioned it when I mentioned I was hanging with him for the day. He arrived at noon and I was at the curb, more for him than me since I didn't want him to feel awkward around my parents. If he felt guilty, it might cause him to have second thoughts. He pulled up to the curb and I knew better than to open the door. He walked around the car and held the door for me. He looked good dressed in jeans that looked newer than his usual faded ones and a button down shirt that was the same color as his eyes.

As soon as he settled behind the wheel, those pale eyes turned to me. "What are you in the mood to eat?"

Me, the one who was always hungry couldn't eat, the butterflies in my stomach made that impossible. "I'm not hungry."

His eyes went from pale to dark in a flash. "Are you sure?"

"Very."

He seemed to debate with himself, the gentleman in him wanting to make the moment special, but it already was special because of him. We didn't speak again until we were in his apartment. He had cleaned, and thinking of Damian Tate cleaning his apartment made me smile.

"What?"

"You cleaned your apartment."

"I had a reason to. Are you sure you want this?"

"Kiss me, Damian."

He didn't need to be asked again. He closed the distance, but this time his kiss wasn't just a kiss, it was a claiming. He explored my mouth as his hands moved over my body, learning every curve. For the first few minutes, I was lost in his kiss and all the feelings it stirred in me, but then I became as interested in learning his body as he was in mine. My touch wasn't as sure as his, my hands touched his sides before moving to his back, up the hard slabs of muscle to his shoulders. His fingers threaded through my hair and tilted my head so he could kiss me deeper as his other arm wrapped around my waist and pulled me right up against him, chest to thigh. Every nerve was on fire when Damian took a step back, thinking he was retreating had me biting my lip to keep from protesting.

He wasn't retreating. He reached for my blouse and slowly unbuttoned it, his finger running a trail down the valley between my breasts. No sooner was my blouse on the floor that my bra followed. The harsh inhale from him not only made me feel ridiculously sexy but rid me of the last of my nerves. I reached for his shirt, pulling it from his jeans and unbuttoned it as slowly as he had mine. He had nothing on under it, so I was gifted with the sight of his muscled chest and abs that formed the eight muscles leading down to the part of him I was most interested in. "You're beautiful."

In the next breath I was in his arms, my breasts pressed against his naked chest and just that contact started a quivering between my legs. He lifted me into his arms, swung me up like I weighed nothing, and walked me to his room. He dropped me to my feet and worked on getting my jeans off, and when he lowered himself down my body to follow the denim down my legs, I moaned feeling the warmth of his breath teasing the curls between my legs.

"Spread your legs for me, baby."

My legs had gone boneless, my fingers digging into Damian's shoulders for balance as I did as he asked, exposing the most vulnerable part of myself to him.

"I'm going to kiss you here."

I knew the mechanics of sex, but it was a whole other matter having a man like Damian on his knees in front of me telling me, in that deep dark voice, what he intended.

"Thea?"

"Don't make me beg."

He chuckled, the sound wrapped around my heart and then his lips were on me, his tongue, and I cried out because nothing had ever felt so incredible. He teased me, touching my clit, moving deeper but never giving me what I wanted. I felt myself falling backwards onto the bed, his fingers on my thighs almost hurt as he yanked me to the edge seconds before his tongue pushed into me. Lights flashed behind my closed lids as the most intense pleasure caused chills to ripple over every nerve ending. I would give him anything. Offer him anything to keep him right where he was, doing exactly what he was doing.

"Don't stop, please don't stop." My fingers curled in the sheets but as his fingers started working in tandem with his tongue and teeth, my hands moved to his head, my fingers fisting his hair as my hips moved against his face. When I came, the intensity of the orgasm brought tears to my eyes even as they rolled into the back of my head. I felt so deliciously sated. He moved and I heard the rustling of clothes stirring me from my blissful moment. The sight of him standing over me, the beauty of his muscled body, his erection that was slightly terrifying in size, sated was replaced with desire so profound I became bold. I moved further up on the bed and spread my legs even wider. It was all the invitation he needed. He rolled on a condom and covered my body with his own.

His kissed me and I tasted myself on his tongue. His mouth moved to my jaw. "You're so sweet. Can you taste it?"

He kissed me again but harder. "One night isn't going to be enough," he whispered.

I pulled my hands through his hair and forced his gaze on me. "I don't want just one night with you."

"I need to be inside you. Are you ready for me?"

"Yes."

His hand disappeared between our bodies and I felt the tip of his cock touching me right where I ached for him. "It's going to hurt."

"I don't care."

He kissed me again, deep and wet, then I felt a burning between my legs as he thrust forward. I tensed as my fingers dug into his arms.

"I'm sorry."

It hurt, I wasn't going to lie, but Damian was inside me. We were connected in the most intimate way possible. It could hurt a thousand times more than it did and I would happily take it to have him part of me.

It was me who ran my thumb over his lips, his tongue darting out to taste me. "You're mine now," I whispered.

He pulled from me then sank in deeper. My legs fell open wider as he slowly moved, turning the pain into pleasure. His dark head lowered and his lips brushed over my nipple before he sucked me into his mouth. I'd heard about this, never thought it could be all that enjoyable. I was wrong. Oh so wrong. It was so incredible I guided my neglected breast to his mouth. Damian was consuming me and still he wasn't close enough, deep enough. My body went tight as I stood on the precipice of the next orgasm.

"I'm coming, Thea. Come with me."

And I did, right before he stilled as pure pleasure moved over his face. He stayed where he was, so still, and I feared guilt was pushing out pleasure. Instead he opened his eyes and smiled at me. The first real smile I'd ever seen from him.

"I'll feed you then you're back in my bed."

"I like this plan."

I had to get home, but I didn't want to leave him. He was sleeping, his face turned to me, his back exposed and the sheet just brushing the curve of his ass. I sat on a chair with my feet on the bed and sketched him.

"I need to get you home."

"Just a few more minutes."

His eyes opened. "What are you doing?"

I placed the sketch on his pillow. He rose to his elbows and studied it.

"You are really talented."

"It's easy when you have a beautiful subject."

Those pale eyes flashed hot then he pulled me onto the bed. "You're right, we have a few more minutes."

The whole week that followed I spent in a daze. I was in love with Damian, deep irrevocable love. I stood near the school and waited for him to get the car, he insisted because rain was threatening. I hadn't been standing there long when the skies opened up and a drenching rain poured down. Damian arrived only minutes later but I was soaked to the skin. I reached for the door, but he was faster, coming around to join me in the rain.

"You're a bit wet."

"You are now too."

"Drowned rat is a good look on you."

I playfully punched him in the arm. "Funny."

He moved closer and right there in front of our school, he kissed me senseless. His lips lingered just out of reach of mine. "Hi."

"Hi."

He held the door for me and grinned. He didn't rush around the car to get out of the rain. He strolled around it and folded himself behind the wheel. "My place. I want to see you wet and naked."

Everything below my waist throbbed.

He touched my chin. "Let me guess. You like this plan."

"Very much."

I rested my chin on Damian's chest, his hand was moving up and down my bare back. We'd snuck away for a few hours. He made me lunch and then he undressed me and took me on his kitchen counter. I would never again see a kitchen counter and not think about him. I was so happy, happier than I had ever been. It had been a month since we first made love and every day I wanted him more, liked him more, but graduation was coming and I worried about what came next for us.

"We haven't talked about what happens in September."

"NYU, you mean?"

"And the army."

"I've been thinking and I might hold off on that, maybe find a job closer to you."

"Why?"

The look he gave me was adorable. "You have to ask that?"

"Is that what you want though, to work at a garage instead of pursuing a career in the military?"

His fingers down my spine were very distracting. "The military isn't going anywhere, but this…" He rolled and pinned me under him. "I want to see where it goes."

"I want that too, more than anything, but I don't want you to have regrets either."

"Regret being with you, no way."

He ended the conversation when he kissed me, but deep down I feared that Damian was lying to himself and me.

DAMIAN

The Aherns were having a graduation party for Cam, Thea and me. They had even invited Anton. I couldn't remember the last time a party was thrown for me. The gesture had rocked me and cemented the familial bond that had been forming since that first dinner I had shared with them. I had just left my apartment when my phone rang, and thinking it was Thea with a last minute menu item had me answering it. I wished I hadn't when I heard my mother's voice.

"You need to come over here immediately."

"No."

"Listen to me you little shit. You either get your ass over here or I'll just show up at the Aherns. I'm sure my invitation got lost in the mail."

I went numb. She would crash the party; she'd ruin the day for everyone just to fuck with me.

"I'm on my way."

She was in the kitchen, digging through the trash looking for any bottle that still had a sip or two of vodka. The Aherns were throwing a party for their children to celebrate their accomplishments and my mother was fucking picking through her trash for a fix.

"I heard through the grapevine you were fucking that Ahern girl." She looked at me from over her shoulder, her bloodshot eyes rimmed with dark circles. "Got that apartment just so you could fuck her, didn't you? I wonder what her father would say."

My hands balled into fists, but I refused to take the bait. "Why are you such a vile bitch?"

She turned and laughed, but the sound wasn't pleasant. "I loved a man and he left me. He was everything to me, I worshipped him, and he fell in love with someone else."

"That's not love. Love lifts you up, you were obsessed with him,

51

clung to him, demanded everything from him, even feeling jealous of your own child and the attention Dad gave to me."

"He was mine! Mine not yours. And he loved you, you who did nothing but shit in your diapers and cry and want attention. He lavished that on you, took his love from me and gave it to you. You didn't hold his interest very long though, did you? Out of sight and out of mind. And don't you act like you are any better than me. You're just the same. Tell me I'm wrong. You are willing to give up everything for that girl, to follow wherever she leads. She consumes your thoughts. A lowlife daring to believe you're good enough for her. She'll realize it, just like your father realized it, and she'll leave you. And it will be you sitting in your shit apartment, drinking yourself to death because you can't live in a world without her."

Ice moved through my veins because as much as I wanted to deny it, there was truth in her words. Thea had become the center of my world, the air I breathed…my own obsession. Would I become jealous of my own child if Thea and I ever had one? Did a scene like the one I had witnessed between my mother and father lurk in my future? I would rather never see Thea again than ever see her look at me the way my dad had looked at my mother. My legs went weak at the thought.

"You belong here with me. We are just alike, you and I."

"Why did you call me here?"

"I'm out of vodka and the electric company is going to shut off my power. You need to take care of it. It is the least you can do considering what you cost me."

Looking at where I came from, the evidence of the darkness in my blood, I wouldn't pull the Aherns into hell with me, and if I stayed that is exactly what would happen. She would make all of our lives hell. But I didn't intend to spend another second with the twisted and pathetic creature whose only legacy was hate. I walked out while she screamed at me to stay and I never looked back.

I had never seen Thea looking as happy as she did during the party. Her face was radiant from the smile that went from ear to ear. She had put herself near me for most of it, but at the moment she stood with her dad—arm in arm. He was toasting her, the pride on his face so clear to see. I would remember how she looked in that moment so I could carry it with me. I loved her, but I had to let her go. I wanted to be better for her and me and to do that I had to leave, even when everything in me wanted to stay.

"What happened?" Anton was a good friend but sometimes he was too fucking observant. I had been to the army recruiter and was getting my shit together. I was leaving. Now that the decision was made I had to just do it, because unlike my thoughts at the beginning of the school year, I didn't want to go.

"Your fucking mom, wasn't it?"

"She's a bitch, but it isn't because of her I'm leaving…not entirely because of her. I need this."

"And Thea?"

And Thea, the ache in my chest just wouldn't fade, but this was the right decision for her too.

"I love her, but she's got NYU in the fall. Our timing sucks."

"I like her for you."

"I like her for me too."

"I think you're doing the right thing."

That surprised me. "Yeah?"

"Yeah. I'll look out for your girl."

Cam was heading to Massachusetts. Thea would be alone in the city. "Don't look too close."

"I won't even tease about it. Besides she only has eyes for you. Can I help you with anything?"

"You already are. Watch out for her. If I know she's got you watching her back, I'll be good."

"Done. You still want Special Forces training?"

"My recruiter thinks it's a good fit."

"So you'll be hitting the ground running. Upside, you won't be deployed."

"Not for a while."

He started for the door. It was harder than I thought it would be. Anton was like a brother and it felt really fucking nice to know he thought of me as one too. "Take care of yourself. When you're ready, I'll give you a ride to the airport."

"Thanks. I mean it, Anton. Thank you."

"You can thank me by coming back in one piece."

THEA

It had been a week since the graduation party and Damian wasn't acting like himself. I was worried about him, but he was never around when I stopped by to see him. I was upset, even scared, because the clock was ticking and we were wasting precious time being apart.

"Hey, Thea," Dad said as he and Mom walked into the kitchen. "I see you're wearing your slippers."

Dad had surprised me with fuzzy bunny slippers after my graduation party. They had made me smile when I saw them, but not even their adorable little faces lifted my spirits.

"Can we talk?" Mom asked, but she was already pulling out a chair.

The last time Mom and Dad wanted to talk, as a unit, it was to tell me that Santa Claus wasn't real. "Ah, yeah."

"We wanted to talk to you about Damian," Mom said.

I assumed this was the sex talk. Damian and I were a couple and my parents knew that. It was fair for them to assume we were having sex and we were. We didn't go out of our way to hide it, but I also didn't talk about it around the dinner table. I loved that they wanted to have the talk, but that ship had sailed.

"Ah...this is awkward, but you're a little late if this is the birds and the bees discussion."

"We know."

I can't say I was surprised, my dad missed nothing, but I could say sitting across the table from my parents while we discussed my love life was definitely uncomfortable.

Dad continued, "Your eighteen, an adult and smart. You are being smart, right?"

"Yes."

"And we like Damian. He's a good guy," he added.

"He is. The best. So if this isn't about sex then what's up?"

"First love can be very powerful and when you add sex into the mix it can be life changing, but you have plans for the fall."

"I'm not changing my plans."

"It's not you we're worried about." Mom said. "It's Damian. His goal is the military, has been for a while, but we heard he's been talking with Cam about finding a job closer to you."

"Yeah. He mentioned that not too long ago."

Dad was giving me his cop look before he said, "You don't agree."

"I would love for him to stay with me, to move closer so we could continue to explore what has only just started between us, but I don't think he would be happy...not for long anyway."

"Have you talked to him about it?"

"I've tried. He's been busy since the graduation party, but we have to talk and soon. It's just..." It hurt; really hurt talking about this because I wanted to be with him, wanted to learn every little thing that made up Damian Tate. It would take me years. I wanted years. I wanted a lifetime. Sometimes I tried to imagine my life without him in it and I actually had trouble breathing. It was going to be unimaginably hard letting him go when the time came, but we were young and in love. My hope was that we didn't end, we'd just put us on hold for a little while.

"It doesn't have to be goodbye."

"I know."

"But at this point in your lives you both need to think about yourselves first, you need to be selfish," Mom finished.

"And love, time only makes it grow stronger," Dad added.

As much as I tried to push the inevitable from my mind, this conversation made it real and I couldn't stop the tears. "It still hurts."

Dad reached for my hand. "Love often does."

I needed to change the subject before I embarrassed myself. "How are you? You've been working a lot and seem kind of stressed too. Is everything okay?"

He didn't answer right away before he smiled. "You're a very astute young woman. Yeah. It's just sometimes we're faced with challenges, temptations, and doing what's right even when it's not popular."

"That doesn't sound good."

"Don't worry about me, kiddo, you have enough to think about."

Damian had called and asked to see me. We were in his kitchen and I knew he had come to the same conclusion about us as me because he looked how I felt.

"My dad left when I was five. He walked out and for all intent and purposes never looked back. Mom fell apart. She worshipped him and he left. It was like her whole life had been wrapped up in him and when he was gone, she no longer knew who she was."

My heart broke. I had known his home life had been bad, but having a dad who walked out and a mom who checked out stirred anger too.

"As the years passed, she lost herself in the bottle and at first she was despondent, but her love gradually turned to hate that spread like a cancer forcing those around her to share in her misery."

What a hateful, selfish woman. There was a special place in hell for people like her. "Including you."

"Especially me. For years it felt as if I would drown in her hate, and then 9/11 happened. The worse act of terror in modern times and I found hope. Hope for a life away from her…a life where I could make a difference."

"The army."

"Yeah. Then I met you and it was like that life was dropped at my feet. All the beauty in the world right there, within reaching distance."

"But?"

"I want you, but you were right. Working at a garage isn't what I want. I need to work on myself first. To be better for you and for me."

Even wanting this for him, I ached inside. I tried to keep the tears from my voice. "You don't need to be better for me, you're already perfect for me, but I agree that you should enlist."

Surprise flashed across his face as did pain. "You do?"

"I want to be with you, the idea of a time when you won't be around is too painful to contemplate, but we both need to work on ourselves. And as much as the idea of you enlisting and going off to war terrifies me, it is what you want. We can make it work. Long distance relationships aren't so long now with technology."

His face closed off and I realized he wasn't just leaving. He was leaving me. "I have to ask something of you. As much as it goes against everything I want, please don't write to me."

I gasped on a sob. "What?"

He stood and pulled me from the chair, right against his chest. "I love you, Thea, more than is probably healthy. I've never loved anyone in my life."

He loved me. I knew that and yet hearing those words was like feeling the magic of Christmas morning times infinity. "You can never love someone too much."

"Yeah, you can, but the military isn't just a job, it's a way of life. Are you going to leave your family and move around with me, or wait by the phone when I'm deployed to hear if I'm coming home? I won't put that on you."

"You don't think I'll be going through it anyway, whether you want me to or not?"

That sadness was buried behind his eyes again. "I can't do this if I'm holding on to you, but I can't let you go. I need you to let me go." It was the pain in his voice, the obvious struggle he fought that had me agreeing even as my heart broke. "I don't want this, I want you to know I don't want this, but I understand why you think you do. So I'll agree to not write to you, but I'll be missing you, worrying for you, loving you and there's not a damn thing you can do about that."

He framed my face in his hands and for a good long time he just looked his fill before he whispered, "This isn't over." His lips closed over mine for a kiss that was more than a kiss, it was a promise. He took me to his bed and all night and into the morning he loved me, like he was getting in a lifetime's worth.

He was leaving. Two days later, I stood on the front stoop of my parents' house and watched as he said goodbye to my family. I bit my lip to hold back the tears that had been threatening, tears that I knew wouldn't stop once they started. When I thought of him gone, away from me, I couldn't breathe. I felt panicked, like I was trapped in a funhouse looking for a way out and not finding one. The idea that tomorrow I couldn't walk to his apartment, I couldn't call him, I wouldn't see his face, hear his voice, I wouldn't get to look into those eyes. I wanted to sob; I wanted to scream at him to stay even knowing he had to go. Four long years until I was out of college, we had four years...so much could happen in that time. It only took less than a year for Damian to change me, totally and completely.

"Thea, come say goodbye," Cam called, but I was looking at Damian who was leaning against his car looking back.

I couldn't say goodbye, we had said our goodbyes, having to do it again would kill me, so I lifted my hand and smiled what I was sure was a sad smile before turning and heading back inside. I didn't even reach the stairs when I felt a hand on my arm. He turned me into him and pulled me close, right up against his chest. I wanted to cry, but I didn't want that to be his last memory of me.

He didn't say anything and neither did I. We had already said everything we needed to. He just held me for a really long time and when he walked away he took my heart with him.

It was hours later and I was sitting on our front stoop. I felt empty inside, had tears brimming my eyes that I fought to hold back. How the hell was I going to get through this? How was I going to learn to live without him? A car pulled up in front of the house and for a second I thought it was Damian coming back to me. It wasn't. Anton climbed from the driver's side. He strolled up my parents' front path and joined me on the step.

He didn't say anything, didn't offer any words of comfort or greeting, he just sat silently next to me. I had been battling back my tears, but it hurt so damn much. I rested my head on Anton's shoulder, a tear escaped and then another. He put his arm around me, pulled me closer, and I lost the battle with my tears.

DAMIAN

Basic training was intense. The hours were long and by the time I went facedown on my bunk I was too fucking tired to think and still when I dreamed it was Thea I saw.

Boot camp was ten weeks and I was nine weeks into it. After boot camp there were several other training programs I had to complete before I was even considered for Ranger school. It wasn't going to be easy. I'd heard stories about Ranger school, it was hard as hell, fucking brutal, but I was so ready to give it a go.

It'd been another exhausting day of training. I headed to my barracks for a shower before dinner at the mess hall. I was surprised to see the letter on my cot and when I saw the return address I actually got a little weak in the knees. Dropping onto my bunk, I ran my fingers over the delicate curves of her handwriting. I hadn't wanted her to write and yet I'd kill anyone who tried to take this letter from me. My hands were actually shaking as I opened it.

Dear Damian,

I know you don't want me to write and so I won't after this letter, even though I don't at all agree with your request.

I love you times 1,460. One 'I love you' for every day over the next four years. I won't be there to say the words and so I'm putting them in the only letter I'm allowed to send. I'm sending kisses too, but not 1,460 because that would look weird, me kissing the paper 1,460 times.

I baked a batch of cookies, but they weren't any better than the last batch, a little less charred but still inedible. I will conquer the cookie and when I do I'm sending you some and you can just deal.

You asked me to let you go, but I can't. You are part of me. Every little thing I want to share with you, which was easy when you were right here, close enough for me to touch, but even with the distance between us you are still the first person I think about when I wake and the last person I think about before I go to sleep. I dream about you too, sometimes those dreams feel so real that when I wake it's hard to accept you aren't here.

I did a little research on the army and basic training, so I could imagine you and what you're doing. I know my imagination doesn't hold a candle to the challenges you'll be facing, but know that I am with you every step of the way. And when the time comes when you're deployed, know that there are people at home thinking about you, praying for you, loving you.

You asked me if I would follow you when you were re-stationed or would I wait by the phone when you're deployed to hear if you were coming home? YES and

YES. Anywhere you lead, I'll follow.

Wherever you are, the places you go, the horrors you'll see, the people you'll befriend, please remember me…remember the girl with the crazy hair who is thinking about you every day. You're not alone, Damian. You'll never be alone again and you are loved…so much.

Please be safe, be happy and until I can see you again know my heart is with you because you own it.

Love always,

Thea

My chest ached and there was a burning behind my eyes. I reached into my pocket for the photograph Cam had given me the day I left, the picture of Thea that had changed my life. I touched her face and was grateful the barracks was empty because I did something I had never in my life done…I cried.

One day we would pick up where we left off.

2005

CHAPTER 3

Six months had passed since Damian left. I put on the brave face, but I hurt inside. I missed him and I worried about him. He never responded to my letter, I hadn't expected him to and yet I wanted him to. I knew we were doing the right thing and yet a part of me thought we had been stupid to not have held on with both hands. I would never be the same, he had changed me in a good way, but I also knew I had to let him go.

"Thea?"

Anton handed me a cup of tea. Since the day Damian left, Anton had become a fixture in my life. Damian brought us together, both of us dealing with the loss of him. We were kindred spirits even if we were the oddest couple, the daughter of a cop and a gangster, and yet he grew to be as close to me as a sibling.

We were at Anton's place, something I found I did often since Damian left. Most days we were in his game room, he had several eighties arcade games with no quarters required. I found joy in kicking his ass at Pac-Man.

"Cam is coming home this weekend," I said.

He settled next to me on the sofa. "We should do something."

"Yeah…oh and Mom invited you to dinner on Saturday."

Dad didn't have an issue with a man of Anton's reputation sharing a meal at his table. I suspected that was because Dad could see beneath the polished man to the damaged soul. Anton had demons, but he had learned to control them.

"I would like that."

"I'll invite my roommate to join us."

Anton grinned at the mentioning of my roommate. Kimber Green was vivacious and fun and the one who forced me out of the dorm, forced me to get involved and to interact. She knew about Damian, we had many tearful nights talking about him, but like a good friend she helped me to pick myself up, shake myself off and live.

Our first meeting, she was hanging an afghan over her bed while listening to Bob Marley. She looked like a supermodel, with her platinum blonde hair and tall thin build. She grew up in New Jersey; her mom was a teacher and her dad a pharmacist. She was a hoot and a lifeline for me. And now we were inseparable.

"Cam will no doubt enjoy meeting her."

"Hands off policy applies to him too." My roommate was seriously sexy, but I wasn't losing her over a fling, and that was all Kimber had—flings.

"Wise." His tone turned serious when he asked, "How are you doing?"

"I miss him. Every day, I miss him. I thought the ache would ease as time went on, but it hasn't. I know why he left, I even agree with him, but I can't help but wonder if he had had different parents, a different home life, would he have been so eager to go."

"Maybe not, but he wouldn't be the Damian you know and love had his life been different."

"I suppose so. Still, his mother should rot in hell for what she did to him."

Anger dripped from his reply, "I absolutely agree with that. Are you hungry?"

"I could eat something."

"I'll order Chinese and then I'll kick your ass in Pac-Man."

He had yet to beat me at Pac-Man, but I gave him credit for trying. And that was the mystery of Anton. Money gained through illegal means and yet he was also the same guy determined to make me smile even if that meant taking a beating at a game. It was the contradiction he posed and the kindness that was ingrained in him that drew me in and kept me there. A finer friend I would never find. And still, there was no chance in hell he was beating me at Pac-Man. "Bring it."

"You're not wearing that are you?" Kimber was clearly not a fan of the jeans and sweater I had selected for our evening out with Cam and Anton.

One of my sweaters used more fabric to make than all of Kimber's clothes combined. She had the body to pull off sexy, but she was constantly trying to get me to dress that way too. Spandex was a privilege not a right.

"Show some cleavage. What's the harm?"

"No thanks."

"Come on. At least wear my fuck me boots."

"Tempting."

"I'll wear you down."

Not likely. She looked sexy in her clothes. I would look like a little kid pretending to be a hooker.

"When are we meeting your brother?"

Cam was at Northeastern studying criminal justice, but he was coming down for the weekend. We had never been apart for so long. I couldn't wait to see him.

"Seven."

"We better get a move on. We don't want to be late."

Kimber was usually late. "Why the concern?"

"He's your brother, the guy version of you. I'm thinking hot as hell."

"No. I told you. My brother is off limits. I'm not sharing you."

"I'm fabulous, but I don't date my friends' brothers. Too complicated. But that doesn't mean I can't look."

"You're ridiculous."

She reached for my hand. "I'm doing my best, but you need your twin." And this was why I loved her. She was a good soul.

We beat Cam to the club, but when he arrived I launched myself at him.

He held me close. "Good to see you too, sis."

When Cam stepped back, he offered his hand to Anton. "Anton. How are you?"

"Good. How's Northeastern?"

"It's a lot more quiet and things move at a slower pace, but I like it."

Kimber's hand shot out to Cam. "Hi. I'm Kimber, her roommate."

I knew that smile of Cam's. Appreciation. His hand closed around hers. "It's very nice to meet you."

Kimber batted her lashes at him. She was flirting, it was in her nature to flirt with every specimen of the opposite sex, but seeing her doing so with my brother was just plain weird.

Kimber linked her arm with Anton. I once thought sparks would have flown between these two, but it was affection and nothing more. "Buy me a drink, handsome?"

"Absolutely."

Cam dropped his arm over my shoulders as we followed the others. "Your roommate is hot."

"Hands off."

He pressed a kiss on my head. "Fine. Hands off. How are you doing?"

"Okay."

"Have you heard from Damian?"

"No. He asked me not to contact him."

Cam's jaw clenched. "He is so fucking pigheaded."

Damian *was* pigheaded and stubborn.

"Next time he's home let's set Mom on him. He won't stand a chance."

I hadn't thought of that. Rosalie Ahern was a force of nature. She could bend you to her will and have you smiling the whole time.

"Good idea. So how's school really?"

"A little lonely. I miss you, Mom and Dad, but I love my classes."

"So you're really going to do it, follow in Dad's footsteps."

"Big shoes to fill, but yeah."

"That makes me nervous, having two cops in the family, but you're so much like Dad. You're going to rock at being a cop."

He pulled me closer. "Thanks, sis. I think so too."

DAMIAN

It was hard work, every second of every day was consumed with rigorous training and I thrived on it—the discipline, the purpose, the feeling of being connected to something so much bigger than me. I had not yet been deployed, was in the middle of Ranger training. My hope was to eventually try for the Green Berets once I met the requirements. Joining the army was the right decision, absolutely, but I missed Thea, every second. I wanted her in my life, couldn't imagine a lifetime feeling the emptiness I felt inside. When she finished school, she and I needed to have a long talk. She had said wherever I led she'd follow. I was calling in that promise.

"Damian, there's a call at the communications barracks for you."

It was either Cam or Anton. They were the only ones who called. It hurt that Thea didn't, but she was just respecting my wishes. Besides, she tried to stay in touch; I was the one who made the conscious decision to not write her back. My logic was simple. I wanted her; she was the only one who could pull me off track. But if I didn't make something of myself, what did I have to offer her? That didn't mean I didn't ask about her, but I kept even that in check…longing was a fucking unpleasant feeling.

The private working the room stepped out to give me some privacy.

"Damian."

"Hey, man. It's Anton."

"Hey."

"Congrats on making it into the Ranger program."

"Thanks."

He sounded off, worried or upset, and thinking it was related to Thea, I was abrupt when I said, "What's wrong? Is it Thea?"

"No. She's good."

The tightness in my chest eased.

"I'm calling because your mother is dead."

My first reaction to that was…finally. Followed quickly with fucking finally. I felt absolutely nothing for her. All those poets had it wrong. Love could fade…it could die. I had loved my mom when I was a little boy, but as a man I felt absolutely nothing.

"She's at the morgue and Mr. Ahern wanted to know what you wanted us to do with her remains?"

"Where did she die?"

"The house. The neighbors complained of a smell. The cops found her. She'd been dead a while."

Fitting. That place was like her tomb. She died the day my dad walked out. "You should have left her in the house and burned it down around her."

"That's what I thought, but I wanted to make sure."

I was wrong. I did feel something, I felt relief and hope that when Thea and I finally got together there would be no obstacles, no fucking skeletons in my closet. And that made me all the more determined to make myself good enough for her...worthy of her. "I don't care what you do with her. Give her body to a local med school or cremate her and drop her ashes in a landfill. I owe that woman nothing."

"I'll take care of it."

THEA

I went with Anton and Dad to identify Damian's mother's body. She was going to Hart's Island, to be buried with the countless other unclaimed bodies in the city. Anton was talking to the medical examiner while Dad filled out the papers. I looked at the woman who had given birth to the love of my life. A lifetime of hard living and the decay of death had turned her into a truly horrid image. Her physical appearance now mirrored her character.

"He's loved, every part of him, deeply and completely. You didn't break him, you damaged him and you hurt him, but you didn't break him. He has family, friends, love and he will be remembered, unlike you."

Anton joined me, reaching for my hand. I felt his anger. It matched my own. "She didn't deserve him."

"No, she didn't."

"It might make me a monster, but I'm glad she can't hurt him anymore."

"Then I'm a monster too." He squeezed my hand. "Are you done?"

I looked one last time at her, but I offered no prayer...she didn't deserve it. "Yeah. I'm done here."

It was Thanksgiving and Mom and I had been up for hours getting the turkey in the oven, preparing the sides and making the pies.

Anton, Cam and Dad were watching the game while setting the table, though I suspected the table was being neglected.

Mom had told me earlier in the week that she had a surprise for me, so my heart moved into my throat when I heard the knock at the door.

"Are we expecting someone else?" I asked, though I already knew the answer. I pulled open the door to find Damian standing on our front stoop. It had been eighteen months so I didn't immediately react because I wasn't sure he was real. But imaginary or not, I soaked up the sight of him.

Anton approached as Damian stepped inside. "Hey man, it's so good to see you." He and Damian hugged; a smile that was so rare for him lit up his face. Cam walked over and the male ritual repeated.

He really was here. Now I couldn't move because I was too overwhelmed with having what I most wanted standing within reaching distance.

Mom hurried into the room, right to Damian. "I'm so glad you decided to come."

"I'm happy to be here."

I had missed that voice.

"Son. Good to see you," Dad said as they shook hands.

Mom turned to me and smiled. "Surprise."

Those pale eyes settled on me. I moved right to him, pressing myself close as I buried my face in his chest. His arms wrapped tightly around me. How I had missed this—his body, his scent… him. This had been my favorite place to be and it was bittersweet to discover that it still was. I tilted my head back and he dipped his chin until our eyes met. "Hi."

A grin touched his beautiful lips as he remembered too. "Hi."

Mom's voice was a bit bright when she said, "Dinner's done. Let's eat."

It was a tight fit getting us all around the table. I was sitting across from Damian and as conversation moved around the table I wasn't really paying attention because I found myself looking through my lashes at him. Watching as he moved the food around his plate, the way he grinned when he thought something was funny, how even being right in the thick of everything he seemed to be alone. A few times when I glanced up at him he was staring back and I felt his stare in every part of my body, a searing right down to my bones that was unlike anything I'd ever felt except for whenever I was in his presence. I wanted to steal him away from the others, wanted him alone so I could ask what he had been up to and how he had been. But the fear that what had been between us wasn't there anymore held me back, because if it had faded all the memories I clung to would fade.

After dinner I was putting the serving platters back in the basement.

"Thea."

I closed my eyes, loving the way my name rolled off his tongue. Wiping the expression from my face, I turned to him. "Hey."

"How's school?"

"Harder than I thought it would be, but I love all the design classes. What about you? Cam mentioned you were a Ranger. Congratulations." I was happy for him, happy that he was finding his place, but it hurt too because he really was making a life in the military, and so the dream I held onto of picking up where we left off seemed more elusive than ever. "Is it what you needed it to be?"

"Yes. It's hard work, grueling, but it's exactly what I needed."

"I'm happy to hear that."

"And you?"

"I love school, love the friends I've made."

"But?"

I never held back with him, I wasn't going to start now. "But when I close my eyes, when I dream, it's about you. That hasn't changed. I don't think it ever will."

There was so much emotion in his soft reply. "I dream of you too."

"You do?"

"Every night."

I let his confession fill me up for a minute before I asked, "Are you still at Fort Benning?"

"Yeah…" A strange look moved over his face before he added, "I'm heading overseas."

My whole body went numb. "Where?"

"Afghanistan."

The blood drained from my face and I couldn't stop my body from shaking in fear of what he would find when he got there. I hadn't allowed myself to think about him in the thick of fighting. I had deluded myself with images of him training, not fighting.

"When do you leave?"

"Two days."

Two days. He was leaving in two days to head to a country ravaged by war, a place where he might never come back.

Tears filled my eyes looking at him knowing it could be the last time I ever did. "You asked me to let you go and I've been trying, but I'm not ready for that. Oh God, I'm not ready for that."

We moved into each other at the same time for a kiss that was more than a kiss. Love and fear for him had tears welling in my eyes and rolling down my cheeks. He broke the kiss, but his expression when his big hands cradled my face and his thumbs brushed the tears away was one I would remember always. He curled his spine and kissed me again, deeper, his tongue exploring and tasting…remembering.

My hands shook as I reached for the snap on his jeans.

"Thea." My name sounded more like a growl.

"I need you."

"I don't have a condom."

"I don't care."

The sound he made was felt in every nerve in my body. His hand moved under my skirt, his fingers curling around the silk of panties before he lowered himself down my body. He kissed the inside of my thigh before he stood, lifted me and pressed me against the wall.

"Are you sure?"

"Please."

It wasn't hard or fast when he joined us; it was deliberate and so beautiful feeling him skin to skin. My legs curled around his waist and my fingers dug into his shoulders. We didn't kiss. It was so much more intimate to watch him as he watched me. He moved slowly at first, each shift of his hips causing immeasurable pleasure. In and out, the friction between my legs, his cock hitting my clit with each stroke started the tingles, the raising of the hair at the nape of my neck, the chills that caused my nipples to harden and my body to spasm. I slid my hands down his back to his ass as his thrusts increased, turning harder and faster. I ground into him as we climbed toward that edge. When I came, his hand covered my mouth to silence my scream and when he came he closed his eyes and lowered his head to my shoulder. For several long minutes after, we stayed wrapped around the other.

I felt the chain around his neck and pulled his dog tags free. My heart ached as I brushed my finger over them. I lifted my gaze to his. "Please be safe. The only thing worse than a life without you, is a world without you in it."

A tear rolled down Damian's cheek and that lone tear decimated me. I wiped it from his cheek and brought the finger to my lips. "Remember me like this. Just like this and know I'm remembering you."

He kissed me, the most poignant kiss of my life.

He left not long after, my heart going with him. That night I prayed for the first time since I was a little girl. I believed when you wanted something badly enough you had to be willing to give up something you loved to see it happen, so I vowed that night that I would give up the dream of a life with Damian and in return all I asked was that he be kept safe.

CHAPTER 4

B ullet gave the silent warning, we'd all come to learn his body
language. The number of times that German shepherd saved
our asses was more than I could count. He was a hell of a soldier.
Matthew, his handler, called him back and we hunkered down
until the threat was gone. I'd made it into the Green Berets; my
team spent six months out of the year in Afghanistan doing special
reconnaissance. We spent a lot of time behind enemy lines. Our
missions were clear, we were to stay undetected and avoid combat
as we gathered intel. I had always been quiet, but I'd learned to
be really fucking quiet. We were on our way back to base camp
now after an op and that was always the part that scared the shit
out of me...being so close to safety. Anything could happen and
had. Bullet kept us out of sight, warned us when enemies were
approaching. We'd wait them out even when most of us wanted to
engage...orders were orders.

I'd met a lot of good guys. Some were here to fulfill their ROTC obligations; some were lifers, and a lot had families at home waiting. I'd learned it was possible to do both, maybe not ideal, but it was possible. Four years it had been since I saw Thea. I knew she was well, that she had graduated last year and was still looking for *the* job. I thought about her every damn day. I pulled out the picture of her. I could spend hours looking at her picture and that letter she had sent. She nearly broke me with that fucking letter. The paper was worn from the amount of times I'd read it. We were heading back to North Carolina for leave, I was now stationed at Fort Bragg after becoming a Green Beret; I was taking my leave in New York though. Thea and I needed to talk. Bullet nudged Matthew the all clear. I tucked Thea's picture away.

It was hot as fuck here and the sand and dust...I would die a happy man if I never saw fucking sand again. Summers in North Carolina were hot as hell as well, but that was a reprieve to this oppressive heat.

A few hours later and after a debriefing, I was off to the showers. We'd been gone for a week. I think I could sleep for a week after I ate my body weight in food. I didn't even make it half way to my destination when the commotion started.

Matthew came running up behind me.

"What's going on?"

"Firefight in the village."

I ran with him to the waiting Humvees. "Locals?"

"Fucking power struggle."

As if there wasn't enough shit going on, local crime lords used the unrest to make power plays and they didn't care if civilians were gunned down during their grab for control.

Poverty, I'd never seen anything like it. Children living with so little, the constant threat of being gunned down by stray bullets and yet they could play, smile and run to us when we rolled into their rural villages. Today was different though. The mud houses themselves weren't burning, but flames were shooting out of the windows. Screams and the smell of burning flesh carried on the wind. It wasn't a smell I was familiar with before coming here and now it was one I'd never forget. The local tyrant had been escalating to this. The building used for the school was where the villagers huddled in times of trouble. That was one of the buildings burning.

"Son of a bitch," Matthew hissed at my side.

"There could be survivors." I was already on the move. Staying low, sweeping for threats, my finger on the trigger of my rifle. Matthew had my back, covering me as I covered him. Bullet barked. There were survivors.

It took three hours to get the survivors to safety, another few to help put out the fires. By the time we returned to base I was moving on fumes. I didn't even shower, went facedown on my bunk and slept for the next twenty-four hours. And even being exhausted, both physically and mentally right before sleep claimed me, it was Thea I thought of.

THEA

It had been a year since we graduated from NYU and Kimber and I had clicked so well as roommates that we now shared a one-bedroom walk up in Chelsea. Cam had found us the place. Kimber won the coin toss for the bedroom. My bed was a daybed sectioned off from the living room and kitchen by a decorative screen. During the day, while Kimber pounded the pavement looking for an entry-level position in marketing, I was submitting my art to agencies in the hopes of getting a position in graphic design.

Cam had gone right into the Academy after graduation and was now a cop. He often worked with Dad on cases and I was a bit envious that they got to see so much of each other. But Dad and Cam's station was in my neighborhood, so even though I didn't get to spend the day with them I did join them for lunch often. We were at Dahlia's, my favorite little neighborhood bistro. Dad looked tired. He put in long hours being a detective, far longer than he ever had as a beat cop. And seeing Cam in his blues wasn't a sight

I was used to yet.

Once we were seated and our orders placed, Dad asked, "Any luck on a job?" I was doing busy work to pay the bills, but I had yet to find *the* job.

"Not yet. I did get a request from a new author to help her design a book cover."

"That's interesting."

"I hadn't really thought of that kind of work when I applied for positions, but I'm finding it challenging to realize her vision through design. How are you? You look tired."

Dad reached for his water. He had recently turned sixty. He looked young for sixty, but I didn't like seeing the stress lines around his eyes. "Detective work is exhausting."

"Are you thinking about retiring?"

"I still have a few more years in me, plus I get to see your brother in action." Dad teased Cam but there was pride in his voice. He loved that Cam was a cop, a chip off the old block.

"Did you hear that Damian is coming home next week for a visit? My best friend, a decorated Green Beret, unreal," Cam announced.

It had been four years and I waited on news about him like a greedy child. I had done as I promised and no longer held onto the hope of Damian and me together, but I needed to know he was safe and well. I had a whole new appreciation for the spouses of servicemen and women and their families. It took a special kind of person to not only put their life on the line for their country, but for those loved ones who stood on the sidelines supporting even while fearing that dreaded call.

I wrote to him, every day. Shared every part of me in those letters. I even addressed and stamped them, but I never mailed them. It was how I coped with letting him go when my heart demanded to have him close.

"Mom will want to make him dinner," Dad said.

"Yeah. She's already planning the menu. You're coming, right Thea?"

I wanted to go to dinner because I wanted to see him, but it seemed wiser to stick to the status quo, so I hedged. "When?"

"Next Saturday."

Then I lied. "I have plans."

"You can't change them? You haven't seen Damian in four years," Dad added.

"I really wish I could."

Neither of them bought my lie but I was saved from a grilling when our food arrived.

Kimber and I were on the hunt for the perfect cup of coffee. The large coffeehouse chains were great, but we wanted something more intimate. A new place had opened in the neighborhood, Cup of Joe, and we were on our way to investigate.

"You're being ridiculous." Kimber had spoken those very words at least twenty times since learning I was blowing off the dinner with Damian.

"I'm not ridiculous."

"It's been four years."

"I still love him but the situation hasn't changed and seeing him will only bring it all back."

And that was the truth of it. I wanted to see him, but I had finally managed to tuck my feelings for him away, stored them in a figurative box much liked Dad's special box in his office. I loved Damian, I would always love him, but I had learned to find happiness without him. It seemed stupid to stir it all up, to open that Pandora's box and let all those emotions out only to have to wrangle them back in when he returned to his life overseas.

Kimber studied me for a minute. "It will force you to feel things you don't want to feel."

"Exactly."

"Love scares the shit out of me."

"Love hurts, but those magical weeks when Damian and I were in sync...I doubt I'll ever feel that way again."

Kimber's eyes looked a bit bright but she had moved on because we had found Cup of Joe. "We're here."

As soon as the door opened, I knew we had found heaven on earth.

"Holy shit. Do you smell that?"

The combination of rich, roasted coffee and something buttery and sinful wafted out to us. "Oh yeah."

It was a small place and the tables were tightly packed together. We reached the counter and were greeted by an auburn-haired woman about our age.

"Hi. What can I get you?"

"Everything," Kimber said before she looked at me for confirmation then said again, "One of everything."

The woman didn't know what to make of Kimber's order, so I added, "We're serious. One of everything."

"Looks like I'm closing up early today. I'm Ryder Chase. The owner."

"Thea Ahern and Kimber Green, coffee drinkers and pastry eaters. We're on a mission to find the best damn cup of coffee in the city and if your coffee tastes as good as it smells, we just have."

She stopped bagging up the pastries and stared at me. "You're not kidding."

"Ryder, I suspect we're going to become fast friends, so let me state right now. There are two things I do not tease about—coffee and sweets. Both are like a religion to me."

"That is true," Kimber added.

"Good to know."

"If you're really closing early, maybe you'll join us so I can pick your brain on how you made the sweets we're about to enjoy."

"You're serious."

"As a heart attack."

Ryder's smile came in a flash, but lingered before she said, "I think you're right, Thea Ahern. We're going to become fast friends."

My own brother outmaneuvered me. I had successfully dodged the dinner with Damian. A week later, Cam invited the girls and me out with him—as predicted we bonded to Ryder like a long lost sister. Accepting his invitation was a no-brainer, but what he had failed to mention was that Damian was still in town and would be joining us.

The girls and I were already at the club. Even feeling nervous and apprehensive about the evening, it didn't keep me from arriving early. "I can't believe my own brother set me up."

Aren't you curious to see him?" Kimber asked.

"See who?" Ryder asked.

"Her ex is coming tonight. And by ex I mean the love of her life who left and stayed away."

Ryder's eyes widened. "You must be curious."

"Of course I'm curious and scared to death."

"Why?"

When we reconnected that one Thanksgiving it was still there—that memory was one of my very favorites—but four years had passed. A lot could happen in that time, people changed and I was afraid we had changed. I would rather cling to what had been than live with what was. "What if it's not the same?"

Ryder simply replied, "What if it is?"

My phone buzzed—Cam. They were parking. I was going to throw up. "I need to use the ladies room."

"Do you want us to come?"

"No you stay. You can introduce Ryder to my brother."

Kimber grabbed my hand before I could walk off. "We're here for you."

"And I have a feeling I'm going to need some girl time after tonight."

After the restroom, I stopped at the bar and ordered a double shot of Irish whiskey. A little liquid courage couldn't hurt. I savored the burn and the phony confidence that followed. I turned toward the table and immediately forgot how to breathe when my eyes landed on Damian. Every cell in my body recognized him even though he was so different from the boy I knew. My legs went a little weak as I reached for the bar top to keep my balance. He was home; so close I could touch him.

I had studied up on the Green Berets so I knew of the rigorous training that turned their bodies into another weapon in their arsenal. The t-shirt Damian wore hugged his massive frame, snug over his wide shoulders and muscled chest; his faded jeans hung from his narrow hips. His black hair was buzzed, which only brought your focus to his pale eyes, eyes I saw every night in my dreams. Nerves kicked in…excitement, anticipation and apprehension.

"I need another double," I called to the bartender as my eyes lingered on Damian, I also witnessed Kimber and Ryder's reaction to him—eyes bugging out of their sockets, tongues dropping. I totally got it.

"Here you go."

I reached for the shot and kicked it back but I wasn't feeling numb yet. I needed to feel numb. "I think I need one more."

She grinned as she filled me up again. "You're not going to drink it away."

Bartenders were rumored to be very astute and she was no exception. "I know. I'm just looking for courage."

"Have you found it?"

I felt a bit light-headed, definitely giddy and oddly relaxed despite the fact that the love of my life was just across the room. "Yes, I believe I have."

"The shots are my treat. Good luck."

I took a deep breath and steeled myself for the encounter. "Thank you. I'm going to need it."

I slowly made my way back to the table and realized I probably should have waited between shots because I was beginning to feel the effects of the whiskey, and damn that stuff was potent. My legs turned all rubbery but at least the stomach twisting nerves had faded. I felt ten feet tall and bullet proof. Damian saw me first, his eyes sought me out like a heat-seeking missile and my body responded, preparing for something that wasn't going to happen again.

"Thea?" Cam reached for my arms. "Are you alright?" He asked this because I sort of stumbled into the table. I was not a graceful drunk.

"I am right as rain. What does that mean anyway? Right as rain. I don't get that expression."

My eyes connected with Damian's and even through the protective barrier offered by the alcohol, that box opened and all the feelings came flooding out. The magnitude of them had my voice dropping to a soft purr. "Hi."

"Thea."

Even swimming in Irish whiskey, his greeting hurt. Hi was our thing, it was how we greeted each other. A hi that meant so much more than hi. I didn't get my hi. And feeling belligerent that he denied me a hi I amended my greeting, "Damian. At least we remember our names."

Kimber's jaw dropped.

"I'd ask if you wanted something to drink, but it seems you're several drinks ahead of us."

"That I am, Anton. Irish whiskey, Dad's favorite. Strong stuff."

Damian walked off and I watched him go because his ass in those jeans was what dreams were made of. Kimber wedged herself between Cam and me before she whispered, "What are you doing?"

"I don't know. I had three double shots, so I'm feeling pretty good right now."

"You're drunk."

"I am and I've never been drunk before. I like it."

"It feels good now. Tomorrow, not so much."

"I leave myself in your capable hands, Kimber. All the times I got you home safe, it's your turn to deal with me."

"Done." She leaned closer. "And Damian. Holy fucking hell. If he wasn't the love of your life, I'd do him right here."

And for some reason I found that hilarious.

Damian returned with a pitcher of water and bread. He poured me a glass then wrapped my hand around it. "Drink."

"If I drink, I'm going to have to pee."

"Drink, Thea."

"Fine."

I drank that glass and the two others he foisted on me and as expected, I had to pee ten minutes later.

"I'll go with you," Ryder offered.

She pulled me away from the table, but I looked back and leveled my best 'I told you so' face on Damian. "I'll be peeing all night now. I might as well set up a table in the ladies' room."

Ryder yanked my arm almost out of its socket. "Ouch."

"You're an idiot. This is the first time in four years you're seeing that incredible specimen of a man and you're drunk."

"He's probably congratulating himself on his escape."

"I don't know if I should take you home or join the fun," Ryder said.

"Join the fun. It isn't likely I'll be getting this stupid again anytime soon, but I have to say. I'm enjoying not feeling."

We reached the bathroom and by some miracle there was no line. She saw me to a stall and shut the door, but I heard her mutter. "Set up a table in the ladies' room."

On the way back to the table a pair of gentleman waylaid us. They were attractive in a muscle head sort of way, but when compared to Damian...they were children.

"Want to dance?" The bigger of the two asked me. I didn't want to dance because I was having difficulty putting one foot in front of the other. Attempting to dance would be a disaster.

Ryder was obviously thinking along the same lines when she said, "We have friends waiting."

The big one looked behind us and I giggled when he looked

up and continued to look up like something you would see in the cartoons. Clearly Damian was behind me. He grabbed my hand and pulled me toward the back of the club.

"I'll just see you back at the table, Thea," Ryder called after us.

"Okay," I called back then peered up at the dark angel that had a death grip on my hand. "He just wanted a dance."

"And the fact you think that, is why I walked over."

"I haven't seen you in four years and I realize I'm not at my best at the moment, but you're being awfully high-handed for a man who ran from me and never looked back."

Did I just say that? By the steam that came from his ears, yes I had. We reached a dark corner and he pressed me up against the wall. The first time he had done that, the night of our first kiss, came flooding back in delicious clarity. "Is that how you remember it?"

It took a minute for my brain to move past the awesome memory and back to the discussion at hand. Right, him running. "Yep. Broke all ties with me, but you stayed in touch with Cam. That doesn't hurt at all. It doesn't really matter, does it? You have your life and I've got mine."

His jaw clenched and for a second I saw that lost look in his eyes. I hated that look. "Are you happy?" he asked.

"I am. I'm finally able to say I'm happy and mean it. Are you?"

"I've found my place."

He hadn't answered my question, but I knew how much he needed to find where he belonged.

I was happy, but I would never be as happy as I had been with him. I couldn't put that on him, not when he had finally found his place. My life was here and his was three thousand miles away.

"Are you going to continue to avoid me when I come home?" His voice was soft, with a hint of the Damian I remembered, and that damn organ in my chest ached. I couldn't lie, he'd chosen his life and it wasn't with me, but I couldn't look into those eyes and lie.

"I'm not happy, not like I could be with you. I wasn't trying to avoid you...well I was, but only because I've only just gotten a handle on it...of learning to live without you, but I'm still not doing so great with that. I miss you. Every day."

And then he smiled and I wanted to weep. Instead I bit my tongue and fought to hold it all in. He brushed his thumb over my lower lip and my eyes closed as reality and an achingly sweet memory collided.

He remembered too because his voice pitched deeper when he said, "I've missed you too."

My eyes flew open. "You have?"

"Every fucking day."

I wanted to kiss him, and by how dark his eyes grew he wanted that too. "I should get you back to the others before I take advantage of the situation."

"I would be okay with you taking advantage of the situation."

His lips brushed along my jaw and my body burned. "It's been four years, Thea. When I kiss you again I want you fully aware of every nuance."

"I'm feeling sober."

"Tomorrow."

I replied on a sigh, "I can't wait for tomorrow."

DAMIAN

It took me years to realize I wasn't anything like my mother and what I felt for Thea was real and not the twisted sick obsession my mother confused for love. Thea still loved me. Tomorrow, after I kissed her senseless and lost myself in her body for a long fucking time, we'd talk. I wanted to start my life with her and I was going to wear her down until she said yes. I grinned all the way to my car.

Four hours later I got the call that on-leave personnel needed to report back to base. My unit was deployed, the first of a dozen missions that spanned the next few years. As much as I tried to deny it, the life with Thea became more and more elusive. A better man would let her go. I wasn't that fucking man.

2010

THEA

Dad was fixing my garbage disposal. I offered to have a plumber come out, but he said plumbers cost a fortune. It was my own fault. I stuffed too many potato peels down the drain, the disposal couldn't keep up, the line clogged, pressure built and I had a pool of water in the cabinet under my sink. It didn't take Dad long and while he worked I whipped us up some sandwiches. He cleaned up in my bathroom before he settled at the kitchenette table. "Pastrami on rye. Your mother would have a cow if she saw me eating this." He lifted the sandwich and took a huge bite. "So good."

Mom had put them both on a more healthful diet, they were inching up in years and Mom wanted them to live well into their nineties. They were really good about their new diet, but splurging a little never hurt.

"You've been so good I don't think even Mom would have a problem with it."

"Likely. So how are you?"

"I'm good."

Dad gave me a look. "Are you seeing anyone?"

"No."

He put his sandwich down and looked at me with concern from across the table. "When was the last time you saw Damian?"

"A year."

"I know how you feel about him, but it's been a long time since he went away and you've been on hold waiting for him."

"I love him." I had given up the dream of him, but deep down I still waited. He was the one I wanted.

"I understand that, but sometimes love isn't enough. Your life is passing you by while you wait for the time to be right for the two of you. The time may never be right, so what are you going to do? Forgo a chance at happiness with someone else because you're holding out for him?"

He was right; I had thought the very same thing myself. But it was hard because he loved me too. It wasn't that we didn't want to be together, we just couldn't get our timing right.

He reached for my hand. "I like Damian. I like him for you, but I don't want you to get to my age and have regrets. To have missed out on so much because you waited for something that never came to be. He isn't coming home anytime soon and as much as you both may want it to be differently, you're not a part of each other's lives anymore. Live your life Thea, and that includes men. You never know, you might find someone. Damian was your first love, that doesn't mean he's your only love."

I thought about the last time I had seen Damian. He had confessed to missing me, but he had also asked if I intended to continue to avoid him when he came home. I had told him I would follow where he led, but he hadn't asked me to come with him. He didn't write, he didn't call and even with there still being love and attraction between us, was that all it would ever be? A hook up when he was home? I wanted more from him, but he knew I did. The ball was in his court and Dad was right. It had been a year since I had last seen Damian and I was no closer to a relationship with him. Maybe it was time for me to do more than say the words that I was moving on, maybe I really needed to make the effort to move on because Damian had.

"I'm not saying you have to get married, but give another guy a chance."

It physically hurt for me to agree because I didn't want to, but Dad was right. Life was passing me by. It was time I started living it again.

DAMIAN

We had been eating dinner in the mess hall when all hell rained down on us. Enemy fire tore through our camp; bombs exploded followed by the screams of soldiers being torn apart. The smell of death saturated the air and when all the smoke had cleared we had lost twenty soldiers. Twenty families would get the call, would learn that their child gave the ultimate sacrifice for their country. One of the fallen was twenty-seven-year-old Johnny Middleton—the newest member of my Green Beret unit. His wife of two years and their baby son were waiting at home for him to return.

I was on leave, so I volunteered to take Johnny home and I'll never forget the silence of the airport as his body was wheeled from the plane. The tears in the eyes of strangers, all taking a moment to pay their respects to a man that gave his life for his country. And I would never forget the look on his young bride's face, the tears that streaked down her cheeks and the pain buried in her eyes that would never fade.

I thought of Thea. She'd been waiting a long time for me, but what if that was my homecoming? All those years she waited, put her life on hold for me, and I came home to her in a box. Or the thought of marrying her, having a family with her, and leaving her...forcing her to live through the heartbreaking scene I had witnessed with Johnny's family. I couldn't do that to her. She was young; it wasn't too late for her to find someone who didn't put his life on the line every time he stepped outside of his tent.

I wrote to her and writing that letter had been the hardest fucking thing I'd ever done. I sealed it, stamped it and sent it off and a part of me died, but when one door closed, another opened.

THEA

I turned the letter over and over in my hand. It wasn't excitement I felt seeing Damian's writing on the envelope. I knew what this was before I even opened it. Tears burned my eyes as I took a deep breath, ripped open the envelope and forced myself to read his words.

Thea,

I'm writing to tell you that I've accepted a post overseas for an indefinite stay. Our younger selves hoped
one day we could pick up where we left off, but as adults
I think we both know that isn't going to happen. I love
you, but sometimes love isn't enough. Be happy. Live
your life, Thea, and know there's a man out there who
remembers you...will always remember you.

Damian

Tears rolled down my cheeks and a little part of me died as
I fisted his letter in my hand and curled myself up into a ball. I
couldn't hold back the sobs because it hurt like hell when a dream
died.

DAMIAN

It was Christmas and my team had just been deployed again. The
mess hall had a Christmas tree and they served turkey and all the
fixings. It was good, but it wasn't the meal Rosalie had always
served. I'd give an arm for a slice of her turkey and one of her pies.

US troops were pulling out of Afghanistan. That was the word
that came down from the brass. Perhaps it was because of that
announcement that insurgent activity had increased, fucking suicide
bombers. As troops left, security teams replaced soldiers—private
firms that could continue the peacekeeper efforts. I liked the idea
of the private security firms, of leading a team. All the money I'd
made from the army had been saved and Anton had helped with
investing it. I was growing a nice sum and had some ideas on how
to use it.

"Mail." One of the private's called as he started calling out
names. "Damian, you've got a package." I had been expecting a

package but I was surprised as fuck to see it was from Thea. It had been a long time since I'd seen her handwriting, but I knew it. I waited until I returned to my bunk before I opened it. Tucked in the box was a tin with a card taped on the top. The paper was wrinkled, as if she'd been crying when she wrote it. My heart squeezed in my chest.

> Dear Damian,
> I've perfected the cookie and wanted to share them with you. Butter cookies, like that first batch I had attempted when we were kids.
> Merry Christmas. I hung a stocking for you in my apartment. Maybe one day you'll come home and see it, share the holiday with me. I know you're moving on and you want me to do the same, so I will. But you're still family. You will always have a place at my parents' table, in their home, in their hearts and in mine. Please be safe and know I'm remembering you too.
> Love always,
> Thea

My chest grew tight. All the times I would have loved a package from my girl at home and I get one when I could no longer call her mine. It had been over a year since I sent her that letter and still I thought of her…every day if I was being honest. I hoped she was happy, that she had found what I hadn't been able to give her. And even wishing the best for her, I hated that it wasn't me she curled up to every night. But that was life. It continued on whether we were ready for it or not.

2014

CHAPTER 5

The rain came down in sheets; the grass under my feet was soggy as the heels of my pumps sunk into the mud. It was cold, Christmas was right around the corner but there was no joy or peace or giving thanks because my dad, my beloved daddy, was gone. The soil covering his grave was freshly tilled, his stone recently carved.

He had been shot on the way into work one night. There had been a rash of shootings in the area, senseless violence, which made his death so much harder to handle. Two days after he died, I received a package from him. I had burst into tears when the mail carrier for my building handed it to me. I saved the box and the wrappings even the mailing slip. Ever since his first surprise with the digital music player we had continued the tradition, one that was shared just between the two of us and one I had really loved. This present was a key, a little brass key on a chain. He had often said I held the key to his heart. I wanted to hate the necklace because I suspected he had been returning from the post office, open later due to the holidays, when he was killed. His gift came at such a terrible cost, but I never took it off because it was his last gift to me. I wore it on a long chain, hidden from view because the memory and meaning was his and mine and I wanted to keep it that way.

We had the city funeral a few days ago, but this memorial was just for the family. Mom was barely holding it together. I hadn't really appreciated what Mom and Dad had until Damian. They had been true soul mates, the kind you read about in romance novels. He had been months from retiring; they had been planning their first of many vacations. It had been two weeks and Mom just wasn't handling it. In her shoes, I wouldn't be handling things any better and still I was worried because it was like she had died with Dad.

Cam stood next to Mom. She clung to him like she needed him to stay upright. His head was lowered, his blond hair falling over his face. He and Dad had been especially close so seeing the devastation Cam was trying so hard to hide so he could be strong for Mom broke my heart. Anton stood stoically at Cam's side, his grief etched in his features. A man struggling to hold the emotions he felt at bay. Uncle Tim was on Mom's other side, Uncle Guy and his family stood next to him. Uncle Tim was still a defense attorney, a partner now at the prestigious firm Wainwright Gallagher and Rembrandt LLP, one of the top law firms in the country. He had come a long way since his humble beginnings. The man was practically a celebrity now and yet he dropped everything to be here for Mom, Cam and me. Just like Uncle Guy, they were both here to pay their final respects to the man they thought of as a brother.

And just behind everyone was the lone figure, standing in the rain in his dress greens. Damian.

My eyes moved to the stone, the final resting place of a man who had been all things to me, who had given me a strong sense of right and wrong, who never wavered in his love, even when that love was tough love, and who had taught through example that a real man could cry. I couldn't believe he was gone, but he would never be forgotten.

"I love you, Daddy."

I stood in Mom's kitchen looking at all the casserole dishes littering the counters, the people milling around. It was late and yet people still gathered to remember and mourn. I wanted them to leave, didn't want to hear another apology over my loss. I had managed to get through the day by focusing on what needed to be done. But it was done now and my family had gone off to grieve in their own way. I needed to do that too.

I started for the door when Damian walked in. He came home as soon as he heard about Dad. It had been years since I had last seen him. We never got our tomorrow because he'd been called back. Five years had passed since that night, four years since his letter. He rarely came home. I had even had a boyfriend for a time, but it ended because my heart just hadn't been into it. I had finally let Damian go; at least I let go of the dream of being with him, of picking up where we left off. And even with that part of us over, the sight of him still brought all those memories back and how for just a little while he had been my Shaun Cassidy, Brad Pitt, Zac Efron and Chace Crawford all wrapped up into one. Once upon a time I had wanted the happily ever after with him and now I just wanted him back in my life any way I could have him. He had been my friend before he had become the love of my life. And after losing my daddy, I needed my friend back.

"Do you want to go?" he asked.

"Yes."

He waited for me to join him, his hand coming to rest at the small of my back to help move me through the crowd, deflecting well wishers with the slight turning of his massive shoulders. He draped my coat over my shoulders before walking me to his car. He had impeccable manners, he always had. He held the door for me before moving around to the driver's side and folding himself behind the wheel.

He didn't ask where I wanted to go. He just drove. And when we parked in front of McGinty's, Dad's favorite Irish pub, I felt the tears burning the back of my eyes and rolling down my cheeks.

Inside he ordered two shots of Dad's favorite Irish whiskey, and without saying a word, he lifted his shot in honor of Dad and kicked it back. This was exactly how Dad would have wanted people to remember him. Not wearing black, eating casseroles and whispering in soft voices. He'd have wanted us to have a drink, laugh, dance and be merry. To celebrate he had lived and not mourn that he had died.

For an hour we silently celebrated my dad. I wasn't in the mood to talk and he seemed to understand that, but then he always had been able to read my moods so easily. His head turned and those pale eyes found mine. "Are you okay?"

"Yes. Thank you for this."

"He was a good man."

"The best."

"Are you ready to go home?"

"Please."

Damian parked his car in front of my building. I had been about to thank him for the ride, but he was out of his car and walking around to me. That gesture brought back countless memories.

Silently we walked to my apartment, but when I unlocked the door I didn't want him to go. "Do you want to come in?"

"I shouldn't."

It was late, I was highly emotional and all those old feelings were stirring a longing I knew better than to feel. It was probably best we ended the night now.

"Thank you for the last hour. It was exactly what I needed."

He was so perfectly still and yet he studied me like I held the answers to the secrets of the world. He was tall, six foot six, and with the body he had now he was imposing, formidable, and yet all I felt was safe. His eyes were hot, emotions swirling through their depths, but what he was thinking I couldn't say. I was about to back into my apartment when his big hands framed my face. He curled his back, lowered his head and kissed me. Not a chaste kiss, a hot, demanding and hungry kiss—a kiss that curled my toes and weakened my knees. He kissed me like he would die if he didn't, and I kissed him back because I had missed this.

As quickly as it started, he ended it…pulling away from me and taking a few steps back. I waited for the apology, one that would have pissed me off, but he didn't apologize. He just looked at me, like he was searching for something.

Quite abruptly he said, "Take care, Thea." He walked away and I so wanted to call him back but I didn't. Nothing had changed; his life was thousands of miles away from mine. I watched him go, knowing he would always be the one I compared every other man to.

DAMIAN

It took effort to walk away, especially when every cell in my body wanted to take her up on her invitation. I wanted to spend hours getting lost in her, wanted to remove the pain and heartache that burned so brightly in her eyes. I wanted to love her enough to heal some of the hurt she felt. Instead I walked blindly down the stairs and out the door as I reached for my cell and called Cam.

"Where are we meeting?"

"My place."

"I'll be there in ten."

Edward Ahern had been like a father to me and through his example I learned that family wasn't the vile shit I had grown up with. That family was synonymous with love and laughter and though there was also pain, when dealt with together it was manageable. He was the kind of man I wanted to be one day. And he had been Thea and Cam's father, their patriarch. And he was gone. Taken from them in the blink of an eye. What was worse,

Cam suspected there was more to Edward's death. That it hadn't just been a random act. And that meant there was potential trouble brewing, trouble that could land at Thea's feet or Rosalie's...even Cam's.

He requested my help to keep what was left of his family safe and together. I didn't even think twice. I was resigning my commission and coming home because they were my family too.

THEA

In the morning, I worried when I went home. Mom was having a really difficult time and seeing her destroyed was so hard and what was worse was no amount of consoling helped. It made me feel so helpless.

It hurt coming home, knowing that Dad wasn't there and wouldn't be again. I understood Mom's pain, could totally sympathize. As soon as I pushed open the door, I smelled bacon and followed my nose to the kitchen. Mom stood in front of the stove but she turned to me when I entered.

"I thought I heard the door. You're just in time. I'm making breakfast."

Who was this person and where was my grieving mother? The back door opened and Cam and Anton appeared.

"The wood is stacked. Hey, sis."

Anton walked to the sink, but stopped to kiss my head. "Morning."

"What's going on here?"

Mom stopped draining the bacon and offered only one word in reply. "Life."

"But..."

"I'll take over, Rosalie," Anton offered and took the tongs from her. She walked to me and took my hands into hers. "Your father is gone. Forty years I shared with him and I could allow my pain to consume me. I could fall into despair and stop functioning, but I have all of you and together we can heal by leaning on each other. Love isn't selfish, so I will mourn the loss of my husband, but I will cook bacon and eggs for my children because that's life."

"I love you."

Mom hugged me hard. "I love you too."

"Breakfast is ready," Anton said.

And so we ate breakfast with two empty chairs at our table, but life went on and we went on with it.

DAMIAN

I never thought I'd find the sight of the old neighborhood welcoming, but I did. We'd just rung in 2017. It had been a long time since I went away and still it all looked very much the same. I bought the gym I used to visit regularly as a kid. Anton had brokered the deal for me, said I needed an investment property. It was good thinking because there was an apartment just above the gym. After dropping off the stuff I'd packed up in my car at the apartment—the moving truck was due tomorrow—I drove to Thea's. The ride was bittersweet. Our reunion wasn't going to be the one we had wanted as kids, but I was home and she was the first person I wanted to see.

I pulled up across the street from her apartment. It took me a little while to work up the nerve to climb out of the car. I'd been in war, I had killed, and yet the idea of seeing the girl I loved had me shaking a little. It took me longer than I would ever admit to get out of the car. Before I started across the street, I saw her walking down the sidewalk. It was her hair I saw first, still as wild as it had been when we were kids. She was smiling, a smile I knew by heart—how it changed the lines of her face and brightened her eyes because I had memorized her picture. So caught up in seeing her again, it took me a little longer to realize she wasn't alone. A man walked with her, her smile that had seen me through so many dark places, a smile I claimed as mine, wanted all to myself, was directed at him.

He held the door for her and they disappeared into her building. There were any number of scenarios to explain what I had just seen, but seeing her with someone else made me feel homicidal… contrary of me because I had been the one who let her go. I climbed back into my car. We'd have our reunion, just not today.

CHAPTER 6

Actuary science is a fascinating field and one that has helped guide my decisions in both my professional and personal life. Everything we do has an impact, the challenge is finding the balance between action and risk. For instance, that's your third glass of wine, which inhibits your senses and increases your risk of injury." He flashed me a smile with dimples. "Good thing for you that I'm here to see you home."

If he didn't have dimples, I might have stabbed him in the heart with my steak knife. He could assess the risk of his death with *that* action. I had been introduced to Derrick Glass, my risk-conscious date, by Kimber and I could see her pulling a joke on me with this set up, but Ryder had encouraged the match too.

Derrick and I had drinks the other night and on first impression he had a toe curl factor. Dirty blond hair cut short around his handsome face, a tall, muscular build clothed in tailored clothes, and he had those dimples. Drinks lasted a few hours and yes he tended to talk about his line of work a lot, and insurance was a very dry subject, but he was so cute I didn't mind. We had decided to try dinner and perhaps it was because we were past that awkward introduction stage, but there was something about Derrick Glass that I just couldn't put my finger on. Under his impeccable manners and elegant dress, I suspected there was something darker. Dad had always said I had an uncanny ability at reading people. Gut instinct, just like him.

I also discovered this evening that he didn't shy away from offering his opinion, but it didn't feel like an opinion. It felt like a pleasantly issued command.

The waitress arrived with the dessert tray.

"We're not interested in dessert." Derrick hadn't even asked me if I wanted dessert.

"I want dessert." I may have shouted that.

"Dessert on top of three glasses of wine? You're thirty-one, but you're never too young to start thinking about diabetes and other weight related diseases."

My jaw dropped and I knew how that looked because the waitress's jaw dropped as well. I was thirty-one, five foot five and a hundred and fifteen pounds. I still had the metabolism of a teenage boy. I ate what I wanted and got away with it. I never exercised because I found it all to be just too much work. Would I get away with my eating habits forever? No, but while I had this super power of eating whatever I wanted and not putting on a pound I planned to enjoy it.

"It's very kind of you to remind me, Derrick, and still I want dessert. I might even get two."

The waitress turned her head to hide her chuckle before she said, "May I suggest the chocolate lava cake and coconut tart. Both are decadent."

"Perfect."

My eyes caught Derrick's and there was that look again. He wanted to put me over his knee. He actually balled his hand into a fist and I grinned. Can you say control freak. Well handsome or not, there would be no third date for us so I, the 'at risk for diabetes alcoholic' stopped trying.

We parted right outside the restaurant because neither of us was interested in pretending any longer. And I had bought a new dress for this date. It was a fabulous dress—shoulderless with bell sleeves and short, just reaching my thighs. I started down the street, preferring the cool night air to a cab, and pulled out my phone to call Kimber.

"How was your date?"

"He spent most of the night discussing actuary science and then pointed out to me, after I ordered my third glass of wine, that I should be mindful of diabetes. Why on earth did you think I would connect with him?"

"He's uptight, but I had the sense there was something else lurking under all that reserved nerdiness."

"There is. The man's a control freak."

That piqued her interest. "How so?"

"Let's just say I think he has definitely got a defiant side."

"Oh, now I'm intrigued."

I exhaled on a laugh. "You date him."

"I just might."

"You owe me a drink."

"We're at Silver City now, come join us."

"There better be a dry martini with three olives waiting."

"It's the least I can do."

"You can say that again."

"Yes, I can add that. When do you need this?" I'd been working with this author for close to a month on her branding, but we had finally nailed it.

"In a week, if possible."

"Absolutely. And you want both black and white and color?"

"Please. I love it, Thea. It couldn't be more perfect."

"I'm happy you like it. I'll get it to you in the next day or two."

Dropping my phone, I studied the brand and it really was awesome. After that first request for a book cover I had found my niche. I loved my job, loved working with a client and capturing their vision through design. And most of all I loved that I could work from home. My apartment was the same one-bedroom in Chelsea that I had shared with Kimber. She moved closer to her job, a marketing job in midtown. I stayed because I adored my building and my neighbors, even being the youngest of them by a few decades.

A story on the news caught my attention. I reached for the remote to turn it up.

"Officials are calling for an investigation. This isn't the first time evidence has gone missing from lock-up in this precinct. We'll bring you more as the investigation unfolds."

That was Cam's precinct, had been Dad's too. Evidence tampering was a serious allegation. Cam hadn't mentioned it, but then I hadn't seen him in a few weeks. He had taken the detective's test and had passed with flying colors. Dad hadn't been alive to see it, but I knew he was watching over us and smiling down at how much his son was like him.

I finished jotting down my notes on the changes to the brand before heading into the kitchen for a cup of coffee, but I was hungry too and Cup of Joe was right down the street. When I arrived, it was packed. It was close to lunchtime so I wasn't surprised. Ryder had been baking something sinful, the luscious smell of buttery pastry had my stomach growling. I hadn't moved far into the line when I saw Derrick Glass. I immediately scoped the place out for escape routes. I was gauging how well I could slide between two tables against the far wall before moving quickly on my hands and knees to the door when I noticed Derrick walking toward me. Busted. I was surprised he approached with how our date ended unless he was preparing to dish out more rhetoric on my looming diabetes and alcoholism.

"Thea. How are you?"

I tried to read any hidden meaning in those words like *are you feeling shortness of breath, any chest pains or arm pains*, but it seemed he wasn't diagnosing me, just being friendly. "Derrick. Hello. I'm good. Just getting some lunch to bring home while I work." Yes, subtle comment that I wasn't staying, even though I had intended to stay but not if it meant I had to share another meal with him. He would probably whip out his calculator so he could numerically as well as empirically determine the shortening of my life span because of a croissant.

"I wanted to apologize for the other night. I was not at my best."

A snarky comment was on my tongue, but I had to swallow it. He noticed when he grinned showing those damn dimples.

"You came here to see me?"

"You mentioned how much you loved this place so I took a gamble that you would be here."

I wasn't sure what to say to that but I didn't have to reply because he continued on.

"You looked beautiful, by the way. I should have said that, but I felt a bit off balance, hence the incessant talk about actuary science."

I made him feel off balance. I didn't think I had ever made anyone feel off balance, well at least not in a really long time.

"Can I be honest with you?" he asked.

"You seem to be doing that already."

He smiled, this time so his perfect straight white teeth showed. "I think you're lovely, but I had hoped when Kimber approached that…"

He wanted Kimber, most guys did. Funny, I hadn't wanted to see him again and now that he was being charming he was interested in my friend. Some people just walked in the light. I was not one of them.

"Ask her, no better yet, tell her she is joining you for dinner."

His eyebrow rose just slightly. "Seriously?"

"Yep."

"And you would be okay with that?"

"It was just dinner. You didn't give me a ring, we didn't declare our undying love, and frankly I can see the two of you together more so than the two of us."

This time there was something wicked in the way he smiled. "I think I will take your suggestion. I really am sorry about the other night."

"Silver lining, you've got me thinking more responsibly about my eating habits."

"Nonsense. There is nothing wrong with them," he said, as he looked me from head to toe. "And you can sure as hell pull off two desserts."

Such a different man from the one I dined with. Charming even. "Good luck with Kimber. I think you will find you and she are more suited than us. Though she is a big sweets fan too so you might want to hold off on your…" I waved my hand since I wasn't really sure how to word his harsh opinion on desserts since I didn't share it.

"I should have gotten you four desserts, two to take home. You're a beautiful woman and I was being a thoughtless ass."

"At least you see that now."

He laughed out loud then pressed a kiss on my cheek. "See you around, Thea."

"Later."

I watched as he walked out and knew I should give Kimber a heads up that he would be calling, but I didn't. I headed for the counter. Ryder was grinning at me.

"What was that all about?"

"Kimber."

"Oh. Oh…"

"Yeah, he's telling her she is dining with him."

"And you aren't going to warn her he's calling."

"Nope. Payback is a bitch."

"Truer words. What can I get you?"

"The most fattening thing you're offering."

I stared at the words on the paper. I had thought briefly that I should stop the letters, but he was still the first person with whom I wanted to share my day. Every happy moment and every heartbreak, it was Damian I wanted to tell.

> Dear Damian,
>
> Anton took me to a fancy French restaurant and he insisted I try the escargot. Don't let Anton talk you into ever trying them. They were horrid. Not even the garlic sauce cut the flavor. He took me to our favorite pizzeria after as an apology. We got pizza with pepperoni and mushrooms, your favorite.
>
> Mom has been threatening to dye her hair that ombré look. She's thinking blonde and blue. I'm doing my best to talk her down, but she's having a midlife thing. I suppose for a midlife crisis, that's not so bad. If it were me, I'd buy a sports car...something sexy and fast.
>
> I had a dream the other night. You knocked on my front door, took my hand as soon as I opened it and slid a ring on my finger. It was one of those dreams that felt so real that when I woke I actually cried when I realized I had only imagined it. Every time I watch a scary movie, I think of you. Every time I eat pecan pie, I think of you. When the first sprouts of spring grass break through the earth, I think of you. I miss you, every day. I pray for your safety every night. I hope you found what you were looking for. I hope you're happy.
>
> We were young, but I still hope one day you come home...to me. I wish for that every day too. I probably

shouldn't. I should let you go like you asked me to, like you have, but you're more than just my first love. I'll never love anyone like I love you. I've come to accept that and so what's the harm in wishing for the happily ever after with you.

Be safe. I love you.

Love always,

Thea

"Thanks for joining me for lunch." Uncle Tim and I were eating at a bistro in midtown. I loved that we were still close to him. He had really stepped up after Dad died, made himself more available to Mom, Cam and me, even knowing he had a crazy schedule. He wasn't just a celebrated defense attorney with an acquittal rating that bordered on magical, he was also a State Assemblyman who had his sights set on the Senate. Due to his hectic schedule, we didn't have lunch as often as either of us would have liked, but it was great that we were still able to occasionally fit it in.

"How's work? You're still working out of your apartment?"

"I am. I've quite a few regulars, mostly authors, and I'm nonstop busy."

"And you are still thriving on the work?"

"It isn't the direction I thought I would be taking when I started college, but I love it. What about you? That case in the news is pretty intense." Cathy McKay was a mother of three that was found dead in the alley behind the diner where she worked. The police had an eyewitness, caught the perp and had evidence that put him at the scene. It was believed by all to be a slam dunk case for the prosecution, but Uncle Tim had successfully poked holes in their theories and their evidence. So much so that people were now tossing around the word acquittal.

"I hate cases like this, but I'm sworn to uphold the law and when civil liberties are being trampled all for the collar, that can't happen. It doesn't make me popular, but I'm doing right by my client."

I remembered Dad often saying the same thing of Uncle Tim. I reached for his hand. "Dad, even being a cop, understood the importance of what you do. Your client is very lucky to have you."

"So let's talk about Cam. What's he up to?"

"Good question. Ever since Dad died, he buries himself in work."

"As a coping mechanism I get it, but it's been over two years."

"I know."

"Do you know what he's working on?"

"No. He keeps Mom and me in the dark, for our own sake, but I miss him. He doesn't come around nearly as much as he should."

"I'll try to talk to him."

"I would really appreciate that. I know he loves the job, I just hope he is not hiding behind the job."

"He's a smart guy, but I'll have a word."

"Thank you."

We were pulled from our conversation when a man stepped up to our table. It took a minute to place the face, but it wasn't hard because his daughter's case was eating up the media. Chris McKay. Uncle Tim stood as soon as he saw him.

"You shouldn't be here."

"How do you sleep at night?"

"Chris, don't make me call the cops."

"She's dead. Your client did it and yet you spend day after day brainwashing the jury that he is innocent."

His eyes raked over me, a chill forming because he looked slightly mad. "Your daughter?"

Uncle Tim stepped in front of him to hide me from view.

"What if it had been her? Would you be so eager to get the one off who had killed her? Left her children orphans?"

"Leave now." I had never heard Uncle Tim sound so furious. He reached for his phone just as the manager of the restaurant walked over.

"Is there a problem, Mr. Gallagher?"

"No. Mr. McKay was just leaving."

"I hope you never experience the devastation." Those were his parting words before he was escorted out of the restaurant. Uncle Tim looked around at our fellow diners offering a nonverbal apology before he settled back in his chair.

"I'm sorry about that."

"Has he done that before?"

"A few times. He's grieving. I understand. He needs someone to blame and right now that's me. It happens all the time."

"I'm sorry."

"All part of the job."

The waitress returned; she looked a bit flustered. You could tell the manager had sent her over. "Would you like dessert? It's on the house."

And in trying to shake off that ugly scene, Uncle Tim and I said at the same time, "Absolutely."

I parted with Uncle Tim and walked home. On the way, I spotted a couple ahead of me on the street. They walked hand in hand and when they reached their destination, he held the door for her. She looked up at him and smiled as she preceded him into the store. The sight hit me right in the center of my chest, as a wicked case of déjà vu swept through me. It was the little reminders of Damian, the ones that snuck up on me out of nowhere that were the hardest. I missed him, every damn day.

I was in my old neighborhood, stopping by to say hi to Mom. I'd been thinking about that scene at the restaurant with Uncle Tim. He had handled it like a man who had been through it before, but to have to face the families of the victims had to be hard. And thinking about Uncle Tim had Dad drifting into my thoughts. When I felt melancholy over missing him, I liked coming back to the Bronx, to my childhood home, because there were lots of really great memories. I had just reached the front steps when I heard my mom scream. I flew up the steps and pushed through the door but the sight that greeted me took a second or two to sink in. My mom was in a pair of Juicy sweatpants, her ass in the air and a very sexy, young man stood over her.

"What the hell is going on here?"

Mom jerked upright and peered at me from over her shoulder. "Yoga lessons."

"Yoga? You?"

Mom touched the younger man's arm. To be accurate in the retelling she was stroking him like one would a cat. "I'll be right back. Let's take a little break."

"Sure thing, Rosalie."

She flashed him a smile before she walked past me, reached for my hand and pulled me to the kitchen.

"Yoga? Who are you and what have you done with my mother?"

She walked right to the plate of donuts on the counter and shoved half of one in her mouth.

"You are having Yoga lessons but on breaks you're shoving your face with a donut. Have you lost your mind? It's happened hasn't it? Oh my God, nothing like seeing what I'll become in thirty years."

"Oh stop being so dramatic. I'm eating this donut because I love donuts, and yoga—downward dog—can suck it."

That sounded more like my mom. I got my exercise habits from her, but considering she was still the same size as she had been when she married my father over forty years ago...whatever pact she made with Satan I hope extended to me as well.

"So who is Mr. Hot and Sweaty?"

"He's adorable, isn't he? I don't even need to do the yoga. He can just sit on the sofa so I can stare. I ran into him at the market; like literally, he wasn't watching and our cars almost collided in the parking lot. We got to talking and he mentioned he was a yoga instructor."

"I'm sorry, you brought home the man who almost ran into you?"

"Yeah, he's charming. I checked his references first."

"I don't even know what to say. Talk about throwing caution to the wind."

"Cam cleared him."

"Cam looked into him?"

"Yeah, I'm not crazy."

"You picked up a man who is more than half your age at the grocery store, after he nearly crashed into your car, and had your cop son run a background check on him before agreeing to have him tutor you in the art of yoga in the privacy of your own home. Yeah, I think the jury is still out on your sanity."

She gave me the mom look, the one that used to bring fear and now only had me stifling a laugh.

"So, he gave you his card and you called him because when your instructor looks like him, yoga can't be all that bad."

"Exactly."

"And he makes house calls?"

"Apparently."

That was unusual but effective. If I could get a hottie like that to come to my place, I might take up yoga too. Probably not.

Mom pulled out a chair and dropped into it. "The truth is I loved your father but he's gone and though I miss him every day, he would be really angry if he knew I wasn't sucking up all I could out of life."

"He would, I've been saying that."

"You have. So I'm finding fun. Yoga isn't fun, but hot pants in there is helping me keep in shape."

"I really hope that's not code for something else."

She slapped my arm. "Get your mind out of the gutter."

"You do realize you're objectifying your yoga instructor."

"Yeah. So what?"

"I came for a visit, but I don't want to interrupt your lesson."

Mom gave me a look I knew I gave often to my friends. It was unnerving when you realized you were more like your mom than you ever thought or even wanted.

"We should do dinner out, something fun and frivolous. Invite the girls."

Mom loved Kimber and Ryder like daughters. "I'll arrange something." I reached for a donut and started from the kitchen.

"He's waiting for you."

Mom eyed the plate of donuts.

"You aren't getting another one down your throat in the time it takes to walk back into the living room. And you have powder…" I pointed to my chin "…here."

She looked seriously upset at the idea that she couldn't have another donut and I could relate because I would be feeling the same way. There was comfort in the knowledge that if I did get diabetes, it was my mom's fault.

"I'll call you about dinner."

"Have you heard from Cam?" She wasn't teasing now. Uncle Tim was right, Cam's way of coping with Dad's death was to bury himself in work—case after case going after the bad guys. It scared the hell out of me because he went after some really bad guys, but it was helping him heal. Downside there was a part of his life that Mom and I were kept from. That was hard because we couldn't just pop in to see him and he didn't drop over as often as he used to. We were adapting, but I secretly hoped he got it out of his system and chilled.

"No. Why don't you call him?"

"I hate bothering him. I know how busy he is."

"He's never too busy for a phone call."

"Yeah. It would be nice if he called me once in a while though."

And there was the heart of it. It wasn't intentional, but I would call Cam and remind him to call home.

"I had lunch with Uncle Tim the other day."

"Oh, how was that?"

"Great until Chris McKay walked up to our table."

"Who's that?"

"The father of the woman his client allegedly killed."

Her face went white. "He actually confronted Tim?"

"Yeah. Uncle Tim said it happens all the time with victim's families."

"That's horrible, for both of them. I understand it is Tim's job, but the man lost his daughter."

"He handled it, but it got me thinking about Dad."

Mom always had the sweetest smile when thinking of Dad. "He would have made a terrible defense attorney. He cared too much about the victim. He always teased Tim, claimed it was black magic that had him winning cases like he did."

I remembered their countless good humored fights on the subject.

"They were best friends, but they were often on opposite sides of cases and your father had a point. Tim wins cases ninety-nine percent of the time other lawyers would lose. He really is that good, but that means more than the innocent are being set free. That always bothered your father."

"It bothers me too." I leaned in and kissed Mom on the cheek. "I'll let you get back to your exercise. I'll call about dinner."

"Thanks for stopping by."

"I could be tempted to stop over more often if he is going to be here. Not doing yoga, mind you, but I could lie on the sofa and watch you two."

"Out. Out of my house, child."

"Bye Mom." I reached the front door and called to Mr. Hot and Sexy. "She just ate a donut."

I closed the door on my mom's rather vocal reply.

CHAPTER 7

Cam had been on my mind since my visit with Mom from the other day, so I called him. No matter how busy he was, he always made sure Mom and I had the most accurate numbers for him in case we needed to reach him.

"Hey, Thea. What's up?"

"You owe Mom a call."

I heard his exhale over the line. "Damn. I do. I've just been crazy busy."

"Yeah, doing what?"

"Juggling a few cases."

"Just like Dad."

I heard the love in his reply. "Yeah, just like Dad."

"You're good?"

"Yeah. You?"

"Right as rain"

He chuckled at the memory too.

"Call Mom."

"I will. Later."

"Later."

I hung up and decided to take the rest of the day off because having talked to Cam had me thinking about Anton and it was close to lunch so he could feed me.

Opal was one of the more posh clubs in the city, offering not just entertainment at night, but a five-star restaurant that was open for lunch and dinner. The place was always packed, but I never had to wait in line—benefits of knowing the owner. Inside it was a place to see and be seen with some of the most beautiful people you'll ever see in real life. I always felt a little uncomfortable, like a daisy in a hothouse of roses.

Locating the man in question wasn't difficult; all you had to do was watch the reaction of the women in the crowd. His presence always caused a stir. As was the case when I saw women's necks twisting…the man was on the move. In recent years, I never saw him in anything but a suit—something Italian and ridiculously expensive. His brown hair was never out of place, his smile was always just a little bit wicked and he walked like he had nothing to fear. And he didn't. Anton Scalene was a dangerous man. He strolled through the club and heads turned, drawn in by the sexy curve of his lips, the swagger in his gait, and the muscular build hidden under tailored clothes. He was a predator, but a damn good one, luring women in with his easy smile and affable nature.

He spotted me by the smile that touched his lips and as was his way, he reached for my hands and brought them to his lips. "Thea, what a lovely surprise."

"Hi, Anton."

He tucked my hand through his arm. "So what brings you here?"

"Mom has taken up yoga."

That earned me not just his face, but also a bewildered look. "Rosalie is exercising."

"I know. Hard to believe, but she's just in it for the eye candy."

He chuckled, "That makes more sense."

"Anyway, I just had a chat with Cam and realized I haven't seen you in a few weeks. So here I am."

"And just at lunch time too."

He knew me really well.

"Now that you mention it, I am hungry. This place is amazing by the way."

Anton looked around, but unlike me he was studying it with a critical eye. "It's getting there." His dark eyes returned to me. "I dined at Clover last night."

"Oh my God, was it delicious? I heard the new pastry chef is amazing."

"Amazing isn't the word. I'll have to take you."

"The waiting list is insane."

"I know the owner."

"Really? You know Trace Montgomery?" I only knew of Trace Montgomery because Kimber dragged me to a cooking lesson at his school. She wasn't interested in cooking, she wanted to stare at Trace and after seeing him, I understood why.

"Anyway, while I indulged in a truly spectacular meal, I had an almost overwhelming desire for your mom's cheeseburger casserole."

"I forgot about that casserole. I'll have to get her to make it for our next dinner."

"Maybe she'll make enough for me to take home a doggie bag."

I couldn't help the smile. The man was wearing tens of thousands of dollars in clothes and jewelry and yet he wanted Mom's frugal, but tasty, casserole.

He looked thoughtful for a moment before he added, "Damian resigned his commission. He's home."

That news came as a complete shock, but right after shock was excitement and anticipation. Damian was finally home. "What? When?"

A strange look swept his expression before he added, "He resigned about two years ago. He's working in the private sector now."

I realized we had both moved on, but he didn't reach out to me in two years? My enthusiasm took a hit but still I asked, "Doing?"

"He leads a team, a kind of security team that runs ops when it is impossible to send the military—retrieving hostages or politically based kidnappings. That kind of thing."

So he was no longer with the military, but he was still doing the same type of work. That explained why he continued to keep his distance.

"You said he was home, so he's based in the States."

"His team is all over and up until recently he was based overseas, but Damian moved HQ here. He's temporarily setup in a gym he owns in the Bronx."

So not just the States, he was back in the neighborhood. That hurt. "How long has he been home?"

There was that look again before he said, "A month."

A month, four weeks he'd been home and he never reached out to me. There was a time I would have been devastated to be out of the loop when it came to Damian. Who the hell was I kidding? It hurt like hell that he was home and never called me…that only I still carried the torch, but a lot had happened in the years that separated us. We weren't the same people anymore. And even reasoning that to myself it did little to ease the ache in my chest.

"Why am I just hearing about this now?"

"Damian didn't tell you he was home?"

"No."

"What the…"

At least I wasn't the only one confused by Damian's behavior. I didn't dwell, there was no point, and moved the conversation along. "A gym doesn't sound like Damian's speed."

"It's on the MMA circuit, so it hosts fights every night."

"That makes more sense."

"I encouraged him to buy the place a few years back as an investment property. He's got a manager running it, so it's minimal work for him but it does bring in a steady income."

"I'm happy he's home."

Silence followed for a second or two. "I'm sorry he didn't tell you he was home."

"That's on him, not you."

Anton didn't press the point. "Let's get lunch."

"I would like that."

Anton touched the small of my back while we maneuvered through the bodies to his private table. "The Angel Network Fundraiser is on Friday."

It was a charity that had been near and dear to Dad. Every year he and Mom had organized the event, but it was too hard for her now. Uncle Guy and his wife Cherie took it over. "I know. I haven't gone since…"

"It's hard for all of you, but I've been going every year so the family is represented."

It warmed my heart to know he thought of us as such because he was absolutely thought of as family by Mom, Cam and me. "You're a good man, Anton.

"Only to those that matter."

"I'd like to join you this year.

"You would?"

"You've been holding down the fort long enough."

There was understanding and love in the smile he offered in reply. "I'll pick you up at seven."

That night I couldn't sleep; I just lay in bed staring at my ceiling. Damian Tate was home. Had been for four weeks with no call. It hurt that he was home and never contacted me. Maybe he had only been keeping in touch with Anton. He been away a long time and had a business he was setting up, one that Anton was clearly helping him with. Maybe the slight wasn't personal. I had to believe that because regardless of our relationship status, he was family.

I had pondered his kiss the night of Dad's memorial and why

he'd done it for a long time after and then I just let it be what it was, a perfect moment.

It would be an adjustment having Damian home. We weren't the kids we had been but he still owned a piece of my heart. I still had the dream sometimes of us together, but it was just that, a dream, because had he still felt what I did, he would have called or visited in the fours week that he had been home. I would fall back on humor though; I had learned the beauty of humor after losing Dad and the debilitating sorrow that followed had eased. The power of a laugh, the finding appreciation in things we often take for granted. I wouldn't focus on what I couldn't have with him, but what I did have with him. We had a history and there was love there too, and that wasn't a bad start to finding our way back as friends.

My cell rang, which had me looking at the clock. It was awfully late for a phone call. It was an unknown number and I thought to let it go into voice mail, but I was annoyed enough to give the caller a piece of my mind. "What!"

No answer and yet the line was open. It was late so that freaked me out. Instead of ranting as I intended, I hung up and blocked the number.

Exactly at seven on Friday, Anton arrived and a half an hour later we were pulling up in front of the New York Public Library where the charity fundraiser was held every year, sparking a pain in my chest remembering Dad. Silas, Anton's driver, helped me from the car before Anton pulled my hand through his arm. We started up the steps to where Uncle Guy and his wife Cherie waited. Uncle Guy was a detective now, got his shield just last year around the same time Cam had. Dad would have been so proud.

"Thea." Cherie hugged me, no air kiss on my cheek like the others in the crowd were doing.

Uncle Guy stepped in for his hug before his attention turned to Anton, his smile never fading. Anton was family. In the beginning, it had been awkward, to say the least, with Anton being who he was and a family of cops, but most of Anton's businesses were now respectable. Not that he was a model citizen, but he knew how to play the game really well and he had us, his family, to keep him from going too far to the wrong side.

"Anton, nice to see you."

"And you."

We walked inside where formally dressed people milled around. Anton turned to me. "I'll get drinks. Champagne ladies?"

"Yes please."

"I'll come with you," Uncle Guy offered as the two headed for the bar.

"It's been too long. How is everyone, how's Trevor?" I asked.

"Trevor and Sara are having their first baby."

"On my God. No way. I remember when he couldn't tie his shoes. Congratulations. What's he doing now?"

"He's working on Wall Street." She leaned in a little. "Between you and me, I am so glad he didn't follow in his father's footsteps. Worrying about Guy is bad enough, I couldn't imagine worrying over Trevor too."

"I hear that."

"And you? I heard your graphic design business is really taking off."

"It took some time, but I've got a great client list and I'm never without work. In fact, I've even gotten to the point that I have to turn some jobs down."

"That's wonderful. How's your mom?"

"She's taken up yoga."

Cherie's eyes widened. "Yoga? That seems…"

"Her trainer is twenty-four and gorgeous."

"That's more like it. And Cam?"

"Working nonstop, determined to single-handedly rid the city of crime." A little melodramatic but it sure felt that way sometimes.

The wife of a cop, she understood. "That's a little scary."

"Yes it is."

A blonde in a stunning silver dress approached. She looked more impressed with herself than what she saw. She didn't excuse herself, just jumped right into the conversation. "Cherie, there are a few people you should meet."

"Thea, Katrina Dobbs. Her husband Miguel is lead detective and Guy's mentor. This is Edward Ahern's daughter, Thea." Dad had been lead detective and I was curious about Miguel, the man who now had my Dad's job, because his wife was a douche.

Katrina gave me a once over and her smile wasn't at all sincere before she said, "A pleasure."

I didn't reply and she didn't wait for one as she started over to the local politicians to schmooze.

"She's an acquired taste," Cherie said. "It was so wonderful to see you."

"And you. Please give Trevor my best."

"And you, give Rosalie and Cam my love."

"I will."

Uncle Guy and Anton returned at the same time I spotted Uncle Tim. He saw me too when he changed directions and headed over. He had his entourage and looked like a man without a care in the world, but I remembered vividly the ugly confrontation with Chris McKay and how the encounter affected him. Uncle Tim would make a fantastic actor.

"Thea."

"Uncle Tim."

He pulled me close and squeezed just before he released me. "I'm happy to see you here."

"It was time."

There was understanding in his smile before his focus shifted to Uncle Guy. "Detective."

A chill iced the air drawing my attention to Uncle Guy. And though he replied cordially there was definitely an edge to him that hadn't been there only moments earlier. "Counselor."

If Uncle Tim noticed Uncle Guy's curt reply he ignored it and greeted Cherie. I glanced at Anton, who glanced back, both of us intrigued by the dynamic between the two men.

"It's nice to see Edward's family so well represented this evening," Uncle Tim said as he shook Anton's hand.

"Indeed," Uncle Guy replied before he touched Cherie's arm. "It was lovely seeing you, Thea, Anton. Please give Rosalie my love."

"I will."

It didn't pass any of our notices that he hadn't acknowledged Uncle Tim and Uncle Tim played it off when he smiled and yet I saw something dark in his eyes as he followed Uncle Guy's retreating form. A smile curved his lips though when he looked back at us.

"A man loses to you at poker and he's never the same again." Uncle Tim's entourage chuckled at his attempt to lighten the mood. One of his men whispered in his ear.

"I'm being told I need to mingle. Enjoy your evening. I'm really happy you're here." He held his hand out to Anton. "Have a good evening."

And then he was gone, lost in the crowd that surrounded him.

"What do you think that was all about?" I had never seen the two of them being so cool and distant. It was unsettling to say the least.

"I don't know, but it wasn't about poker."

"I wonder if Mom knows."

"I always had the sense your Dad was the glue that kept the three of them together."

I hadn't really thought about it growing up. If Uncle Guy was around so was Uncle Tim, but Dad and Uncle Tim were childhood friends and Uncle Guy his partner so yeah, maybe it really had been Dad keeping that friendship going. That was kind of sad. They both had lost a dear friend; they should be looking to each other to help ease that loss.

Anton pulled me from those thoughts when he flashed me a smile. "Alright let's rub some elbows and then get out of here. I have someone's ass to beat at Pac-Man."

"Dream on."

"Damian's home."

Kimber almost dropped the bagel she was smearing cream cheese on. We were having breakfast at Cup of Joe, something we tried to do at least once a week. Ryder joined us, a perk of being the boss. "He is?"

"Yeah."

The way they looked at each other and then at me and back again was like something out of a sitcom. "Since when?" Ryder asked.

"A month."

"And we're just learning of this now?" Kimber had a wicked evil eye.

"I just learned of it."

"He's home, Thea. You're both living on the same continent now." Ryder was a hopeless romantic.

"It's been a long time, lots of water under the bridge. We're different people. I'm happy he's home, but don't start planning a wedding."

"Maybe you'll discover you're not that different." Ryder and I both just stared at Kimber because it wasn't like her to be so optimistic.

"Where did that come from?" Ryder took the words right out of my mouth.

"I've never been in love but I have to believe it doesn't give up without a fight."

Who knew that Kimber was also a romantic, and I really liked her take on the situation, quite a lot.

Ryder changed the subject. "So we're taking Mom to dinner tomorrow night?"

"Yes. To Dahlia's and then Opal."

"Are the guys joining us?"

"No. Cam has work and Anton has a meeting, but he did reserve us a table."

Kimber flashed me a smile. "No line…awesome."

The night out with Mom had been a blast. I was home and getting ready for bed, but I was feeling edgy and Damian Tate was the reason. He was home. Anton had mentioned his gym hosted fights every night, which meant it was likely still open. It was kind of late, so heading to an MMA fight on my own was a bit reckless, but I couldn't settle. The sensation similar to when you're vacillating over the purchase of a ridiculous pair of shoes that you adore but the price tag stops your heart, but you make the decision that you have to have them. You want it done, you don't want to wait, you want those beauties on your feet and in your closet. I could pop in, check him out and leave and he never needed to know I was there. In and out, what could go wrong?

I liked that he had chosen the old neighborhood to set up his gym. The cab pulled up to the curb in front of his place and based on the look of the outside, I was very surprised by the number of people squeezed into it. The cage was upfront; the opponents engaging in bare knuckle MMA. It seemed fitting that Damian was a part of this culture since he had spent so much of his youth participating in fight clubs that were far less civilized than this. I remembered Damian that night I had seen him fight. He had been methodical, calculating and cold. He had destroyed his opponent but he wasn't fighting the flesh and blood, he was battling whatever haunted him. Had he finally made peace with that?

This fight didn't look as primitive, but it was a raw sport; the testosterone and pheromone levels in the room were off the charts. I sought Damian in the crowd, he was tall so he wouldn't be hard to locate. It took a while before I saw him coming from the back, talking to someone—likely the manager of one of the fighters. I felt him, like a moth to a flame. It was him because of how my body reacted to him, but he was different...no longer the boy I knew but a man. He was home, within reach and I wanted so badly to push my way through the crowd to get to him, but I didn't. My feet wouldn't move because I feared how he would react, feared he wouldn't be as happy to see me as I was him. We waited so long to be here, and now we were and I couldn't get my damn feet to move. So instead of going to the one person I wanted more than breath, I held back and just stared my fill. He looked good, really good, and that body after years of military training had been crafted into a work of art.

All those old feelings were there, but they were mellowed... like slipping into a favorite pair of slippers. The memory of the first time I had visited him on fight night teased the corners of my mind. The memory bringing a smile and it also had me turning for the door because if he caught me he would likely be just as pissed now as he had been then.

Distracted, I walked right into someone—a man in his thirties, wearing a suit but he'd removed his tie and unbuttoned a few buttons. Dirty blond hair, hazel eyes and a long, lanky body...he was cute if you were into the mature frat boy look. There was a smile on his face, but it was a lascivious smile that had me itching to cover myself from his view. "Sorry. Excuse me."

"Where's the fire?" He moved to block my exit, which just irritated me. Why did some men assume they could get up in your face because they wanted to? And this dude was drunk or high so this wasn't personal. I was a female and alone which made me easy pickings. I needed to get a t-shirt made up, something like, 'Yeah you, fuck off'.

"You can't walk into a man looking like you do and not at least give your name."

My skin crawled. "I didn't see you."

"You see me now. What's your name?"

"I'd like to get by please."

"So proper." He gave me a look that had bile rushing up my throat. "I think I'd like to hear you say please in a few different contexts."

I moved around him, but he grabbed my arm and pulled me back. "A name."

"Get the fuck off me."

"I just want a name."

"Now." I had learned self-defense, my dad and Cam had insisted. I could take this clown out with little effort, particularly since he was not in his right mind. I didn't really want to make a scene, drawing attention to myself, more specifically drawing Damian's attention.

Before I could formulate my next move, a deep and raspy voice came from over my shoulder. A voice I remembered, a voice I heard sometimes in my dreams. My body broke out in chills as my heart tripled its speed. "Fuck off."

In super slow motion I looked behind me to find Damian standing menacingly over me like some avenging angel, and though his glower wasn't directed at me at the moment, it would be after he dealt with the jackass still trying to get my name. I didn't even look back at the drunk because I was mesmerized at the sight of Damian. The years had been good to him, freaking fantastic, but at the moment he looked about as approachable as a rattlesnake.

"I saw her first, man."

"You're leaving here on a fucking gurney if I have to say it again."

The man released my arm and leveled a glare over my head then one at me before he turned and stumbled away. I felt another hand on my arm, gentler but still firm, as I was pulled across the room to the office in the back. The door had only just closed behind him when I turned and looked up into Damian's furious face. It was a beautiful face though, even more so now with the signs of living etched here and there. He didn't say anything, just gave a withering stare that had me breaking out into a sweat. He moved closer so that I could actually feel the anger coming off him. "What was that?"

Yes the feelings for him had mellowed and still it felt like my blood ignited and his voice was the match. It had been two years since Dad's funeral, the last time I had seen Damian, so his greeting was anticlimactic to say the least. "A drunk who didn't understand the meaning of the word no."

"Are you here alone?"

"Yes."

"At this hour?"

I supposed there was comfort in the fact that time didn't change some things, namely the overprotective nature of the men in my life. "I don't really need to answer that, right?"

"Thea." I had never heard my name said in quite that way before, an expletive.

"Damian."

"Why are you here?"

"Really? You have to ask that? You're home. I was curious."

He had a thought on that because the harsh lines of his face smoothed out some. And still he asked, "At one in the morning."

It wasn't one in the morning when I arrived. Sharing that seemed like a bad idea too. "Is that all you have to say to me? I haven't seen you in years, my timing could be better I agree, but I would have thought you would have more to say than a few curt words and a glower, though it is a respectable glower you've got there."

He pushed his hands into the pockets of his jeans and rolled back on his heels as he let his eyes wander down my body. "I'm still processing you standing in my office."

What did that mean? I waited for him to clarify, but he didn't and instead said, "I'll take you home."

"Thanks, but that's not necessary. I'll get a cab." The words were out before I appreciated what I said. I wanted him to drive me home, but it was a knee-jerk answer because my brain was still trying to decipher his cryptic comment.

"I'm not asking."

So typical. "I'd forgotten how pigheaded you were."

"That's the pot calling the kettle."

I wanted to stick my tongue out at him, when I was younger I would have. "Fine."

He grabbed his keys, reached for my hand and walked me through the gym. I forgot to be annoyed because I had missed having my hand held in his. Déjà vu swept through me remembering the countless times we had done this when we were younger, but the difference was now he was pulling me away from him, not drawing me close.

We stepped outside and around the building to the sexy, black car parked at the curb. A Maserati? He owned a Maserati? How the hell did he own a Maserati? Did he turn to the dark side, skirting the law like Anton? He held the door for me before coming around and folding himself behind the wheel.

"Nice car."

The engine purred to life and seeing him behind the wheel, the picture he made, I kind of just stared at him for a good portion of the trip. To be honest, I stared at him for the entire trip so I was more than a little surprised when we pulled up in front of my apartment building.

"How did you know I still lived here?"

"Same way you knew where my gym was." He climbed out while I pondered that. We didn't speak again until we reached my apartment. I unlocked my door and turned to him and that night from two years ago—the last time I had seen him—came back in technicolor. Mellowed feelings or not, I wanted a repeat performance. I wanted that so badly I just stared at him like a lobotomy patient.

"Lock your door."

I felt like Ralphie from *A Christmas Story* when he finally got to see Santa Claus to ask for his Red Ryder and he froze up. I just stared like a deer caught in headlights, so his suggestion of locking my door was one I grabbed onto. I stepped into my apartment, closed and locked the door. I heard the sound of his heavy footsteps retreating. It was about ten minutes later when my brain reengaged. And that's when I banged my head against the door, repeatedly. "What's the worst thing that could happen? Nice job, slick."

CHAPTER 8

W hy did you go so late?" Ryder asked. She and Kimber were over and I was sharing the disastrous reunion between Damian and me from last night. It hadn't been a complete disaster because I got to see his beloved face again. And despite our reunion, I got weak in the knees knowing he was finally home. It was his response to me that wasn't so great; it sucked if I was being honest. He treated me much like Cam and Anton did...affectionate in a familial way. I didn't want Damian as another brother, but it had been a long time. That might be all that was left of our relationship. The man had been home for a month and never once contacted me. That said a lot and it hurt. His silent acknowledgment that we were no longer a we. But I had learned the hard way that life was short, so I'd take Damian however I could get him.

"I was curious and I tried to reason with myself that a visit during a more reasonable hour, like daylight, was smarter, but I couldn't get the notion of seeing him out of my head."

"I know that feeling…like that bartender at the little place in the Village. You remember him, right? I couldn't get the idea out of my head that I needed to blow him. I did, right there behind the bar. That's a good memory."

"Only you would equate a reunion with someone's first love to a blow job." Ryder rolled her eyes at Kimber before she added, "How did he look?"

"Fantastic…older, sexy, hot as hell. Anyway, I was leaving when a drunken dude got in my face. You know the type, arrogant and on the prowl, looking for the lone female."

"He didn't hurt you, did he?"

"No, he was just a pest, but one that was persistent until Damian stepped in."

"Oh shit. So not only busted for being out late but caught in the exact situation of why you shouldn't be out late."

"Exactly. After scaring off my unwanted suitor, he scolded me like a child."

"I would have scolded you too." Ryder had a good angry mama voice. "There is more."

"He's been home for a month, but he never called me. Why wouldn't he have called? And his greeting last night was lukewarm at best."

"Oh, Thea."

"I knew we were over, he made that very clear in his letter, I'm just surprised how much it hurts getting the confirmation from him."

"Maybe he was just caught off guard. You'd be shocked senseless if he showed up unannounced at your doorstep."

"I hope so." I didn't want to think about my reunion with Damian because it was depressing, so I moved the conversation along. "Anyway, my plan had obvious flaws, but I'm not the first one of us to come up with a half-baked idea all in the name of a hot guy."

Ryder squeezed my hand in comfort at the same time she tried to dismiss my comment. I didn't let her. "You know what I'm talking about. Doing the drive by of the parcel store repeatedly just to see the man working the counter instead of shipping something so you could actually talk to him."

Ryder tried for nonchalance but failed. "That's different."

"How?"

"He never caught me except for that one time."

My head jerked to Kimber's, hers to me. It was my voice that pitched a bit higher with incredulity. "The time you drove into the back of the UPS truck that was parked at the curb loading up packages. That one time you mean?"

"It was a small dent."

"Small dent my ass," Kimber said then added, "I have some bad news."

My heart dropped. "Derrick?" She had been out with him several times and from the way she glowed when she talked about him... she liked him, a lot.

"No, he's great." She lowered her voice, like she didn't want anyone else overhearing what she said next, which was weird because it was just the three of us in my apartment. "I have a gray hair on my..." Her comment completely threw me. Made evident when I almost spit out the wine I had just sipped.

"Do I want to know why you were inspecting your lady garden?"

"My vagina and me class."

"Your what?"

"Yeah, a friend took it. She said it changed her life."

"As in she no longer has one because she is someone who spends time getting acquainted with her vagina?"

"No, it's not so much a mystery anymore."

"I wasn't aware the vagina was a mystery at all. There are tons of books on the subject that not only explain what it is and what it can do, but also how it is different from the penis."

Kimber glared. "You're teasing me."

"Oh, yes. I am teasing you. I will continue to tease you about this until you are all gray down there."

"Whatever. Doesn't change the fact that I have a gray hair. I plucked it, but it'll come back."

"Are you worried that the next time Derrick heads south he will see the gray hair and realize he is in bed with one of the *Golden Girls* and flee?"

"You're just full of snarky comments."

"The subject makes it very easy."

"You're awfully quiet, Ryder. Don't you want to add your two cents like this one?"

Ryder was trying very hard not to laugh. "I honestly have nothing to say."

The lead story for the eleven o'clock news playing on the television in the background caught my attention. "Turn that up."

Ryder reached for the remote.

It was the McKay case, the one Uncle Tim was defending. My stomach twisted seeing Cathy McKay's father, Chris, in the courtroom especially after the confrontation I had witnessed between him and my uncle. He looked destroyed, his daughter was dead and her children orphaned and my uncle was working hard to get her killer off.

"The prosecution has rested. The defense, led by Timothy Gallagher, starts tomorrow. Once again, the prosecution in the case of Cathy McKay and Jacob Hunter has rested. The defense team will start opening arguments in the morning."

I wasn't listening to the report because I was too busy staring at the picture in the courtroom, specifically my uncle. He looked smug and the juxtaposition he made next to the devastated father turned my stomach.

That night something jarred me from sleep. I was groggy and in the middle of a really great dream that starred Damian. A part of me was still dreaming, wishing it were him sneaking into my apartment to have his way with me, but lust subsided as that sixth sense kicked in. I had the distinct feeling that someone was in my apartment. I should have locked my bedroom door and called 911. I didn't. I reached for the bat I kept near my bed and went to investigate. When they found me dead, my ghost could berate my dead form on how foolhardy my action had been.

I cracked the door to my bedroom and smelled coffee. Someone broke into my apartment and started brewing coffee? There was a part of me that had to give the home invader points for having their priorities straight, but that was my coffee. Damn it. I smelled bacon and that was the last straw. Fear gave way to anger. It was one thing to break into someone's home and kill them, but you were stepping over the fucking line eating their bacon and drinking their coffee. And yes I knew a therapist could have a career treating me for *my* messed up priorities, but we were talking about bacon and coffee.

I moved from my bedroom, saw the man standing at my stove and lifted the bat.

"I'm making some for you too, sis."

Cam. Then I screeched, "Cam!"

"Keep it down or Mrs. Cooke will be over and there's not enough for her too."

Mrs. Cooke was my seventy-year-old neighbor.

"What are you doing here at this hour?"

"I was in the area and I was hungry."

"So you break into my house and eat my food? What if I called 911?"

He gave me the look, the one that said he knew me better than that. "You're not really mad and even if you were, I'm making bacon and coffee."

He was right. They were my Achilles heel, bacon and coffee and Damian. I moved to the cabinet for the plates.

"Did you call Mom?"

"Yeah."

"Did she mention yoga man?"

Cam stopped dishing out the bacon to stare at me like I had grown horns. "Yoga man?"

"I visited her a couple weeks ago and she was doing the down-ward dog with a young, twenty-something trainer. I now know what I will be like at her age. You'll have to kill me before that."

"Mom is doing yoga? That's unnatural."

"It's a sign of the pending apocalypse. Have you been following Uncle Tim's case?" I asked.

"Hard not to. It's all over the news. Tough case. I wouldn't want to be him."

"The father confronted Uncle Tim not too long ago."

Cam followed me to the table and set our plates down. "How do you know?"

"I was there."

He tensed as every muscle in his body went hard. "He approached Uncle Tim while you were with him?"

"He was upset. Can you blame him?"

"No, but there's a line."

"Had it been you or me, I think that line would get blurry too."

"Likely."

"Do you think they have the wrong guy?"

"I wasn't in on the bust, but the evidence seemed pretty damning."

"It is kind of a testament to Dad and Uncle Tim's relationship that they could be on such opposite sides and still stay close all those years."

"I know. Personally, I think it would eat me up, arresting assholes only to have my best buddy getting them off. Dad was always more level-headed than me."

"And yet, you're a lot like him. You and Anton, you a cop and him a…"

"True." He reached for his coffee. "Damian's home. Have you seen him?"

I didn't go into detail since his reaction would be the same as I got from Damian, a scolding. Not to mention there wasn't much to share about our lackluster reunion. "Yeah, the other day. Why didn't you tell me he was home?"

Surprise flashed over his face. "You didn't know?"

"Not until Anton told me the other day."

"Sorry. I just assumed Damian contacted you. What's that all about?"

"Your guess is as good as mine. Mom is hosting a dinner."

Cam's smile was a little sad because he was thinking as I was. All we were missing was Dad. "I've started going through the files Dad left for me."

"Dad left you files?"

"Cold cases he was working on in his spare time."

"I didn't know Dad was doing that."

"And going through his stuff…" Cam leaned back in his chair, "…I want to know what happened to him."

Unease moved through me. "You don't think his death was random violence?"

"No."

At first, I responded to his news with my breakfast wanting to come back up my throat, but this was actually a good thing. If his death was related to the cases he had been working on then there was a chance we could bring his killer to justice. A remote possibility when his death was believed to have been a random act.

"This is why you've been so busy."

"Yeah, I'm working his case on my down time."

"You must have some theories."

"I do, but maybe we can hold off having that discussion."

"Okay, but when you're ready to talk, I am ready to listen. Have you talked to Uncle Guy about this?"

Cam stood and reached for his plate. "I'm keeping it on the down low."

"Even from Uncle Guy?"

"Yeah."

"Is something going on with him?"

"Why do you ask that?"

"I saw him at the fundraiser and the tension between him and Uncle Tim was intense."

"That's interesting."

"I suspect it's more interesting to you because you know more than I do."

"I'll share and soon."

"Fair enough."

I popped the last piece of bacon in my mouth. "You always did make it better than me."

It had been a few days since Cam's visit and I found myself mulling over our conversation often. Dad had been working cold cases. That didn't surprise me. He had definitely been an advocate for the victim. I wasn't even surprised to learn he left his files with Cam, knowing how he was following in Dad's footsteps. Hearing that whatever case Dad had been working on might have led to his death was harder to process. He was gone, I had worked through that grief, but knowing there was a chance I could look his killer in the eyes, could watch as he was sent to prison. It was closure I never thought any of us would have. I was sure Cam had not mentioned this to Mom. She too was healing, but this would definitely be a setback for her. It was better to wait until there was a resolution before pulling her into it.

To take my mind from questions I had no answers to, I distracted myself with baking a batch of oatmeal raisin cookies. Unlike my failed attempts in my youth, I had become quite the baker. And though I vowed to not share my cookies, I did. The scent filled my apartment, so I wasn't at all surprised by the knock at the door. Mrs. Cooke lived right next door. She had moved in just last year after she lost her husband of close to fifty years. She was lovely, very friendly showing up on my doorstep her first day with a smile on her face and a homemade Bundt cake. Since that time, she had started dieting, which I didn't really understand because she was seventy; at her age I think I'd be eating whatever the hell I wanted. But because she was always dieting, she didn't buy or make sweets anymore, so she came here and ate mine. I guess the calories didn't count if you weren't home when you ate them.

"Mrs. Cooke. Come in."

"Hello, dear."

"I was just about to pull some cookies from the oven. Would you like some?"

"Oh I shouldn't."

Even though that's the reason she was here. She probably smelled them and followed her nose to my door. "I know, but with a cup of tea."

"Twist my arm."

She settled in the living room while I went to put on the water. "Have you met our new neighbor?" she asked.

"New neighbor? No."

"I saw him the other day. He's very handsome. You should stop by with a pie."

I loved my neighbors, but I was the youngest of them by decades. If there was a new neighbor, he was probably closer to Mrs. Cooke's age than mine. "I realize I'm not dating much, Mrs. Cooke, but I think I would like to date someone closer to my own age."

"He is your age, well close. He's probably in his fifties."

I choked on my own saliva, but close to my age. Fifty? Really? "You do realize I'm only thirty-one."

"Well, yes, dear but anyone under sixty is a youngster as far as I'm concerned."

"I appreciate that, but fifties is not close to my age. He's probably closer to you in age than me."

She pondered my words. "I guess you're right. Maybe *I'll* bring him a pie."

The fact that she could tease about bringing another man a pie was huge. She and my mom had connected, both losing their husbands, and I was happy to see both of them were healing. Which had me wondering how long she intended to stay. She had a lovely place in Westchester, one that she let the staff and lawyers take care of while she mourned. I had seen a few pictures in her albums and the place was amazing.

"Have you given any thought to moving here permanently?"

Her smile dimmed a bit and I got it. There were memories in her home, lots of them. "Our home, you mean."

"Yeah."

"I certainly can't keep the estate myself. And it is a lot of money to keep going."

Money she apparently had. Her husband had been an investment banker on Wall Street.

"Can I ask why you have kept it going?"

"Mitchell loved that house. He did much of the work on it himself. I wasn't ready to let that piece of him go. But you're right, I need to make a decision on the place."

"Well you don't have to make that decision right now."

"True, especially since those cookies smell done."

And she wasn't wrong when the timer for the cookies went off a few seconds later.

Mom had managed to find a date for dinner that worked for everyone, well everyone but Ryder and Kimber. The guys were on their way...*Damian* was on his way. And I could talk a big game about mellowed feelings and being friends, but my heart was pounding in my chest with excitement at the thought of seeing him again. Tempered only by the lukewarm response I had received from him that night at his gym and the fact that he had neglected to tell me he was home.

I tried to distract myself by helping Mom. I stood in her kitchen whipping up a salad.

"I'm sorry the girls couldn't make it."

"They're sorry too. But we'll get them here the next time. How did you tie these three down?"

"Anton took care of it for me."

He would. He loved Mom.

"And they're all coming?"

"Yes. It'll be nice having a house full of voices again." Her voice broke a bit and I reached for her hand.

"He's here too." I was referring to Dad.

"I know."

The doorbell rang. "Can you get that? I need to warm up the buns."

"Sure."

Unlike Thanksgiving from so long ago, I was prepared for the sight of Damian. And even being prepared, my body went haywire. Our eyes locked and all those old feelings came flooding back. I wanted to jump into his arms, but like he was reading my thoughts he pushed his hands into the pockets of his jeans. My heart cracked at his rejection.

Cam pulled me close for a hug. "Twice in as many weeks. You're going to get tired of seeing me, sis."

I tried to play it off, tried to be as remote as Damian and turned my attention on Cam. "Not likely."

Anton sniffed the air before he pressed a kiss on my cheek and started for the kitchen. "Is that the cheeseburger casserole?"

"Yes."

I heard Mom's delighted laughter. He probably just kissed her in appreciation.

"I'm starved," Cam said then walked to the kitchen, which left me alone with Damian.

He had always been a huge presence but now it was like he sucked all the air from the room. The need to curl up against him was strong, like the pull of the moon on the tide. And I loved knowing that hadn't changed, that he still tugged on all the right strings for me even if he didn't feel the same anymore.

Hi was on the tip of my tongue, but remembering how sweet and erotic that one word could be coming from his lips, I swallowed that greeting and instead said, "Damian."

He studied me for a second or two before my name rolled off his tongue in a sexy whisper. "Thea." It was almost as good as hi.

We heard Cam's greeting when he entered the kitchen. "Yo, Ma."

"Cameron Edward Ahern. You give me a hug this minute."

"She'll want one from you too."

Damian smiled, the sight making my heart slam into my ribs because I could count on one hand the number of times I'd been gifted with one from him. Then he followed after Cam. I wanted a hug from him too, but I didn't think it was wise to say as much.

DAMIAN

Fuck. For all the training and discipline I'd developed over the years, one look at Thea and it all went to shit. We weren't teenagers anymore. Our lives went in very different directions, but seeing the woman, the girl I loved grew into, was bittersweet because even with all the time that separated us, and the circumstances, I was still in love with her. So instead of yanking her into my arms and keeping her there, I pushed my hands into my pockets.

THEA

"It was just as good as I remembered," Anton said as he leaned back in his chair. "Thank you, Rosalie."

"My pleasure. It's so good having you all under the same roof again. Damian, I heard you've come home for good."

"Yes ma'am."

"And you're settling down here in the Bronx?"

"That's the plan."

"I like this plan. You've been gone long enough. Don't you agree, Thea?"

I had been looking at Damian. It was safe because he was looking at Mom, but with her last comment his attention shifted to me. My eyes lowered to my plate. "Yes."

"I'll get the dessert," Mom announced.

"I'll help you," Anton offered.

"I need to make a call. I'll be right back," Cam said as he too walked from the table while reaching for his cell.

Damian sat across from me. His long fingers playing with the tines on an unused fork, his focus on what he was doing. I liked the signs of aging on his face, the lines at the corner of his eyes and near his mouth. I hoped they were laugh lines…hoped that he'd found what he'd been missing. The man in front of me was practically a stranger and that observation twisted my heart. I knew how many times he had been deployed and I had a theoretical idea of what his unit did overseas, but what had it really been like? What had he endured to forge the man that sat across from me now? And even with him being different, with us both being different, I still felt that pull and connection. I still loved him.

The words were out before I could stop them. "I can't believe you're here. I have so many questions and yet I could happily sit across from you and say nothing and just look my fill. I've missed you."

His focus shifted to me and I was treated to the beauty of those pale green eyes, but it wasn't sadness I saw in them like I had when he was younger, instead I saw nothing. No emotion at all. He wasn't just older. He was harder and more closed off. And considering how he had spent the past thirteen years, I understood. "Cam mentioned you were a graphic designer."

I tried to keep the disappointment and pain from my voice because I wanted him to say he had missed me too. "I do mostly book covers and branding, but I love the work and the commute is ideal because I get to work from home. And you? I heard you were a Green Beret? What was that like?"

"Have you been back to McGinty's?" That was the bar he had taken me that night, Dad's favorite watering hole. Clearly he wasn't big on conversation that revolved around him.

"On his birthday. You?"

"On the anniversary of his memorial."

"But you were overseas."

"Some things are more important."

Tears burned the back of my eyes. He and I had missed our chance, but I loved hearing his loyalty to Dad even now. "You should have called me. I would have joined you."

"That's why I didn't."

I managed to control my reaction to that, my harsh inhale was muffled as I glanced down at the table. I never knew words could feel like a slap in the face. What the hell had he meant by that? He didn't want me to join him? Before I could call him on his comment, Mom and Anton returned.

"Who wants coffee with their cake?"

Damian was once again looking at the table. We might be different and what had been was no longer, but he sure as hell would be explaining that comment.

I was working, finishing a book cover for a paranormal themed book but the dinner at Mom's consumed my thoughts; particularly Damian and how different he was. It was naïve to believe things between us would be as they had been, but never once in all the times I imagined our reunion did I imagine the cold and impersonal conversation we had shared at dinner. Regrets sucked.

I didn't usually have the television on while working, but the verdict to the McKay case was about to be read. I was conflicted because of course I wanted to see Uncle Tim win, but in this case I really did believe they had found the killer and he was going to walk. News crews were lined up outside the courthouse just waiting to get first reactions.

The jury filed back in as the cameras panned from the prosecution to the defense to the McKay family. Chris McKay upfront, his eyes blank as he waited for the verdict. I couldn't imagine what was going through his head. The lead juror handed the verdict to the bailiff who carried it to the judge. He silently read it before folding up the slip and handing it back to the bailiff.

"Have you reached a verdict?"

"We have, your honor."

"And how do you find?"

"We find the defendant, Jacob Hunter, on the charges of murder in the second degree, not guilty."

The courtroom exploded with shouts, but the camera was focused on Chris McKay. The person behind that camera would likely receive accolades because he caught the single tear that rolled down the older man's face. The judge called for order, the juror was reading off the lesser charges and all the while Chris McKay sat like a statue. The camera then panned to Uncle Tim and his client, both had the biggest smiles on their faces and I actually felt a sharp pang of anger. I understood it was a victory but we were talking about the murder of a young woman. It seemed to me it was more humane to curtail the celebrating until after the cameras were off.

The judge dismissed the case, released the defendant and about a half an hour later Uncle Tim and his client were standing on the steps outside the courtroom. There were camera flashes and reporters shouting questions as Uncle Tim took the podium.

"Justice was carried out here today. The verdict may not be the popular one, but it was the legal one."

"And what about Chris McKay, his grandchildren. What words do you have for them?"

"This isn't personal. I'm very sorry for their loss. I've been there and know the helplessness, the anger, the need to find someone to blame. Unfortunately, the law proved beyond a reasonable doubt that my client is not that person."

"And what of popular opinion that the cops had it right? That they are even now following a few leads that may prove he did in fact murder Cathy McKay."

"It's neither here nor there. A jury of his peers found him not guilty. He can't be tried again, double jeopardy. The case, as it pertained to Jacob Hunter, is closed. Thank you."

I really hoped Jacob wasn't the killer because not getting

another shot at him if new evidence did come to light, that he was protected by double jeopardy, would be a really hard pill to swallow for Cathy's family.

CHAPTER 9

I had spent the morning running errands and was now famished. I had stopped off at Ryder's for a large coffee and something sinful, grabbing a treat for Mrs. Cooke too. I had just left Cup of Joe when my phone rang. Seeing it was Cam, I rearranged my bags so I could answer.

"Hey, Cam. What's up?"

"Just saying hi. What are you doing right now?"

"I was running errands, but I'm on my way home. Why?"

"Want to grab a bite to eat later?"

"Yeah."

"Damian is joining us too."

Excitement rushed through me before I could stop it. "Sounds good. Where were you thinking?"

"Opal. We might get Anton to put his quest for world domination on hold to join us."

"I'll meet you there."

"Catch a cab. I'll cover it."

"I can afford a cab."

"And I'm your brother so shut up."

"You're so sweet."

"See you soon."

He was seriously a clown, but the idea of dinner with my three favorite guys had me walking with a little extra pep in my step.

At Opal, I was shown to our table. I was the first to arrive and while I waited the hostess sent the waitress over to take my drink order. I wasn't there long when Cam arrived and with him was Damian. I felt a wicked case of déjà vu seeing the two of them together and how similar and yet different the picture was that they made now.

"You beat us," Cam said as he bent in half and pressed a kiss on my forehead.

"Not by much."

"Thea." Despite myself, I really liked this new form of greeting—my name from his lips.

"Damian."

"Have you seen Anton?" Cam asked.

"No."

"I'll go hunt him down," Cam said, but he was already on the move. Damian took his seat, leaned back and leveled those eyes on me.

I didn't hedge because I didn't know how much time I would have him alone. "You said you didn't call me when you came home because you knew I would want to join you. What did you mean by that?"

He didn't answer right away, just kind of studied me like someone would a painting or in my case a large slice of cake. "Considering how it ended the last time it seemed wiser to avoid temptation."

His or mine? Before I could ask, Cam returned with Anton

and instead of clarification I was only more confused. We seriously needed to work on our timing.

Anton greeted me with a kiss on the head. He always did, so did Cam. Not Damian, at least not now. But when we were younger, those hands had roamed over every inch of me. And just the memory had an ache forming between my legs. I shifted in my seat and reached for the cold water. My eyes collided with Damian's. I would have sold my soul to know what he was thinking.

"Any preference on food or should I just have them send out a sampling?"

"A sampling works," Cam said and since that sounded good to me too I just nodded a reply. Besides words were difficult with how parched my throat had grown thinking about Damian and his hands.

Anton took his seat and folded one leg over the other. "You're ready to catch Thea up?"

I'm sure I looked comical with how fast my head whipped around to Anton. I made myself light-headed. "Catch me up?"

"You wanted to know what I had learned about Dad's death."

"Yeah. I do." Anton's choice of words penetrated then. Catch *me* up. "Why do I have the sense that this is solely for my benefit?"

"It is. Anton and Damian are already in the loop."

I wasn't sure how I felt about that…them being in the loop but not me. "How long have they been in the loop?"

Cam pulled a hand through his hair, a nervous gesture. "Since Dad's memorial."

"Both of them?"

"Yes."

Anger whipped through me as I glared at Damian. "You've been communicating with Cam for two years, but you never contacted me?" It was fucking personal him not reaching out, but I forced myself to shake it off. "Never mind. So the three of you have been playing *Hardy Boys* for two years and no one thought to include me?"

"We needed to get a handle on what we were dealing with."

"And do you have a handle on it?"

"We're getting there."

"What do you know?"

"The pending investigation at the precinct into evidence tampering, there's a link to that and some of the cold cases Dad was investigating. I think he might have uncovered some dirty cops."

That was not at all the direction I thought this was going. Dirty cops. I felt ill at the implication.

"I haven't shared this with Mom and I don't intend to until I know more."

"Are these cops we know?"

"So far, no. But I'm still digging." He leaned closer to me. "I don't know the extent of this, how far up it goes. I'm being discreet, so I don't expect blowback, but I want you to be extra cautious. Don't take any unnecessary risks."

"Like paying someone a visit at one in the morning." The words were barely off Damian's tongue when Cam and Anton started talking at once. To be accurate in the retelling they were shouting at me, but I was fuming that Damian could ignore me but he didn't have a problem with ratting me out.

"If you hadn't kept me in the dark about being home, letting me learn you were finally home from Anton, I wouldn't have needed to make that late night trip." Silence fell over the table and two very angry sets of eyes turned on Damian. "It's not important. Ancient history, right Damian?"

If that comment had any impact on him, I couldn't tell.

Cam was still glaring at Damian but it was me he reprimanded. "You can't pull that shit, Thea. I'm serious. I don't think this will touch you, but you need to be smart."

"I am smart, I just act foolishly sometimes."

"Don't be fucking foolish."

Damian's comment had my temper boiling. He left, chose to stay out of my life, demanded I stay out of his, and yet he was sitting here like he had any say in my life now. The rational part of my brain acknowledged we were family, but the emotional part of my brain thought he should mind his own fucking business because he had been communicating, probably daily, with Cam for over two years and had been home for a month but never called me. The emotional side won.

"You gave up a right to thoughts on my behavior a long time ago."

"Let's calm down." Cam directed that at Damian because he looked stupendously pissed at me. So that comment got through.

Anton was as always the calm presence. "Alright, she knows. Leave her alone." And then he took my chin between his thumb and forefinger. "You ever pull a stunt like that again though and I'll put you over my knee."

"Why couldn't you have been girls?"

DAMIAN

My muscles ached as I hammered into the bag. My body was exhausted and still I kept at it because the pain helped battle the ghosts. This time the ghosts were my own fucking fault. After that first attempt at seeing Thea, I had picked up the phone countless times to call her, but I never did. I reasoned that she had to have known I was home, Anton or Cam would have told her, and she made no attempt to contact me. She had done it before, sought to avoid me because it was easier than dealing with all the emotions stirred up at seeing me. I didn't realize she didn't know I was home. She must think I was a real fucker being home for a month and never calling her. I was a fucker because I'd acted like a fucking pussy and in the process I hurt her. Her comment that I lost my right, she wasn't wrong, and yet I refused to accept that because she was mine. Always had been. There was more than anger in her words though—the shadow just behind her eyes...pain or maybe regret. I had regrets, a whole fucking footlocker full of them, but dwelling on the past was pointless.

She'd been beautiful as a teenager, but she was exquisite now.

I'd bet money she still took a moment to appreciate the bloom of a rose and the flight of hummingbird. That genuine love of life had been one of the things that had drawn me to her. It still did. Regrets sucked, looking back on your choices and knowing you made some of the wrong ones. Especially when they cost you the one you wanted more than breath, they really fucking sucked.

Trouble was brewing and the priority was to keep it from touching her. And if that meant I had to watch her from the sidelines—the life I had foisted on her—that was my penitence for not holding on with both hands to what I had when I had it.

Checking my watch it was after four. The cleaning crew had finished an hour before. I locked up and headed upstairs, stripping on my way to the shower. Thinking about Thea that night at my gym, the man that had his fucking hands on her, touching her like he owned her, had bloodlust burning through me. Did she deal with that shit often? It was part of the reason I wanted her brought up to speed. She was a trusting soul and would unknowingly welcome the fox right into the hen house. She had said the only thing worse than a life without me was a world without me in it. I hadn't appreciated how right those words were until she was the one flirting with potential trouble. Her apartment still had only that one piece of shit lock. A lock I could kick in with little effort. How had Cam let that go all these years? I intended to rectify that immediately.

It was only after six when I left my apartment. Thea wouldn't be up yet. Tough shit. Her safety was more important than her fucking beauty rest.

THEA

I woke in the morning to the sound of someone pounding on my door. It was too early for this, particularly since I hadn't fallen asleep until three in the morning. I grabbed my robe and on the way to the door I formulated all the nasty comments I intended to share with whatever asshole felt it okay to bother me so early. Yanking the door open, all those scathing remarks went right out of my head at the sight of an irate Damian. His expression was so sour he would make a flower wilt.

"It is too early for this."

He pushed into my apartment. "You need better locks."

What? Where the hell did that come from? Yes it was true I could use better locks on my door, but why the hell did he feel the need to share that discovery with me at this godforsaken hour.

"Why are you here now?"

"Stupid that you've been living here with that shit on your door."

"What is stupid is that I have to deal with an enraged and unwelcomed Neanderthal first thing in the morning. This could have been discussed later, like after lunch. Why are you here now?"

He ignored my question. The man was on a mission to lock down my apartment when he said, "I'll send someone over later to add the locks and a security system."

"That's very kind, but not necessary."

"I'm not asking, Thea."

"You never do." I could argue with him but it would be about as productive as slamming my head into a wall, repeatedly.

He seemed to be assessing the safety of my apartment, walking around the place like he owned it. He even walked into my bedroom. And me, the fool that I was, watched him because despite why he was here, I really liked seeing him in my apartment…specifically my bedroom. Now I was tired and horny. Fabulous.

"I would like to go back to sleep now that we've taken care of this most pressing issue, so I'll show you to the door if you're done."

He was already making his exit. "I'll be back with my guy later today."

"Yeah, you said that already, I'll be here."

He walked out without another word. What the hell had that been all about? Sure, I needed better locks, it was something I should have taken care of before this, but the building had never had any trouble. That wasn't an excuse, but I had only just learned of the need for extra caution. My temper had definitely been stirred by Damian's continued high-handedness, but I acknowledged he was acting as he was because he still cared.

Damian had shown up with his friend as threatened. He stayed only long enough to get his man into my apartment. Carlton had spent hours installing the alarm system and then another hour teaching it to me. It had been two days since I got my alarm and even though I had already felt safe in my apartment, I felt even more so having the place locked up like Fort Knox.

I was at the grocery store in need of a sugar fix, scanning the offerings in the bakery, when the kid behind the counter asked, "Thea, what can I get you?"

We were on a first name basis. "Hey, Kenny. I'm thinking the sticky bun cake because that icing looks good, but I had a date not too long ago and he went on and on about risk. Now he's got me thinking about what I eat. I'm only thirty-one, but it's a downhill trip to forty and then fifty and even though fifty is the new forty, it's still fifty. Which apparently my neighbor thinks I look close to, trying to hook me up with our new neighbor who *is* in his fifties. Not to mention I've had to deal with a blast from the past, a very welcomed, sexy and slightly irritating blast from the past."

"So am I boxing one of these beauties for you or do you want something else?"

He looked humored by my indecision; the line of people behind me waiting for their sweets looked annoyed.

"I'll get the sticky bun cake."

"Good choice."

I apologized to the people waiting. I tended to get carried away when sweets were involved. It was while I stood waiting that I saw Damian. At first I thought he was a hallucination because I had started to daydream about him, thought about him at night too, but I realized he wasn't a figment of my imagination. The man

I was even now trying to forget through a nearly lethal dose of sugar stood in my grocery store. The sight itself wasn't a foreign one because he and I had done countless trips to the grocery store for Mom growing up, but looking at his body I suspected the experience would be a very different one now.

He walked toward me and I had always loved watching him move, but seeing all that was Damian Tate now moving in my direction was a sight I could seriously get used to. He curled his back to lower his head and the scent of him had a moan burning in the back of my throat because I remembered that scent, thought of it often while in bed. "You're using the alarm?"

Not the words I wanted to hear. I would have much preferred my name or something sweet and dirty or better yet no words at all—just the lowering of his mouth another inch so he could kiss me. My reply wasn't very enthusiastic. "Yes and thank you."

"Anton and I want to talk with you."

"Okay."

"Is now good?"

I guess I wouldn't be indulging in my nearly lethal dose of sugar. "Sure."

"Kenny, I can't take that with me right now."

"Do you want me to hold it?"

"Yeah. I'll be back later."

"You got it."

Damian and I didn't speak as we walked to the car. We also drove in silence. When we reached the club he led me to Anton's office, which was located in the back, and still I saw quite a bit. Anton's associates had gathered, some of which I recognized from pictures on the news. These men were what legends were made of—the kind of mobsters depicted in the movies and books...the kind who would kill their mothers to secure a deal. I had only caught a glimpse, but they were very easily recognizable, because like Anton, they were practically celebrities...Dominic Ferrari, Salvatore Federico and Sylvie Dane. It was the juxtaposition of Anton against the older men that held my attention. He was younger and unlike the big brawny bulldogs, he reminded me of a dagger, a dangerously sharp, but beautiful dagger. When he struck, I bet you didn't see him coming. He might look cultured, but Anton came from a place far worse than most would ever see. I didn't know the specifics, but I did know he had clawed his way out of a dark and ugly place. And even with all the polish he had now, those demons he had battled back and leashed still lived inside him.

I was shown into Anton's office, the man himself appearing a few minutes later.

"What's going on, Anton?"

"Please have a seat."

"I have a feeling I need to be standing for this news."

Anton and Damian shared a look before Anton said, "What Cam didn't share with you the other night is part of what he's investigating involves an associate of mine who isn't a fan of NYPD poking their noses into his business."

The first trickle of alarm moved through me and I did sit, dropped right into the chair behind me. Cam wasn't just looking into dirty cops but also gangsters. Had Dad been too? Was that why he'd been killed?

"Thea?" I focused back on Anton before I slid my gaze to Damian, who was leaning up against the wall opposite the door. The pieces fell into place. "That's why you resigned your commission, why you moved back home. To help Cam figure out what happened to Dad."

"Yeah."

I was up and across the room wrapping my arms around his waist and pressing my face to his chest to hide my tears. "Thank you. I'm sorry I gave you a hard time the other night."

I'd caught him off guard, but he didn't hesitate in pulling me closer. I didn't want to let go, but I did. And a glance at him showed he wasn't unaffected by the moment because his eyes were darker than usual. My legs were just about useless so I didn't walk back to Anton's desk and instead took a seat on the much closer sofa.

I had forgotten Anton was in the room until he said, "Damian is helping Cam with ferreting out some information." There was understanding in his expression as he studied me. "We're concerned about you."

"Me? Why?"

"Your Cam's sister and if those he is investigating catch wind of what he's doing, it is possible they will seek leverage to make him drop the case."

That had a shiver of fear moving down my spine. "You think it's possible someone might come after me?"

"Remote, but it's not a chance we are willing to take," Anton said.

I was a little slow, but I was catching up. "That would explain your early hour visit from the other day about the locks on my door."

Damian didn't reply but he didn't need to.

"That was all you had to say as to why you were so insistent on the alarm system." I raised my hand to stop his interjection, not that he was falling all over himself to reply. "I realize the man you are now seems to hoard words like a little kid with a shiny new toy. Still when you drag a woman from bed before the sun rises, it is best to be clear as to why you are doing so."

His grin in reply mesmerized me, enough that I just stared at him until the grin turned into a wicked smile then I shifted my attention back to Anton because I was feeling reckless and now was not the time. "Do you think Mom, Kimber and Ryder are on the radar?"

"Kimber and Ryder probably not, but your mom…we've got her covered."

"You have someone watching my mom?"

"Her trainer is one of Damian's."

My head once again jerked to Damian. "Yoga man is one of yours?"He was stuck on the nickname; me, I was relieved to hear of the connection to Damian because otherwise the way they met was just plain weird.

"Did you have someone on me?"

"We've all been, Cam, Damian and me but doing it on the down low. We're stepping that up and Damian wants point."

Damian had been acting rather distant with me so hearing he wanted point both puzzled and excited me. I couldn't focus on that though because I was worried about why they felt they needed to up their game. "If this conversation was meant to reassure me, I'm not feeling very reassured."

"The more information you have the better prepared you'll be to protect yourself."

"True, but you're only giving me bits and pieces."

Anton walked around his desk and settled on the corner of it. "Think it through, Thea. Your dad was working on a case that might have involved dirty cops. In the middle of that investigation..."

I had already thought of that and yet hearing it spoken out loud wasn't easy.

Anton noticed because he softened his voice when he added, "It can't be overlooked. Plus, you were the executor of your dad's will."

I had been staring at my lap as I twisted my fingers, but that comment from Anton earned him my attention. I had been executor. Dad knew Mom wouldn't be able to handle it. And in her shoes, if it had been Damian, I wouldn't have either. "Someone might think he left something regarding the investigation and I found it while going through his things?"

"It's all conjecture, but we would be fools to not consider all the possibilities and plan accordingly."

"What about Cam? Wouldn't it be more likely that they would go after him, like they had with Dad?" The thought had tears stinging my eyes.

"He's smart and knows the kind of people he is dealing with." My dad had been smart too. Anton waited until my gaze met his. "These precautions are likely all for nothing, but it is better to be safe than sorry."

"Does Cam know you're talking to me?"

"Yes. He wanted to be here but he couldn't get away and didn't want us to wait."

"I'll do whatever you think is necessary."

"I don't think it will be for a long duration." Anton checked his watch. "But sadly, I have other business to see to."

"I'll take you home," Damian said as he moved to join me.

"Do you also have other business?"

I got a raised brow from Damian in response.

"What I mean to say is if you need to come back to this part of town, seeing me home is silly…not with rush hour traffic. I'll get a cab. You can walk me to it and I'll even call you when I get home."

Anton and Damian shared another look before Damian lifted his chin in agreement. Anton pressed a kiss on my cheek, looked behind me to Damian, and then walked from the room.

Damian and I didn't speak as we walked outside and waited for a cab. A yellow car turned the corner and Damian stepped into the street. He didn't need to put up a hand or whistle. His sheer size alone commanded attention. The cab pulled up.

"Your phone," he said.

I handed it to him and he punched in his number. "Text me when you get home."

"I will."

He responded with a chin lift. He held the door for me, paid the cabbie and walked back inside before the cab even pulled from the curb.

That night the girls came over and we had margaritas and painted our nails. I filled them in on the unnerving meeting I had had earlier with Anton and Damian. I hadn't been able to think of much else. The idea that my dad could have been targeted, that Cam was following in those footsteps was terrifying. But the longer I thought on it, I just wasn't so sure things were as dire as Anton made them sound. It had been over two years and if people feared Dad had information, information I might discover, wouldn't they have approached before this?

"Based on what you've shared, you seem pretty mellow," Ryder said as she salted the glasses for the next round of drinks.

"It could be the margaritas," I said.

"True."

"Seriously, I can't think about Dad being targeted. It was hard enough losing him the way we did, but the idea he was killed because he was doing his job, and worse by another brother in blue, I can't entertain that idea. Not yet."

"You might have to."

Ryder was right, at some point I might have to, but that point wasn't now. "I know and I will if that time comes. And I'm completely willing to do whatever they think is necessary for me to stay safe, which is why I asked we hang out here tonight. But it is possible Anton and the others are seeing more danger than there is because they are conditioned to see danger."

Kimber reached for a nacho. "You mean the cop, the gangster and the black ops dude."

"I don't know that Damian was in black ops, but yeah. It's like conspiracy theorists that see something in everything. They are trained to see all the pitfalls even when they don't exist."

"Possibly, but I'm glad you are listening because if they aren't wrong…" Ryder said then added, "Does Mom know?"

"Not yet. Not until they know more."

"Makes sense. I want to know about Damian. What is he like now?"

"He has always been intense but he is even more so because he has such a commanding presence, even being a silent one."

"And?"

"He told me that he came home on the anniversary of Dad's memorial to raise a glass at McGinty's. I told him I would have joined him if he asked. He said he knew which was why he didn't invite me."

"What the hell does that mean?" Kimber asked.

"Your guess is as good as mine. I asked him to clarify, not that it helped, he said after the way the last encounter went it seemed wiser to avoid temptation."

"Oh my God. That's so awesome." Ryder was jumping up and down, slushing her drink over the side of her glass.

"Is it? He has been home a while and I've only just connected with him. And I know he's working with Cam, but it only takes a minute to call. I can't help but think he's avoiding me, though he is going to be my shadow for the foreseeable future." I took a sip of the sweetly sour drink; the icy concoction went down very smoothly. "I'm not going to lie. I've waited a long time to be this close to him, to have him back in my life, but he's different now."

"Different how?"

"He's in his head more. Not that he was ever big on talking but he seems even less so now. There is a very good possibility that I'll slowly go insane from all the silence."

"I think insanity is a small price to pay to be in the company of a man like that."

Ryder tossed a chip at Kimber's head. "You're an idiot."

Kimber grabbed her glass. "Come on. *No Tomorrow* is starting."

And even if Damian was in his head more, he was back, he was home and he was going to be my shadow. I couldn't wait.

CHAPTER 10

The following morning when I stepped outside it was to find Damian leaning against his black Maserati, looking at his phone. What a sight he made—all that beautifully muscled man leaning against a ridiculously sexy car. I indulged both my imagination and libido with the image of me flat on my back on that car and Damian over me, in me, all around me. My body burned at the thought. I should invest in one of those handheld fans because I predicted a lot of hot flashes in my future.

He looked up and that face, those eyes, it was like coming home. He opened the passenger door and like a favorite scent, that gesture brought back so many memories.

"Damian."

I waited, and he didn't disappoint. "Thea."

The way he spoke my name conjured images of him buried deep inside of me right at the moment he climaxed. I might need more than a fan, maybe an ice suit.

I climbed in and waited for him to fold himself behind the steering wheel, then waited for him to engage me in conversation, but he pulled from the curb without so much as a *how are you?* This older and sexier Damian really did seem to be a conserver of words, like if he hit some unseen limit each day he would disintegrate like vampires in daylight, but he had to conform to at least some social niceties if we were going to be spending time together.

I tried to encourage this when I asked, "How are you this morning?"

Crickets.

"I like your car." I would like it even more screaming his name while he fucked my brains out on it or in it. I wasn't picky. *Don't go there, Thea.*

That comment earned me a glance, but he still said nothing.

I continued on because I was Rosalie Ahern's daughter and had learned tenacity from her. "Have you ever heard of actuary science?"

He didn't even give me his face for that question. Pity because it was a nice face.

"I had a date not too long ago with a man who assessed risk for insurance companies. It's the first date I've ever been on that I pondered killing the person sitting across from me. He wasn't going to let me have dessert. And yes, the operative word there is let. I had two desserts just to show him. I would have really pushed him over the edge if he discovered I didn't exercise at all. He would have all kinds of thoughts on that I'm sure. I'm thinking dating isn't for me. I might join a cult. That sure would keep future boyfriend prospects scratching their heads…me bragging about being in a cult. Oh, we should get coffee. I know the best little place. Do you want coffee?"

We were at a light. I'd been looking out the side window while I verbally assaulted him with every thought in my head. Well, not every thought because I could have gone on for hours about him. But doing so in front of him just seemed tacky. I turned to find him staring at me and I'd bet money the bubble over his head was saying something along the lines of. "What the fuck."

"Coffee?" I asked again.

"Cup of Joe?"

"You know about Cup of Joe?" That was a stupid question. Of course he knew. He was trained to know and he was Damian.

He had been going to Cup of Joe anyway because minutes later we were parking in front of it. He climbed from the car and walked around to join me at the curb, held the door for me and somehow we managed through the small, tight space of the café to the counter. As soon as Ryder saw me she smiled then did a double take at my coffee drinking companion, followed shortly with the crash from whatever she had been holding dropping from her hands.

"Hey, Thea." Her eyes took their time moving down Damian's body and I got it, he had a damn fine body, but I didn't like her looking. "Who's your friend?"

She knew who he was, but they had only met that one time, years ago. It was possible Damian would buy that she didn't remember him. Not likely. I played along anyway. "Damian, Ryder, Ryder, Damian."

A chin lift was his greeting. A saucy smile was hers. "How do you know each other?"

As soon as the words were out of her mouth, her eyes bugged out of her head. I could only chalk up her behavior to temporary insanity. Damian had rendered me stupid on many occasions, but he was going to be suspicious as to why my best friend was pretending she didn't know who he was, as in he would deduce that we'd spent the night, many nights, talking about him. It was time for diversionary tactics.

"We met over a pigeon. He flew into a shop window, the pigeon not Damian, and Damian here was just heartbroken. I mean tears, manly tears, just coursed down his cheeks. I was a distance from him, but he carried on in such a way I thought I better check it out. And when I saw the little bird in his big hands..." That had me looking at his hands—big, blunt cut nails, wide palms and long fingers. I remembered those hands wrapped around my face possessively, those fingers inside me. The memory had my mouth going dry. I rallied, "Long story short there was no saving the pigeon, but his death wasn't in vain. We roasted him over a trash can fire and shared him with some of the locals. Squab, it's quite good."

Damian and Ryder were both looking at me like I'd lost my mind, but at least I had successfully taken the focus off Ryder.

She grabbed onto the figurative raft I had tossed her and asked, "Do you want your usual?"

"Yes."

"And you Damian?"

"Large black."

My head jerked to Damian because he answered her. Maybe that was the trick, I needed to work in the food industry.

I said to Damian, while Ryder went to get our coffee, "It has been a long time, but I remember you speaking more."

There was laughter in his eyes when he turned them on me.

"Are you going to be picking me up often?"

"Yes."

"So maybe you could rethink your vow of silence and make an exception for me."

Nothing.

"You are doing it on purpose. Aren't you? You want me to go insane so I can talk to the voices in my head and yours."

No reaction. He was like a freaking cyborg. "Are you here for Sarah Connor?"

I thought he wasn't listening, but he chuckled at my *Terminator* reference and I felt immensely pleased with myself.

"You could start with a *good morning*. It's not hard to say the words. They slip so easily off the tongue. Do you want to try it?"

He had something on his tongue now, but it wasn't good morning.

"We can work toward *have a nice day* or even my name. I don't know that I have ever heard you call me by my full name. Do you remember my name?" I asked that like I was talking to someone who had just suffered brain trauma and again I got those laughing

161

eyes.

"It's Thea Ahern. You are Damian Tate and I am Thea Ahern." And girls have a vagina and boys have a penis. *Kindergarten Cop*. I was on fire with the Arnold movie references.

I patted his arm but feeling the hard muscles of his biceps I wanted to stroke him. My voice was a little funny when I added, "We can work up to my name."

He paid for our coffees, which I thought was lovely, and headed for the door. Ryder caught my attention before I followed him. "You're right, he is aging really well."

"Yeah, I saw you looking."

"I was just looking, hard not to."

"You're sounding more and more like Kimber."

Ryder shuddered. "Don't say that. I'm not that bad." She then lifted her chin. "He's waiting for you."

I liked the sound of that. "Later."

"Later."

Damian *was* waiting. He held the door for me. I strolled through. "Thank you, Damian."

I almost dropped my nectar of the gods when he answered, "You're welcome, Thea Ahern."

DAMIAN

Anton had called a meeting with Salvatore Federico. His link to the cases that Cam was investigating couldn't be ignored, but having Anton approaching him instead of the NYPD was smart. He would still be pissed having an outsider digging into his business, but it should take some of the sting out of it.

I wouldn't be in on the meeting, but I intended to be close because you could read a lot about people just from their body language, like Thea. I had always thought her eyes gave her away, but her body was even more telling. And it was a fucking fine body too.

That whole scene the other day at Cup of Joe, she had always been offbeat but she was fucking hilarious now with her efforts to get me to talk. Over the past thirteen years I had been in countless situations where silence was necessary, a matter of life or death. I had grown accustomed to observing more than talking. The fact that she had picked up on that and was determined to get me to speak had the contrary ass that I was more determined not too. It was like fucking foreplay; waiting to hear what ridiculous thing would come out of her mouth next and I couldn't wait, getting to know the woman she had become. I suspected I was going to like her even more than the girl she had been.

THEA

It had been a few days since Damian appeared outside my apartment ready to assume his bodyguard duties. He was quiet, sure, but that day with him had been one of the best days I had had in a long time. I wanted to call him, just to talk, like how we used to, but I wasn't sure he would be amendable to that.

I needed groceries and there was a convenience store right down the street from my apartment that took minutes to walk to. If I called Damian, I would turn a twenty-minute errand into an hour. I wouldn't mind spending that hour with him, but asking him to drop everything because I was having a hankering for ice cream seemed wrong. I suspected he would want me to call, my safety his primary concern, but I was living on the edge and headed to the store alone. I stocked up and headed home, my arms were killing me when I reached my building. I guess I didn't need four half gallons of ice cream. I sensed someone coming up behind me and panic hit first then shame. All of the caution being forced on me by those who knew the situation better than I and I shrugged it off. I was going to be murdered right in front of my own building. It would serve me right.

"Let me help you."

Uncle Tim. I tried to shake off the fear, but it was a sign that I needed to listen to the guys despite my feelings on the matter. And that was the problem with conspiracy theories…they drove people crazy.

"Thank you."

"Maybe you should have made two trips."

"I will next time." There wouldn't be a next time with me alone. I would wait the hour for Damian and then let him carry all of it. The image of him loaded down with my groceries was a good one.

We stepped into the foyer of my building and Percy, our mail guy, was filling the boxes. "Afternoon, Miss Ahern. Would you like yours and Ms. Cooke's mail?"

"Please."

He piled it together and I lifted my elbow for him to tuck it under. "Have a good day."

"You too, Percy."

"What brings you here?" I asked Uncle Tim as we made our way to my floor.

"I was in the neighborhood, so I decided I'd stop by and say hello. I thought I'd have a good chance at catching you since you work from home."

"I was working, but I got a hankering for ice cream."

"He flashed me a grin. "Ah…gotcha."

We reached my apartment; he took my key and unlocked the door. I dropped the mail in the pile accumulating on the counter and headed to the fridge to unload.

"That's a lot of mail," Uncle Tim said as he started sifting through the pile.

"It's mine and Mrs. Cooke's. She has a bunch of mine too. Once a week we go through the pile."

"And you're not concerned about bills."

"I auto pay all my bills and her accountants handle hers." I finished in the fridge and turned to get my first good look at him. "You look tired."

"I am."

"Congratulations on the McKay case."

"Cases like that are hard. It was a win, but it doesn't feel like one."

"I understand that." I thought to mention Cam and how he was looking into Dad's death. Uncle Tim could help with that, had very expensive PIs on retainer who could do the legwork for Cam, but I hesitated because Cam was keeping it on the down low, including not sharing with Uncle Guy, so it was a good guess he hadn't shared with Uncle Tim either. I wasn't sure I agreed with Cam, but I would stay out of his investigation.

Uncle Tim shifted a bit from foot to foot, a sign that he had something on his mind. He caught himself and grinned. "I'm announcing my candidacy for Senate in a few weeks and I would really love to have you and Cam at my side when I do. I've already contacted Rosalie."

Pride burned through me along with sorrow that Dad would miss this. "Absolutely, but you seem nervous about asking. Why?"

"I think of you as family and if you stand up with me, you'll be announcing that to the world."

"We are family."

"I don't want to overstep."

"You were Dad's dearest friend and Cam and I have known you all of our lives. There is no overstepping."

"Thank you for that."

"You've got to be on cloud nine. At the top of your profession with the McKay verdict and now this."

"It's a dream, so it feels a bit surreal that it is coming true."

"Dad would be so proud."

"I miss him."

"Me too."

He glanced at his watch. "I've got a meeting up town. I'll have my assistant send you the information on the gala."

"We will be there with bells on."

He pressed a kiss on my cheek then walked to the door. "Lock your door."

No matter how old I got all the men in my life were determined to protect me from the boogeymen, and as stifling as that could be at times, I wouldn't change it.

"Yes, sir."

I had previously mentioned that my luck was not great and this was made abundantly clear when I ran into my mom on the streets of Manhattan. Damian had joined me for a day of errands. I didn't know who was more surprised when she called my name from halfway down the block, Damian or me. What was worse, she wasn't alone. Kimber was with her. No good came from putting those two together.

"Just keep walking," I said.

"It's your mom." He said that like I was slow. I knew it was my mom and I also knew she was unpredictable especially when accompanied by Kimber. Who knew what would come out of their mouths and since Ryder, the more levelheaded one of us, had gone all batshit crazy when in this man's presence, there was no telling what those two would do. I wasn't sure I had a good enough imagination to smoke and mirror him after the nonsense they were sure to spiel.

"If we hurry to the car, it isn't likely she'll chase after us. Not in those heels."

I was looking right at him so I saw the smile that touched those lips. I wasn't sure if that smile was aimed at me or my mom because when I followed his gaze she was hurrying down the street, waving one hand over her head while hollering my name. Kimber was grinning and moving just as quickly, but her attention was fixed solely on Damian.

"We could have totally reached the car," I muttered just before Mom stopped in front of us panting like she'd just run a marathon.

"I didn't think you heard me."

"Mom, half of the city heard you."

Kimber didn't even say hi to me. She looked Damian up and down, biting her lips as she did before asking in a voice that sounded more like a sexy purr. "Who's your friend, Thea?"

Seriously? Her too?

"Who? Him? I don't know. We just left the bank at the same time."

As I hoped, her attention snapped to me and she glared. "And that's why he's standing here with you now."

"I think he's a little slow," I whispered then added, "I didn't want to be rude."

"I'm sorry for my daughter, Damian. I really did try to teach her manners, but she is just so damn stubborn."

I hadn't witnessed Mom and Damian's reunion the night of the cheeseburger casserole, but I got to see it now and not only was I flabbergasted, I was jealous because he took my mother's hand, smiled and said in the sweetest voice, "It is lovely to see you again, Rosalie."

I remembered that voice; it was usually followed with us getting naked. Oh dear God, I was having sex thoughts in front of the man in question and my mom. Kill me now.

"And you, sweetie. You need to come to dinner more often now that you are home."

"Absolutely."

Kimber wasn't going to be ignored. She thrust her hand out to him so fast she almost punched him in the gut. "I'm Kimber."

Damian took her hand. "We've met. Nice to see you again."

I lowered my head, what else could I do. That was Damian's way of saying he knew we were up to something and was calling me on it. I needed new friends.

"What do you do, Damian?" My head jerked to her. *Abort. He knows you are full of it.* She didn't even look at me, too consumed with undressing the love of my life with her eyes.

"Ex-military, in the middle of transitioning jobs." He was playing along. We were doomed.

"Transitioning into what kind of job?" Kimber asked.

Had she never heard the expression beating a dead horse? Which was a terrible expression. I jumped in. "He mentioned a phone sex operator for a 1-800 number."

"Are you ever serious?" Mom was giving me her narrowed eye look. She should be giving that look to Kimber.

"No."

Mom's narrowed eye look morphed into a devious twinkle, which was never good before she said, "So you and Thea are making up for lost time."

It was tempting to kick my mother in the shins and make a run for it. Make up for lost time…I needed to find a manhole and throw myself into it.

Mom and Kimber then did the weirdest thing. They both studied Damian like a zoo animal so I too looked to see what held them captivated only to see the smile that was so rare for him. "Even all grown up you are still just adorable," Mom said.

"Oh yeah." That was Kimber's eloquent contribution to Mom's observation. Damian was adorable? If they meant in a scary, dangerous, rip off kittens' heads sort of way.

"Has Thea made you dinner? She's become quite the chef."

My childhood meals were pretty terrible. I had learned a lot since, not that I had any intention of sharing my culinary skills with Damian.

Damian replied, "No. The last meal I had from her was in high school."

"She was a pretty dreadful cook, but she was persistent, was determined to take care of you…and Cam."

My jaw hit the pavement. Mother—she was called that when I was displeased—was rehashing the past. I wasn't prepared to stroll down memory lane. I looked up to determine which building was higher so I could toss myself off it. Or better yet toss her.

"Get her to make you dinner. She cooks almost as well as she draws."

"I will. Thank you for the tip."

"Now that you are home don't be a stranger. I'll make cookies, I know how much you love my butter cookies."

"Yes, unlike the ones Thea burnt past all recognition." He then took her hand and brought it to his lips. "I'd like that."

Fiend! He waited fourteen years to take his shot at the cookie disaster of 2003. He just made my list. No cookies for him! Especially since he just kissed my mother's hand, Mr. Charming who turned into a cyborg when we were alone. Kimber offered hers too, though he didn't kiss it, and her crestfallen look pulled a smug grin from me. They walked away all flustered and I just stared at him. Oh, I'd feed him. There was that rat poison buried in the back of the cabinet under the sink.

"What the hell was that? You barely speak to me but you fawn all over my mom."

"She's your mom."

"So."

That was the only explanation he felt the situation called for because he started for his car. I followed after him, but it wasn't until we were driving back to my apartment that I said, "I'm sure you don't really want dinner."

"Dinner would be good." He glanced over at me. "Tonight works."

He was going to be in my apartment with me. I didn't see good things coming from this, but to him I said, "Tonight it is then."

Damian was just finishing his stew, and it was a damn fine stew if I did say so myself; he thought so too because he had three helpings. I served it with warm crusty French bread, which he didn't eat, and a salad that he devoured. All through dinner I barely ate because I was too busy watching him. He was in my apartment. I liked seeing him in my apartment.

Someone knocked at the door.

"I'll get it." I dragged my feet to the door because I had been contemplating jumping him and seeing what happened. "It's just my neighbor."

Damian stood. "Check first."

It was Mrs. Cooke, looking into the peephole. I pulled the door open and she didn't even wait to be invited in. Breezing into my living room like she owned it, her attention going right to Damian. I'd bet money my mother called her. And I'm guessing by the look on her face she agreed with whatever my mom had said about him.

"I'm Miranda Cooke. And you are?" I had never mentioned Damian to her because by the time she came into my life, he had been placed firmly in the box.

He got her first name and on first meeting. I had to wait a few weeks and still I felt more comfortable calling her Mrs. Cooke, and Damian, like he had with my mom, turned on the charm. He reached for her hand and said in a voice that was the softest I'd ever heard come out of his mouth, even gentler than the one he had given my mom earlier, "Damian Tate. A pleasure."

First with my mom and now with my seventy-year-old neighbor he was flirting and yet he conserved his words around me, only gifting me a few in every conversation, which had me coveting the ones he did say like they were a rare gemstone. I was calling Anton later and requesting a replacement.

"Thea failed to mention how handsome you are."

I hadn't mentioned him at all, my mother had and knowing my mother she not only mentioned how handsome he was, she had probably gone into detail. I snorted again then reached for a cookie and shoved it in my face so I didn't say something I might later regret.

Damian gestured to the sofa and Mrs. Cooke sat like she was wearing one of those bustle skirts, just on the edge of the sofa all dainty and ladylike. I couldn't believe I was being forced to watch this and what was worse, I was jealous. I was jealous of my senior citizen neighbor. I was pathetic.

"What did Thea make you for dinner?"

"Beef stew."

"Oh, her beef stew is delicious. Nearly as good as her chicken potpie."

Damian glanced at me before he said, "I'll have to get her to make that for me next."

My mouth opened, chewed-up cookie may have fallen out, but I didn't care. He was speaking in full sentences. There was even a sexy lilt of humor in his tone. I reached for the bottle of wine and poured myself a glass that could rival the one Brody had poured himself in the first *Jaws* movie. Then I glared over the rim at my neighbor and bodyguard as I drank it.

"Have you had dessert?" Mrs. Cooke asked, and she would because she had a sweet tooth that rivaled my own.

"Not yet. Thea was just putting on the coffee."

Oh was I? Funny, he didn't mention wanting coffee or dessert.

"Would you mind making it decaf, Thea?"

I resisted the urge to slam my glass down on the table and stood, muttering, "Not at all. It would be my pleasure."

I may have banged a cabinet or two but they didn't hear me because they were talking. I had spent the past two hours prying words from the man and now he had verbal diarrhea. I hated my life. And I was particularly irritable because as the cyborg stuffed his face with my stew, I had been entertaining thoughts of ripping his clothes off. I needed to cool down so I opened the freezer and stuck my head in.

"What on earth are you doing, Thea?"

"I read once if you open the freezer really quickly you can catch sight of the creatures that live inside it."

She gave me that tone, the one that worried if I was mentally okay. I got that tone from her a lot. "I've never heard of such a thing."

Damian on the other hand knew exactly what I was doing because he looked downright edible.

"Did you see one?" he asked.

"Not in a long time."

His eyes went dark. "Really?"

We weren't talking about freezer creatures, we were talking

about cocks, so I replied, "No, but I really want to."

He slid his gaze over my body and lingered a second longer on my breasts. "It's all about timing."

I moaned.

"Can you draw me a picture of these creatures? I haven't a clue what you're talking about."

And at her innocent comment, Damian and I broke out into laughter.

CHAPTER 11

I can't believe I have to wear this," Cam said for the seventh time as he adjusted his collar.

"It's a tux, not chain mail. Deal."

"I don't want to deal."

I glanced over at Anton. "It's like he's three."

We were in Anton's Bentley on the way to Uncle Tim's gala. Cam, Anton and Damian were all dressed in tuxedos. I'd lost the ability to speak when Damian arrived earlier. Even now I kept sneaking glances at him through my lowered lashes.

"Uncle Tim picked up Ma?" Cam asked.

"Yeah, but she's excited for the ride home in this baby."

Anton grinned. "She's already called with the directions Silas should follow to get her there. It's definitely the long cut."

Cam laughed. "That sounds like Ma."

Damian was next to me and his large body dwarfed mine on the super comfy leather seats. I had never seen him in a tux and now thought he should wear one at least once a week. "You look great. That's a good look on you."

Those pale eyes moved slowly down my body and were a shade darker when they returned to my face. "So do you."

Three words should not make a person want to spontaneously combust but when those words were issued from a man who rarely used them; yeah, my blood was boiling in my veins.

We pulled up in front of the swanky hotel off Central Park. Damian climbed out first and I swear it was like watching the Secret Service. All he was missing was that thing in his ear. When I was standing next to him at the curb, he tucked my hand through his arm. There was a part of me that let myself have a girlie moment over his actions even knowing they were more protective in nature than romantic. I did have a moment's pause over how serious he was being. He wasn't one for dramatics and so I had to believe there was more I didn't know that warranted such caution and that was a thoroughly unnerving thought.

We headed inside. I was wearing four-inch spiked heels and had piled my hair on the top of my head, which gave me a few more inches, and I still felt petite next to the giants I was walking in with. The gala was in one of the larger ballrooms that was decked out in cloth covered tables, arrangements of red and white roses in modern black vases and several bars were set up around the room with people milling around them. The room was nearly packed and to see the turnout of support for Uncle Tim was heartwarming.

Damian lowered his head when he asked, "Champagne?"

"Please."

"I'll help you," Cam said as the two walked to the nearest bar.

"You look beautiful tonight," Anton said when we were alone.

I was wearing my favorite black sheath dress. It was simple, but hugged my figure in all the right spots. It was definitely the one dress in my closet that never failed to make me feel sexy.

"Thank you. So do you. If the people knew the well-dressed you lounged around in ripped-up sweats and dripped pizza on your tees, they'd never believe it."

"Or that a woman who looks as stunning as you do tonight could belch out the alphabet."

"I only did that once."

"Once was enough."

He dared me, but it had been gross...fun too, in a disgusting way. "Do you see Mom and the man of the hour?"

"Not yet."

"Are you surprised by the turn out?"

"Not really. He's got just as many friends on the force as he does on the other side of things. I'm more surprised that so many from both sides came tonight."

It was true Uncle Tim had many unsavory people as clients. That was part of the reason Anton agreed to join us for the gala because with his background he could have been a strike against a man looking for a seat in the Senate, but Uncle Tim had a very colorful following. Anton's presence wouldn't even turn a head. Well, he'd turn the ladies' heads but that was nothing new. And still the idea of cops and gangsters in the same room made me nervous.

"You don't think there will be trouble, do you?" I asked.

"No."

I hadn't meant to sigh, but I did.

"There's Rosalie."

Mom arrived with Uncle Tim. She looked beautiful in the silver silk gown she wore, but there was sadness coming from her, not something most would pick up on. She was thinking about Dad.

"Your mother is a beautiful woman, more so when she's not sad."

It shouldn't have surprised me that Anton would pick up on Mom's mood so easily, but still it did. "I love you, Anton."

That surprised him, but surprise shifted to love. "The feeling is mutual."

Damian and Cam returned just as Mom and Uncle Tim joined our little group. There were handshakes and kisses before Uncle Tim said, "Thank you for coming."

He looked nervous, so I reached for his hand and squeezed. "We wouldn't have missed it."

Damian handed Mom a glass of champagne and me the other. "You look beautiful, Ma."

Mom flashed Cam a smile. "This old thing."

I happened to know that 'old thing' had set Dad back a few thousand dollars.

Uncle Tim scanned the room. "It's a good turn out."

"Are you surprised?" Mom asked.

"A little bit."

"That's nonsense. Someone is waving you over or she's having a seizure." Mom gestured to the tall woman near the podium.

"It's time. Ready?"

"Yes." Mom spoke for us all as we joined the woman at the podium. I was happy to see that Anton and Damian didn't stay back. They shouldn't have because they were family too. Flashes from cameras went off around the room as Uncle Tim took his place behind the microphone.

The voices hushed as he spoke. "I lost my oldest and dearest friend two years ago. His family is here with me tonight as I announce my intention of running for Senate for the fine state of New York."

Applause broke out as more camera flashes went off. This was Uncle Tim's moment and how I wished Dad were here.

Later in the evening there was dancing and you could have knocked me over with a feather when Damian requested a dance. We hadn't gone to prom, what we had done was so much better—his apartment, a scary movie, takeout and clothes optional—so we had never slow danced. It was a crime we had never slow danced because slow dancing with him was incredible.

We *were* dancing so it was okay for me to rest my cheek on his chest and inhale his scent—a scent that had haunted me. During the harder parts of our separation I had contacted Yankee Candle hoping they could take his scent from a t-shirt of his I had and turn it into a candle. My very own Damian Tate scented candle. It was a surprise that a paddy wagon didn't come for me after making that request, even more of a surprise to learn I wasn't the first one to ask that of them.

I ran my hand down his back, a back that was different from the one I had touched, tasted and explored every inch of.

Lifting my eyes to him, I asked, "What was it like over there?"

His chin dipped and his jaw clenched as the muscles under my touch turned rigid. "The very worst of humanity and the very best."

"You don't want to talk about it."

"I don't talk about it."

"I wrote to you."

If I thought his muscles were rigid before, they were like rock now and his inhale sounded painful.

"You told me not to, but I did. Every day, still do. Some were just telling you what I was doing or what I had to eat that day and others…I never mailed them. I have them, all of them."

His voice broke on just one word. "Why?"

"The Thanksgiving you told me you were leaving, I prayed for the first time in a long time. I asked that you be kept safe. I wanted that so badly I was willing to let go of the dream of us together. And I did let it go, but I couldn't let go of you because you own my heart, you have since I was seventeen, so I wrote letters you wouldn't ever read just to feel closer to you."

I couldn't really describe his expression. It was harsh and pained and yet beautiful. "I came back for you."

I stopped moving, my mouth opened but no words came out.

"That night at the bar, when you were drunk. I waited to return to duty because I wanted to ask you to come back to North Carolina with me."

Tears filled my eyes. It hadn't been just a hook up that night. He had wanted forever too. "But you didn't."

"You were drunk, I was going to wait until the morning and then

I got called back for duty." There was something else he wanted to say, but seemed to think better of it. It was just as well because I was still reeling from what he had said.

"I would have gone back with you."

He pressed my face to his chest, holding me so close I could hear the strong, uneven beat of his heart. "I lied before. I'm here to help Cam, to find out what happened to the man who was like a father to me, but I resigned my commission and came home for you."

He had come back for me. That night so long ago I had been a drunken fool, but even I remembered every word we spoke. He had been called away, but why hadn't he tried asking me again? Even being puzzled over that, I replayed Damian's soft confession over and over in my head. I got nothing done, lost huge hunks of time, because maybe we were still a we; maybe we were finally at a place to pick up where we had left off. That thought made me deliriously happy.

My stomach growled. I hadn't eaten today. I couldn't help the smile because only thoughts of Damian could distract me from food. It was too late to make something. I could order takeout. I wondered what Mrs. Cooke was doing about dinner. She cooked like a goddess. It was dinnertime. I could invite myself over. And if she hadn't made dinner we could get takeout together. Stepping into the hall, I noticed immediately that her door was ajar. She often walked down the hall to visit her friend Betty and left her door propped open.

"Mrs. Cooke?" I called as I pushed open the door. I wasn't prepared to find her motionless on the floor. "Mrs. Cooke!" I ran over and dropped down next to her. I felt for a pulse and nearly wept when I found one. I reached for my phone and called 911 and then I called Damian.

"Thea."

I sounded a little hysterical when I said, "Mrs. Cooke. I've called an ambulance. She's unconscious. It looks like she fell."

"Go with her in the ambulance. I'll meet you there."

"Okay."

The paramedics arrived and not even ten minutes later they were loading her into the back of the ambulance. By the time we reached the emergency room of Mount Sinai, Damian was already waiting. She was wheeled to the back as Damian joined me at the nurse's station.

"What happened?"

"I don't know. I spent the day working and decided to invite myself over to her place for dinner and saw that her door was ajar. I thought maybe she was down at her friend's place, but when I entered I saw her on the floor."

I had seen Damian intense, but I had never seen him scary. He looked scary in that moment. He reached for his phone and stepped away from me while he spoke. I settled in a chair but my thoughts were on Mrs. Cooke. She didn't have family. We were her family. I should call my mom, but this was the hospital where Dad had been brought, where he had died. I didn't want to put her through those memories unless I had to. Damian joined me in the waiting room when he finished his call. He took the seat next to me and held my hand while we waited. About an hour later the doctor appeared.

"How is she?"

"Just a bump on the head. We'll keep her for a few days for observation, to make sure the fall wasn't a symptom of something else."

"Is she awake?"

"In and out, we're not allowing visitors tonight. In the morning we will reassess."

"Thank you, doctor."

Relief was like getting pummeled by a crashing wave. She was going to be okay, but anger replaced relief. I had been home. Right down the hall and yet I locked myself in my apartment to work. How long had she been lying there?

"I was home. I should have checked on her sooner."

"Don't do that to yourself."

"She is elderly. I should have checked on her."

"Has she ever fallen before?"

"No."

"From what I've seen she's a spry elderly woman and suspect she would take issue with you acting like she's an invalid. You got her here and she is going to be fine. Don't harp on what could have been."

He was right, damn it. Mrs. Cooke would box my ears if she knew I hinted that she was in any way limited. "Thank you for coming."

He didn't answer, but he did reach for my hand again and led me to the car.

I had missed this, having him close. Having him to lean on. And I was grateful that he had dropped everything to be there for me. "What were you doing when I called?"

"Running."

I hadn't expected that answer particularly since I detested the idea of running. "At seven at night?"

"Whenever I can fit it in."

Green Berets had some serious training requirements; one such requirement was running two miles in something crazy like 12 minutes. That took some serious stamina; well at least it seemed so to me. I researched Green Berets after learning Damian was one. "And after your run what would you have done?"

"Catch the news then sleep."

"Thank you for coming."

We reached the car but instead of opening the door he turned into me and touched my chin with his thumb. "What happened to Mrs. Cooke wasn't your fault."

"I know."

His eyes moved over my face and I really liked the way he

looked at me. "I want your letters."

My heart melted. "They're yours, so absolutely."

Mrs. Cooke was doing well. A week after her fall and she was home. She didn't remember much from that night and seemed confused with what she did remember. I didn't push for answers. I was just happy she was on the mend. Her friend Betty and I were taking turns staying with her so she wasn't alone. We also thought it best to keep it to just one visitor at a time so we didn't overwhelm her with us both doting. Betty was on tonight, so I was having dinner with Anton. It was something we started years ago and tried to manage at least once a month. We had agreed on Dahlia's, and despite him offering to pick me up, I was right down the street. I did, at his insistence, take a cab. I was there before him, so I waited at the bar and ordered a glass of wine. The turning of heads a few minutes after seven meant he had arrived, his focus going around the restaurant until it landed on me. The smile was instant as he moved through the tables.

"I'm sorry I'm late."

"Only a few minutes."

"I'll see about our table."

"Would you like me to order you a drink?"

"Please, Maker's Mark, on the rocks."

He walked to the hostess station and the women in the restaurant followed his every move. I chuckled before ordering his drink.

"Our table is ready."

He reached for his glass while addressing the bartender. "Add these to our tab."

He led me through the restaurant, his hand on the small of my back as he maneuvered us through the tables to ours, one tucked in a dark corner.

He held my chair before taking his seat. Gracefully was how he moved when he pulled out the chair and folded his large body into it.

"I'm finally eating at your favorite restaurant." He looked around. "It suits you."

He was right; it did suit me because it was quaint, eclectic and artsy.

"The food is amazing," I added.

"Any suggestions?"

"Everything on the menu is delicious."

For the next few minutes we looked over the options. The waitress approached, falling over herself to get to Anton. He didn't even look at her when he placed our orders and requested a bottle of wine and two glasses. Based on her expression, the bottle was clearly an expensive one.

"How's Mrs. Cooke?"

"She's good, thank God. It's so scary. I think she should get one of those alert bracelets. I don't know how long she was like that and I was home and didn't know she needed help."

"That's probably not a bad idea. I can help you look into it if you want."

"I'd like that."

The waitress returned and uncorked the bottle. After pouring a splash, Anton lifted the glass. He had elegant hands, which was deceiving since I knew those hands were capable of some very bad things. He brought the glass to his lips. Something I had seen countless times and yet when he did, it was an elegant motion. He swished the wine around his mouth for a second before lowering the glass.

"That will do."

The waitress poured a glass for me before topping his off then left the bottle and hurried away.

"Try it. It's quite good." I lifted the glass and took a sip and then almost died and went to heaven. My appreciation was clearly seen on my face when Anton smiled. "You like it."

"Like it? I'd have an affair with it."

"Damian is looking into what happened to Mrs. Cooke."

I parroted his comment because I had no idea where it came from. "Looking into what happened to her. What do you mean?"

"It could be nothing, just a fall like the doctor said, but it is in Damian's nature to learn for himself."

"Is he thinking it wasn't an accident?"

"You live in the same building, on the same floor, and are friends with her. There's a connection and Damian would like to rule out other possible scenarios."

"But she's just an old woman. Why would anyone want to hurt her?"

"Most likely no one did, but that's not something he would assume."

"I'm not complaining. I'm grateful that he's so cautious, but I can't help but think the three of you find trouble in everything, even when it doesn't exist. There has been nothing, no attempt at all. A lot of attention is being paid to my safety for what seems like no reason."

"I'm sorry to say that isn't the case. When you are around danger long enough, it is easier to spot."

"So there is trouble brewing?"

"Yes."

That was not a comforting thought, but I wasn't going to obsess. The guys were on it and I would do my part and be careful.

Anton didn't elaborate on the trouble. He seemed to be of the same mindset as me, of not making me worry. He brushed past that topic and instead said, "And he cares. This is how he shows it."

I knew that and knew of several other ways he liked to show he cared that I liked even more.

Our meals arrived and for a little while we ate in comfortable silence, though my thoughts lingered on the news that Damian thought there might be more to what happened to Mrs. Cooke. I hated the idea that she could have been hurt because of me. I put it from my head and hoped he was wrong. After our dishes were removed, Anton reached for his glass of wine. He looked so relaxed and yet I knew he was taking in everything around him. "What do you want for dessert?"

"The crème brûlée is killer here but the pumpkin tart with nutmeg ice cream sounds delicious too."

"Get both and we'll share."

"Yay! Exactly what I hoped you would say."

"So how has it been with Damian?"

Just hearing his name pulled a smile. "We're older, but we're not so different. Why didn't you tell me sooner that he was home?"

"I thought you knew. I thought he came to see you, so I was more than a little surprised by your reaction when I did."

"Cam didn't tell me either. He assumed too." I reached for my glass of wine. "Damian is definitely more reserved than he was and keeps his feelings really close to his chest. We allowed doubt to dictate our reunion, at least I did, because what we felt as kids was so intense. But it is still there, the love and attraction. He told me he had intended to ask me to come back with him that night so long ago when I was a drunken fool. I would have gone with him. I wish he had asked, wished he hadn't been called away before he could." I took a sip of my wine, lost in thought before I added, "I don't understand why he never tried asking me again."

"Have you asked him?"

"Not yet, but I will."

"And now?"

"He is home, back in the neighborhood, and we both still feel it, so I think we have finally gotten our timing right."

His smile in reply said it all.

Our desserts arrived. The waitress put the crème brûlée in front of Anton and the pumpkin tart in front of me. I split the tart and ice cream, putting his half on the unused bread plate and slid it over the table to him before I tasted a forkful and moaned in sheer bliss when the flavors exploded on my tongue.

"It's better than sex."

I hadn't realized I said that out loud until I heard Anton's reply. "You're not doing sex right if that's the case."

My eyes flew open to find him grinning at me. When it came to sex, I was seriously out of practice. He made a good point though. Sex with Damian had always been mind-blowing. I really hoped I got a refresher on that and soon. "I need a filter."

"I like that you say exactly what you think."

"It's a condition actually, Tourette's." I glanced up from my dessert, but he wasn't eating. "Aren't you going to try it?"

"I'm enjoying watching you, ever the enthusiast for sugar."

I glared and he chuckled again before he lifted his fork. "It's very good," he said as he pushed the crème in my direction and having the metabolism that I had, I finished off both desserts.

A little while later, Anton signaled for the waitress. I reached for my clutch to pay. He glared. He handed over a black credit card. I thought to argue with him but he wasn't a man one argued with and won. "Thank you."

He stood then pulled out my chair. He kept me close, like right up against him as we left the restaurant. When we reached my door, Anton didn't immediately release me. "Thank you for joining me for dinner."

"Thanks for suggesting it."

"I'm really happy that you and Damian are finally getting a chance."

That was the understatement of the year, but to him I said, "Me too."

"Lock your door and arm your system."

Our conversation earlier about Mrs. Cooke and how it was possible she hadn't just fallen freaked me out, which why I answered with just, "Okay."

"Sweet dreams."

"Night."

I closed and locked my door and set the alarm and still I pushed a chair under the knob.

It was late when the phone rang. I reached for it cursing under my breath because I had finally fallen asleep after tossing and turning for most of the night due to Anton's dire prediction of looming trouble.

"Hello."

No answer. It was likely a sales call, the cold dials that took a beat or two to actually patch through to a representative, but doubt wiggled in because this wasn't the first late night call like this I'd received. And Anton had freaked me out a bit at dinner. Not to mention I had felt on several occasions someone watching me. If this was related, how did they get my cell number? What did they want? Or was it just plain old drunk dials. I rolled over, closed my eyes and tried for sleep. I was just on the cusp of it when the phone rang again. Fear had my hand shaking and like before there was no answer. I hung up then looked at the number. Private. I turned off my phone. I needed to tell Damian about the calls, it wasn't a coincidence I was receiving them now. And that thought kept me up for the rest of the night.

In the morning I was dragging. I had planned to get an early start, but I needed more sleep. Damian needed to know about the calls though, so I called him and got his voice mail.

"Hey, it's Thea. I just wanted to share that I got two wrong numbers last night around three and half past three in the morning. Private number. This isn't the first time either, it happened a few weeks ago too. It seems like something you should know. Later."

I left my phone on the counter and headed back to bed. I was ripped from sleep an hour or so later by the pounding at my door. I had been in true REM sleep so I felt a bit drunk as I stumbled to the front door. I didn't even bother looking out the peephole when I yanked open the door while saying. "What the fuc—"

It was Damian and he looked pissed, but his expression changed as he moved his gaze slowly down my body. It was only then that I remembered I was wearing nothing but a pair of boy shorts and a tank top. Oops.

"Where's your phone?"

"Good morning to you too."

He actually fisted his hands and those hot eyes fixed on me. "It will be a fucking hell of a lot better than good if you don't cover yourself up."

It was tempting to pull my tank off in invitation, but now wasn't the time. "My phone is in the kitchen."

He didn't wait for me and was already looking at my call list when I joined him, after detouring for my robe. "Would you like some coffee?"

"Just the two calls?"

"Yes. Is that a no for coffee?"

He looked up from the phone. "Yes to the coffee."

"Have you determined what happened to Mrs. Cooke?"

"Yes. I'm taking this." He pulled out his phone. "Take mine for the day."

It didn't pass my notice that he didn't answer my question. "I don't need it, I'm not leaving my apartment."

"Take it anyway. You leave the apartment, you call me first."

I wasn't going to argue with the man. It was too early and I didn't have caffeine coursing through my veins yet.

"What do you know about your neighbor Jerry Castile?"

"I don't know him. He moved in about a month ago."

"In his fifties?"

"Yeah. I never met him, but Mrs. Cooke did. She was trying to hook me up with him. Why?" I was in the middle of adding sugar to my coffee when I answered my own question. "He was the one to hurt Mrs. Cooke?"

"Yes."

"Who is he?"

"He has a rap sheet as long as my arm. A history of moving into buildings and robbing them."

"Oh my God. Don't they do background checks on potential tenants?"

"They're supposed to, but his information was pretty well hidden."

"He was right under our noses the whole time. Do you think she walked in on him robbing her?"

"She's vague on the details, but yeah. She probably startled him."

"I was right here. I never heard a thing." I was sick in the stomach knowing I had been so close while she fended off an intruder.

"Don't."

"It wasn't my fault, doesn't change the fact that it sucks I was here and was unable to help her."

I put his coffee in a travel mug since I knew he wasn't staying. He would want to follow up on this Castile guy. I handed it to him. He had the oddest look on his face.

"You're not staying, but you wanted coffee."

"Thanks. Do not leave with—"

"Without calling you, I know."

He started for the door. "I like your pajamas. There's only one thing I like on you more."

That comment was unexpected and tummy flipping, especially recalling how he had looked when I opened the door. "What do you like on me more?"

He had reached the door and was halfway through it when he looked back and grinned. "Me."

The door closed on his chuckle and I headed to the bathroom for a nice cold shower.

CHAPTER 12

Mom showed up on my doorstep the following morning, but instead of her normal wackiness, she was frighteningly serious. She pushed into my apartment before spinning around and leveling her no-nonsense look at me.

"What's going on? I had the most unusual conversation with Miranda the other day."

Betty and I were still taking turns spending time with Mrs. Cooke. She didn't want to be home alone and we didn't want her to be home alone either. What I hadn't known about her was that she *was* a conspiracy theorist and under the circumstances she wasn't wrong, but her theories were so far from the reality of things…little green men, spaceships. I believed in aliens, don't get me wrong, but the man that attacked her had been human, not a bloodthirsty extraterrestrial. He was also gone. I didn't know what happened to him, suspected Damian and Anton were behind it, but Betty, who had been crushing on the man, informed me that he had all but disappeared.

"I don't believe aliens invaded her home, but someone did. What happened?"

"One of the tenants who recently moved in had sticky fingers."

Mom's face paled since she caught on immediately. "She walked in on him robbing her."

"Yeah."

"Where is this pillar of the community now?"

"Gone. My guess Damian is 'questioning him'."

"I think I'd like to see Damian questioning him."

"You and me both."

"Miranda is going to stay with me for a while. I know you and Betty have been taking turns, but I think she'll feel safer being away from here completely."

"I think that's a great idea."

"Maybe you should too."

"I rarely leave my apartment and when I do I have to call Damian first."

"That's not a hardship, but why do you have to call Damian? Is it related to what Cam is investigating?"

"Yes. They told you?"

"He hadn't intended to share, but I'm Rosalie Ahern."

"You badgered him until he cried uncle."

"Exactly."

"So you know that yoga man—"

"Is one of Damian's, yes I know."

"What is yoga man's real name?"

"Mark," Mom said, looking a little worried.

"Are you okay?"

"What, that Cam is looking into your Dad's old cases? Yeah, I remember your dad right before...he had been working late a lot and was rather disheartened. If Cam can bring to light whatever that trouble was, I'm all for it as long as he is being smart about it."

"I think he is being smart."

"I know he is. He has Anton and Damian watching his back and ours."

"True. Be careful, watchful."

"Are you kidding? In our neighborhood? People know what's happening to you before you do. We'll be covered."

Yeah, they would be.

She pulled me close. "I love you, Thea."

"I love you too."

She took my hands into hers. "And Damian? What's going on with you two?"

"What we felt as kids is still there, but stronger. And I love him. I've always loved him. Getting a chance to be with him, the man he is now. I've waited a long time for him and he was worth waiting for."

Her smile took up her whole face. "I thought so. The sparks between you are like the Fourth of July." She squeezed my hands. "I'm glad something good came out of this."

"Me too."

She started for the door. "I need to introduce Miranda to yoga man."

Poor Mark, he would forever be yoga man to Mom and me.

"If you get her doing yoga, you have to call me. That is something I need to see. I'll help you get her packed."

"She'd like that, so would I."

Mrs. Cooke was going through her photo albums when we entered her apartment. She loved her photo albums because they were filled with pictures of her husband. I hated seeing the bruises on her face, knowing it could have ended so much worse. She was looking through an album that was older than ones I'd seen before.

"What have you got there?" I asked as I settled next to her on the sofa.

"Have I not shown you this?"

"No, I don't think so." I pulled the book over so it sat on both of our laps.

Mom headed into the bedroom. "I'll pack your bags."

"Everything is already out on the bed."

"Is that your husband? I didn't know he was a cop, why didn't I know he was a cop?"

"Oh yes. Mitchell was a cop for a few years before he retired."

"Why did he retire?"

Clearly what she had to say was painful because her hands shook a little when she flipped the page. "We had had four miscarriages, both of us were convinced it was the stress of his job and we so wanted children. He didn't hesitate to resign. His father and grandfather had been investment bankers, they wanted him to follow in their footsteps. He wanted to be a cop, but he quit and joined the firm for me...our family. As it turned out, it wasn't the stress of the job."

It seemed wrong that such a lovely woman had been denied a family, something I knew she very much wanted. We thought of her as such, I think she thought of us that way too.

"We're not your blood, but you're family to us."

Her smile was a touch sad. "You are family to me too."

"Okay, we're good. We need to boogie, Miranda, or we're missing happy hour."

Happy hour was a tradition on our street. The neighbors poured themselves their beverage of choice and everyone mingled. It was a tradition I really liked. I would have joined them now, since it had been quite a long time since I had been to one, but I was looking forward to watching a movie and going to bed early.

I walked them to their cab, waved as they drove off. The postman was filling the boxes when I entered. I wondered if Mom had forwarded Mrs. Cooke's mail. I would have to remind her to do that.

"Afternoon, Percy. Could I get my mail and Mrs. Cooke's?"

"Sure thing, Thea."

In my apartment, I locked my door and dropped the mail on the counter then retrieved my phone and remote—Chinese food and a movie. Now all I needed to make it the perfect night was

Damian. We'd get there.

I stopped by Mom's a week later and was greeted to the sight of Mrs. Cooke and five white-haired friends, hunched over playing cards drinking milk in lieu of whiskey.

"What's going on here?"

"Bridge." I was surprised at her abrupt answer, but then Mrs. Cooke realized it was me. "Thea, dear. It's so good to see you."

"And you. You're in the zone."

"I am." She was a card shark; her eyes were shining in victory. "I see you're fitting right in."

"Indeed." But her focus was on her game and I would hate to be the reason she didn't clean house.

"I'm going to hunt down Mom."

"She is in the kitchen. That lovely Guy fellow is over."

Uncle Guy. I hadn't seen him since the charity event. "Don't take all of their money, Mrs. Cooke."

"But it's just so easy." That earned her looks and grunts from around the table. I was laughing when I entered the kitchen. Mom and Uncle Guy were sitting around the kitchen table, drinking coffee.

"Hey."

Mom turned then stood for a hug. "What a lovely surprise. Would you like coffee?"

"Thanks, but I had my two cups for the day." I limited myself to two cups or else I'd be drinking the stuff all day long.

"So what's new with you?" Uncle Guy asked as he claimed a hug. We settled at the table.

"I wanted to see how Mrs. Cooke was doing, but she looks like she's having the time of her life."

"She's got a ruthless streak, that one. It's a little scary." Mom said feigning a shudder.

"I just witnessed a bit of that."

"And you? How are you?"

"I'm good. I miss my neighbor, but I'm happy she's adjusting so well. It's nice to see you, Uncle Guy. How's the detective business?"

A strange look moved over his face but it was gone so fast I wasn't sure I had actually seen it. "It's a lot of work, shocking some of the cases you see, but rewarding when you tie all the pieces up and hand it over to the DA."

"I bet."

Mom reached for her coffee. "You saved me a call. I have a friend whose son is interested in graphic design. He's been dragging his feet since he graduated college and his parents are trying to get him to make a decision on his career."

"Dragging his feet. How long as he been out of college?"

"Four years."

"Let me guess. He's living in their basement."

I totally saw the answer on Mom's face, but she tried to sugarcoat it. "He's not as bad as that."

Uncle Guy and I shared a look.

Mom confessed, "Oh, all right. He's a twit, but would you talk with him?"

"Fine."

"Good. Friday at Seven at Delaney's. His name is Kit."

"You already set it up?"

"Millie can be quite determined."

"Not determined enough to get her son out of her basement."

Mom grinned over the rim of her cup. "Touché."

It was Friday and I met Kit at Delaney's, but only a few minutes into the evening and I knew I had been hoodwinked.

Kit started the evening by suggesting we blow off dinner and head to a club. I didn't understand how a club would be conducive to talking, but he didn't want to talk. He was on the prowl. Luckily I was not the focus of his attention, but it did mean I got dressed in my business-like attire for nothing. Plus I was hungry because we had skipped dinner.

"Hey, you don't mind if I take off with Candy here, do you?"

Candy, seriously? Her name was Candy. I bet with an *i* and a heart over it. "No, by all means please…"

My phone interrupted us, thank God. It was Damian calling; he saved me a call. It had been decided that I could attend this meeting without the need of a shadow. I had been dropped off though, with instructions to call when I was done.

"Perfect tim—"

"Are you still at Tansy's?" I had called him earlier to share we had changed venues.

"Yes."

"Stay inside, by the bar, and wait for me. I'm only ten minutes away."

It was his tone that had fear running like ice through my veins. "What's wrong?"

"Just stay visible."

"What's happened?"

"By the bar, Thea. No bathroom, I'll be right there."

My hand actually shook when I put my phone away. Kit and his hook-up were gone. Damian wanted me by the bar so I walked on unsteady legs toward it and grabbed an empty stool at the end. The bartender appeared—long hair pulled back into a ponytail, a full beard and mustache, and tats down his arms. But it was the size of him that comforted because it wasn't likely anyone would approach with him near.

"What can I get you, babe?"

"Just water, please."

"You got it."

He placed the water before me and flashed a smile. "You need anything, I'm Sully."

That was good to know. "Thank you."

All kinds of scenarios bombarded me and with each one I grew more and more scared. Before I went into freak-out mode, Damian appeared. It was the manner in which he appeared though that was alarming.

"We need to go." But Damian was already pulling me from the club and at a pace I couldn't keep up with.

"I can't walk that fast."

His head jerked back to me and I honestly think he was contemplating tossing me over his shoulder. He didn't though; he slowed his pace but not by much. We hit the front of the club and I tried to pull free, but he wasn't letting go.

"You are going to rip my arm out of the socket. What is going on?"

"Someone took a shot at Cam. He's fine."

The only thing that kept me together was his hand wrapped around mine, without that I might have shaken apart. "Where is he?"

"At the precinct. He's fine. Pissed as hell though."

Thinking about Dad, the possibility that history was repeating itself, I grew hysterical. Mom, did she know? Someone should be with her.

"Mom?"

"She doesn't know."

Tears fell as I tried to pull from Damian. "Thea, he's fine."

"I'm not losing him too."

His hand tightened on mine at the same time I saw his jaw clench. He yanked me into a bar a few doors down from where we had just been and pulled me back toward the bathrooms. He pushed me up against the wall. "Thea, calm down. He's fine."

"He could have died."

"He didn't." He moved into me as he curled his big body around mine. "I won't let anything happen to him or you."

I wanted to press my face against his chest, to borrow some of his strength. Tears burned my eyes as my body shook in fear.

"Thea." There was so much emotion in that one word. He wrapped my face in his hands as his thumb brushed over my cheek. And then he rocked my world when he closed the distance between us and captured my mouth with his. All my questions and fears evaporated when his lips touched mine. The kiss started as a diversion to calm me, but after so many years of waiting and wanting it turned very real as everything, including the trouble that led us here, faded. His hands moved down my body to my thighs as he lifted me and pressed his body deeper into mine, but he still wasn't close enough. I curled my legs around his waist and wrapped my arms around his shoulders. His cock was hard and hitting me right where I ached, our bodies moving together in that ageless dance. His mouth moved to my neck where his teeth grazed my skin as his hips continued to grind into me. I dug my nails into his shoulders right before I came and when the orgasm crashed over me I had to bite my lip to keep from screaming. He didn't stop, his hips continued to move against me to prolong the pleasure and it was pleasure, a pleasure so intense it brought tears to my eyes. The Pandora's box in my mind flew open and every heartbreakingly beautiful detail, every feeling and every memory, came flooding back.

Damian had stopped moving, his eyes were closed and there was such stark desire on his face and yet he denied himself the release we both knew he wanted and needed.

I cradled his face in my hands "Why?" I whispered.

"I've waited a long time for you. When I come, it'll be inside you." His eyes opened, those pale eyes dark like an emerald. "And once won't be enough."

Before I could reply he kissed me again…deep, wet and perfect. I didn't so much unwrap my legs from his waist as they just went boneless. He lowered me to my feet, but he didn't release his hold on me until he knew I had my balance.

"Give me a minute."

He was as affected by our kiss as me and the wanton part of me wanted to be reckless, wanted to drop down to my knees right there, but instead I attempted to distract him in another way. "I watched a video of a snake eating a rabbit. It was disgusting seeing the whole rabbit moving down the snake's body."

It was a little known fact that badass, ex-Green Beret Damian

Tate was not a fan of snakes.

He knew what I was doing when his head tilted and I got a crooked grin. "Nice try."

"I can help you with that. I really want to help you with that."

And he really wanted my help by the hot possessive look that swept his face. "Rain check."

Best rain check ever. "Are you okay?"

"Manageable."

He pulled me from the bar.

"If exercise felt like that I would do it every day, all day long."

His hand tightened on mine. "Not helping."

"Right. Sorry."

It was only after we reached his car that I began to recall the events that led up to the best orgasm of my life while fully clothed. Damian was thinking about the troubling events too because as soon as he pulled from the curb he said, "You're staying at my place tonight."

For just a second I thought he wanted to finish what we had started, but by the way he held the steering wheel in a death grip that seemed unlikely. It had been a long time since I had been in Damian's domain and I really wanted to see where he lived and how he lived now.

"Okay." The troubling news about Cam couldn't be ignored. "What happened tonight?"

"He was returning to the station when someone took a shot at him."

I went numb. Someone was copying my dad's murder. "He's okay?"

"Yes. We think it was a warning."

"And related to Dad."

"Yes.

It was shock that kept me from completely flipping out. Cam was okay. I repeated that over and over again in my head. I could dwell and really freak myself out, but me losing it wasn't going to help the situation. I tried to distract myself.

We reached his gym. I had noticed the apartment above it and wasn't surprised to learn Damian lived there. He pulled around back to the spot that must have been his designated spot because it was where he had been parked that night I stalked him.

"You are not worried about leaving this car in this neighborhood."

"It helps when people know whose car it is."

Right. He was an ex-special ops badass. People probably gave him a wide berth. There was a door at the back of the building that led to stairs. Damian hit the lights in his apartment and I just took it all in because it was awesome. Open floor plan, like a converted warehouse. All the rooms flowed together into each other except the bedroom, which I guessed was behind the barn door at the far end of the space. The décor was very urban with lots of metal and reclaimed wood. A huge television took up one quarter of the floor plan; a large leather sofa shared the space. The kitchen was smooth lines, concrete countertops and stainless steel appliances. The difference between this and his first apartment was like night and day. Yet I found I preferred his old place because we had made some really great memories within its walls.

He stood with his hands pushed into the front pockets of his jeans and he looked as vulnerable as I had ever seen him. An ache started in my chest because to look at him he seemed invincible and yet under that was the boy with the sad eyes who had irrevocably changed me. "This is amazing, but I still like your old place best."

Understanding moved over his face as the sweetest smile touched his lips. "Yeah, that place was pretty great."

I wanted to kiss him, and I knew he had read my mind when his sweet smile turned wicked. He abruptly changed the subject. "The bedroom and bath are back there."

"I would like to take a shower if that's okay."

He growled then muttered, "I'm a fucking saint."

I wanted to giggle. Mom was right; he was adorable especially when he was sexually repressed. He started across the room, taking my hand as he passed. "I'll grab you some clothes."

The memory drifted into my mind, the day in the rain after we had made love for the first time. He *had* gotten me wet and naked and after he gave me a pair of boxers and a t-shirt to wear while we waited for my clothes to dry. I kept them, stole them was more accurate, shoved them in my backpack when he wasn't looking. I sometimes slept in them when I wanted to feel closer to him.

He didn't walk with me to the bathroom, the man had his limit and I suspected we had passed his. He headed for the kitchen and I was just closing the door when he said, "You are safe here."

I glanced up to see he had stopped, his head twisted and I had his complete focus.

"I never questioned that."

I closed the door then pressed my forehead to it and tried to calm my wildly beating heart before I stripped and climbed under the spray. The showerhead was one of those rainwater ones and Damian's soap, the subtle scent of it on my skin had my senses on overload. Once I changed into his clothes, clothes I wasn't giving back, I rolled up my dress and left it on his hamper. He was in the kitchen on the phone when I joined him. He held the phone out to me.

"It's Cam."

"Oh God, Cam, you're okay?"

"Yes, I'm fine. They weren't trying to hurt me, just scare me."

"Well, they scared me."

"They only pissed me off and made me more determined because I'm getting close. Stay near to Damian."

Since that was where I wanted to be, near Damian, that was an easy request to agree to. "I will."

"You sound tired."

"I am, and in shock. I know you guys deal with this kind of thing all the time, but for me it is just a little hard to process."

"I'm fine. Get some sleep. Love you, Thea."

My heart twisted because he was more rattled than he was admitting to speak those words. Cam loved me, I never doubted that, but he rarely spoke the words. "I love you too."

I handed the phone back to Damian.

"Do you want something to drink?"

"Water would be great." My stomach growled. I forgot I hadn't eaten yet.

"Have you had dinner?"

"No, my dinner meeting turned into a hunting session for Kit. Then you called."

"How about eggs and bacon?"

It was just eggs and bacon and yet my chest grew tight because eggs and bacon was our thing, the one meal he made and often. Part of the reason I loved bacon now was the memory it stirred of him…us. I missed his eggs and bacon. I missed him.

"I want to say I waited. That I didn't let another man touch me, but that would be a lie. There was one other. He was kind and good. I tried to love him. I really did, but your ghost was always in the room."

He didn't make an audible sound, but it felt as if his inhale sucked the air from the room. He lowered his head and pressed his hands to the counter like the very act of breathing brought him pain.

"I'm telling you this because I didn't mail those letters and I didn't call. I even avoided you, but I never stopped thinking about you. I never stopped loving you."

I needed to retreat, needed to pull myself together and wrangle those emotions back into the box. "I'm really not that hungry anymore. Thank you for tonight."

He hadn't moved, standing alone in his kitchen with the weight of my ghosts on his shoulders too.

I didn't know what woke me a few hours later. The apartment was very still and I assumed Damian was sleeping. The living room was lit enough for me to see that the sofa was empty. There was a second door near the one we had entered. It didn't lead to the back of the building but to the gym. Silently I descended and noticed a cleaning crew had been through after the fights from earlier. It was quiet but for the man working the punching bag. Damian wore running pants and a black tank and as beautiful a sight as he was, that wasn't what held my attention. He looked as he had when we were younger; his punches directed not at the bag but something that haunted him. Seeing him in the empty gym, a single light illuminating just him…he looked so alone. Tears burned my eyes and I so wanted to wrap him in my arms and hold him. I didn't though. I watched him for a few minutes hoping whatever he battled he succeeded in holding it at bay then I turned to head back upstairs.

"Couldn't you sleep?" I'd always loved his voice. I let myself feel everything this man brought out in me and the strongest of those feelings in that moment were safe and loved. It took very little effort on my part to turn around and walk the distance to him. He stood near the punching bag, his hands fisted but at his side as he watched me, like a predator tracking his prey.

"Dad encouraged me to live my life, to stop letting it pass me by. He liked you, liked you for me, but he worried we were both waiting on something that might never happen."

"He wasn't wrong to encourage you."

"I didn't move on, not until I got your letter." Pain moved over his expression. "I hated that letter."

"I hated writing it."

"Why did you?"

His shoulders tensed as the muscle at his jaw knotted. "I escorted a fallen brother home to his young wife and baby son. Her pain and grief were palpable and thinking one day that could be you… that you waited so long and that was our ending. I couldn't do that to you."

Tears burned the back of my eyes. I couldn't even imagine so heartbreaking a scene. "And now?"

He touched my chin to keep my gaze on him. His eyes softened and a smile touched his lips, which made what he said more harsh…but in a really freaking awesome way. "I hate that another man knew you in the way only I want to know you. I fucking hate him. I want to take you right here, everything in me demands that I reclaim you, brand you as mine, but you're not just a fuck. The priority right now is your safety." His voice lowered before he added, "But after, I want it all—every kiss, every breath, every moan, every orgasm, every memory…good and bad."

He already had all of me, but I nodded my head because words simply weren't happening.

"Have you kept up with your self-defense?" Priorities and his right now were for my safety.

"Dad and Cam insisted."

"Have you ever had to use it?"

"A few times."

Concern shifted to really scary in a blink of an eye. "It wasn't anything as terrible as I am guessing you are thinking. Just over-zealous boys who needed to step back."

"Have you ever worked a bag?"

"A little."

"Do you want to give it a go now?"

"It helps you?"

"Yeah."

Fighting always had been an outlet for him. "The night of our first kiss, I was mesmerized watching you fight and heartbroken at the same time. I wanted so much to hold you, to love you. It was a stroke of luck that you were thinking the same."

The sound that rumbled up his throat was sexy as sin. "When this is all over…" He let the promise hang in the air between us before he moved to stand behind the bag. "Show me what you've got."

And I did. I channeled all of it; fear, anger, confusion even love, into the bag and he was right, it did feel good.

I slept until lunchtime before Damian drove me back to my apartment. We pulled up in front of the building; Damian hit his hazards before climbing out and meeting me at the curb. At my door he waited for me to key into my apartment. "I'll see you tomorrow night."

I didn't know why he was seeing me tomorrow night, but I loved that he was seeing me tomorrow night. He clarified, "Your friend's show."

Sunshine's show, I'd forgotten all about it, but under the circumstances I think that was to be expected. "Yes, tomorrow."

He waited for me to close the door and lock it and I didn't move until I heard his heavy footsteps retreating. I stripped as I made my way to my bed then dropped facedown. I woke when it was dark outside and my stomach growled.

I pulled on my pajamas and headed to the kitchen. I didn't have much to eat so I grabbed a pack of crackers and a glass of wine before settling in front of the television. I tried to watch a movie, but I was on overload between the fantastic moment at the club, the heart to hearts and the news that someone tried to scare off my brother. The wine took the edge off, so I finished the bottle before I fell asleep on my sofa.

I woke on my bathroom floor in a puddle of my own drool. A bottle of wine on a relatively empty stomach and no water spelled hangover. The cold tiles felt so good on my clammy skin. And it was while I lay there in a pathetic bundle that I remembered the showing…a showing Damian was joining me for and I felt like death warmed over. I pulled myself up and looked into the toilet bowl wondering if the suction was enough to kill me. I would love to read that police report.

There was only one thing to do about my hangover. I reached for my phone and called Anton.

"Thea, good morning."

"It's not. I need the remedy."

I heard the slight chuckle. "Oh, Thea. You are drinking alone now."

"I don't need a lecture, just the remedy."

"I'll be there in ten."

Anton arrived ten minutes later, but he didn't come alone. Damian was with him. Of course he was with him. Why wouldn't he be with him? Anton gave me a once over before tsking. He actually tsked me.

"I've arrived just in time."

"Funny."

"Seriously, Thea, what the hell? You look like something my dog threw up."

"Anton! That's a horrible thing to say." But he wasn't wrong.

"How much did you drink?"

"Not as much as you're thinking."

Damian didn't greet me, only gave me a once over before he headed to the kitchen.

"Drink it fast." Anton handed me the glass with the piss yellow liquid. The ingredients of the evil brew were a mystery, but it worked like a dream. Tasted like shit going down, but relief was almost immediate.

"You have that show tonight." Anton would of course know my schedule and not just because he likely discussed it with Damian. It was just his way.

"Hence the need for that," I said while glaring at the glass, the yellow liquid clinging to the side. "You need to tell me what is in that."

"Then I can't see you at rock bottom. No way."

"I hope to return the favor one day."

The remedy was working when I rushed to the bathroom, part of the cure included vomiting. Lovely, because it wasn't like I hadn't sunk low enough.

I felt strong hands holding my hair back and assumed it was Anton. A cool towel was draped over my neck. "Thank you."

"You need another dose," Anton called from the living room, which had my head jerking to Damian. He watched me with concern in those pale eyes.

"You didn't drink water."

If I didn't drink the same amount of water as I did alcohol I was ill the next morning, even with just one glass of wine. I had experimented a few times in high school with beer and wine. I hadn't gotten drunk and still I woke the following day sick. Damian remembered. One more reason why I was crazy about this man. "No."

"Are you hungry?"

"Yes."

"I'll make you something to eat. Remedy, water, coffee then food."

"Okay."

"You good?"

"I need a minute." I needed to brush my teeth.

He seemed reluctant to release me, but he did. "I'll make you some eggs and bacon."

My heart sighed. "Thank you."

I would have kissed him right then, but not in the state I was in. I washed my face, brushed my teeth and pulled my hair back before I joined the guys in my kitchen. The smell of the bacon had my stomach growling.

Anton pointed to the chair. "Sit and drink this. Were you drinking alone?"

"Yes."

"Why?"

"I didn't realize how stressed out I have been about the events of late and with the news about Cam, I was letting off some steam."

Damian placed the plate of food in front of me before pulling out a chair, turning and straddling it. Anton also took a seat but it was the way they stared that made me nervous.

"What?"

"Are you up to hearing what we know?"

The knot caused by the situation with Cam had only just eased, but being ignorant was stupid. "Yes, but I'm hung over so use small words."

Anton chuckled but turned serious a heartbeat later. "Cam has made some good headway into the investigation on the corruption at the precinct."

"Meaning he has the names of the dirty cops?" I asked. Dirty cops that knew Cam was looking into them, maybe even that Dad had been too. History *was* repeating itself.

"Yes."

"Who?"

"Miguel Dobbs."

"He's Guy's mentor."

"As lead detective, he mentors all the new detectives, including Cam, but he is definitely moonlighting. He is also recruiting from within."

"Recruiting other cops?"

"Yes."

"Who are they moonlighting for?"

"Salvatore Federico."

It just went from bad to worse.

"Did Miguel kill my father? He has Dad's old job. Did you know that?" I was getting pissed, really fucking pissed.

"He has an alibi for the time of the shooting, but it doesn't mean he didn't pay someone."

Anton was hedging. "There's something else."

"The man that broke into Mrs. Cooke's place, Jerry Castile, his arresting officer was Miguel Dobbs."

It took me a minute to make the connection, but when I did I wanted to throw up for an entirely different reason. "So Mrs. Cooke's attack was related to me."

"It's a connection that deserves further investigation. It could be that Jerry was just back to his old ways and his link to Dobbs is completely coincidental." Anton was trying and I really appreciated it, but he didn't believe what he was saying either.

"And that's what Cam is looking into, digging deeper into Dobbs?" I asked.

"Yes, there is still the possibility that your dad's death was random."

That bastard had taken my dad. He wasn't taking my brother too. "You know they are linked. It's why you're both worried now. You're worried about Cam. And after the other night you have a reason to be."

"Nothing will happen to him." Damian sounded quite sure of that. I was glad he felt so confident.

"As we learn more we'll keep you posted, but we were in a meeting when you called. We really need to get back. You'll be okay?"

"Yeah, I'll be fine. Thanks for bringing the remedy."

Anton kissed my head. "Anytime."

Damian hunched down next to me. "I'll be back later."

"Okay."

"Eat."

I nodded my head, but I wasn't hungry. Anton and Damian were at the door when I called to them, "If it was Miguel who killed Dad, he has to pay."

Damian didn't miss a beat. "Abso-fuckin-lutely."

DAMIAN

The door had just closed behind us when I asked Anton, "She ever do that before?"

"Get drunk alone? No. But considering the circumstances, I think letting off some steam is okay."

There were other ways she could let off steam, ways I could help her with...fucking wanted to help her with, but losing focus now was not an option. "What's your take on the shit with Cam?"

"We're making people nervous."

We reached my car. I leaned against the hood and looked across it to Anton. "We know Dobbs is dirty and that he's recruiting, but him taking a shot at Cam...he's got to be really fucking stupid to bring that kind of heat down on himself when he's already in the crosshairs."

"Or someone is setting him up."

"I want Dobbs in a room. A few broken bones and he'd sing like a fucking canary."

"That would bring blowback on Cam, but Federico is fair game." Anton had the look in his eyes. He was formulating a plan.

"Will Federico talk to you?"

"He's a miserly fuck, but I can be persuasive. Before I approach him again, I want backup. We need to make a stop."

I didn't pretend to understand the food chain as it pertained to gangsters in New York, but I did know for all the polish Anton had on the outside, he was a scary motherfucker. I'd seen the other side of him a few times and knew he wasn't jesting when he said he could be persuasive. I was curious as hell by the stop we needed to make because it was a club in Soho.

"Do you want to fill me in on what we're doing?"

"Federico is a dinosaur. He's desperate to hold onto his waning empire. He's old school in his beliefs and his methods, but times are changing. He's been a thorn in my side for years. Holds properties that I'm willing to legally buy from him, but he won't sell because they're drug dens...keeping his customers satisfied. I don't have much of a moral code, but fucking drugs...I draw the line there."

"So you've been looking to take him down."

"Yeah, but he's got some connections and any attempt I make could start a turf war. I'm not interested in adding to the bloodshed of the city. I need more leverage."

"So what's the plan?"

"Some of these buildings are near schools and I know a guy who's been as vocal as me about Federico's crack houses, but like me he knows he needs to pick his battles. However, he has a friend who's father was a cop?"

"Was? Did he die on the job?"

"No retired, but this friend isn't going to like the possibility that Federico could have been involved in a cop's murder. That's a battle he'll definitely pick."

"So who's this guy?"

"Lucien Black."

I pulled up to the curb outside the club Allegro and Anton climbed out. I followed. The inside was weathered and worn with a scarred wooden bar and a stage up front. Tables and chairs packed the place. A woman stood behind the bar, drying glasses. She glanced up, her eyes hitting me before moving to Anton where they lingered.

"Can I help you?"

Anton didn't move, even the air around him seemed to still. I looked over to find him studying the blonde. I had never seen him look as he did just then. It was subtle, only those who knew him well would pick up on his intense mood of the moment. And yet when he spoke his voice gave nothing away.

"Anton Scalene to see Lucien Black."

She recognized his name with how her eyes grew wide. She moved from around the bar. "I'll let him know you're here."

At that moment a woman came from the back hall tying her black hair into a ponytail. "Tara, is there more coffee?" She stopped short when she saw us. "Oh. Hi."

The Tara chick said to the woman, as she walked around her heading to the offices in the back, "This is Anton Scalene."

The second woman's reaction wasn't like Tara's. Her eyes didn't widened; they narrowed. "Darcy Black. So what trouble are you looking to pull my husband into?"

"Behave wife," a deep voice said just before a man, I assumed was Lucien, appeared. He stepped up next to his wife and pressed a kiss on her forehead before he turned his attention to Anton. "Good to see you."

"And you. This is Damian Tate, a friend."

Lucien extended his hand to me. "Nice to meet you."

I jerked my chin in greeting as I took his hand.

Anton asked, "Do you have a minute?"

"Yeah." Lucien turned to his wife. "I won't be long and then we'll go over the report. Line by line."

His wife blushed and lowered her lashes before she whispered, "Don't do anything crazy."

Lucien gestured to the room down the hall before he said to his wife, "Me? Doing something crazy? Never."

In his office, I stood near the door while Anton took a seat on the sofa. Lucien followed us in and closed the door. He didn't mince words. "Why are you here?"

"Salvatore Federico. I need your help convincing the man it's in his best interest to talk to me. I've had one sit down with him, but he wasn't very forthcoming."

"Why do you want a sit down?"

"Damian's girl's dad was a cop, murdered in the line of duty. I think Federico knows more about that than he's saying."

I didn't know this Lucien dude, but I did know rage when I saw it. He turned his attention to me. "I'm sorry." His focus shifted back to Anton. "Alright, tell me what you know."

THEA

I had spent the day thinking about Dad. He was the kind of man who would have absolutely looked into bad cops. He loved the job, the badge, and anyone tarnishing that would have been high on his list. But the idea it was a fellow man in blue that was responsible for his death was sickening and infuriating. And I felt helpless because there was very little I could do but sit back and wait for the guys to piece it all together. It was enough to make a person crazy, but tonight was a big deal for a friend and client, so I had to put all of it on the back burner and focus on making her night as special as possible.

The remedy had done it again. After the breakfast Damian had made and a nice long shower I felt great. I finished dressing in my sassy little black dress and left my brown curls down because Damian had always loved my wild hair. And yes I was preening for him. I added a little makeup to bring out the green specks in my brown eyes and slipped on my black sandals. I was just switching out my purse when Damian arrived. I pulled the door open, he didn't come in, but he did give me a once over. My face was down as I organized my bag, but I felt his eyes. I liked having his eyes on me, and the heat that followed his gaze down my body as he took his time to appreciate.

"I'm ready." I reached for my keys then finally looked at him and it was me who took my time appreciating him. He was dressed in a black suit, charcoal gray shirt unbuttoned at the collar. There was something ridiculously sexy about a man like him dressed like that. And while I looked with unabashed interest and want in my expression, his expression looked pained. "What?"

"It's cold."

"Outside? It is fall, but we'll be inside with lots of people."

"You should cover up."

Understanding dawned and with it I felt smug and sexy as hell. With feigned innocence I looked down at myself. "Is there something wrong with what I'm wearing?"

"Sainted, I should be fucking sainted."

The ride to the gallery was a silent one. We pulled into valet and as he walked around the car, women were checking him out. I didn't like their blatant show of interest, but I understood it because I was tempted to worship him myself.

"You want a drink?" he asked.

"Red wine, please."

"You made it!" Sunshine threw her arms around me. Her name was fitting because she was as bright and warm as the sun. Her auburn tresses were long, to her ass, and plaited. She wore a flowing dress and had a band of daisies circling her head.

"Thank you so much for coming."

"I wouldn't have missed it."

"Even though you don't get my art."

I didn't. We'd discussed it. Art was art, but where some could study a dot on a white canvas and get immeasurable knowledge from that dot, all I saw was a dot. But I loved Sunshine so even if she drew only stick figures, it would be a work of art to me…a fact I had shared countless times with her. Damian approached with two glasses of wine and handed one to each of us.

"Oh my God. Where did you find him?"

"I hired him for the evening." It seemed the easiest way to answer to avoid questions that would take the whole night and then some to explain.

"You need to tell me what agency you used if they have hotties like this in their stables."

Damian had no reaction, but I was struggling not to laugh.

"I have to go mingle. Check out the painting on the end. I dedicated that one to you. Thanks for the wine, cutey."

Before I could reply, she skipped away.

There was humor in Damian's eyes when I glanced at him. "Shall we?" I asked.

He touched the small of my back and walked us toward the first painting and all the while I worked on keeping my balance because the heat stirred from his touch was nice, really, really nice.

"I think it speaks to the darkness in all of us. What do you think young lady?"

It was a black canvas with a white question mark in the center. I thought that Sunshine painted it while watching her favorite show, *Gravity Falls*.

"Um, it's…" I tilted my head, like that was going to bring me clarity, but the older couple followed my lead. "I think…" I tilted my head the other way and they followed. I glanced at Damian. To the casual observer, he looked uninterested, maybe even bored, but I knew better. I would have paid handsomely to know what he was thinking because I swear he looked to be enjoying my discomfort.

"To me it speaks…" And then inspiration struck. "What do you think it means, darling?" And as I hoped, I successfully turned the elderly couple's attention away from me and onto him. They waited with bated breath for the perils of wisdom he was about to bestow on us.

"I think it speaks to the ageless question…is there something after death?"

He said it so matter-of-factly; it just rolled off his tongue like he spewed nonsense like that every day—the man who didn't speak except when it was absolutely necessary. The older couple looked at him like he was the messiah. I swear they were getting on their knees if we stayed much longer. But we didn't, he led me away, giving them time to ponder his words.

"Where the hell did that come from?"

He shrugged, but his lip twitched and when he glanced down at me there was laughter looking back. I teased him. "You're about to smile, you might want to pull it together." But I was hoping he would smile—seeing every aspect of his face brightened by a genuine smile, one directed at me—because it was my very favorite of his expressions.

CHAPTER 13

It had been two days since Sunshine's show. The painting she had dedicated to me was of actual stick figures. I could still see Damian's laughing eyes every time I closed my own. We were older and different but I liked the man he had become. The one who could spout that shit about the ageless question, could find humor in me suggesting he was an escort, could take me up against the wall and give me the best orgasm of my life while we were both fully clothed, held my hair back and made me greasy food after a night of overdoing it. Like the boy he had been, the man he was now was someone well worth knowing.

I finished the work I had planned for the day. I wasn't in the mood for a movie because I was feeling a little too wired given the state of things. I needed a release and since sex with Damian was off the table, it was zombie-killing time. I fired up my Xbox, checked my arsenal and got to it.

I was a little rusty but into the second hour I was on a roll. I felt fairly confident that when the zombie apocalypse came I would make a dent in them before I turned into one myself. At first I thought I'd want someone to lop off my head because who wanted to be a zombie, but then it might be cool to see what it was like. A mindless, brain addicted fiend. There were worse things to be. When my phone rang I almost didn't answer it, but it could be important. I put it on speaker.

"What the hell are you doing, having an orgy?"

"Only you, Kimber, would hear the surgical and precise sounds of a master taking out a zombie horde and mistake it for a sex fest. What's up?"

"Just called to see how you were doing."

"Why? What did you hear?"

"You are paranoid."

"No, I'm not. Someone got to you. Who? Mom?"

"She was worried, she hasn't heard from you in a few days."

"I'm fine, just releasing some tension by killing the undead. It's very therapeutic. You should try it."

"Nah, I like my method of relieving tension."

I was only half listening, so I walked right into it when I asked, "What's your method?"

"Sex and lots of it."

"Right."

"Let's get together for dinner."

"Sounds good. How about here on Friday."

"I'll call Ryder."

"Thanks, Kimber, for checking in on me."

"That's what friends are for. See you on Friday. Have fun with your brain eating friends."

The knock at the door came about two hours later and I was still killing those bastards. I hadn't eaten, except for some pretzels and canned cheese. I had also closed my blinds because the glare from the sun hurt my eyes. I looked like an insane shut-in. I paused the game and checked the door then felt my pulse jump when I saw

Damian on the other side.

I yanked it open and he walked in then stopped and just stared. I didn't doubt I looked slightly wild.

"I'm killing zombies. There's no room for vanity."

"Zombies?" There was definite interest in that word.

"Are you a brother in arms? Do you also kill those brain sucking monsters?"

I realized I was talking to someone who probably killed people every day, well not every day because that's excessive. The deli man didn't put enough rare roast beef on his sandwich and so he slit his throat with the dagger he had hidden up his sleeve. I giggled at the thought.

Again I saw the humor in his eyes in response to me calling him a brother in arms. I asked, "Do you want to play?"

"Yeah."

"You do?" And that was said almost identically to how Farmer Ted said it in *Sixteen Candles*.

"Come on in."

He strolled into my apartment, shrugged off his leather jacket exposing the black t-shirt that just hugged his body. I wanted to be that t-shirt. I really wanted to be that t-shirt. He was wearing cargo pants and boots, he looked like a zombie killer. He reached for the controller, his arms flexed and I had to bite down on the moan. I wasn't going to be killing zombies, I was going to be watching him and wishing he were wearing me like he was that t-shirt.

He glanced over, his sign that he was ready, so I grabbed my own remote and started the game. At some point I just stopped playing because the man was…lethal. I realized it was just a game and there were countless people out there, living in the basements of their parents' home, who could kill as efficiently as Damian. But they were gamers, this man hunted for a living. His skill didn't come from hours and hours of play. It came from real life. Damian was a lethal weapon. And fear stirred in me thinking about the situations he had been in that turned him into the man he was now. That part of his life was in the past and still it was terrifying to think it could have ended very differently.

I didn't want to think about that, so I indulged myself a little. My eyes moving over his perfectly sculpted arm, the biceps and triceps, his wide shoulder and the bulging muscles of his middle back that tapered to a flat stomach. I loved the view, but I was getting turned on, so I focused back on the game. He was on a level I had never seen, would never again see without his help. I wasn't thinking about the game anymore though.

"I'm hungry. Do you want to order a pizza?" It wasn't pizza I wanted.

"Yeah."

"Pepperoni and mushroom?" I hadn't realized his attention had shifted to me, so I was surprised to look over and see him staring. "What?"

He said nothing but there was a softening around his eyes. "Yeah."

I ordered the pizza and grabbed two beers before settling back on the sofa. Given the situation I found myself in, my thoughts often detoured to Cam's investigation. "Do you think it was Miguel who killed my dad?"

"It points to him, but the pieces don't all fit."

"And so until they do you'll be looking at other possibilities."

"It's what I'm trained for."

"And we have to be careful of which cops we involve because we aren't sure who we can trust."

"Exactly."

"You gave up a lot to come back and help Cam. Thank you."

He stopped the game and turned his focus on me. "I gave up a lot when I left home all those years ago and I told you, I didn't come back for Cam."

"If that's the case, why didn't you let me know you were home?"

I couldn't quite read his expression, his gaze shifted to the floor. "I stopped by the day I got home, but you were with someone. I intended to reach out again, but the truth is I didn't like seeing you with another guy."

Another guy? There had only been the one, Ethan, and that had ended years ago. "Whoever he was, he wasn't a boyfriend. He was probably a client. I learned if I couldn't be with the one I loved, I wasn't interested."

His eyes turned back on me and I liked the hot possessive look in them.

"I want to kiss you so badly right now, so I'll get us another beer instead." I jumped from the sofa. A few minutes with my head in the freezer would help take the edge off.

I knew he had joined me because every part of my body responded to him like a mare preparing for a stallion to mount her. He pressed into me, sandwiching me between the fridge and his body, his chest to my back. He rubbed his cheek against my head, his forehead touched my shoulder and yet it was only his body holding me in place, he had yet to put his hands on me. His discipline was warring with instinct and the breath caught in my lungs as I waited to see which would win. The second his hands touched me I knew that instinct had won. He turned me into him and right before he kissed me I saw the wild look of him. He hadn't just given in to instinct; he'd given in to his baser needs. His hot, wet mouth closed over mine, his tongue driving into my mouth while his hands ripped at the barrier of my clothes. We were frantic; both of us crazed with the need to taste and touch after so long a fast. I heard the t-shirt tear before he yanked my bra down. My whole world was focused on my breasts and the need to have his hot mouth on them, but instead he lifted the key hanging from the long chain.

Pain moved into his expression when he asked, "What's this?"

"It was from my dad, his last gift to me."

Understanding replaced pain as he let the key drop back into place. He moved his hands up my body and cupped my breasts, teasing my nipples with his tongue. I was so wet and the need to rub myself against him was strong. He sucked one of my breasts into his mouth and my eyes rolled into the back of my head. He dropped to his knees, taking my sweats with him, and buried his nose between my legs to smell my arousal. With a tug, the thin layer of silk that separated us was gone and his tongue was inside me as my body splintered apart from the orgasm. I went boneless and my head fell back against the fridge because I had missed this. He lifted me into his arms and carried me to my bed. My back hit the mattress as he stripped and then he was all over me, hands, lips, teeth and tongue and I was just as frenzied trying to taste and touch as much of him as I could.

"I need to be inside you, feel you. No condom. I'm clean."

Unlike the last time we had had unprotected sex, I was on the pill. But even if I hadn't been, I would have thrown caution to the wind. "Please."

The word was no sooner out of my mouth when he lifted my hips, looking me right in the eye, and surged into me. For just a second we both stilled at the beauty of being here again, but the beast that ruled him took over as he lost himself in my body. Right before he came his mouth found mine for a kiss that was poignantly tender. He buried his face in my hair and for several long, blissful minutes we stayed just like that…replete and connected.

His head lifted and tenderness stared back.

"I never knew that zombie hunting was an aphrodisiac."

He chuckled.

"What changed your mind?"

He brushed my hair away from my face, his hand settling on my cheek as his eyes took a slow journey over my features. "You remembered what I liked on my pizza."

I almost laughed, but I realized he wasn't entirely kidding. I got it because I felt it too. We were connected, bound, and had been since we were seventeen. Even after all these years, our bond was still just as strong.

A wicked smile spread over his face. "You do remember what I told you."

I was too wrapped up in how he was looking at me to really follow along with the conversation. "What?"

"Once wasn't going to be enough."

I *followed* that and he knew how his words affected me because he was still buried in the part of me that shuddered. He shifted his hips. "You like this idea."

I had always been a fan of his ideas. "Very much."

"Do you have condoms?"

"In the bathroom, but they're like four years old."

He liked hearing that by the cocky grin he threw me before he climbed from the bed. And that was when I saw his back. He had the most beautiful back, defined muscles that cut to his narrow waist and smack in the middle of all that beauty was a tattoo of the devil—a horned, winged beast of a man with red eyes. His tail curled between his legs at the small of Damian's back.

"When did you have that done?"

He looked confused for a second and then something dark swept his face. "After I enlisted."

"It's beautiful."

I had the sense it wasn't intended to be beautiful and the idea that he marked himself with something that was like a brand, a reminder of something ugly, upset me.

But he turned my thoughts from that when he said, "We might as well shower first." He didn't wait for my reply when he grabbed me and threw me over his shoulder.

For two days we stayed in bed...the best two days ever. Damian had even blown off a few things, and knowing his need for me was stronger than his incredible discipline was very heady. I had invited him to join the girls and I for dinner, but responsibility reared its ugly head and he went off to do all the things he had let slide.

I had been devastated when Damian had left at eighteen, but he wouldn't be the man he was now if he hadn't gone. And I could say in all honesty that though I had loved the boy he had been, I was crazy out of my head for the man he was now. Everything happened for a reason.

The ladies were on the way. I had cooked dinner, chicken potpie and a big salad loaded with so much extra stuff it wasn't at all healthy. I was just uncorking the bottle of wine when my house phone rang.

"Miss Ahern?"

"Yes."

"You are listed as Ryder Chase's emergency contact."

My legs nearly crumbled out from under me. "What's happened?"

"Time is critical. Can you get to Mount Sinai immediately and please bring identification."

"Yes, of course."

I hung up then checked the caller ID and it was in fact from Mount Sinai. Fear whipped through me as I grabbed my purse and flew out of my apartment. I was in so much of a hurry, I had only the sense to turn off the stove and lock the door. I reached for my phone when I stepped outside and called Kimber.

"Hey woman."

"Something has happened to Ryder. Meet me at Mount Sinai."

"Are you pulling my leg? Ryder is right here."

My hand had been up hailing for a cab, it dropped. "What?"

"We're on our way to you now."

Something sharp dug into my back. "Hang up."

"Who is that?" Kimber asked, but my mind was going numb with fear.

"Now," he hissed.

He took my phone and hurled it across the street. My first thought was it was a mugging until he called someone and said, "I have her."

Those three words resonated down to my bones.

Fear had my body feeling all funny. We had just reached the alley next to my building when fight or flight took over. I had to get away from him because this wasn't a mugging. Thank God for the self-defense classes Cam and Dad had forced on me. I lifted my elbow right up into his nose causing him to stumble and lose his hold on me. I ran down the alley to the fire escape. If I could only get back inside, but I didn't get far when he grabbed me by the hair and yanked me back to him. He jerked me around just as his fist connected with my jaw, my vision going black from the pain before I was jarred back into consciousness when my head slammed into the wall behind me. Lights flashed in my vision as my stomach pitched violently and my legs gave out as I crumbled to my knees. This man looked ready to carve me up as he held the knife so tightly in his hands his knuckles were turning white. At least the bastard was bleeding. I had made him bleed.

I was literally paralyzed with terror, but not my vocal chords as I screamed, loud and long hoping someone would hear. That earned me a kick in the gut. And as I doubled over in pain, coming to grips with the very real possibility that I was about to die, Damian appeared. I didn't know how he was there or if I was wishing so hard for him to be there I was seeing things. But the sight of him, looking like an archangel, or maybe even the devil he had depicted on his back, had tears filling my eyes. He hauled my attacker off me and threw him against the wall. Damian's eyes connected with me for an instant, making sure I was still breathing, before he moved soundlessly like a predator. The deadly energy coming off him was as mesmerizing as it was terrifying. The punch was so vicious that my attacker's head jerked back hard from the blow and while he was disoriented Damian grabbed his head, and with a quick jerk he snapped the bone. The man dropped to the ground in a boneless heap. He didn't move, didn't make a sound. He was dead. Instead of fear of the situation, I feared for Damian because he had just killed someone.

Damian's back was to me as he stood over the dead man. He reached for his cell and made a call. I started to shake, the reality of the situation settling over me, not because of the attack, but of losing Damian again while he spent twenty-five to life upstate all because he had saved me. And I hurt, oh God did I hurt everywhere.

He moved soundlessly, hunching down to look me over. He took several deep breaths through his nose and still the rage coming from him was palpable.

"How did you know?"

"Kimber called, but I was already on my way."

How did Kimber know his number? "You were?"

"Your mom was right. You cook almost as well as you draw."

Only Damian could make me smile with the circumstances being what they were. And even with his teasing, he was furious and yet very gentle when his hands roamed over me feeling for breaks. He lifted me into his arms.

"He's dead?"

"Yeah."

I started to cry and even though it hurt like hell, I wrapped my arms around his neck and buried my face on his shoulder, holding him as tightly as I could so no one could take him away from me.

"Thea?"

"They're going to take you away from me."

"No they won't."

"But you just killed a man."

"No body, no crime."

My head jerked up at that and even knowing it was wrong, hope stirred. Yes, he had killed someone but the man had it coming. "That was Anton you called?"

"He'll take care of it."

"Meaning?"

"Cleaner is two minutes out."

My lower lip started to tremble. "You are ex-military, Mr. Discipline, a follower of law and order and I've made you a criminal."

"If you think wartime is law and order, you are very mistaken and that fuck would have killed you. My conscience is clean."

He had killed for me. I was sure it wasn't the first person he had killed, but I hated that because of me he had another ghost. "Mount Sinai called, said Ryder had been brought in. I checked the caller ID, it really seemed to have come from them. I'm so sorry."

Every muscle in his body went hard as stone and yet he said nothing as he started for the front of my apartment. And even being gentle, I still had to bite my lip to keep from moaning in pain. "He got your head and your jaw…" He said that through clenched teeth. "Where else?"

"He kicked me in the stomach."

"Motherfucker." He stopped walking, like he was contemplating killing the man again. Love burned through me as I curled deeper into his big, strong body. We reached the front of the building as Kimber and Ryder came jumping out of a cab.

"Oh my God," Ryder said through tears.

"Where is the fucker?" Kimber looked ready to kill someone.

"Inside," was all Damian said and they followed.

Damian lowered me to the sofa then hunched down in front of me. "We have to call the cops."

"I know."

His hand was actually shaking when he brushed the hair from my cheek. And there was something brewing behind his eyes, but before I could ask about it he said, "After, we're leaving."

"Leaving?"

He didn't answer, I didn't press. After that ordeal, getting away for a while sounded really nice.

"I need to make a call. Are you okay?"

"I am now."

He looked over at Ryder. "Tell the cops what you know."

"Okay."

He walked from the room as Kimber and Ryder hurried around the sofa to sit on either side of me.

"Is he dead?" Kimber asked.

I nodded, but my attention was on Ryder. "What does he mean tell the cops what you know?"

"A man came in a few times asking about you. I didn't like his interest so I told Damian."

"How did you have his number?"

"He gave it to us a while ago. Told us to call if we saw anything unusual. Anyway, he had someone tracking the guy. He hurt you." Ryder looked ready to kill someone too.

Damian had recruited my friends with keeping me and all of us safe. Love for him burned through me. "It could have been so much worse."

"I'm glad he's dead. Asshole."

"Me too," Kimber chimed in.

"I won't be mentioning that to the police though," Ryder added. Yep, these were my girls. I loved them.

DAMIAN

I walked from the room, so I didn't upset Thea, and almost punched the fucking wall as I struggled to pull in my rage. The sight of Thea in that alley had my blood boiling. I curled my fingers into fists, my nails biting into my palms. I wanted to kill that fucker again, more slowly. It wasn't just rage, but also anguish at the thought of a world without her in it. She could have died. That was on me. I was supposed to have her back and I failed. I wouldn't again. No fucking way.

Taking her away for a while was smart because the game had just changed. And I knew just where we could lay low.

I reached for my phone and called Cam. "We have a problem. There's another player."

THEA

The paramedics insisted I go to the hospital, but luckily I escaped the harrowing experience with only a mild concussion and lots of bruises. After being checked by a doctor, and happily numbed with pain meds, the cops escorted me to their precinct where I was questioned.

"Did you know him?" Detective Baker seemed like a nice man, someone closing in on retirement. He had a friendly face and an easy disposition. His partner, detective Locke, was a bit more uptight and suspicious.

"No. I've never seen him before."

"So work it for me one more time."

"I received a call from Mount Sinai saying my girlfriend had been brought in and since I was her emergency contact they asked me to come. I stepped outside and called my other girlfriend and she informed me Ryder was with her. That was when the man put the knife to my back."

"And you've never seen him before."

"No."

"How does Damian Tate fit into this again?"

How did I answer that and not implicate Damian? I wasn't a great liar. "He was coming for dinner. He heard me scream. The man didn't want an audience I guess because he ran, but then I think anyone would have. Damian is rather intimidating."

"Are you involved with Mr. Tate?"

"We're friends, have been so since we were kids." I wasn't sure they were buying my story. I had seen in countless movies how the interrogated went on the defensive to throw the cops off their game. I decided to give that a try. "I don't understand why you're grilling me when whoever did this is still out there." He wasn't still out there. He was dead and buried wherever cleaners buried bodies. Or maybe they didn't bury them. Maybe they put them in acid or something and got rid of them completely. It was a disgusting thought and yet a fitting end for that bastard in the alley. Fucker.

It looked as if Detective Baker wanted me to go through it all again when the door opened and a man entered with Anton just behind him. "Enough. She's answered all your questions. She needs rest." The man was probably Anton's lawyer and from the look of him, a very expensive one.

Anton helped me to my feet then wrapped me protectively in his arms.

"Mr. Scalene." Detective Baker was salivating over the idea of grilling Anton.

"I'm taking her home."

"Leave a number where we can reach you."

Anton didn't acknowledge him as he led me from the room.

Damian was waiting at the door. Anton walked me right to him and did the hand off as Damian gently pulled me close, right up against his body...exactly where I wanted to be.

"Where are Kimber and Ryder?"

"One of my men drove them to your mom's," Damian offered.

Once we were in the car, Anton said, "We're taking you home to pack. You won't be going back there for a while."

"Kimber and Ryder, my mom?"

"We'll stop at your mom's so you can see them before you go." Anton said.

"I'm sorry about all of this."

Both looked pissed. It was Anton who replied, "Don't. This isn't your fault."

"Feels a bit like my fault. I was so gullible. I didn't even question the call."

Anton gently took my face in his hand. "Anyone would have done the same."

"You wouldn't have, Damian wouldn't have. And what about Cam? Damian killed someone and you helped him cover it up. His two best friends and he's a cop."

"We saved him the trouble."

Damian wasn't wrong. I suppose that was the silver lining. Cam was a cop, but he would have hunted that man down and he wouldn't have been as methodical because he didn't have the training Damian had. And a cop killing someone would have been front-page news.

Anton ended the conversation when he said, "None of this is your fault, Thea. Let's get you safe and then we're ending this shit."

"Be safe. Listen to Damian. Do exactly what he says." Ryder said as she gently hugged me being mindful of my bruises.

"What she said. And try not to worry." Kimber drew me in and held me close. "We'll keep an eye on your apartment, get your mail."

Mrs. Cooke didn't know what was going on, at least not to the extent of the others, but one look at my battered face said it all. She looked older as worry creased the area between her eyes. "Please be careful, Thea, and stay close to your young man."

"I will. And make sure Mom doesn't have too many wild parties."

Mom didn't laugh at my attempt at humor. She stood with Cam, but it was the expression on her face as she took in my appearance that broke my heart.

"Look what they did to my baby girl. They won't get away with it, but I'm glad Damian is taking you away from here. You'll be safe with him." A tear slipped down her cheek before she gingerly wrapped me in her arms. "Please be safe."

We were both thinking the same thing. Yes, I looked terrible but if this was related to Dad, it could have been so much worse.

Mom had no sooner released me that I found myself pressed against Cam. "I'm sorry," he whispered.

"Not your fault."

"Anton and Damian will share what we know. I promise you I will find out who was behind your attack. Fucker is going down."

"I know you will."

Anton approached. "We've got to go, Thea."

"What about the cops?" Mom asked.

"That's where I'm going now. I'll take care of it," Cam said.

I hugged everyone one last time then walked to Damian who stood by the door. He led me out, but I looked back, saw my peeps and hoped like hell it wasn't the last time I did.

The safe house was tucked in a neighborhood in Elizabeth, New Jersey. Once we arrived, Damian checked the place top to bottom making sure windows were locked, doors barred. He pulled all the curtains before moving to the kitchen, one that was stocked with food. He grabbed a frozen bag of peas and handed it to me.

"For your jaw."

I settled at the kitchen table, Anton joined me. Damian leaned against the counter across the kitchen from us.

"They wanted me. He called someone and said he had me."

"Fucking hell," Damian hissed.

Anton's expression was nearly as scary when he said, "The cleaner checked the phone. It was a burner. We've been tracking Dobbs, Federico and the man that approached Ryder. We're missing a piece."

"What do you mean?"

"It's not adding up, there's another player that we don't know about. And since these fucks have made a move on you, until we figure out what we don't know you need to disappear for a while. I don't even want to know where you are." Anton looked a bit rattled and that really freaked me out.

"Do you really think that's necessary?"

Damian sounded really scary. "Look in the mirror."

I didn't need to look in the mirror because I ached everywhere.

"I was attacked, I get it, but to go on the lam…" I couldn't believe I could actually say that statement and it was true.

"The lam?" There was humor in Anton's expression. Damian looked ready to skin something.

"You know what I mean."

"They came at you so there's no reason to believe they won't again."

"But shouldn't Damian be there to help you find the bad guys. It is what he does."

"I'm with you." Damian's tone left no room for argument.

"I'm sorry, this all is just so unbelievable. Dad's gone, Cam's hunting dirty cops and has people shooting at him, and someone wants something from me and is willing to hurt me to get it. I'm just a graphic designer with an addiction to coffee and sugar. I feel like I've stepped into someone else's nightmare."

"We're going to deal with it and while we do, you'll be somewhere safe. I suppose we should mention that you and Damian will be posing as a married couple. You'll draw less suspicion."

The situation was suddenly looking up. Away from danger with the man I loved pretending we were married. Yes, things were definitely looking up.

CHAPTER 14

I was beginning to think death wasn't so terrible a fate. If I had to listen to the deafening silence for much longer I might off myself and save whoever wanted me dead the trouble. I had my suspicions as to the cause, but Damian had done a complete one eighty. We had been in the car for almost nine hours and he had said exactly five words to me. When we left, I got a *let's go.* Twice in our journey he said *gas* meaning we were running low and in need of some and I had been gifted with *food* because *his* tank was running low. I appreciated the gravity of the situation, the constant knot in my stomach was proof of that, and I even liked that Damian was taking the matter seriously, but the silent treatment was getting old and fast. I would have better conversations with my shoe and had been tempted to hold a few to stave off boredom. Silver lining, he was breathtakingly sexy. I had studied him while we were confined to the small space of the car. He wasn't using them now, but he had magnificent lips. His lower lip slightly fuller than the upper, lips that begged to be bitten then licked then sucked on. And yes, I thought about that and the two days of sexual bliss we had shared before he turned into a cyborg again because otherwise I would have gone mad from the silence.

I was taking the Scarlett O'Hara approach on this entire mess, *tomorrow is another day*, in that I'd worry tomorrow. Shock helped with this plan because I felt like I was in a perpetual dream-like state…that none of this was real and I would wake up from it at any time.

It was late, close to eleven, when Damian pulled into a motel. "We are stopping here?"

I didn't expect an answer from this new and less improved Damian. In fact, I had started holding both sides of the conversation because it entertained me and I suspected irritated him.

In my best interpretation of his voice I said, "Yes, Thea, we have traveled hard today and you have had a trying week. You need a good night's sleep."

"Oh, Damian, that is so thoughtful of you. I would love a shower and eight hours of sleep."

He threw the car in park and shut off the engine before turning to me, but I hadn't a clue what he was thinking. Without a word, he climbed from the car and headed to the trunk. I joined him and looked around at the five-star establishment he had found us. It felt kind of like a scene from *Pulp Fiction*. All it was missing was the blood splatter on the office door and the severed head by the ice machine.

"This is really nice. How did you find it? Did you Google worst motel imaginable?"

He handed me my overnight bag, grabbed his own, before shutting the trunk and headed to the office. I followed after him. "You're armed right?"

This earned me a look from over his shoulder.

We entered the office to find a man sitting behind the counter, and calling what we saw a man was stretching the word to its limit.

Very little hair was left on his large, bulbous head, his gut stuck out in the stained wife beater he wore and his eyes were glassy, either from lack of sleep or alcohol. Normally I wouldn't disparage someone based on their appearance, however since his entire office was papered with bare-chested women, the gratuitous display eased any guilt I might have felt.

"We need a room."

The manager sized me up. My skin crawled at the scrutiny. "Twin beds or king-sized?" He asked that as he adjusted himself. Seriously how the hell had Damian found this place?

"King-size and if you look at my wife that way again I'll rip your fucking eyes out of their sockets and feed them to you." My head jerked so hard to the left I felt light-headed. My expression matched that of the manager's, but for different reasons…obviously.

Damian paid for the room, grabbed the key before reaching for my hand and pulling me from the office. Our room was the last room, the opposite side of the building from the office. Done on purpose I was sure, the manager probably wanted Damian as far from him as possible.

Despite the unwelcoming appearance of the outside and the manager, the inside was surprisingly clean. Dust-free, new carpets, and with a check of the mattress I discovered no bed bugs and no mold on the shower curtain. Things were looking up. But then I realized he had asked for only one bed. This would have started the tingles of anticipation, but the man wasn't talking to me so it was highly unlikely he intended to do all those wondrous activities that inspired the tingles.

Damian grabbed his bag and headed to the bathroom. He didn't close the door, left it open, so I had a front row seat to the show. He grabbed the back of his tee and pulled it over his head, gifting me with the view of his beautiful back and that tattoo that I both loved and hated. I hadn't been sitting, but my knees gave out and I dropped down onto the edge of the bed when he dropped his pants affording me the sight of the sexiest ass I had ever seen. Heat burned up my neck, my cheeks were on fire and my nipples went hard and still I just stared because staring was all I was getting these days. He didn't turn and I was grateful because I didn't think I would be able to handle a full frontal. He climbed into the shower and almost as an afterthought he reached for the door. He didn't shut it. He just closed it enough that I was left staring at the scarred wood, but all I saw was Damian's very fine body. We were sharing a bed where we wouldn't be touching; he'd probably even build a wall with the extra pillows.

He wasn't in the shower long, came strolling out with a pair of running pants on and nothing else. He was built like he had been airbrushed to perfection. His shoulders were unimaginably wide, but then with how effortlessly he had tossed my attacker in that alley, I couldn't say I was surprised. His pecs, his abs, he was the perfect example of the male form. I dragged my eyes from him because I was feeling aches in places that he wouldn't be helping me ease, and reached for my bag.

I headed to the bathroom and he called after me. "No lock."

I knew his instruction was only because he needed to be able to get to me just in case someone came in through the window. But for just a second I let myself believe he intended to sneak in while I showered and have his way with me, like he had the other day. I liked the idea of that so much, as soon as the water rained down on me I eased the ache the thought stirred. I bit my lip, lowered my head and hoped the sound of the shower drowned out my moan when I came.

I finished in the shower and dressed in my shorts and tee. I thought to enter the room naked and see if that stirred anything, but when he rejected me, which I knew he would when he saw the bruises, it would hurt even more than the injuries I had sustained in the alley.

He was already in the bed, resting on top of the covers, his focus was on the news playing on the television. I climbed under the covers, rolled on my side away from him. I wanted to scream at him, to snap him out of it, but this particular ghost he was mentally battling, my attack, was too fresh and raw. He needed time in his head to deal, so instead I whispered into my pillow. "Good night."

I wasn't expecting sleep so was shocked when I opened my eyes to find light streaming in through the crack in the curtains. Cautiously, I turned toward Damian only to discover his side of the bed was empty. I stretched then climbed from bed, grabbed my stuff and headed to the bathroom. I was just finishing up when I heard him return. Peeking around the door, Damian was dropping the key on the bed but it was the sight of the coffee that almost had me shouting in glee.

"Did you get one for me?" I asked.

He looked over and took his time moving his gaze from my bare feet slowly up my body until he finally reached my face, a face that was now burning because damn I felt that like a caress.

"No."

I almost said thank you because I wasn't expecting him to say no.

"No?"

He moved to his bag, ignoring me. I wasn't going to be ignored. I walked into the room, right up to him, and poked him in the chest with my toothbrush. "No?"

His focus was on my toothbrush.

"You went out for coffee and didn't bring me back a cup? It is bad enough you have decided to stop speaking to me, but that is just rude."

He looked me right in the eye before shifting his gaze back to my toothbrush—his nonverbal way of telling me to back off. I pressed the brush harder into his chest.

"We are stuck with each other for the foreseeable future and when you are my only hope for conversation, the damn cat has got your tongue."

His eyes went all dark as they speared me with a look but I hadn't a clue what emotion was behind that look. "Next time you get coffee, in case your memory has also been affected, I take mine black with two sugars." And then I grabbed his coffee and disappeared into the bathroom, slamming the door behind me for emphasis. It felt good for the two point three seconds that it lasted. The door flew open; the coffee I hadn't even sipped was removed from my hand before I saw nothing but his back as he strolled to the door. I hurried with dressing because I wouldn't put it past this less friendly Damian to leave me here.

He was standing by the trunk when I stepped outside, drinking his coffee. I hoped he choked on it. Dropping my bag in the car, I took a play from his book and said nothing as I yanked open the passenger door. And that's when my eyes landed on the second cup of coffee, one that had Thea written on the side.

He climbed in, keyed the engine. "Black, two sugars."

I was gushing a bit. He hadn't forgotten about me. I belted in, reached for my coffee and flashed him a smile.

"Thank you."

He didn't answer. I hadn't expected him to.

Deadwood, South Dakota. I had no idea how he found this place, but as we drove through town I couldn't deny it was the perfect place to lay low. Quaint, off the beaten path, and looking similar to what I imagined it looked like in the day of cowboys and the Wild West. Stretches of land for as far as the eye could see and brilliant blue skies and mountains hugging the horizon. It was gorgeous. The air was cleaner; everything was cleaner.

We reached the house, a charming little cottage. "Are you going to carry me over the threshold?"

At my question, he spared me a glance and shook his head, but he wasn't answering me, it was more like he was wondering how he'd drawn the short straw. I wanted to shout that he had volunteered but it was pointless. He climbed from the car.

"I'll take that as a no."

I walked to the trunk to retrieve my bags, but he had already grabbed his stuff and mine and was heading for the door.

Instead of following him in, I meandered a bit in the front gardens. Mums had been planted and the window boxes on the front windows were overflowing with ornamental cabbages and pumpkins. A stone path guided you through the garden beds, most of which had been cut down in preparation for winter. Turning toward the house, I noticed Damian had left the front door open for me. As soon as I entered the cottage, I immediately fell in love. Oak floors, whitewashed walls and an exposed beam ceiling. Furniture in fabrics of pale blues and yellows, coffee and side tables painted in a buttery yellow, a kitchen with wood countertops, white paned glass cabinets, a farmhouse sink and windows all along the back wall overlooking nothing but wilderness. The bedrooms were all done in soft colors with sheer curtains on the windows to add a touch of privacy but still allowing for the breeze from the mountains. Since my bags were in the room with the Wedgwood blue walls, I could only assume that was where I was sleeping. My room had a private balcony. When I stepped out on the balcony, I realized that it wasn't so private because a second room shared it and somehow I just knew Damian was taking that one.

Settling on one of the chairs, I looked out at the view of nothing but mountains and trees and tried to come to terms with how royally screwed up my life was now. A few weeks ago my biggest concern was making sure my DVR recorded *Game of Thrones* and now I was hiding out in Deadwood, South Dakota with bad people wanting to hurt me, the love of my life killed a man, my best friend covered it up, my brother was getting shot at and my mom and dearest friends were out of reach.

I didn't know when the tears started, but I moved back into my room, climbed on the bed and muffled the sound of my tears with the pillow.

An hour later, I headed to the kitchen in time to see Damian reaching for his keys. "Where are you going?"

"Town. We need supplies."

"Can I come?"

In response, I got the chin lift. I had learned, during the long car ride with the Damian looking cyborg, meant affirmative. I belted in and asked, "So what's our story?"

He responded with the best blank look I had ever seen. I had received this stare many times during the course of our journey and yet it didn't grow old.

I clarified, "We're married, so how did we meet? Why did we move here? People are going to ask."

"No one will care. We're just here to lay low."

Words. He spoke actual words. I couldn't bask in his temporary case of verbosity though because his comment was nonsensical.

"What do you mean people won't care? Deadwood has a population of fewer than thirteen hundred people and we're strangers. People are most definitely going to care. Okay, I know. We met at Dahlia's and fell in love over chocolate cake."

My eyes were trained on his profile, but the only reaction I got from that was the jump in the muscle of his jaw, so I continued. "We had only dated for a few months when you realized you could not live another day without me as your wife. We married in a private ceremony and after three years of wedded bliss you whisked me away to Deadwood because you know of my love of wide-open spaces. We don't have children, but we are actively pursuing that..." It hurt because my fake life sounded an awful lot like how I wanted my real life to be, so I turned my head and looked out the window. I felt Damian's stare, but he kept his thoughts to himself.

No one will care, right! That belief of Damian's was dispelled immediately upon parking along Main Street. People stared at us. Some were even talking behind their hands. We were most definitely news. Damian came up on the curb and opened my door for me. Even when he wasn't speaking to me, he still had impeccable manners. We walked toward the market and I reached for his hand. He didn't hesitate to link his fingers with mine. We were supposed to be married after all. He didn't hold my hand long though, releasing it almost as soon as we entered the market so he could push the shopping cart.

Half an hour, that was how long we spent in the produce aisle. The man wasn't a vegetarian. I had shopped often with him as a kid and had witnessed him eating countless meals featuring meat, the latest of which was watching him stuff a double cheeseburger with bacon in his face during a rest stop at a diner on our way here. But he was packing up the cart with a variety of lettuces and kale, beans and peppers and fruit. I was all for eating your greens, but really. Where was the bakery?

Next came the milk and cheeses, the man apparently had a fondness for dairy products and lastly he selected meats, all of which were lean.

"What about bread?" I asked.

"I don't eat it."

I wanted to step on his foot because he knew damn well that I did. "Well, I do." I left Mr. I Don't Eat Bread in the middle of the meat aisle and went in search of bread and cake. Maybe I'd even get a pie. The bakery wasn't what I was hoping for, there were no assortments of cookies, the cake selection was limited as were the breads, but at least I'd have something for my sweet tooth. In the midst of debating over the coffee crumb cake and the orange glazed cake, I met my first resident of Deadwood. She was older, maybe early seventies, with whitish gray hair that leaned more toward purple. She was dressed in a blue housedress and sturdy, thick soled shoes.

"Hello. You are the new gal who just moved to town with her beau."

"Yes, I'm Thea. Damian is here, somewhere." The words were barely out of my mouth when I felt Damian come up behind me. His arm wrapped around my waist as he pulled me close to his side. The gesture to this woman would look like a loving husband, but I knew it had nothing at all to do with that and everything to do with his job of protecting me, even from friendly older women with purple hair.

"Damian this is...I'm sorry I didn't get your name."

"I'm Madge, Madge Littleton."

"It's nice to meet you, ma'am." A full sentence, she got a full sentence, but Damian wasn't done. "Do you need a hand with those groceries?"

Here was the charming Damian, like he had been with Mrs. Cooke and my mom, and I had the same reaction I had then... jealousy. He had it in him to speak, even be charming, very charming, he just wasn't bothering doing so with me now. Jerk.

"Thank you, young man, but Billy at the counter always carries my bags home. There's a square dance tonight at the tavern starting at seven; it will be a good opportunity for you to meet some of your neighbors."

I felt Damian go rigid at my side, so immediately I responded before he could say no because frankly I needed some human interaction. I could only take so much of the cyborg act. "What a wonderful idea. There is nothing my husband likes more than a good square dance. Maybe we will see you there."

"Oh, I'll definitely be there, at least for the first few dances. I'm not as young as I used to be."

"You'll have to make sure you save a dance for Damian."

His fingers on my hip were now digging almost painfully into my side.

"I'll do that, looking forward to it."

And she was because you could feel her excitement. "It was very nice to meet you, Mrs. Littleton."

"Please call me Madge. See you tonight."

She rattled when she departed, and so focused on what she could be wearing that would rattle, I didn't immediately sense Damian's mood until he said in a voice that was a little scary, "You enjoyed that."

"Oh I did, Damian, very much." Then I too walked away because it wouldn't do for him to see me grinning and I was, from ear to ear.

Damian went for a run as soon as we put away the groceries. I tried not to think about the man in the alley and how if Damian hadn't shown when he had, I wouldn't be sitting here. I had something some bad people wanted and they were prepared to kill me to get it. That is not something most people can say and so my overactive imagination took a stroll down memory lane. Were there other people in my life who would like to see me facedown in a river?

Initially, I couldn't imagine anyone wanting to kill me. I was very unassuming. I didn't get into people's business. I kept to myself. I sent thank you notes and Christmas cards. I was really very uninteresting. The biggest drama I'd ever been in was breaking up the fight between Mrs. Cooke and Betty when The Bachelor ended and the outcome was not one either of them liked.

I was convinced the list would be very short, maybe even nonexistent, but as I searched my memories I discovered that there were more people than I was comfortable with who might wish me harm. I looked down at the names under the column, PEOPLE WHO WANT TO SEE ME DEAD. There were too many names on that list and it was while I stared at the possible harbingers of my death that Damian returned from his run. He headed to the fridge first for a bottle of water before he joined me at the table, though he didn't take a seat. Since I was looking right at him, I saw the frown as he studied the sheet of paper in front of me. His focus shifted to me.

"Facing down death I wondered if there could be others in my life that would like to see me dead. A little morbid, but then that scene in the alley was definitely morbid."

He flinched, subtle but undeniable, and I felt badly for mentioning it.

"Old lady in the yellow car?"

"I didn't know her name, but I took her parking spot. I mean technically I was there first, but she was elderly and it would have been the polite thing to let her have the spot because it was closer to the store. But I'd been circling for a while so I took it. She actually flicked me off when she drove past."

"And you think she would want you dead?"

"Probably not. She's probably dead. The incident was several years ago and she looked like the crypt keeper even then."

"Man on the corner?"

"He's a panhandler, who asks me for money every day, which I refuse to give and not because I'm a mean person, but a panhandler who drinks Starbucks every morning and wears nicer clothes than me, I don't think so. After months of being denied, when I walk by him now he starts mocking me by chanting *no* in the most annoying way. I think if he had the means, he would kill me then steal my purse and get the last laugh."

"Do I want to know about the dog gang?"

"Stray dogs that walk the streets in my neighborhood. It's the look in their eyes I don't trust."

"Me?"

It was in poor taste for me to put him on this list since he was acting as he was because of that alley and how I had almost bought it. I got that, understood what motivated the change in him, but his silence hurt and I was childish enough that I wanted to hurt him back.

He walked out of the kitchen before I could answer, not that I intended to.

CHAPTER 15

The town of Deadwood was a very friendly one. The dance had only just started and already we had met nearly half of the town's population. I imagine some found it stifling, but the idea of knowing your neighbors, really knowing them and their families, was one I liked a lot. The Sharptons were neighbors of ours who lived a few miles from the cottage. Bobby, the father, owned the hardware store in town. Missy, his wife, worked at the grain depot and their children, Hank who was ten and Wynona, who was six were in fifth and first grades respectively.

"You should come for dinner tomorrow night. It's hard work moving and I'm sure you don't have your kitchen organized yet."

The house was fully furnished and the kitchen was stocked after our trip to the grocery store, but it was the thought of conversation that had me immediately agreeing. "That would be lovely, thank you."

"We'll arrange something. I'll get your number before you leave."

"How long have you lived in Deadwood?"

"All my life, same as Bobby. We couldn't imagine raising our kids anywhere else. Everyone knows everyone and unlike some small towns, that isn't a bad thing. The only downside, jobs can be hard to find. I would give anything do something other than work at the depot. There's very little human interaction, but we need the second paycheck."

I wasn't sure what a grain depot was, but I could believe it wasn't a thrilling job. "It is a beautiful looking town."

"Especially just outside of it, the views are spectacular. You should take a picnic lunch for you and your husband. It's very romantic."

Yeah, the last place Damian wanted to be was somewhere romantic with me. I had been gifted with the cold shoulder during the ride here, but now he was being downright frosty after the faux pas with the death list. He'd probably tie me to a tree and leave me there.

But to Missy I said, "I can't wait to see it."

"Oh, there's Bobby. I owe him a dance. I'll find you later to get your number." And then she was off, moving through the crowd with surprising finesse. Damian had left earlier to dance with Madge. It was mean of me, but I had been anticipating him fumbling the steps, but he was a quick study. I think as payback for roping him into that dance, and for putting him on my harbingers of death list, he was avoiding me. I hadn't seen him since we arrived an hour ago.

I scanned the crowd and located him near the makeshift bar. He was leaning up against it, a beer in one hand, but it was the smile on his face that nearly took my breath away. I loved when he smiled. And then I realized he was smiling at two women, twenty something's that he appeared to be engaging in conversation. I knew he was playing the part and yet I still wanted to stab him in the eye. He could chat up the entire town for all I cared. And since

I was feeling like a petulant child, I acted like one and walked right out of the square dance. I didn't even care about being cautious. It would serve him right that I be killed while he pretended to flirt with coeds. I started to mutter. Something I did often when irritated. "I should frame him for my death. I could scroll his name on the sidewalk in my blood just to give the local authorities a direction to focus their investigation."

Spending my days where the only noise heard was the settling of the house held no appeal. I had work to keep me busy during the day, but the evenings were going to be tough. The silence was bad enough, but the longing and sexual tension…the need to be as close to him as possible when he was trying to keep me as far as possible. Yeah I needed to find something to do with myself during the evenings, a social outlet. I took note of what shops lined the street so I could inquire about available positions with evening hours.

I passed a hotel. Good to know. If things got really unbearable I could get a room, one with room service and movies still playing in the theaters, and charge it all to Damian—my loving husband. The thought had a giggle burning up my throat. Married to Damian, the one I was stuck with now, I think it would be more fun to be buried alive. And speaking of Damian, had he not noticed his charge was gone? And on that thought someone came up behind me. My whole body tensed. "Scroll my name in blood?"

I jumped out of my skin, then turned and pushed him, but he didn't move, I did. The man was solid muscle. It was only after my heart rate went back to normal that I realized he had been following me from the moment I left the dance. And even being annoyed with him at the moment, my heart warmed.

"How the hell are you so quiet being as big as you are?"

"I can't protect you if you walk off."

"You can't protect me if you are too busy flirting with the locals either." Did I just say that out loud? I was grateful for his muteness so I wouldn't have to hear his thoughts on that.

"Jealous?"

"Now you decide to speak. Is it going to be like this from now on with you? Having to drag the answers out of you? It is really rather exhausting."

His demeanor changed in an instant, but it was the devastation buried in those eyes that had the air stilling in my lungs. "You could have died."

"But I didn't."

"I lost focus and you were the one who paid."

"That's bullshit."

"It's a fact."

"So the plan now is to ignore me?"

He moved so close I inhaled the air he exhaled. "I've tasted you. I've been buried inside you. I know the sounds you make when my cock is driving into you and the look on your face when you come. Staying away had been hard when it was the memory of us I was battling, but your taste is still on my tongue. I'm ignoring you because otherwise I'll give in."

"What's wrong with giving in?"

"I know how it feels to lose someone, I'm not losing you too."

Rocked to my core by that statement I had no words.

"Ready?" he asked.

He didn't wait for an answer and led me back to the car. It was me who stayed silent. He had lost someone, someone important. Not his mother or father, surely he wouldn't shed a tear for them. So if not them, who? The fallen soldier he had mentioned? Based on the pain I heard in his voice, I didn't think so. It was love and lost I heard and I knew how that sounded because I had been there. So it was likely a woman. He had never discussed the years we were apart, not personal things anyway. Was it possible he too had found someone, but unlike me she had meant something to him? I wanted to ask whom he had lost, but if he wanted me to know he would have shared. His unwillingness to share something that would bring me pain further suggested to me it was a woman. I went right to my room when we got home and spent the night coming to terms with the idea that Damian had loved another. I knew how he felt about me, but for a time he had loved another. It hurt, it fucking killed, knowing that he had loved someone else and it gutted knowing he had lost her. But under the pain there was contentment because he hadn't been alone, he had been happy, at least for a little while. It was more than I could say for myself.

"You were the one who said we needed to have a presence in town. Dinner with the Sharptons gives us a presence." I was in danger of actually morphing into Scarlet O'Hara with the number of times I had adopted her *tomorrow is another day* philosophy in the past week, but I couldn't think about Damian and the woman he had lost. It was in the past but the pain was very real for me in the present. I pushed it as far back in my mind as possible and fell back on the humor I had once sought comfort in after Dad had died. To laugh instead of cry and with how I was feeling I should have my own stand-up show.

Damian grumbled at me and it was like I asked the man to walk over hot coals while watching *Pride and Prejudice* with my mom. It was dinner, one we didn't have to cook.

"We won't stay super long."

No answer.

"I understand why you've resorted back to conserving your words like someone squirreling rations away for the zombie apocalypse, but if you spoke to me I wouldn't have been so eager to accept their invitation. You have only yourself to blame."

He was annoyed, but he said nothing—big surprise—and reached for the keys before holding the door for me. It was while we were in the car that I asked, "What is the significance of your tattoo?"

His head jerked to me in surprise. "Why do you think there's a significance?"

"A man like you doesn't mark himself, especially not that severely, without a reason."

The lines around his eyes and mouth softened a bit. I was guessing because I was right and he liked that I knew him so well. "I heard it enough growing up. I embraced it."

Now I was the one who was pissed. I turned more toward him as I worked to control the anger his matter-of-fact statement caused. "Your mother."

"Yes."

I knew his mother was vile, but to call him the devil? "Why did she call you the devil?"

"She hated my father and since I was his son."

I curled my hands into fists, my nails digging into my palms. "How old were you when she started calling you the devil?"

"Six or seven."

"And later, when you were older and didn't want me to meet her. What was she doing then?"

"Whatever the hell she wanted. She was a vile, vindictive bitch who manipulated her own son to get what she wanted."

It happened so long ago and still I ached for the boy he had been. "Manipulated you how?"

"Why are we rehashing this?"

"Damian, how?"

"Filed false reports with the police about abuse so I'd pay her bills, be her beck and call boy, but the bitch enjoyed hurting me. Got off on it because hurting me in her twisted mind was hurting my dad."

"Oh my God." My whole body started to shake at the truth I only then understood. "That was part of the reason you left. If she knew about me, she would have hurt me to hurt you."

"Yeah."

"Stop the car." I needed air. "Stop the fucking car." I didn't even wait for it to come to a complete stop and I was out and moving with no destination in mind. My chest ached as my heart pounded against my ribs, and the rage, the most acute and potent rage burned through me thinking of a sweet, six-year-old Damian being told he was the devil by his own hateful mother. The sadness behind his eyes, that pain that never faded when he was younger. I understood it now and it lingered still. No amount of fighting, or punching a bag or military training and discipline erased the damage she had inflicted because he had marked himself with the only legacy his mother had left him…the belief that he was bad, evil…the devil.

Damian caught up to me and pulled me into his arms. "What are you doing?"

I jerked free and put distance between us because in his arms was a safe and happy place and right now I wanted to hurt something. "I know she's dead, but I want to bring her back to life just so I can kill her in the slowest and most painful way possible. She was a hateful person and right now she's burning in hell for what she did to you. Mom loves you, so did Dad. If they thought you were evil, they would never have opened their home to you. You are not evil and you are not bad. You have spent your life helping people, saving people. Your tattoo is beautiful and in many ways you're like him—dark, dangerous and beautiful, but you are not bad. Tell me you understand that."

"Thea." I couldn't take tenderness right now, not the softness of his voice or the love I saw burning in his eyes.

"Tell me you understand."

"I do."

He reached for me, but I pulled away. Pain flashed in his eyes. "Being in your arms has always been my very favorite place to be, but if you held me now a part of me would always think of her and I am not giving her anymore of you."

Devotion stared back, but he gave me my minute to calm down.

We rode in silence the rest of the way to the Sharptons, but as we drove down their drive heartache eased at the beauty before us. The Sharptons lived in a rancher on sprawling acres with a barn and horses. Garden beds filled with mums in the colors of rust, burgundy, yellow and white wrapped around the house.

"This is beautiful."

Damian parked next to an older model Ford F-150 and climbed from the car. He walked around for me, but I was already out and looking around. "Can you imagine calling this place home?"

He was as captivated by the scene as me. He touched the small of my back and led me to the front door. We hadn't even rung the bell when a girl, who looked just like her mom, opened it.

"They're here Mommy!"

Missy appeared with a red apron around her waist that she was wiping her hands on. "Let them in, Wynona."

The little girl turned and started skipping down the hall screaming. "Hank, they're here."

"We don't often get visitors since we're so far from the heart of town. Wynona is a very social little girl. Please come in."

"Your house is beautiful," I said and realized it was on the inside too. Hardwood floors, beautifully designed rooms, comfy furniture, family pictures on the wall, houseplants scattered here and there.

"Bobby's getting the grill started. We're doing steaks. I hope that's okay."

"Sounds delicious."

"Can I get you something to drink? Wine, beer?"

It was Damian that answered. "Thea likes red wine, I'll take a beer."

"Sure. Let's go to the kitchen."

We followed her as I took in everything because it was so perfect it felt as if it were staged, but in a good way. She got my wine and Damian's beer.

"I'll see about helping Bobby with the grill," Damian offered and disappeared outside.

"Can I help with anything?"

"No. It's all pretty much done. So how are you finding Dead-wood?"

"We love it."

"It's a great little town. I didn't realize the cottage was on the market."

"I'm sorry?"

"It's been sitting empty for so long, it's nice to see people living there again."

"What happened to the previous owner?"

"She died. Cancer. It was very sad."

My heart twisted thinking about the cottage and how picture perfect it was. How had Damian found the place?

"Let's take our drinks and join the men. This time of year is just perfect for outdoor dining."

Especially when they had an outdoor area like theirs. Teak furniture—tables and chairs and lounges—all resting on a slate patio, which also had an outdoor kitchen and fireplace. And there was Damian with Bobby, sitting in chairs looking out at the amazing view. Damian looked good in this setting. He looked good in the city too, but there was something about him here, like he had come home. Did he want this at some point, like when he retired? Did he see himself settling in the country, raising horses or pigs or cows? I could see him, Mr. Badassery, becoming a farmer. Those big hands gently caring for the animals in his charge. I wanted to see that, wanted to be a part of that.

"This is amazing."

"Bobby built it."

Missy took the arm of Bobby's chair, his arm immediately went around her waist. I took the seat on the other side of Damian, felt a pang of jealousy seeing the obvious affection between them. Footsteps sounded as Hank and Wynona came running outside with a ball and baseball mitts. I wanted to reach for Damian's hand, but before I could his strong fingers linked with mine. He was watching the kids, and yet he held my hand tightly in his. My heart squeezed in my chest. It was still there…every emotion he stirred in me, had stirred in me since I was seventeen. I truly was irrevocably in love with this complicated man.

Dinner had been delicious and not just the quality of the steak, but Bobby was a true grill master. We were sitting inside; the kids had gone off to watch a movie. I had had two glasses of wine so was feeling rather mellow. Bobby and Missy were adorable together, often affectionately teasing one another as they were now. I shifted my focus to Damian and felt a jolt to find his eyes on me. I rested my head on my hand and stared back. He was beautiful, even more so when he was relaxed, and he was definitely feeling relaxed right now. I wanted to crawl into his lap. I wanted to leave here, go back to the cottage and rip each other's clothes off. He clearly read my thoughts because his pale eyes turned darker. He made some sound from deep in his throat, but it was the accompanying look that had heat pooling in my belly, and a little lower if I were being completely truthful.

"It's getting late."

I felt giddy hearing Damian making an excuse for why we needed to leave and energized because I so wanted that look he had given me to mean what I really hoped it meant. Jumping up and running to the car wasn't cool, so I managed to pace myself, but my heart was galloping in my chest.

"Thank you for a wonderful evening."

"We should do it again," Missy said as she walked with me to the door.

"Our house next."

"I'll bring dessert."

We hugged. She actually hugged me and yet I barely knew the woman. I waved to Bobby who was shaking hands with Damian. When I reached the car, Damian was already pulling the door open. I watched as he walked around the car, felt my heart move into my throat. He started the car and pulled down the drive. My brain went completely blank. I couldn't grab onto a subject if my life depended on it. By the time we reached the cottage my body was so over-sensitized that I wanted my clothes off because they were actually hurting my skin. And how badly I hoped Damian would be the one to remove the offending articles. He shut off the engine then looked over at me and there was no mistaking what was going on in his head. Before he could act on the heat I saw burning in those pale eyes, his phone rang. Talk about a buzz-kill.

He glanced at the number and all that was hot turned ice cold. My heart stopped, but now it was worry causing it.

"What's wrong?"

"I've got to take this?"

"Is it Cam?"

"No. It's personal."

Those words ricocheted around in my head. *It's personal.* And feeling what I was feeling those words cut deep so I was just as abrupt when I said, "I'll leave you to it then."

I strolled inside and headed right to my room. I showered, changed and lay in bed staring blindly at the re-runs of *How I Met Your Mother* but thinking about his personal call.

The following day, I invited Damian on a picnic to the place that Missy had mentioned. I was surprised he agreed. He didn't mention his phone call, even when I asked if all was well. That bothered me, but it wasn't my business even though there was a huge part of me that didn't agree with that statement.

The view was beautiful, Missy wasn't wrong about that. I had really enjoyed our dinner with the Sharptons. They were such down to earth people. The food had been delicious, the children engaging and sweet. The night had been close to perfect except for the scene before dinner and his damn personal call after it. He wasn't one to keep things from me. Quiet and reserved, yes, but not secretive and I had to say I really didn't like it.

Again I adopted the no worries attitude and tried to enjoy the beauty around us. We left the picnic basket near a tree. I had even brought a blanket. I didn't think for a minute that Damian would sit on the blanket under a tree sharing a meal with me, but I planned on being comfortable.

"Anton mentioned you ran a team of ex-soldiers, a security firm in the private sector. How did that come about?"

I hadn't expected him to answer and was pleasantly surprised when he did. "After I resigned my commission I needed a liveli-hood. I've got the gym and that helps but not enough to build a life on. The only things I'm good at are fighting, fixing cars and running ops. The military has been a part of my life since I was eighteen years old and like a lot of guys, I felt displaced when my career was over. There's money to be made in the private sector for men with our skill sets and it helps with adapting to life outside of the military."

I didn't want to think about the ops he ran, I had convinced myself he was out of danger when he left the military, but that wasn't the case and it was scary to think about. His claim of being only good at a few things was bullshit, but telling him that would be a waste of time.

"What about you? I knew art was your passion, but what made you decide to focus on graphic design?"

"I'm not limited in my medium or the scope. I can work market-ing campaigns, book covers, technical drawings for architects and I get to choose the work and the client."

"Your work is beautiful."

I turned to find him watching me. "You've seen my work?"

I wouldn't say he was embarrassed, but he was definitely off-bal-ance when he confessed, "I own every book you've worked on."

Love washed over me. "You do? How did you know?"

A little grin tugged at his mouth. "Cam. I haven't read them, but I own them."

His clarification made me laugh because I couldn't see him reading romance novels.

"You used to doodle all the time, sketched me and Cam on scraps of paper, your house, a slice cake you were about to eat. Your life as seen through your eyes and hand, do you not doodle anymore?"

"I haven't. Not in a long time."

"Your work is very artistic and probably challenging, but your personal sketches, the ones that reflect you and your life, I think that's a show people would line up to see."

What a thing to say. I was moved to the point of speechlessness and he used the silence to steer us back to our picnic.

He ate his sandwich while standing. His attention focused on our surroundings. His words from earlier were still swirling around in my head.

Our meal was quiet and yet perfect, the silence not frustrating but comforting. When he suggested we leave a little while later, I didn't argue with him and walked silently next to him as we made our way back to the car. I thought about a showing of my own art. I forgot that I used to sketch my family. They were usually goofy caricatures but I had loved doing it. After Dad died I stopped doodling. I loved my work, but I wasn't passionate about my work and Damian picked up on that without me even having to say. We pulled into the driveway and I turned to him.

"Maybe tomorrow we could go into town for a sketchbook and pencils."

Love looked back at me. "Absolutely."

CHAPTER 16

The house was quiet, the sun had yet to rise, but I was awake. I headed to the bathroom. I loved having a bathroom in my room, but I didn't love that Damian had one in his room because that meant I was not treated to the sight of him taking a shower. The memory of him showering at the motel had been burned into my brain and I could recall it with astounding accuracy, and had, several times late at night, as I made myself come.

Moving quietly down the hall, I was surprised to find the kitchen empty. I was sure Damian was up, he was the one to wake the damn rooster. As I prepared the coffee, I wondered how he found this place. Was there a *www.safehouse.com* that people in the business could search when in a pinch and needed a place to flee? That was a stupid thought because they wouldn't really be safe houses if there was a listing of them. Silliness aside, the cottage was picture perfect, charming and quaint and so not the kind of place I would expect Damian Tate to secure. Missy had mentioned the previous owner had died. Was it possible she was the woman he had lost? Were we even now living in the house he had shared with her? My stomach roiled at the idea, though I wasn't sure if it was because of heartbreak or jealousy over a dead woman.

I moved to the sink to fill the carafe with water, looked outside and saw Damian. I thought the sight of him preparing for the shower was hot. He was all sweaty—I was guessing from a run. He wore running pants and sneakers. His bare back, and that tattoo I wanted to study up close, was facing me. I didn't know when he had done it, but there was a pole between two trees and he was doing pull ups so every muscle that I could see flexed. The man was strong. I had firsthand knowledge of this from the scene in that alley, but seeing all that power as his muscles bunched and corded was seriously sexy.

I needed to make a pie, needed to keep myself distracted because what I wanted to do was walk outside and climb that man like a tree. I got the coffee on and then started pulling what I'd need for the pie from the pantry and refrigerator.

I was in the middle of making the crust when he entered from the back door. My greeting was a little too bright due to lust because while I prepared the crust I was thinking about squeezing his buns, rubbing my naked body against his, riding his cock until we both passed out from the pleasure.

"What are you making?"

"Pumpkin pie. Two actually since the crust recipe makes two crusts and pumpkin pie only needs one." I was rambling. "Did you go for a run?"

He walked to the coffee. "Yeah."

"Is it as nice a morning as it looks?"

"Yes."

"Do you take the same route every morning?"

"No."

I wanted to pull my hair out. I was growing tired of the one word answers, particularly since he had slipped a few times while here and forgot to be a cyborg. "No one is breaking through the door, I'm not going to throw myself at you. You can talk to me and not fear you will morph into a lust monster."

"Lust monster?"

"You remind me of the Hulk with your belief that there is a trigger that turns you from all disciplined to reckless in a heartbeat."

"There is a trigger. You."

My body throbbed. "Are you feeling reckless now?"

That earned me a hot glance from over his shoulder. And it was a really nice shoulder, bare, wide and it so beautifully blended into the muscles of his biceps and triceps. I yanked my eyes from his exquisite arms to find his were on me.

"I understand what is motivating you, but it has been difficult with the wall you've put up to keep me out. Maybe if we could define what I do that is considered a triggerable offense, we could spend time together without you shifting into a horny caveman. Though I would like to say I am all for you turning into a horny caveman. And by that look, I'm guessing me saying that is a trigger."

"Fucking hell."

"I'll take that as a yes. Okay, well I can't believe watching a movie with me would trigger your inner beast."

"You curled up against me, your hands on me, your breath teasing the skin at my neck. Big fucking trigger."

They were all the reasons I really liked watching movies with him. Okay so movie watching was out. "What about me joining you for a run? Not that I'm thrilled with that plan because I don't believe in running as a rule, feel it should only be done when being chased. But if it gets me time with you, I would consider it."

"You dressed in a sports bra and shorts. Trigger."

"Baking?"

He eyed the pumpkin mixture I was whisking. "I want to dribble whatever the fuck that shit is on your breasts, down your stomach to your pussy and take my time licking it off."

I stopped whisking, needed to brace myself on the counter because I just had a mini orgasm at the thought.

He then added, "Smelling your arousal is a definite fucking trigger."

"Then you should leave the room because I'm so hot right now I'm going to combust."

And yet he stayed where he was, across the kitchen leaning against the counter sipping his coffee like he didn't have a care in the world.

"How do you do that? Look so calm."

"Years of military training."

"Talking has to be safe. What harm is there in talking? What are your thoughts on the expression lipstick on a pig? I find it insulting to pigs, but it doesn't really make sense because pigs are adorable. Now if it was say, lipstick on a cockroach I get that, but the visual is a nasty one not to mention who the hell would want to be that close to a cockroach to put lipstick on it?"

His mug was halfway to his mouth when he answered. "I don't have a thought on lipstick on a pig, however lipstick on your lips and those lips around my cock. That's another trigger."

"Everything is a trigger."

"No shit. Why do you think I've been avoiding you?"

"I get it now. But I'm going to throw it out there. When horny Damian wants to come out and play, you know where to find me."

He left the kitchen on that note, but not before he called from over his shoulder. "Trigger."

After our conversation that morning on triggers, I needed to get out of the house because I was definitely feeling a little hot under the collar. I left a note for Damian, grabbed the bike from the garage and headed to the nursery we had passed the other day when we went into town. The place was huge compared to what I was used to in the city. I was wishing I'd brought the car. Strolling around the tables outside, the premade pots were beautiful—aster and millet, mums and ornamental cabbage. Fall was definitely in the air, freshly cut cornstalks were tied in bundles and resting against the wall. There were tables and tables of pumpkins of all sizes, shapes and colors and a table of nothing but Indian corn. It was while I moved through the army of scarecrows that someone approached me. She was in her sixties, dressed in jeans and a flannel shirt and had the biggest smile on her face.

"Hi. Can I help you find anything?"

"I'm just looking."

"I don't recall seeing you before. Are you new to town?"

"I am. My husband Damian and I just moved here last week." The lie so smoothly slipped off my tongue. I offered my hand. "I'm Thea Tate."

"Maureen Petersen."

"Is this your nursery?"

"It is."

"It's lovely. I'm wishing I brought the car."

"I may have gone a little overboard, but I just love decorating for fall."

I did too.

"I'll leave you to browse. If you need anything, I'll be inside."

"Thank you, Maureen."

It was amazing to me how nice people were here, so genuinely friendly. If I was more of a cynic, I'd been suspicious about what it was in their air supply that had them acting so nice.

After the nursery, I went for a ride. Maureen wasn't the only one who liked decorating for fall. Practically every house I passed had mums and pumpkins which got me wondering who had decorated the place we were staying at. Unless the neighbors took it on themselves so the house didn't stand out.

Two hours after I left the house, I returned to find Damian pacing in the living room. I hadn't even closed the door and he was on me. Right up in my face, pinning me to the wall. "Where the fuck were you?"

In the alley when he'd killed that man I hadn't been afraid, but I was afraid of him now. "The nursery. I left you a note."

"I was at the nursery. You weren't there."

"I went for a ride."

"Until this is over, I want to know where you are every second of the day."

"Okay."

He rubbed his hand over the back of his neck, the first sign of frustration I had seen from him.

"I'm sorry."

"No, I'm sorry. I just...when you weren't there..."

"Maybe we should find something to do with our evenings. Being platonic and alone together is taking a toll on both of us, but maybe we could find an activity or even a job."

"You want to get a job?"

"I want to get out of the house and talk to people."

"What kind of job are you looking for?"

"I don't know. I'm busy during the day with my design work, but something fun and easy."

"There's a bar on Main Street, Janice's. That place looks pretty happening."

"Waitressing is hard work, but it's a thought. I'm going to pound the pavement tomorrow and see what's available."

"Bring your cell and check in every half an hour."

"Okay."

"I'm going for a run."

"Again?"

"Yes." I could have sworn he added, "And a cold shower," as he walked out. He wasn't going to be able to keep his hands off me for much longer and that thought had me heading to my bathroom for a cold shower too.

"I'm sorry. It's all I have right now."

My first stop of the day in my hunt for a job was Charlie's Chicken Hut. I had thought I could work the register or fry up some chicken since I had worked in the fast food industry in college, but the only job available was a two-day a week afternoon gig of wearing the Charlie Chicken costume while walking up and down Main Street handing out free samples. I wanted social interaction but badly enough to wear a chicken outfit?

"Thank you for taking the time to talk with me."

"I hope you find something else, but if not, I'd be happy to have you."

Stepping outside, I put a question mark next to Charlie's Chicken Hut and moved to the next stop on my list. For the next two hours I was told thank you, but no thank you in more ways than I thought the words could be spoken. My future in Deadwood was not looking bright when Charlie's Chicken Hut was the best I was going to manage. I was taking a break, having a coffee at the local café, which had me missing Ryder and Kimber. We hadn't been here all that long and already I was homesick. I noticed the bar, Janice's, that Damian had mentioned, at the end of the street. It was only two in the afternoon and yet the foot traffic was impressive. He was right, the place was happening. It was hard work, but imagine all the people and conversations. I finished my coffee, popped a mint—coffee breath wasn't pleasant—and hurried across the street. I pulled the door open and immediately my eyes had to adjust to the dark interior. There was a huge, scarred wooden bar that ran along one whole wall and behind that bar were shelves of liquor that would put to shame many of the more upscale places in Manhattan. Tables dotted around the open floor plan. There were no cloths or flowers decorating them. It was just condiments, napkins and menus. Many of those tables were packed and based on the smells coming from the kitchen, I wasn't surprised. Two women, around my age, moved through the tables, collecting empties, dropping off lunches, topping off drinks. A man worked behind the bar, cleaning, refilling…obviously preparing for the evening. If the place was this packed during daylight, it was probably shoulder-to-shoulder at night. A woman appeared from the back and how I knew she was Janice, I couldn't say. Maybe by the way she moved like she owned the place or maybe in the confident set of her shoulders, the arrogant tilt of her chin, the no-nonsense look in her eyes. She was tall, five feet ten at least, long brown hair, but not brown like my hair, auburn brown that hinted at red from the lights shining down on it. Thickly lashed eyes the color of a forest shared a face with features that alone were perfect, put together were exquisite. I felt like a wilting flower, was beginning to think Charlie's Chicken Hut was not a bad idea.

"Can I help you?"

She even had a sexy voice. I felt a bit like a Disney character, cute in my perky way, but completely out of place next to this simmering diva of sexuality.

"I just moved to town and am looking for a job. I'm hitting the pavement today, popping into as many establishments along Main Street as I can."

She'd been carrying a tray of glasses, like forty or so, and she hadn't dropped a one. Settling the tray on the bar, she walked around it and I discovered she wasn't wearing heels.

"Do you have experience working tables?"

"Yes. In college."

"You went to college. Why do you want to work at a bar?"

I was surprised at how easily the white lie slipped from my tongue. I could totally rock this *on the lam* shit. "My last job burned me out and I love talking to people."

"When can you start?"

"Now."

She studied me for a good minute. "Ricki and Dee."

The waitresses appeared at her side. "What's your name?"

"Thea."

"Thea's going to take station three."

The girls smiled. If they were angry I was cutting into their tips, I couldn't tell.

"Alright, Thea, grab a tray and apron. We'll do a trial run and see how you do."

I was surprised she'd offered but I didn't hesitate to act. "Thank you."

"Thank me if you get the job."

She returned to the bar as one of the women reached for a tray and an apron and handed them to me. "Hey. I'm Ricki and this is Dee."

"Hi."

"You're the new girl who just moved here with your husband?" Dee asked.

"Yes."

"He's hot," Dee said. Ricki hit her in the arm. "What? He is."

"Station three is that far corner. If you need anything, just ask. The specials are on the board. Soft drinks and coffee are refilled for free. If anyone gives you any trouble, Mic…" She gestured to the bartender, "…will take care of them. But we don't usually see trouble, at least not with the locals."

I wasn't used to such solicitous people. It was refreshing how friendly everyone was in this town. "Thank you, Ricki."

"You bet. Welcome to Deadwood."

It had been a long time since I had worked as a waitress, but it was like riding a bike. The locals were very friendly, some of them a little too friendly but considering the real flirts were also pushing seventy, their attentions were charming not creepy. I was just finishing hour three of work when the door opened and Damian came barreling through it. It was only the sight of his unbelievably pissed off expression that I remembered I was supposed to be checking in every half an hour. I hadn't called him in over three hours. I waited for the bellow that would shake the building; he certainly looked like he could at that moment. Instead, he grabbed my arm with surprising care considering he looked about ready to flog me, and pulled me to a quiet corner.

"What the fuck."

"Sorry. I forgot."

"Sorry?"

"Yes, sorry."

It was fascinating watching him because he really looked like a man who was in imminent danger of his head flying off his shoulders. He wasn't wrong to be angry. We'd just had this conversation yesterday.

"How did you know I was here?" Sure he had suggested I check the place out, but how did he know I was actually here?

No answer, not surprising. I did feel badly so I sought to explain. "I took your suggestion and I'm interviewing for a job, trial run, and I've been moving nonstop for the past three hours, but I should have remembered to check in. I really am sorry, Damian."

"Where's your phone?"

I reached for my phone that was in my pocket. It was dead. I had forgotten to charge it. In fairness to me I wasn't big on cell phones, I rarely used it, but I had to get used to using it at least for a little while.

"I forgot to charge it."

He looked about ready to explode again.

"I'll charge it when I get back to the house."

"Charge your fucking phone." He pressed closer to me and lowered his voice. "And don't fucking forget to call me."

I said I was sorry. And so on principal I bit my tongue on the sorry I almost offered again.

Janice called my name but I knew she was there before she spoke because Damian's attention had turned from me to someone just behind me. I could not describe the look he gave her, but never once had his head turned when we were together, so seeing it turn now was like taking a kick to the gut. And to add insult to injury, we were supposed to be married and yet my husband was eyeing my potential boss right after he had disciplined me like a child.

"Could you not do that?" My whisper was more a hiss.

His eyes came back to me.

"We're supposed to be married. I realize I'm not in her league, but could you at least fake it."

He didn't answer. Big surprise. I turned as Janice approached and she looked hungry. I didn't want to watch Daman and Janice because there was something there. I hated witnessing the love of my life having a moment with another, but he was having a moment and he did nothing to stop it.

"I was just going to offer your wife a job."

Great now they were talking about me like I wasn't there. I eyed the door. Perhaps Charlie's Chicken Hut was the way to go after all. I could totally rock that chicken costume—a little swagger, a little attitude—totally doable.

Her next question had me seeing red. "Is that a problem?"

Was it a problem? She wouldn't offer me the job if Damian had an issue with it? Seriously? Sure, he stormed in here like a bull and they didn't know the real reason for his anger, but still her question pissed me off. Or maybe it was the way she was looking at him that pissed me off.

"You know what? I don't need his approval for a job, and I don't want to work some place where the idea that I did was even considered. Thanks for the opportunity, but no thanks." I handed her my tray and apron, gave Damian my best withering glare, and walked out. It was Charlie's Chicken Hut after all because there was no way I was going to be alone in that house with that man. There had been countless emotions Damian Tate had brought out in me over the years, but he had never acted in a way that hurt me. But whatever the hell that was in there just now with Janice fucking hurt.

Standing on the corner, peering down the street at what would be my catwalk as Charlie the Chicken, the temptation to walk into traffic was strong. And why the fuck if you were selling chicken would you make your mascot a chicken? A chicken promoting the eating of other chickens was just so terribly wrong in a Hannibal Lecter kind of way.

"Don't do it."

I turned at the humor-laced voice to find Maureen standing

behind me.

"It can't be that bad."

"You're looking at the new mascot for Charlie's Chicken Hut."

"Oh…on second thought."

Her response was not what I was expecting. I laughed, like a real belly laugh. Humor once again eased the pain. "Thank you, Maureen, I needed that."

"Instead of becoming a hood ornament, how would you feel about working for me at the nursery?"

Sure I met her once, but I was a stranger on the street, literally, and she was offering me a job. You had to love this town. "Seriously?"

"I can't offer much, but Charlie." She shivered.

"I'll work for free."

"No I couldn't."

"I have a job, graphic design, I just want to get out of the house and interact a bit. You would be doing me a huge favor."

"Okay. Why don't you stop by tomorrow around noon?"

"I'll be there. Thank you."

I watched her walk away, spotted Damian and for the first time ever, I didn't wait for him to open my door. I climbed in, folded my arms like a petulant child and glared out the window.

"What the hell was that?" he asked as soon as he climbed into the car.

The shoe was on the other foot because it was me who gave him the silent treatment. I said nothing the entire way back. It was only when we reached the cottage that I opened my mouth. "For someone all pissed that I hadn't kept you posted as to my whereabouts, it doesn't take much to distract you. Shiny red ball or in your case a pretty face and a nice rack. Fucking triggers my ass."

I climbed from the car but Damian appeared, right in my face. "You don't know shit."

It was tempting to holler at him in the front yard, but we were supposed to be a happily married couple. I held my tongue until the door slammed at Damian's back. "I don't know shit? Okay, well here is what I do know. I know that you can't string more than a few words

268

together to me because of your fucking triggers, but seeing you being solicitous, hell downright friendly, to others really pisses me off. It pisses me off that I've shared everything there is to know about me and yet you've shared nothing personal. You drop the bomb that you lost someone, but you don't say who. And how the hell did you find this place? And what the fuck was that with Janice? You know what? I don't fucking care." I detoured to the kitchen for a bottle of wine, a glass and a corkscrew then retreated to my room—locked the door, turned on the television and drank the whole damn bottle of wine.

It was late when I left my room. I hadn't heard Damian since I stormed off like a child. I was hurt, there was no way around that. I hadn't handled that hurt very well, but what was done was done.

I walked out back, stepped off the deck and strolled through the gardens. Solar lights were set up strategically so even at night the gardens were showcased. For a safe house it was charming and so not Damian. And the reminder that there was more to this place than he had let on brought a fresh wave of pain.

It hadn't even been two weeks since the attack in the alley. It seemed almost like a dream now, a nightmare that felt real. And even hating that my life had been turned upside down, I wanted to go home. I needed my mom.

I strolled around for a while before I turned to head back inside and that was when I saw Damian. He was on the balcony that we shared. His long legs stretched out in front of him, a bottle of beer dangling from his fingers and his focus was completely on me. I didn't raise a hand, I didn't smile and I didn't offer him a good night. I just walked back inside, locked the door, filled a pitcher with water and went back to my room.

In the morning I woke to the smell of coffee. Walking from my room, like a child to the sound of the pied piper, I entered the kitchen to see Damian at the stove frying up some bacon. His diet was the healthiest diet I'd ever seen and even he couldn't resist the deliciousness of bacon.

The coffee was done. He had a mug next to him. He was showered and dressed and I suspected he'd even had his run already and it was only half past six in the morning.

"Do you want breakfast?" That was his olive branch.

"Sure."

I walked to the coffee maker, noticed the second mug on the counter, sitting right next to the sugar bowl. The gesture from Damian was like a declaration of love from someone else. I looked at that mug as tears burned the back of my eyes. My fingers were trembling when I reached for it.

"You don't want the job at Janice's?"

Like fucking ice water. "No."

"You misunderstood the situation."

"I don't think I did. I'm meeting Maureen at noon at her nursery outside of town."

He turned to me. "Maureen?"

"While you and Janice got acquainted, I ran into her on the street. I met her that day I went to the nursery. Learning my only job prospect was Charlie of Charlie's Chicken Hut, she offered me a job."

"I would rather you were at Janice's."

"And I'd rather work at Maureen's."

"Why are you always so fucking stubborn?"

"Can you get in touch with Anton?"

My sudden subject change caught him off guard. "Yeah."

"Fabulous. Next time you talk to him tell him I think I'll take my chances in New York because being here with you is intolerable." I almost hurled the mug at his head before I stomped from the room. I didn't get far before I was whirled around and pushed up against the wall. I couldn't tell if he wanted to kiss me or shout at me. His fingers tightened on my arms, his body pressed into mine, but it was his hard stare that pinned me in place.

"I should put you over my knee."

It was my reaction to that threat that fueled my anger. When my date Derrick, the actuary, had given me a similar look it repulsed me, but the idea of Damian doing it, I liked…a lot. "Go to hell."

"You have no fucking idea."

"About what?"

It was on the tip of his tongue, whatever it was I didn't know, but he won the struggle for control. Somehow I knew what followed wasn't what he had almost let slip. "Maureen's is outside of town, very little foot traffic, easy for a grab. Janice's is always crowded, lots of eyes on you."

"How do you know Janice's is always packed? How did you find this place?"

"Not important. Take the job at Janice's."

I couldn't argue with his logic and being stubborn because I hated the idea that by me taking the job it helped to put him and Janice in the same room together was just stupid.

"Fine."

He didn't release me. I didn't want him to. I wanted him to close the distance between us and kiss me like he meant it, like he used to. And I hated myself for that weakness.

"You won. You can let go of me."

It was only seconds, his hesitancy in releasing me, but for a man as disciplined as him that small hesitation meant something. Trouble was, I didn't know if it meant he wanted to kiss me too, or snap my neck. Looking at him, it seemed the latter was more likely.

He put space between us. "I'll take you to the nursery."

"What?"

"Maureen. She's expecting you at noon."

"Yes. Maureen." And thinking of Maureen had thoughts of Janice and how I had tried my hardest to burn that bridge. "How do you know that Janice will still offer me the job?"

"She'll give you the job."

"And you won't share whatever the hell it is I don't know."

No answer.

"You say you want me, all of me, well that's a two way street Damian. We won't work if you won't do the same."

I didn't wait for a reply I knew would never come and went back to my room.

It was the longest day of my life. Maureen had been very gracious about me turning down the job. And as predicted Janice had hired me, but I think that was only because Damian also got a job working as a bouncer and the idea that I would get to watch them every night was worse than the silence I was running from.

I didn't leave my room after we returned from town. I lay on my bed trying to distract myself with a movie but it wasn't working. I needed air. I grabbed my robe and stepped outside on the balcony to find Damian sitting there, looking out at the darkness.

"Sorry." I turned to head back inside but he stopped me.

"It took her years to get this place the way she wanted."

My heart cracked open at the pain I heard in his voice, the anguish.

"Amelia always loved it here. I didn't know she was sick. She had kept it from me. I was off saving the fucking world and she was here dying. She called when there was no time left, just enough for us to say goodbye."

Amelia. The love he found after me. I couldn't breathe past the sob that caught in my throat.

"She was only twenty-seven when she died. We only had a few years."

She had been so young. I ached for her and him, but what completely broke me was the painful truth that I only had him now because she had died. No wonder he hadn't shared, I wish now that he hadn't. God help me, but I couldn't comfort him when I was dying inside. My legs were unsteady as I stood. Our gazes collided and I couldn't control my emotions any better than him.

"Thea?"

"I'm so sorry…so, so sorry."

And then I fled, down the stairs and right out of the house—trying to run from his words, from his pain, from his past that hadn't included me. I only got a few houses down when I doubled over in pain, the weight of my despair too much to handle.

Seconds later I was lifted and pressed against a familiar chest. He grabbed my face and forced my eyes on him. "Amelia was my sister." He looked almost as destroyed as me. "You thought she was my wife?"

The house, the way he mourned her, the affection…I did. I thought he had married someone else and the idea of that shattered me.

He pressed my face to his chest and held me so tightly. "It has only ever been you." The floodgates opened. Happy tears, sad tears, I cried for Damian and his sister, I cried for losing all the years I had with him, I even cried for my dad. He carried me back inside and settled on the sofa with me in his lap. He said nothing, just let me cry it all out and with the tears the vice that had been squeezing my heart eased and all the while he watched me with those beautiful eyes.

In a whisper, I said, "I thought you were married and I can't even describe how it…"

"I didn't need words, your expression said it all." He touched my chin. "It has always been you."

"For me too."

He kissed the tip of my nose. "I know."

"You had a sister?"

"Half sister. She lived for a time with my dad growing up, but sought me out when she learned of me."

"Your father never told her she had a brother?"

Pain moved over his face, like an old wound that never healed. "No."

"They didn't deserve you, neither of them. Why didn't you tell me about Amelia?"

"She died around the time you lost your dad. You had enough to deal with."

"And now?"

"You didn't even know I had a sister and I'm going to tell you she's dead. I know you, Thea. You would have mourned her, a woman you didn't know because of her link to me."

He wasn't wrong.

"I didn't want to put that on you with everything else going on."

"And Janice?"

A dark look swept his face. "Janice now owns the bar. She worked for Amelia, managing the bar, and now she owns the place."

"Wait? You think she…"

"Conned my dying sister out of it? Yeah. She didn't know about me so she was very surprised to see me at the reading of the will. That's where I learned she had been given power of attorney over Amelia's interests and the addendum to her will."

"An addendum?"

"Leaving Janice the bar."

"Holy shit."

"I didn't think much of it at the time, it made sense that Amelia would leave the bar to her manager who was also her friend."

"So what made you suspicious?"

"When I was making arrangements for Amelia's funeral, I reviewed her will for her wishes regarding her burial, and it was reviewing the will that I learned I originally had been left everything, including the bar. Janice was in the will. She was left money and her position as manager was hers for as long as she wanted it. And then an addendum is added to the will leaving the bar to Janice right after Janice is given power of attorney, but it was the timing of Janice being given power of attorney that raised a flag. Amelia would have been highly medicated."

"You would have thought the lawyer would have been suspicious of the addendum and Janice's gain from it, given the circumstances."

"He was a neon sign over the door kind of lawyer. He didn't

know Amelia or Janice only that they were close enough that Amelia had her in her will, so trusting her with her estate wasn't a leap. There was no one else but me to question it. I suspected Janice had abused her position, but she was keeping Amelia's dream alive. Underhanded and illegal, yes, but Amelia's went on."

"But it's not Amelia's anymore."

"And not just in name. It's time to shake it up."

"That's why you wanted me to work there."

"Two birds."

It all started to make sense. They hadn't introduced themselves that day at the bar and his expression hadn't been interest, it had been contempt. "So it wasn't lust I saw in your eyes, it was hatred." Talk about a twist on the expression a fine line between love and hate.

"I've only ever felt this emotion toward one other woman, but yeah to manipulate a dying woman for personal gain, I fucking hate her."

Janice was a lot like Damian's mother, I understood the hatred, but we weren't going down that dark road. "Thank you for telling me."

"Don't ever run from me." He spoke the words so softly but it wasn't anger that fueled them, it was pain.

"I promise."

"And I won't keep anything from you."

I touched his chin to hold his gaze on me. "Not ever."

"Promise."

Damian was on a run when I woke. He had lost his sister. That news was more devastating than believing he was married. He had family who had wanted him, had loved him, who had sought him out, and he lost her. I had to believe that everything happened for a reason. I had to believe watching someone like Damian constantly getting knocked down and kicked in the gut, that there was some cosmic scale that would balance so that he would know love and happiness to the same degree he had known heartache and pain. Maybe I was his scale, because I loved him to the very deepest part of my soul.

I was putting on the coffee when Damian came back from his run. He was on the phone that he handed to me on his way to the shower. "Anton."

I seriously needed an Anton fix after learning about Amelia.

"Hey, Thea."

"Hi."

"You sound funny, what's going on?"

"I just learned about Amelia."

There was a note of surprise in his voice. "Damian told you about her?"

"Yes. You sound surprised that he did."

"Her death hit him hard. They'd only just found each other and then she was gone. After the funeral he kind of closed that part of his life down, but considering who you are, you're the only person he would open that old wound up for."

Even hating what we were discussing, I loved his thoughts on it. "Was Amelia the reason Damian's dad left?"

"Yeah. He'd fallen in love with Amelia's mother."

I squeezed the phone so hard I was surprised it didn't break. "So that's why his mother kept Damian because his father started over with another and she couldn't torture the man, so she tortured his son."

"Exactly."

"If she wasn't dead, I would kill her."

"Get in line. I've got to go. Damian will fill you in on what we've learned."

"I miss you."

"Ah, love, I miss you too."

I needed to bake something. Baking always soothed me; it was my form of yoga. I pulled out the ingredients for oatmeal raisin cookies. Damian came in while I measured out the dry ingredients.

"I'm making oatmeal raisin cookies. I picked that over say chocolate chip or butter because they have oats so you will be more inclined to eat them even though you don't eat carbs or refined sugars."

He leaned up against the counter and crossed his arms over his chest, but he was smiling at me. My knees went weak. "Should I get the fire extinguisher?"

Would I never live down my first attempt at making cookies?

"Careful or I won't share. The trick to the perfect cookie is to slightly undercook it."

"Yes because we've seen what happens when you overcook it."

I wanted to laugh, but instead I glared.

Teasing turned serious when Damian said, "They found who hired the fuck from the alley."

I stopped whisking the dry ingredients. "Who was it?"

"He's a CI for Dobbs."

"So the attack was linked to Dobbs."

"I don't think so. I think someone wants us to think that."

"You think whoever hired this CI knew of his connection to Dobbs and used it to throw us off his scent."

"Exactly."

He came up right behind me and pulled the hair from my shoulder to kiss my neck.

My mouth went dry. "That's a trigger for me."

He looked very naughty. "Good to know. How can I help?"

"Cookies? We're talking about cookies, right?"

He chuckled, and then he rubbed his thumb over my lip. "Yeah, babe. For now, we're talking about cookies."

"Cookies instead of sex, I suppose there are worse substitutes."

CHAPTER 17

It was our first night of work. Janice had a dress code—short skirt and tank top that showed off cleavage. Boobs sold drinks; Janice's words not mine. I wasn't thrilled working for the woman, knowing what I did about her, but Damian would get to keep an eye on her so there was the silver lining. I checked out my appearance in the mirror. I liked the jean skirt; I had purchased it from a cute little boutique in Soho. It was short with a frayed edge, sexy but not gratuitous. The tank though, a white ribbed tank with a scoop neckline low enough that my girls were definitely on display. I pulled my hair into a ponytail and didn't bother with very much makeup because in this outfit no one would be looking at my face. A few swipes of mascara, some lip gloss and I was good to go.

Grabbing my apron, I walked into the kitchen and stopped dead. Damian was leaning up against the counter. He was in faded jeans and that black tee of his that was more like a second skin.

Every bump and ridge of muscle was on glorious display. I reached for one of the cookies we had baked last night, our substitute cookies we called them, and stuffed it in my mouth so I didn't do what I really wanted to do, which was lick every inch of his body. He looked up, his eyes hitting mine before he moved them down my body…lingering a moment longer on my breasts.

"I know." I gestured to my décolletage. "Boobs sell drinks." Then I looked at him through my lashes. "Why? Is this a trigger?"

He answered by grabbing a cookie on his way out of the kitchen.

"I need your keys, Pat. I'm not giving you another drink until you hand them over."

Pat was fifty-eight, divorced with three kids in college. He worked as an insurance agent and as soon as the clock struck five, his butt was on a stool at Janice's bar. He was sweet, a flirt and really enjoyed his beer.

"Just one more. Please, Thea."

"Give me your keys and I'll get you one more."

"I have work in the morning."

"Then maybe you should stop now."

"I just had to write three checks for fifteen thousand dollars each. College is expensive. I need to numb my senses so I don't freak out over the hit to my bank account."

I couldn't fault him that, but he'd had four beers already. Driving was out of the question.

"You can't drive. You know you can't drive. I'll call a cab for you when you're ready. I'll even walk your keys over to your office tomorrow morning."

"You drive a hard bargain," he moaned, but he handed me his keys.

"I'll be right back with your beer."

Someone dropped some coins in the jukebox as Pink's 'Trouble' started pumping through the place. Ricki and Dee were dancing as they delivered their drinks. The folks at the pool tables at the far back were getting rowdy, but in a good way. The place was electric. It could hold its own with the best clubs in Manhattan and my guess was it was Amelia's legacy and Janice was reaping the rewards. Damian would make it right.

Stepping up to the fill station, Mic dropped his elbows on the bar and leaned into me. "What can I get you, babe?"

"Another one for Pat, two gin and tonics with Bombay Sapphire and a Maker's Mark, neat."

He grinned, "You got it."

After dropping off Pat's beer, I moved to the pool tables to collect empties and that was when I noticed Janice wasn't in her office, she was up front with Damian. And now that I understood the situation, I couldn't believe I had confused his expression for lust. He looked to be skinning her alive in his mind. I almost felt sorry for her because she had no clue who she was dealing with. And what was she up to? Damian didn't contest the will, as far as she knew. She had gotten away with it. He was out of the military and home where Amelia hoped he would settle. So was she hoping to not just get Amelia's bar but her brother too? From the way she practically licked him when she spoke, I was thinking yes.

"Hey, babe. When do you get off?" I turned to see a biker—long hair and tats all over. He had come-hither eyes and the sexiest smile. The girl hanging on him shot me daggers and I understood. She'd been working him all night, so his invitation to me was a real blow—unless he wanted to party.

Resting my hip on the pool table, I flashed him a smile. "One." I was digging getting into character, being me but not me.

"Are you doing anything after?"

"I'm going home with the husband."

"Husband? You're not wearing a ring."

"I still have one. That's him by the door." I gestured with my head and watched as both the man and his groupie followed the direction.

"He's hot." Damian was hot, but I had a feeling this chick's standards were really low.

"He doesn't look too thrilled that you're talking to me."

I glanced over, he was right, Damian looked annoyed. I flashed him a smile. "He's the jealous type."

"You ever looking to party, sweetheart, alone or with your man, give me a call." He handed me a business card. What kind of biker had business cards? His had a skull on it and his name was Razor. Razor. I was being propositioned in the town of Deadwood by a biker named Razor who owned business cards. I seriously needed to take up writing because you couldn't make this shit up.

Having fun, feeling flirty and playing the part—three weeks ago someone tried to kill me so why not—I glanced up at him through my lashes and smiled. "Sure thing." Then tucked the card in my cleavage, his eyes like heat-seeking missiles following my hand as I did so. The girl hissed, he growled, I waved then sauntered off and knew he was checking out my ass as I did.

On my way to the bar, Damian waylaid me. He pulled me into a dark corner, and pressed me up against the wall. For just a second I thought he was going to kiss me. My entire body burned at the thought. His head lowered, my lips parted and he said, "You looking to get raped?"

I went from hot to ice cold in a heartbeat. "Excuse me?"

"Flirting like that will get you in trouble."

"It was harmless."

"You know that guy?"

"No."

"How do you know he's harmless?"

"It was a little flirty banter."

"Dude has been in prison twice for sexual assault."

A shiver went through me. "How do you know?"

"My job to know."

"Someone should tell that girl."

"She knows."

"How do you know she knows?" I swear it felt like we were

having a *Three Stooges* conversation.

No answer, so I answered for him, "Your job to know."

Poor timing, but the way his big, hard body dwarfed mine and how he had to curl his spine to look me in the eyes made me feel not just delicate, but seriously turned on by the power of him. Those hands could kill without mercy, but I knew they could roam over his lover's body with finesse.

He moved in, his mouth only inches from mine. "Flirting with another man…" He bit my lower lip. "Definitely a trigger."

Before I could respond a ruckus broke out and caveman Damian morphed into warrior Damian. "Stay here." Then he was gone.

"How did you meet him?" I hadn't heard anyone approach so was surprised to see Janice standing there. It wasn't any of her damn business so I lied.

"Through a friend."

"He's something."

What a bitch. She didn't know the truth about Damian and me, but she did believe we were married, so her comment was completely out of line. "Yes, he is."

"I can't imagine it's easy holding onto a man like that. He seems quite virile, must be exhausting keeping him satisfied."

Motherfuc…There was a challenge in her statement, but she was trying to goad me and I wasn't taking the bait.

"Excuse me." Damian was just coming in through the back door. I walked over to him and he tracked me from across the room.

"I just had words with Janice. She's a fucking bitch. I'll help you bury the body."

He had no reaction at first and then he tilted his head back and howled with laughter. And if I thought that was glorious it didn't hold a candle to him grabbing my upper arms, lifting me to my tiptoes and kissing me senseless to the whistles and catcalls of Janice's patrons. When he released me I was a bit unsteady on my legs. The smile he gave me didn't help with my balance.

"I think I need to splash my face with water."

He touched my shoulders and turned me in the direction of the restroom. "It's that way, babe."

On the way to the restroom, I spotted a man hanging just outside of it. I didn't like the look of him. He looked like someone on the prowl. Two girls came out and the way he stared at them gave me the creeps. They seemed to sense it too and hurried it along. I decided against the restroom and walked to the bar.

"That dude is creepy," I said to Mic as I set down my tray.

"How so?"

"It's like he's hunting."

Mic's voice went hard even as he turned his attention on the guy. "I'll keep my eye on him. Might help to tell Damian to do the same, that is if you can get a word in with all that kissing." He ended that suggestion with a grin.

I grinned back because I really liked all that kissing.

It was a beautiful fall day and I was enjoying it while sitting out back with a blanket, a cup of hot chocolate and my sketchpad. Damian and I did not kiss more after we returned home from work. Instead I took a very cold shower then slept like a dead person. He was off running when I woke, so I retreated to the backyard to draw. My focus was the garden, but the beds were covered in leaves. I had never raked a yard and it was such a fall thing to do. From the garage, I retrieved not only the rake and the garden bags, but some gloves I spotted on the potting shed.

Two hours into the backbreaking work, I had to stop. I never appreciated how much work it was to rake leaves. I had callouses on my hands, my back hurt but there was a sense of pride in seeing what I had accomplished. And it was while I pulled the leaves from the garden beds that I made a discovery. There was a hollowed out tree trunk in the garden that was tucked under a bush. It looked like Plexiglas covering the opening to keep the elements out. I got down on my stomach. Amelia had had a whimsical soul because it was the most elaborate fairy garden I had ever seen. Fairies having a tea party around a small fire pit, little houses and shepherds' hooks with lanterns, flowers and a stream made from blue stones, fences and benches. It was beautiful, enchanting and charming. I wondered if Damian knew this was here. He had returned from his run and was in the living room, on the phone talking business. He saw me and abruptly ended the call, probably because I looked slightly wild.

"What's wrong?"

I was so excited, I didn't answer with words but grabbed his hand and pulled him from the room.

We reached the spot and I immediately resumed my position of lying down on my stomach. I looked up at him, but he just stared down at me with that blank look of his.

"I know you're a badass, but no one will see. Get down here."

"Why?"

"Just do it."

I heard the growl, but he did it, mirroring my position. He didn't ask again what I wanted because he saw it immediately.

"Beautiful, isn't it?"

His voice sounded a bit gruff when he said, "Yeah."

"I would have very much liked to have known your sister."

His head turned and there was a look in his eyes that settled quite happily in my chest. "You were raking?"

"Yes. It's hard work."

"I'll help you."

"Maybe I should put on more hot chocolate while you rake."

Mischievousness moved over his features and then he moved so fast, grabbing me around the waist before he dropped me right into the middle of the pile of leaves I had yet to bag.

"I can't believe you ruined my pile," I screeched.

He grinned, the sight making my heart sing, and then he reached for the rake and said, "That's a good look on you."

Later that night we were working. We'd spent the rest of the afternoon cleaning up the yard. We even took a break for hot chocolate and a slice of pie.

Janice's was busy and after a day of yard work, I was dragging. "Hey, darling."

Mic walked by with a rack of glasses. "Hi, Mic."

"Take a break. You haven't stopped since you arrived. I'll bring you a soda."

He was right. I hadn't taken a break because the place was crazy tonight. I didn't take a seat, feared I wouldn't be able to get up again, but I did stand near the fill station. Mic brought me a soda then rested his elbows on the bar. "You liking Deadwood?"

"Very much. Madge cornered me the other day and twisted my arm into participating in the reenactment."

"Have you ever done one?"

"No."

"It's fun, something you should do at least once."

"So you're a veteran."

"I've done several and if you're doing this one I might have to give Madge a call."

I was so excited at the idea of having someone I knew doing it with me that I reached for his arm in my excitement. "You totally should."

It felt like heat boring a hole in my back. I glanced over my shoulder to see Damian leaning up against the wall, but his attention was completely on me.

Mic asked, "How long have you and…" He lifted his chin in the direction of Damian "…been married."

"Three years." That was how many years we were married in the fake life I had made up that first day. It seemed smart to stick to that even though Damian was sure no one would care.

"I wouldn't have thought that long. The man hasn't taken his eyes off you."

Damian hadn't taken his eyes off me? I couldn't keep my eyes off him so it seemed fair.

"Still feels like we're newlyweds." I felt his comment needed a reply.

The smile he flashed me was pure sex. "I believe that."

I felt Damian before I heard him. Turning in time to see the expression on his face. I was momentarily speechless because he wasn't just pissed. He looked like he was going to kill someone. And since I knew from firsthand experience he was more than capable of killing someone with his bare hands, I put up my hand as he approached. He could have walked right through me to get to Mic, the target of his malice, but he stopped as soon as my palm hit his muscled chest. His eyes jerked to me.

"Mic and I were just discussing how it still feels like we're newlyweds. Isn't that right, baby?"

I would sell my soul to the man depicted on Damian's back to know what he was thinking because the heat that fired in his eyes was arousing. The accompanying chills that moved through me became visible when my nipples went hard, and since I was wearing a tank, my arousal was very easy to see. Damian's gaze dropped and my clit spasmed. Oh dear God, I was going to come from nothing more than a heated looked from the man.

In the next second, he gestured to someone behind me. "Take this. She's taking a break."

He didn't wait for an answer as he grabbed my hand and pulled me right out the front door, around the side of the building to the alley in the back.

"What are you doing?"

He didn't answer, well not with words. He pushed me up against the brick of the building; pressed into me, his hands coming to rest on the wall near my head. He looked at me with such hunger my knees went weak. For a good few minutes it was like he was debating about what he wanted to do.

"Fuck it," he said as he threaded the fingers of one of his hands through my hair to palm the back of my head. In the next breath, his mouth closed over mine. Not a kiss, a conquering. His tongue invaded, tasting me with a thoroughness that left me weak. His free hand moved up my body, under my shirt. When he palmed my breast and swiped his thumb over my nipple, a moan caught in the back of my throat. His knee moved between my legs, his lips pulling from mine only long enough to say, "Ride it."

And I did, I rubbed myself against him. My panties were drenched; his jeans were going to be drenched and still my hips rocked into his leg because it felt so freaking good. I was so turned on I came on a scream, one muffled by his tongue and lips. I reached for his zipper, dropping it and pulling him free. He moaned and buried his face in my hair as he moved his hips finding that rhythm. He tried to move away from me before he came and even then he was being a gentleman. I didn't want him to pull away, I needed him closer so with uncharacteristic skill, I pulled my apron off, dropped to my knees on it and took him into my mouth. I couldn't believe what I was doing, never in my wildest dreams would I think I'd be blowing a man in an alley, but it wasn't just any man. His hands slammed against the brick wall a second before he came. He tasted so good, I swallowed and he moaned and then I was being hauled up against his body for his kiss, his tongue sweeping my mouth tasting himself and me.

"That won't happen again. I'm sorry." I thought he was pulling away again so I prepared to argue the point. Then he added, "Blowing me in a fucking alley."

Oh. My behavior had shocked even me, but honestly it turned me on too. "Out of character, absolutely, but really awesome."

"It was a hell of a lot better than awesome." He kissed me again, longer and sweeter, before he said, "We better get back inside before we're missed."

I glanced down. "You might want to take care of that." Or else I'd be tempted to give him awesome again.

CHAPTER 18

I tried running it off, tried working my body until it was too tired and sore to feel anything. But just the memory of the alley, her lips around my cock, turned me rock hard. I ran twice as long the following morning hoping to ease the ache, but it didn't help. Thirteen years of wanting, when the lid came off that sexual geyser it was going to level cities. We weren't at a place where we could spend weeks or months in bed riding that wave, and I knew it would take weeks or months to sate us.

She was in the kitchen when I returned, sitting at the table as she had a habit of doing. She was looking over some tourist book. Fucking hell, don't tell me she wanted to play tourist. I was battling blue balls and she wanted to buy souvenirs and t-shirts.

"I'm visiting the gold mine today."

"What time?"

"There's a tour starting at one."

"I need a shower."

Her expressions were so transparent, every thought in her head showed on her face and right now I knew she was thinking about me in the shower, more specifically us in the shower and since that was where my head was at too, I walked away. Closing the bedroom door I walked right to the shower, stripping on my way. How the hell I managed to walk with the hard on I sported was a mystery. Stepping under the spray, I pressed a hand to the wall, lowered my head, closed my eyes, as my other hand moved up the length of my cock, fisting the shaft as Thea took over my thoughts—her tits, her ass, her hair, her laugh, her smile. I was yanking so hard the fucking thing should have ripped right off. And even after I came I still wasn't satisfied. We were going to need to bake a fuck load of cookies.

"We can pan for gold? Oh, I so want to do that. Do you want to do that?"

She asked but she wasn't really asking. She was doing it with or without me. I wouldn't allow her to go alone, so I was doing it whether I liked the idea or not.

"This is going to be so much fun."

I seriously did not understand how this woman was like a sister to Anton. Two more opposite people never existed. As we waited in line it was like she was at a starting line, her body primed and ready to go as soon as the gun sounded. She reminded me so much of Amelia—a way of looking at the world. Not innocently, neither of them had been sheltered, but like they could take the hits and keep coming back for more. Optimistic. Amelia had been too fucking young. She should have had a full, happy life before dying of old age in her bed at ninety. Instead, fucking cancer took her too damn young. My father had turned out to be no better a parent than my mother and just as shitty a human as her too. He had had a mistress for years while he was living with my mom, had even gotten his mistress pregnant only a year or so after he had gotten my mom pregnant with me. There was no way she knew that because she would have gone homicidal. The man had a short attention span with not only the women in his life, but also the offspring he brought into the world. Amelia hadn't known him any better than I had, but for a little while we had had each other. Watching her take her last breath, helpless to ease her pain…I would rather walk into a firefight unarmed than go through that again. And Janice. I'd set the ball in motion. Her world was about to collapse. She shouldn't have become greedy. She had a good thing going, but she pushed too far. It was time to push back.

"It is a real gold mine. Imagine the stories it could tell." Thea looked around all wide-eyed. I saw a rock depleted of whatever value it had and left as a reminder of the greed of people and their thirst to own more, to have more. And she thought of the lives of those who had mined it. I had no doubt she romanticized it too and not the grueling, early death, sweaty shit job it was.

Her voice turned a bit dreamy as her fingers ran along the walls. "I think I would have liked living back then. There were problems then too, but the simplicity of it. You worked and you loved. I would have liked that."

And it was because of the ease that I could imagine her with me in Amelia's cottage that I ignored her. That pissed her off. And I was clearly a masochist because I enjoyed getting a rise out of her, watching that fire spark in her eyes. She leaned in and whispered in my ear, "I know what you're doing, but there aren't enough cookies in the world to erase that moment in the alley. And it will happen again because you are just as addicted to me as I am to you. But I can wait because I know you're worth it."

An elderly couple was in front of us; she left me to walk with them, which was a good thing because we almost had our own reenactment of that alley scene right there in the gold mine.

One thing was for sure. When this was all over I wasn't letting her out of my bed for a fucking year.

THEA

The man was impossible. If I didn't think I'd break every bone in my foot, I would kick him in the shins or maybe the nuts, but I suspected they were just as hard as the rest of him. He was more determined than ever to keep me at arm's-length, and considering our moment in the alley, I understood. Distracted wasn't strong enough of a word. I even agreed with what he was doing, but it didn't mean I had to like it.

He was running more, and I got a sick sense of satisfaction that his body wanted me to the point that he was trying to physically exhaust himself.

Madge had called and asked me to visit. She wanted to discuss the reenactment. Damian had dropped me off, but Madge was having a hankering for soup and since she was right down the street from the Tavern, I offered to pick her up some. I was on my way back to her house when a motorcycle pulled up alongside me. Razor.

"Hey, babe."

I was a little cool in my reply remembering what Damian had told me about him and his sexual appetites. "Razor."

"Want a ride, babe?"

"No thank you."

His face split into a smile.

Maybe I was getting rusty but I didn't get the rapist vibe from him. I wasn't willing to put that theory to the test though. "Madge is waiting for me."

We were now in front of Madge's house. He looked up at Madge before lifting a hand in greeting. What surprised me was she not only returned it, she called, "Join us, dear."

"You don't have to ask me twice."

Razor touched my arm as we ascended the steps up to Madge's porch. It was odd, a gentlemanly act like that from a man like him. Maybe I misunderstood what Damian had meant about Razor because he really didn't seem the type to hurt women.

"Razor, dear, you know where the cookies are. Could you please bring them out and put the kettle on for tea. Oh and take the soup from Thea."

"Sure thing, ma'am."

He didn't fit with Madge's floral décor in his faded jeans and leather jacket, the long hair and massive frame.

"He's a good boy."

"He is?"

She looked at me funny. "Of course. You can see it in his eyes."

Not according to Damian.

"Thanks for the soup."

"My pleasure. You wanted to talk about the reenactment."

"Yes. I need your measurements for the costume."

"Do you make the costumes every year?"

"I do. As one of the founding families of this town, I like to be involved."

"You had family who lived here back in the day."

"I did."

"I'd love to hear about it."

Razor returned, the cookie jar in one hand, a half eaten cookie in the other. He sat on the steps, leaning back against the railing and bending one leg. He looked to be settling in for a while. He looked at me and winked. I thought he was charming in a roughneck kind of way, which didn't jive with what I knew about him from Damian.

Madge put her knitting down and started to rock. "It's probably best to start when the town was founded."

And I understood why Razor had settled in because for the next two hours Madge told us everything there was to know about the town and it had been a wonderful way to pass the afternoon.

"You keep missing your mark. You need to walk from the saloon and end here." Dinky, owner of the saloon in town and director of the reenactment, said as he once again indicated the road where the x was located.

Reenactments were much harder than I had thought, particularly since the people I was doing this one with became thespians as soon as the figurative costumes went on.

"Sorry."

"Let's try this again."

I waited for my cue and hit my mark. I got a thumbs up and then he was off directing someone else.

Maureen walked over dressed as a gunfighter. "How did you get that role and I have to be some damsel?"

"Years of participating."

"I don't even know what I'm supposed to be doing. Why would a woman in full formal attire be standing in the middle of the street during a gunfight?"

"Drama. How are you enjoying Deadwood?"

"I like it very much. It's a great town and after talking with Madge, I know it's also a town rich with history."

"That it is."

"How's the nursery?"

"We're slowing down, people are preparing for winter, but I do sell trees and poinsettias so we'll be gearing up again after Thanksgiving."

"I'm sorry again that I accepted and then backed out."

"I really didn't have much for you to do with the season coming to an end, but anything is better than being Charlie."

She wasn't wrong about that.

"Thea, I need you to swoon," Dinky said as he came hurrying over to me. "Your hand to your forehead and then crumble, but daintily."

"I don't want to swoon. Give me a gun. I'll hide it in my garter. No one will be expecting that."

"You're the damsel."

"I want to be a gunfighter."

"Your job is to faint."

"Then shoot me. We could get one of those prop bags. A hit to the stomach and I can die slowly while the fighting is going on around me."

Dinky lowered his clipboard. "You're a bit bloodthirsty."

"I just want a role I can really sink my teeth into."

"And when you've got a few reenactments under your belt, we'll discuss that. For this one, you'll elegantly faint."

The urge to kick the ground in frustration almost had me doing so, but when I got my cue, I fainted demurely.

I had just gotten back on my feet when Maureen muttered, "Brace yourself." Before I could ask her meaning, Janice appeared in my face.

"Where's *your* husband?"

Like I'd tell her anything about Damian.

"He won't get away with it?"

"With what?"

"That place is mine. I own it. He's not taking it from me."

"The bar?"

"Don't act like you don't know what he's doing. It's the only reason you came back here, to take it away from me. I earned it."

I saw red. Earned it. She stole it. "Earned it how?"

"She brought me out here and then she died. I should be compensated."

I wanted to punch her in the face "His sister? She died a horrible death from cancer and you should be compensated. Is that what you're saying?"

"Well, yeah."

I made a move toward her, but felt strong hands on my arms pulling me back. Snapping my head around it was to see Razor. He wasn't looking at me. He was glaring at Janice.

Turning back to her, I shook Razor's hold but I didn't make a move toward her. "I not only hope he does take it away from you, I'll do everything I can to help him."

She lunged at me, her claws out. "Bitch."

In a flash I was behind Razor. The sheriff appeared, probably summoned by one of the onlookers because there were a lot of onlookers.

"Maybe you need to cool your heels at the station." The sheriff said to Janice.

"What about her? She threatened me."

"I didn't hear a threat." Maureen said.

"Me either. You're the one who approached her. Then took a swing. I've the scratch to prove it. I'm sure my skin is still under your claws," Razor added.

"Let's go, Janice. Don't make me have to cuff you in front of all these people. You can calm down at the station."

Razor dropped his arm around my shoulders. "You *are* blood-thirsty. I like you, Thea."

Damian appeared a few minutes later. He was livid. "Where is she?"

"The station," Razor said as he stepped in-between Damian and me.

Damian wasn't having that. He swatted Razor aside like he was nothing more than a fly and glared at me. "And you provoked her?"

"I stood up to her. There's a difference. She said she earned the bar because Amelia brought her out here and died. That pissed me off, so I called her on it. I'd do it again."

I wasn't sure what he intended, but I wasn't expecting him to pull me into his arms and kiss me right there in the middle of town. Not that I minded, not in the least. We were both breathless when he ended the kiss.

"Are we good?" I asked because I couldn't read him at all.

"We're a whole hell of a lot better than good."

"Drinks are on me." Razor said, which were the magic words

since the crowd dispersed and headed to the Tavern.

"Thanks for stepping in." I didn't know where Razor had come from, but he'd taken the cat scratch meant for me.

He winked. "Anytime."

Damian and I were hosting a dinner at the cottage. We had offered it that first night at the Sharptons, but I found I was looking forward to doing something so normal and with people I was growing to really like. We were having it outside...barbequing, a fire pit, pumpkin carving and bobbing for apples for the kids, though many of the adults were joining in too. Bobby was helping Damian with the grill and I found myself stopping throughout the evening to watch him. He would never be the affable guy who talked up everyone; he'd always be in the shadows, but watching him grilling up the burgers and chicken, grinning at whatever story Bobby was sharing and seeing him happy made me really happy.

Madge had brought baked goodies, Maureen contributed wine, Razor—yes I invited Razor and Damian didn't protest, weird—and Mic brought the beer and Dinky brought a box of cigars. Missy, Ricki and Dee were helping me in the kitchen, finishing up the sides that would accompany the grilled meats Damian and Bobby were responsible for.

"I love this. I'm so glad you two moved here," Missy said. I felt badly that I couldn't be completely honest with her, but I agreed. I was happy we had moved here too even if it was only temporary.

"It's a great town. You were right."

"Maybe Hank and Wynona will have playmates soon."

I'd been slicing a tomato and almost took off my finger. Children with Damian, just the idea made me want to cry. Thinking of a little boy or girl with his eyes made my chest grow tight. I was saved from answering when Wynona entered the kitchen.

"Mommy, I want to carve a pumpkin."

"Okay, give me a minute and I'll help you."

"Oh…okay. One minute."

Missy glanced over at me and rolled her eyes heavenward. "And she'll hold me to that. She learned to tell time solely for that reason."

Children were the best. We finished in the kitchen and I followed Missy to the carving station.

"I want to make Cinderella's coach."

"Oh, honey, I'm not good enough to do that."

Wynona's big eyes turned to me. "Can you?"

I could draw the carriage, but no way could I carve it. "No, a jack-o-lantern is about as good as I get."

Her lower lip quivered when she looked back at her mom. "Can we try?"

"Sure, sweetie. We can try."

It was pretty clear that Missy was in over her head. Damian and Bobby approached.

"What's going on here?" Bobby asked.

"Wynona wanted to carve Cinderella's coach, but I'm just not that skilled.

"Daddy has two left hands," Bobby said to which Wynona nodded, so apparently he tried and failed at some craft. Though did he do it on purpose so he wasn't roped into being the designated helper? I had been guilty of that a time or two growing up.

Damian stood quietly next to Bobby, his hands in his pockets, observing the scene. I couldn't tell what he was thinking, but then he pulled up a chair and reached for a carving knife.

"Can you?" Wynona asked him and the hope in her voice nearly broke my heart.

"Got a picture?" Damian asked.

"Mommy, your phone."

Missy took out her phone and pulled up a picture of the elaborate coach made from a magical pumpkin. Damian studied it for a few minutes and then got to work.

I watched mesmerized at the skill Damian had with a knife, knew it stemmed from his line of work, and still he methodically carved that pumpkin, the detail unbelievable. It took him almost an hour but when he was done, Wynona had her replica of Cinderella's coach.

"It's perfect," Wynona squealed as she clapped her hands together. "Oh Mommy, look at it."

Damian stood, his hands covered in pumpkin guts, but before he could make his escape Wynona jumped from her spot and wrapped her arms around one of his legs. "Thank you, thank you."

My heart ached in a really good way seeing Damian getting love from a little girl because he had carved her a pumpkin. She eventually released him and when she looked up, he smiled.

I followed him into the kitchen. He was at the sink washing his hands when I moved up behind him and mirroring Wynona, I hugged him, around the waist because I was taller. "I loved every second of that."

"It's just a pumpkin."

I pressed a kiss right where I knew his devil tattoo was. "It was so much more than that and you know it."

I didn't wait for his reply and left the kitchen, wiping my happy tears from my eyes.

Toward the end of the evening I was sitting around the fire pit with Ricki and Missy. The guys were inside watching a game. We were bundled in blankets, hats and gloves, but it was such a beautiful evening with the clearest sky above, that we weren't ready to go in.

"It's so beautiful here."

"I told you." Missy's comment brought a smile.

"I didn't know Damian was Amelia's brother," Ricki said.

My eyes moved from the star-filled sky to Ricki. "Did you know Amelia?"

"Yeah. She hired me. Great lady. It was so sad watching her fight so hard only to lose. The bar was amazing when she owned it."

"How so?"

"She had the coolest stuff, vintage—an old jukebox, framed baseball cards. She was a collector and most of her stuff she kept at the bar. It made sense because she was there all the time."

"Where's the stuff now?"

"Piece by piece it's been removed."

I didn't like where this was going. "By Janice."

"That would be my guess. She's selling it and pocketing the money, which makes her lowering our wages just bitchy."

"She lowered your wages?"

"When she took over, she dropped it to just over minimum wage, said we would make it up in tips. The tips are great, but with the amount of money that flows through that place why is she docking us a couple dollars an hour?"

Because she was a greedy bitch.

"She docked their pay. She's selling off your sister's things."

Damian and I were in the kitchen after everyone left. He didn't seem surprised by the news.

"You knew?"

"I suspected. She's been selling off the stock too. She's getting ready to run."

"What the hell was that scene then the other day?"

"She's not one to take things lying down. She thought to intimidate you to get me to back off."

"That didn't work."

His smile was wicked. "No it didn't."

"So what are we going to do?"

His expression changed for just a second or two, the way he studied me left me feeling all gooey inside. "The sheriff should be picking her up soon for felony fraud and theft."

I was sure I looked like a guppy, but I shouldn't have been surprised that Damian was on top of this, that he could multitask. Still it felt good knowing Janice wouldn't be getting away with it.

"So it hasn't just been Cam's stuff you've been working on."

"She went about it underhandedly, but she was the right person to run the place. She knew Amelia, she knew the bar so I sat back and waited to see how it would play out. In the beginning she kept to the status quo, but she got comfortable and cocky. I have a list of every item sold and to whom."

"How's that possible?"

"Mic. I did some recon, discovered he was ex-military and offered him a side job."

"To keep an eye on Janice."

"He was a computer systems specialist, so he's compiled quite a nice dossier on her. She's getting ready to run, but she's not going anywhere." He grinned then said, "I like hearing you say what are we going to do about it."

"We've been a *we* since we were seventeen."

CHAPTER
19

T he light kept flickering, the fluorescent bulb humming as it illuminated Federico at his favorite table, at his favorite restaurant. As was his way, the place was closed so he had the whole restaurant to himself. The man was wearing a bib, a fucking paper bib as he cracked the shells of the crab and slurped the meat into his mouth. Juice dripped down his chin onto that bib, but fucking hell, he was grown man. His security team surrounded him, providing him a false sense of security…a man past his prime but holding on too tightly to the last threads of his glory days. He had finally agreed to talk with Lucien and I, but I should have known the man wouldn't make it easy. He cracked another crab leg and sucked up the meat.

"You've got to have rocks in your heads thinking I'm going to discuss my business with you. That first meeting I gave you as a courtesy. You shouldn't have asked for a second."

I brushed the lint from my pant leg, had to control the urge to slam the fucker's face into his plate. "You didn't tell me anything I didn't already know during that first meeting."

"And I ain't telling you now."

"We know you've got Miguel Dobbs by the short hairs, but there's someone else. We want to know who?"

"I want that bitch over there to come over here and suck my cock. It's nice to want, don't mean you're going to get it."

I glanced over at the woman, all curves and blonde hair. It'd be a cold day in hell before she voluntarily sucked him off.

Lucien reached for his whiskey, the ice rattling in the glass. "Who's your bed partner?"

"Are you hard of hearing? I've already answered that." Federico reached for his wine and drank the entire contents in one swallow before he signaled for his man to refill it.

"There are seven," I said to Lucien.

"Eight, one in the back."

"I like those odds."

Lucien lifted his glass. "Let me just finish this. It's exceptional." He finished off the amber-colored liquid before placing his glass down and looking over at me. "Let's not kill them. I promised my wife I would play nicely with others."

"It's too much work getting rid of bodies anyway."

"What the fuck are you two talking about?" Remnants of crab shot from Federico's mouth when he asked that.

Lucien and I moved at the same time, the element of surprise worked in our favor. Five were down before they knew what was happening. The man standing just at Federico's right took a gunshot to the thigh and dropped. Federico's fat hand went for his gun, but I grabbed the steak knife and pinned his palm to the table as the man bellowed in pain. Lucien disabled the last two thugs before he returned to the table, reached for the decanter of Chianti and poured us each a glass. We both settled back in our chairs.

"My hand, you motherfuckers."

"It's just your hand. You have two," I said before I leaned back in my chair and swirled the Chianti in the glass. "I'll ask again. Who are you working with?"

"Fuck you."

I was out of my chair, yanking the knife from his hand. He howled in pain, but went silent when I pressed the tip to his throat.

"Make no mistake. One swipe and you're a memory. I'm going to ask you one last time who you're working with before I make you a casualty."

His eyes bugged out of his head and I smelled his fear, a scent I was very familiar with as the memories I buried deep itched to break free. I pressed the knife harder against his throat. His voice broke. "Guy Hartnett."

It was only because I had years of discipline that I managed to control my reaction to that. Guy Hartnett was dirty? He was working with Federico? And yet it all made sense, he was the point where it all intersected. Fucking Guy Hartnett. This was going to kill Thea and Cam.

I lowered the knife. Lucien studied me before his eyes moved to Federico. "If you think to retaliate, think again."

"You won't get away with this," Federico hissed.

"We already have. Hartnett contacts you, I want to know," I said blandly as I dropped the knife on the table.

"Why the fuck would I tell you?" Federico hissed.

Lucien moved swiftly, grabbing the older man around the throat and squeezing. "Because deep down you're scared. And you have every reason to be. One of us coming at you, you might survive, the two of us coming at you and you don't stand a chance. You cooperate and we'll leave you out of it, you don't cooperate and we'll bury you. Understood."

Federico's face turned purple from rage, but he nodded his head. The man wasn't as stupid as he looked.

"And those crack houses. You close that shit down or I'll fucking burn them to the ground."

"That's my livelihood."

"Find another livelihood."

Lucien stepped back. "Are we done here?"

I drained the last of the wine from my glass. "Yeah."

On the curb, Lucien looked back at where we'd just come from before he turned his attention on me. "We just made an enemy. I'll put some guys on him and tap his phone. Just in case the man grows a set and tries to strike back."

"Good idea."

"Who's this Hartnett guy?"

"Former partner and best friend of the cop that was killed."

"Shit."

"Yeah, that about sums it up."

I waited until I was back in my office before I called Damian. I didn't even wait for a greeting before I said, "It's Hartnett."

Silence for a beat before Damian said, "Come again?"

"I just had the chat with Federico. It's Hartnett."

"Son of a bitch."

"I'll tell Cam, but I'm guessing you'll want to tell Thea."

"Fucking hell," Damian hissed before he added, "Fucker is going down for this."

"Yeah, he is."

CHAPTER 20

I was scrolling through the channels looking for something to watch, my mind replaying Damian's heroics to little Wynona the other day and the pumpkin that she even brought to school to show the other kids. I was surprised there wasn't a line of first graders at the door looking for him to work his magic on their pumpkins.

Seeing him hunched over that pumpkin—big, badass Damian carving Cinderella's carriage—warmed my heart. And he thought he was evil.

I stopped channel surfing at *The Blair Witch Project*. Memories bombarded me, pulling a smile because this was the first scary movie that Damian offered himself as my security blanket.

"Hey, Damian." Yes, I screamed that because I was very comfortable and I didn't feel like getting up.

Soundlessly was how the man moved. One minute he wasn't in

the doorway and the next he was. He looked around and I swear he reached for his gun even though he wasn't wearing one. After a quick scan he turned those eyes on me and it was very clear what he was thinking....*What the fuck?*

"*The Blair Witch Project* is on. Do you want to watch it with me?"

I saw his slight reaction to my news...he remembered too. He walked into the room, grabbed a blanket from the basket as he passed—my heart melted—then settled next to me just like he had done all those years ago.

I curled up against his body, wasn't at all shy about wrapping my arms around his waist, pressing my cheek on his shoulder, draping my legs over his lap. He was wearing me like another blanket. It was perfect. And I knew this was a trigger for him, but there was no downside for me. I either got to snuggle against him or he'd rip off my clothes and have his way with me.

I wasn't watching the movie and I suspected he wasn't either. He then did exactly what I had hoped he would do all those years ago. He shifted us, pulling me under his big body. Our gazes locked.

"Do you know how badly I wanted to do just this that day?"

The words got stuck in my throat hearing he had been feeling what I had even then. "I wanted that too."

His head lowered and my breath caught as his lips came down to mine. His hands framed my face as he took the kiss even deeper. I lost his mouth right before his forehead touched mine.

"Tell me to stop. You've got to tell me to stop because I can't."

"Please don't stop."

The look that transformed his features I would never forget. Damian—disciplined and controlled—gave in to his own wants for the first time in his life and it was a beautiful and deeply arousing sight. His hands moved down my body before he lifted my tank up and over my head. His eyes followed his hands on their journey back down my body, taking his time to cup my breasts, swiping his thumbs over my nipples. He yanked my shorts down my legs then reached for the back of his tee and pulled it off before he dropped his running pants. I whimpered. He was large and hard everywhere. His hands moved to my thighs where he spread me like some offering before he knelt between them.

He thumbed my clit, his other thumb slipping inside me, my hips lifted as a moan pulled from my throat. He watched his hands as I watched him. His eyes grew dark, the tip of his cock glistened. I wanted him inside me, but he lowered his head and touched my clit with just the tip of his tongue and yet my entire body shook from the pleasure. He took his time tasting, moving lower until his tongue replaced his thumb. I cried out as my body braced for the orgasm and knowing how close I was he gripped my thighs and yanked me to him as he thrust into me. The scream ripped from my throat, my back arched as the most intense pleasure rippled down my spine.

"Cup your breasts," he demanded in a gruff voice as his hips continued their assault, drawing out the orgasm.

They were heavy in my hand and felt so good.

"Do you feel how perfect they are? I'm going to spend hours on just them, my tongue, my teeth, my cock buried between them."

His words triggered another orgasm, less intense and still magnificent.

His body stilled, his eyes closed and I was gifted to the beautiful sight of him finding his own release.

His voice was sexy as hell when he said, "Let's move this to the bedroom."

Damian had me pressed tight to his body, I listened to his heart beating, the strong even beat.

"Do you remember the first time you came to my house, the night I cut your meatball? You must have thought I was a nut."

I felt him chuckle.

Resting my chin on his chest, I asked, "You did think I was crazy, didn't you?"

"No."

"I didn't make a very good first impression that night."

"That night wasn't your first impression."

"What do you mean?"

"The first time I saw you was a picture in Cam's wallet. He lent me money and when he opened his wallet I saw you. All hair and limbs but it was the smile on your face. You were fucking glowing and all you were doing was getting your picture taken. My home life was shit and there's this picture of you so happy. I wondered for weeks what could make someone that radiant? Then Cam invited me to dinner. I said yes because I wanted to see you. I wanted to see if you were really as vivacious as that picture made you seem. I had never met anyone like you."

"I didn't know that." I loved knowing this.

"Cutting my meatball...I fell a little bit in love with you that night."

He touched my cheek to wipe the tear that rolled down it. "The day you stepped in when I was getting taunted. Do you remember that?"

He answered by mirroring what he had done that day and took a curl between his fingers.

"I fell a little in love with you after your silent rescue."

"I wasn't going to enlist. I had been looking for a job closer to you at NYU, but my plans changed the day of the graduation party after a call from my mother."

She was dead, she couldn't hurt him any more, and still dread moved through me. Her fucking legacy. "What happened?"

"It was a typical call, trying to get me to do shit for her by being a manipulative bitch. But it was the comment she made about my feelings for you. She twisted what I felt, had me questioning if what I felt was healthy or the sick shit she called love. The idea that one day you and I would end the way my parents did. I never wanted to see that day."

My heart ached. "That's why you didn't just leave, you ended us."

"Leaving you was the hardest thing I have ever done. I didn't know at the time that it would be so long before our lives finally got back in sync."

"And now? You have been very determined to avoid just this."

"I'm only fucking human and you're right, there aren't enough cookies in the world." He stroked my cheek. "What were you smiling at in that picture?"

I knew the exact one he spoke of and I wanted to lie because it was a profound moment for him, but the reality was far from profound. "You're going to be very disappointed."

"How so?"

"Mom had made her coconut cake and she had called to say it was done right before Dad took the picture."

He dipped his chin down, I tipped mine back and we just stared for a beat or two before he laughed, a deep rich sound that was glorious to hear.

"I'm not disappointed at all, that sounds exactly like you." His smile faded and his voice pitched deeper. "One look and I was a goner."

I woke in the middle of the night to Damian's mouth on my neck, his hand between my legs. He moved over me and framed my face with his hands as he joined us, slowly, almost lazily, and so very sweetly. We moved together finding that perfect rhythm, and after, he wrapped me in his arms.

"I need to talk to you about Guy Harnett."

All the sweet feelings fled and my body went cold. He wanted to talk about Guy? "Why?"

"Cam has been following the money, something your dad started. Money from dummy accounts set up for Salvatore Federico to pay off the low-level enforcers and informants he has around the city. One of Salvatore's moles is Miguel Dobbs. We know he acted as hired muscle for Salvatore, we also know he recruited from within his precinct."

"You're saying he recruited Uncle Guy."

"He's not on the books, like some of the others, but a look at his financials shows he is floating more money than he reports to the IRS."

I needed to move, I jerked from his hold, pulled his t-shirt on and started to pace. Uncle Guy was dirty. Dad's friend, his partner was dirty. I didn't know what I felt more of; rage, betrayal or gut deep sadness. Uncle, he was no fucking uncle to me. "How did you see his financials?"

"Not important."

I snapped my head in his direction. He was out of bed and had pulled on his jeans, but he stayed on the other side of the room because he knew I needed space. "Illegally. That will impact the case when it goes to trial"

"Not if the arrests aren't made off the illegally obtained information and at this point Cam is focused on the cops he can prove were taking bribes, which includes Dobbs. Here is the interesting part. Salvatore cut ties with Dobbs as soon as he learned of Cam's investigation."

"Understandable."

"But why? Dobbs is a very small fish and Salvatore is well protected. A small fish isn't taking him out and still he erases every connection to Dobbs, every paper trail."

"He's not worried about Dobbs, but someone Dobbs' services were used for."

"Yeah."

"And Guy?"

"Anton had a sit down with Federico. He confirmed that he's been partnering with Hartnett, scratching each other's back as it were. Dobbs isn't the ringleader, he's the puppet."

Pain ripped right through me. We trusted him, loved him and he was deceiving us the whole time.

"Why would Guy do it?"

"Around the time of his cash infusion, his son and wife were getting treated by a very expensive fertility specialist. It would seem Hartnett and Federico struck up a deal. Guy keeps legal shit from landing on Federico and his minions and Federico throws him some moonlighting opportunities."

"Oh my God. Guy's family loved Dad, Trevor especially. How's he going to feel when he learns of this, looks at his child knowing his son cost a man his life. Why would Guy do that to him?"

Damian didn't answer that, but he did say, "He's dirty, but we're having trouble pinning anything on him."

"So what happens now?"

"Cam is working with the DA to build the cases against Dobbs and the other dirty cops. He expects warrants to be issued within the week."

"And Guy?"

"He is still trying to build a case against him. We can't count on Federico's testimony so we have to keep digging."

I did move then, right to Damian and pressed my cheek to his chest. "He knew. Dad knew he was playing with fire and planned for the worst case scenario by sending Cam copies of his files."

"Yeah it looks that way. You okay?"

My heart ached so I did what I always did. My arms went around him and I borrowed some of his strength as I allowed the full impact of what he shared to settle over me. Dad's former partner, one of his best friends, played a part in his death.

It wasn't yet morning, but I was awake. I was angry, so fucking angry, and sad and hurt. I thought about the night of the charity function and how Guy had been so solicitous, and sitting in the kitchen with my mom being all friendly, and yet he had a hand in Dad's death.

"Are you okay?"

My attention jerked to Damian to see he was awake and watching me.

"I don't know what to do with the rage and the anger." I climbed from the bed. I needed air. I yanked open the balcony door and stepped outside. I was just settling in the chair when Damian joined me. He stepped to the railing, checking the scene I was sure. Even now he was watching and protecting. I studied his tattoo until he turned, leaned up against the railing and pushed his hands into the pockets of his jeans.

"Talk to me."

"He was like family. His family was an extension of ours. He had been a pallbearer at Dad's funeral, he's Cam's godfather, and if he wasn't the one to kill dad, he played a part. How do I process that?"

"I wish I could answer that. He won't get away with it. I can promise you that."

I stood, feeling too restless to sit. "Can I see your tattoo?" But I didn't wait for a response. I walked to him and traced the devil on his back. It was beautiful. "Your Mom was wrong to call you the devil. People like Guy are devils. He was my father's best friend and he threw it all away for money. I don't care why he needed it. The price he paid to get it was too fucking high. You're nothing like that." I kissed him right in the center of his back. "This tattoo shouldn't be an albatross; it should be a talisman to your strength, your character, your integrity and your beauty because you are beautiful, Damian, inside and out."

I pressed my forehead to his back, wrapped my arms around his waist. "Do you think he knew? Dad? Do you think he knew it was his friend, his brother that betrayed him? The one he had walked the beat with, the one who had his back as much as he had his? The man who stood up with him at his wedding, promised to care for his children if something should happen to him. Do you think he knew?"

Damian turned into me, his voice harsh. "Don't do that to yourself."

"I don't just want him to get caught, I want him to hurt. I want him to know we know and I want him to hurt. What kind of person does that make me?"

"Human."

A thought had fury slipping to fear. "What about Mom? She has to be told something? What if Guy makes a play for her? She won't know."

"Your mom and Mrs. Cooke were moved to Mrs. Cooke's home in Westchester."

"They were?"

"As soon as Cam learned of Guy's involvement. Kimber and Ryder are being watched, if necessary they'll be joining them."

"I've never felt this kind of blinding rage before. I've never wanted to come out of my own skin from fury. I want to hit something, hurt something." Tears filled my eyes as I looked pleadingly into his. "Please make it go away."

Without a word, he pulled me close and kissed me deeply. My hands sought him, fury turning to passion. I couldn't touch or taste him enough. I wanted him, every part all at once. My mouth moved over his shoulder, my tongue darted out to taste the salt on his skin. He tasted good, so fucking good. My hands started a journey down his chest, my mouth following. The hunger for him grew to the point that I bit him, right on the pec and hard enough that I drew blood. I froze. I had never in my life bitten a person and certainly not during sex. His hand wrapped around mine and brought it to his cock that was straining the denim. "Do that again and I'm coming on you not in you."

He carried me to the bed and lowered me to my feet before yanking the tee over my head. He dropped his jeans, hooked an arm around my waist and pulled me down onto the bed.

His hands slid down my back to my ass where he squeezed, separating my cheeks as his cock pushed between my legs and he rubbed himself in the spot I wanted him to take.

"Please."

"What do you need, baby."

"You—hard, fast…I want it to hurt in a good way."

He flipped me and pressed my chest into the mattress while

holding my hips up high.

"If I'm too rough, say."

He couldn't ever be too rough.

"Thea?"

"Okay."

The tip off his cock moved between my ass cheeks to my core that was already starting to spasm. I cried out when he rammed into me, filling me so completely it hurt to accommodate him.

"Are you okay?"

"Please don't stop."

He pulled out, my body desperate to hold him inside and then he was thrusting forward again. In and out, over and over, he slammed into me until the pain and pleasure blended into one life-changing orgasm. My limbs went weak, my mind emptied, but Damian wasn't done. He pulled from me and settled on the edge of the bed.

"You fuck me now."

I crawled to him, threw my leg around his waist and straddled him, holding myself just out of reach for a second before I sank down on his cock. His mouth found my breast, sucking hard as his tongue swirled around my nipple. I didn't think I'd come again, but my muscles tensed, my body making the climb until I went off like a firecracker. His hands on my hips kept me moving as he found his release. The growl that rolled up his throat was the sexiest sound I'd ever heard.

My head dropped on his shoulder, his arms came around me. "Better?"

"Yes. I'm sorry."

"Best fucking sex of my life. You better not be sorry."

"I'm not really."

He stood, carrying me since I was still wrapped around him, and climbed under the covers. I fell asleep. My body spent, my mind overwhelmed, but the one light in the darkness that my life seemed to have been plunged into held me as tightly as I held him.

CHAPTER 21

I'm leaving for New York tomorrow." Damian dropped on me at dinner the following night.

"What? New York? Why?"

"The late night phone calls you received were tracked back to Chris McKay."

I'm sure I looked confused because I sure as hell felt it. "Chris McKay?"

"It's a piece that doesn't fit. I had someone on him, but he's disappeared."

"What do you mean he's disappeared?"

"He's gone under and well enough that I can't find him. That says to me someone forced him to go under. I want to know who and why?"

"What are you thinking?"

"He was harassing you because of his daughter's case and your link to Timothy Gallagher. My guess, he was doing similarly to Timothy Gallagher, but he has clients that would not be thrilled to have someone nosing around."

"Are you saying you think he's dead? What about his grand-kids?"

"They're staying with a distant relative. He hasn't been to see them in several weeks. It's more than likely that he isn't tied to Cam's investigation, but with his link to you I want to know exactly what his involvement is. I've gotten a lead on a possible direction as to who is pulling his strings."

"And you have to go?"

"Everyone else is working on other things. Besides, he harassed you. That makes it personal for me."

"How do you do that?"

He lifted his brow in question.

"Make me want to smile even when I'm feeling slightly terri-fied."

He brushed his thumb over my lower lip. "Terrified?"

"For you."

It was his turn to smile. "I love that you're concerned for me, but I'm good, babe. And you will be too. You're covered."

"I'm covered?" I was slightly distracted from his smile.

"Yeah."

"Mic?"

"And Razor."

It took effort to keep my jaw from hitting the table. Razor worked for Damian. "Razor?"

He was enjoying my befuddlement.

"I can't believe I didn't see that."

"One of them will stay at the cottage with you while I'm gone."

"What about work? I don't imagine Janice wants me in the bar?"

"She doesn't have a say."

"Seriously?"

He didn't answer but I didn't expect one. And then a thought turned me cold. "Are you not coming back?"

That earned me an exasperated glare. "I'll be back in three or four days. The timing sucks, but I have to go."

"So, you're not running?"

That pissed him off. "I'm going to put you over my knee."

My body went up in flames at the thought. Damian grinned. "I like that look on you."

"What look?"

He leaned over the table. "Hot."

"Well, you're in luck since that's a condition I feel around you all the time."

"I know."

"You're not immune."

"Fucking hooked too."

"Good answer." I looked down and then up at him through my lashes. "Maybe we should get our desserts to go."

Damian's voice carried through the restaurant. "Check."

I was thankful for work, both my graphic design responsibilities and the late hours at the bar, because it kept me busy and being busy helped distract me because I missed Damian. And I worried for him and the others and the shit storm they were wading into at home. Chris McKay had been the one calling me. He had been distraught and angry after his daughter's murderer had been set free, I understood. But had he intended to do more than harassing phone calls? That thought caused a chill to move through me. And who was behind him disappearing? I hoped he was alive. He'd acted carelessly and emotionally, but he didn't deserve to lose his life for being in the wrong place at the wrong time.

I was working the area by the pool tables when I noticed a girl that was being backed into a corner. It was the expression on her face that had me walking over.

"Can I get you something?" The girl's fearful eyes latched onto me.

The guy barely glanced at me when he said, "We're good." It was the creep from the other night who had been hunting.

And even feeling alarm, and a touch of fear, anger had the next words bubbling up my throat. "You don't look good to me. Why don't you back off there, pal."

That got me his face and he was not pleased. "Why don't you?"

"I'm not the one cornering that poor girl. Step back or I'll bring one of the bouncers over to make you."

He stepped back, the girl ran away. "No means no, you know that right?"

"We were just having fun."

"When you have to force your companion into having fun, that's called rape."

"She was playing coy."

"I'm going to walk over to that big guy at the bar and share with him that you blur the lines from consenting to coercion. Do yourself a favor and get the hell out of here and don't come back. In fact, why don't you crawl back into whatever hole you came out of. I'll be calling the sheriff and giving him a full description."

"I've done nothing wrong."

"And we're going to make sure it stays that way."

"Bitch."

"Yes I can be. So get the fuck out."

"What's going on over here?" Razor asked as he stepped up next to me.

"Nothing, just encouraging Don Juan here to move it along."

"I'll be seeing you again." The threat was clear. Razor went on alert.

"I won't be as nice next time," I replied sweetly.

He strolled toward the exit; Razor and I followed him. Mic stopped me from walking him to the door. He signaled to the bouncer to make sure the guy left.

"What was that?"

"He had some girl pinned up against the wall. She didn't want to be there, he didn't care."

"Son of a bitch." I thought Razor was pissed at the guy until he said, "And so you just strolled up to him and got in his face."

"Someone had to."

Mic didn't look any happier. "Next time flag a bouncer. It is why they're here. I don't imagine your husband would be thrilled to hear you did that."

"You can cut the shit. I know you work with Damian."

Contrition on their faces was very funny. "We were just following orders."

Mic leaned closer to me. "You're changing the subject, next time get a bouncer."

"Fine. I'll leave it to the bouncer."

I turned back to Razor. "Can I get you something?"

"A Guinness."

"You got it. And thanks for stepping in." A pattern seemed to be forming in our behavior.

"No problem."

Razor moved back to the pool tables and I watched as he did. "Damian told me he had a record. Why would he do that?"

Mic dropped his elbows on the bar top. "What kind of record?"

"He said he was a sexual predator."

Mic's expression went blank for all of three seconds before he howled with laughter. Like so loud every head in the place turned in his direction. I went beet red and lowered mine.

"A sexual predator? Oh my God, that's good. Razor," Mic hollered across the bar, which wasn't necessary because Razor was already on his way back. I'm sure curious as to what had Mic behaving as he was.

"What the fuck is wrong with you?" Razor barked at Mic.

"Damian told her you were a sexual predator."

"Why the hell would you tell him that?" I screeched. Razor joined Mic in laughing, a loud belly laugh.

"I'm missing something," I muttered, but they still heard me.

"I wondered what bullshit he fed you, you were pretty icy to me that day on the street."

"He shouldn't have done that."

"In his shoes, I would have too."

"Why?"

"You got to ask me that, babe, no point in me answering."

"Wait." I looked back at Mic. "You knew that Damian and I weren't married so why did you ask me all those questions about how long we'd been together."

"Because it pissed him off."

"What pissed him off? You talking to me?"

"Yep."

"I think you are all a bit crazy. I have to get back to work."

I walked away to them laughing again, probably at me. Whatever.

Mic had a cabin outside of town and deep in the woods. Mic thought it might get my neighbors talking if he or Razor stayed with me at the cottage while Damian was gone, so we stayed at his place. We were really in the middle of nowhere, which I supposed was good, but I had nightmares about running into a black bear and after watching *Back Country*, I did not want to come face to face with a black bear...ever. I spent the days working on my graphic design projects and the nights at the bar.

Mic was working and I wasn't due in for a few hours. Razor and I were playing Monopoly. Truth be told, I was kicking his ass at Monopoly.

"I'm going to figure out how you're cheating because I know you are."

Razor was not a gracious loser.

"How am I cheating? You're the banker."

"I don't know, but you are."

"Sore loser."

"I heard a rumor that you make a killer chicken potpie."

"Is getting your ass kicked making you hungry?"

He lifted his middle finger, but smiled to lessen the insult. "I love chicken potpie."

"You're goofy."

His smile turned into a stern line, but his eyes were still laughing. "I'm scary as fuck."

"Okay. You're scary. If we're having potpie, I need to make the crust."

"I'll oversee."

"You mean sneak some."

He winked. "Nothing gets past you."

I liked Razor, so outspoken and crass, so very different from Damian. "How did you and Damian meet?"

"I used to be a bounty hunter and was working a case. Found myself in a situation of six against one. I really thought that was it for me, and then Damian appeared, emerging from the shadows like a demon. I swear to fucking God I didn't think he was real. He took out four of my attackers with his bare hands. I'd never seen anyone fight with such cold calculation. Turned out he was hunting the same guy. He let me collect the fee then offered me a job. He saved my life that day, figured I would return the favor by watching over his."

I'd seen that cold calculation in Damian before and maybe it was wrong but I was happy he had found a way to funnel that into something good.

"I'm happy you're watching his back."

"I'll be happy when you start making that pot pie," He offered that with a smile.

DAMIAN

My team had intercepted an email to Chris McKay's grandkids. They traced the origin but it was a dead end. Whoever had him knew their shit. What I wanted to know was what the hell he knew that made him interesting to anyone? He'd harassed Thea and that was enough for me to have a private word with him, but the fact that he was being sequestered suggested the authorities had him. But why?

My phone vibrated on the seat next to me

"Cam, what's up?"

"It's done."

It was about fucking time. "How many arrests?"

"Seven."

"Hartnett?"

"I couldn't pin him to it, which just pisses me off. We know he's the missing link, even without Federico giving him up. He ties it all together…the dirty cops, Dobbs, Federico, even Thea's attack in the alley using Dobbs' CI so if it went to hell the blowback landed on Dobbs. And he was Dad's best friend, he would have known his schedule, he would have been able to get to him, and Dad was investigating dirty cops. Guy is dirty. He's the common denominator and yet I can't pin anything on him." I felt the rage I heard in Cam's voice. The man had been family and he betrayed us. "I want him."

"Fuck yeah."

"What happened with the tip on McKay?"

"It didn't pan out. I think the cops have him. What I can't figure out is why."

There was silence for a moment before he said, "She's my sister, but hear me out before—

"No."

"I didn't even—

"You want to use her as bait."

"Arrests are being made, he has got to be getting nervous. He wanted something from her and if she returns now he'll likely react."

"By putting your sister right in the fucking crosshairs."

"She would want to be."

"She doesn't get a choice."

"Our dad was killed. His best friend killed him. Keeping her from this will only piss her off. You know I'm right."

"I don't give a fuck."

"You will when it puts a wall up between you."

I knew he was right. I fucking hated that he was right.

"Let's bring her home," he said.

"We have to tell her first. She has to agree to this or she stays where she is."

"Agreed."

"I'll let you know." I disconnected and tossed my phone on the seat. We did all of this to keep her safe and now we were leading her right into the lion's den.

CHAPTER 22

My legs felt like noodles and I ached in places that felt so good to ache in. Damian got home last night and we spent all night and the early morning celebrating his homecoming. He was putting on the coffee but I hadn't been able to climb out of bed. My body just wasn't responding yet.

The door opened, he walked in with two mugs of coffee that he placed on the dresser. Seeing him made me feel energized because I needed a shower and I was certain I could get him to join me. I climbed from bed.

"Shower?"

In answer he stripped out of his jeans. It was not a sight I would ever grow tired of seeing. He grabbed me around the waist and tossed me over his shoulder as a laugh bubbled up my throat. I loved when he was being playful. He didn't release me when we reached the bathroom and with my ass in the air and my stomach pressed to his shoulder, he turned on the shower.

"I heard you approached a potential rapist on your own."

Oh crap. Suddenly I didn't want to be over his shoulder. Downstairs or in the next state would have been preferable.

"Two of my best guys were there and you decided to handle it on your own."

His hand moved over my ass and realization dawned a second before it came down hard on my left ass cheek.

"Ouch."

He didn't stop after one, he smacked my ass—a few hard hits on each cheek, and even as my ass stung in pain, I was so wet.

"I've waited for you for half of my life. I want a lifetime with you."

"You just spanked me."

He smacked me again. "A lifetime, so that means you don't confront potential felons on your fucking own."

He rubbed my tender flesh, his finger moving between my legs where I was soaked. I never would have thought a spanking would make me hot, but I was so turned on.

"You liked that." He was as surprised by my body's reaction as me.

He rubbed his finger over my clit and I couldn't stop the moan, didn't try to when he started finger fucking me. Right before I came he yanked me down his body and onto his cock. My eyes rolled into the back of my head.

He pressed me to the wall, held both of my hands in one of his high over my head, lifting my breasts to his mouth. His hips moved hard and fast, his cock hitting me on the clit as he moved in and out, his mouth taking turns teasing and sucking on my breasts. I came apart in a dizzying orgasm. He stilled, his cock jerked as ecstasy rolled over his features.

"A lifetime, Thea." He kissed my neck and carried me into the shower.

It was while we cleaned the dishes after breakfast that Damian shared, "It's over."

I stopped drying the glass. "Cam has made the arrests?"

"Yeah."

"How many?"

"Seven."

"Was Guy...?"

"He couldn't pin anything on him, but we've linked him to all of it. He knew Dobbs, the dirty cops, the man who attacked you in the alley."

"There's more."

"Cam believes Guy is the one who called out the hit on your dad. Your dad must have figured it out that Guy was the common denominator."

We had already been thinking this, but hearing it spoken out loud was shattering.

"Guy wants something from me, so let's use me as bait."

His face went dark, but he looked conflicted.

"That's the plan, isn't it?" I asked.

"I don't fucking like this plan."

"I'm in."

"Think about it first. I dragged you here to keep you safe and now we're asking you to walk right into the middle of it."

"Guy ordered the hit on my dad and if we can't flush him out he'll get away with killing him. That's not an option."

He rubbed his hands over his face. "We orchestrate this op, right down to the smallest detail."

"Okay."

"You don't take any chances. I'm not kidding, Thea."

"I won't." I realized then what fueled the spanking from earlier. It wasn't so much what I did, but what I might do. "I won't be careless, Damian. I promise."

He reached for his wallet, pulled something out and handed it to me. It was the first letter I had written to him and the picture of me from Cam's wallet.

"Do you know how many times I looked at these? Waiting out

insurgents, sitting in foxholes…how many missions the thought of you got me through. You have been in my head since the first time I saw that picture. And having that letter…fucking Christ. And now you're in my bed and my heart and…" He rubbed his head before his hot stare speared me with its intensity. "I fucking hate this plan, making you bait, but I swear to God if you take any unnecessary risks…"

"I won't. I promise."

He moved so fast, pulling my body into the cradle of his. "I'm holding you to that, because you own me. Every dark part of me."

"I thought we were leaving?" Two days after he returned, we were heading back to New York. Mic, who had accepted a job with Damian, and Razor were joining us. Damian had spent most of the day yesterday out of the house while I packed my stuff. Whatever he was up to, he wasn't quite done.

"We have to make a stop first." He said as we parked down the street from Janice's. I was surprised to see Missy.

"Thanks for coming," Damian said to her as we approached.

"Thank you," Missy replied then turned to me and surprised me with a hug. "I'm going to miss you. Damian filled me in."

She surprised me again with that confession. "He did?"

"It's like a episode of a crime drama." She took my hands into hers. "Please be careful."

"I will."

"I'll fill everyone else in."

"I'd really appreciate that, thank you. Can I ask why you're here?"

"Damian offered me the position of manager for the bar."

Damian's absence yesterday was beginning to make sense. "That's wonderful. But that means…"

As if on cue, Janice was brought out in handcuffs. Unlike the overly confident woman I interviewed for, she had her head down. I had a twinge of pity for her to be so publicly humiliated, but then

I thought about Amelia and how she had conned a dying woman. Actions had consequences. She needed to man up to hers.

Damian walked over with a man I didn't recognize. "Missy, this is James Stiles. He was Amelia's accountant. He can bring you up to speed on the bar. I'm closing it, you reopen when you're comfortable. And you'll need to hire a new bartender. We'll be back as soon as we take care of the situation at home."

"Don't worry. I managed the grain depot for years. It's the same concept. The bar is in good hands."

"I know it is."

"Would you like to go through the books now?" James asked Missy.

"I'll put on some coffee." Missy looked back at me. "When you return, I'll make dinner."

"We'd love that."

Damian took my hand and led me to his car. "How did you know she was looking for a new job?"

"I asked."

"You're a good man."

He held the door for me. "Only to those who matter."

That wasn't true, but I didn't press the point.

We didn't go right home, we made one stop. Mrs. Cooke's house. I didn't even wait for the car to stop before I jumped from it and ran to my mom. She caught me into a tight hug. We were both crying.

"I've missed you," she whispered.

"I missed you more."

Mom released me and I reached for Mrs. Cooke's hands. "Oh Mrs. Cooke. I've missed you. How are you with being back here?"

"I'm good, dear. The memories bring a smile not pain."

"I'm so happy to hear that."

Anton and Cam came strolling outside. "Finally," Cam said as his arms went tight around me. "How you doing, sis?"

"Better now."

"You must be tired," Anton said as I moved into him and kissed his cheek. "I'm happy you're home. I missed you."

"I've missed you too, Anton."

"There are refreshments inside," Mrs. Cooke announced.

"Thanks for letting us stay here."

"Nonsense. It's a big, drafty place that has gone too long without having life in its halls."

Razor, Mic and Damian joined us and I knew this because my mom made a sound in the back of her throat, which had me wondering about her own personal hottie. "Where's yoga man?"

"Inside helping the girls with dinner. Who is this?" Mom asked, but she was already offering her hand to Razor.

"My mom, Rosalie, and Miranda Cooke, this is Razor and Mic."

"Just delighted to make your acquaintance." Mom was batting her lashes, but it looked like she had something in her eye. Confirmed when Razor asked, "What's wrong with your eye?"

Mom gasped, Mrs. Cooke looked flabbergasted and I roared with laughter. It was good to be home.

My smile was so big my face hurt when we stepped into the kitchen to see my two besties making dinner. As soon as they saw me they dropped what they were doing, screamed and ran to me. We hugged, jumped up and down and spoke in a language no one but us understood. And then they pulled me from the kitchen. "We'll bring her back," Kimber shouted from over her shoulder as Ryder dragged me upstairs.

"We have so much to catch you up on," Ryder said as she dropped on the bed. The room was amazing, spacious with antique furniture, muted-gold papered walls and a fireplace.

I stood in the middle of the room and spun in a circle. "I can't believe she let this sit vacant for so long."

"I know. The place is amazing."

I dropped down on the bed too. "How were things here? Any trouble?"

"No. None. We heard about Guy, we can't really believe it."

My happy glow soured. "I can't talk about that right now. How's Mom?"

"She doesn't know."

"That's probably for the best because she would absolutely hunt him down."

"That's what your brother is afraid of," Ryder said.

"So what's up with Damian?" Kimber asked.

"It's a long story, but he wants a lifetime with me."

They both squealed so loud I was sure they heard it down the block. "Oh my God. He said that?" Ryder gushed.

"Yeah. It's still there, what pulled at us when we were younger, but it's so much more now."

"I love that something good came out of all this shit." Ryder was right about that.

I wanted to tell them about Amelia and the friends I had made, but I was exhausted and that was a conversation that would take hours, so I moved the subject off me. "How's Derrick?"

Ryder released a breath, Kimber's expression turned sad. "We split up."

"Why?"

"It just wasn't working."

"Bullshit," Ryder shouted and since she was sitting right next to me my ear was now ringing.

"What's bullshit?"

Ryder pointed accusingly at Kimber. "They were working just fine until this one got cold feet."

Kimber was studying the lines in the comforter. "Kimber?"

"I like...okay I love him. That scares the shit out of me, so I ended it."

"You fell in love for the first time in your life so you broke it off with the man."

"Yes. Coward." This was clearly an argument these two had

been having for a while.

"Sticks and stones," Kimber said then stuck out her tongue.

"And how did Derrick take the breakup?"

"He hasn't."

Remembering the man in question, yeah he didn't seem the type to give up if he wanted something. "He'll break you down, particularly since you want to be broken down."

"I know."

Ryder jumped from the bed. "We should join the others because dinner is almost ready."

Before we went to dinner, the guys and I sat in the library as they once again briefed me on what to expect.

"Once you know the restaurant, my team will setup the surveillance. You will not be alone with him. Silas will drive you and my men will be posing as waiters. You'll be covered every second."

"I'll be fine."

I had never seen Damian like this. And I appreciated that I'd be feeling the same had the roles been reversed, but Guy wasn't getting away with this.

Cam reached for my hand. "I get what you're feeling. We all are, but control your temper until we have him. He wants something from you so make him feel comfortable to ask for it. Anything he says could help us with nailing him. We only need one thread and his shit will unravel."

"I got this."

They all looked grim, but it was Anton who said, "We know you do."

Cam then did the weirdest thing. He stared at Damian then me and back again.

"You and her finally got it together?" he asked.

Damian didn't even blink. "Yes."

"What are your intentions?"

"Are you serious, Cam? Ignore him, Damian. My brother's a moron."

"I'm not kidding. What are your intentions?" Cam demanded.

I rolled my eyes because honestly. "You're being an idiot, Cam."

"Damian?" I knew that tone of Cam's and couldn't believe he was actually being serious.

"Cam, cut the shit." I was getting pissed now.

Damian's focus shifted from Cam to me. The hard lines smoothed out and warmth moved into his gaze. "To offer her a blanket and my body when she watches a scary movie. To hold her hair when she is sick and to supply the water when she drinks. To keep the house stocked with cookie ingredients and working fire extinguishers. To make her eggs and bacon and two cups of black coffee with two sugars every morning. To fall asleep next to her every night and to wake to her beautiful face every morning. To plant my babies in her, to build a life and family with her, to grow old with her...watching as life etches itself on her face. My intention, Cam, is to spend the rest of my life with her."

No words would come after that breathtaking vow, so instead I stood and walked on unsteady legs to the man I loved and buried my face in his chest.

"Fucking finally," Cam said after a few minutes.

I had just climbed into bed when Damian entered. I hadn't stopped playing his vow over and over again in my head. For a man who conserved words, he sure as hell could string some really fucking great ones together. Still I teased him. "Did you and Cam agree on my dowry?"

"He loves you."

"I know that. I love him, doesn't mean he wasn't being an idiot."

"Concern for his sister does not make him an idiot."

I was reminded of Amelia and how Damian wouldn't ever get to have that with her, so I changed the subject.

"Mrs. Cooke is very forward thinking with her room assignments."

That earned me a look from over his shoulder. A shoulder that was now bare since the man was undressing for bed. I suddenly felt overdressed in my nightshirt.

I waited for him to finish preparing for bed because that included getting naked. Yes, the man slept in the nude. I had said once I didn't walk in the light. I would like to retract that statement.

He climbed into bed and pulled me under him, his hands brushing my hair from my face. "Follow the plan."

"I will."

"Don't take any chances."

"I won't."

"And if you feel uncomfortable, drop your napkin."

I ran my hand down his face, brushed his lips with my fingers. "You will be right there. I'll be fine."

"I want a lifetime, Thea."

"We'll start with that."

And then he kissed me.

It was weird being home, but I had missed it. I had called Uncle Guy as soon as I got home and scheduled the dinner. The man would make an incredible actor because he sounded so happy to hear from me, so familial and yet the bastard killed my dad. We were meeting in two days, Damian was even now wiring the restaurant and setting up the surveillance, drilling the teams. While he was busy doing that, I went about business as usual and spent yesterday cleaning the apartment and stocking my fridge. While cleaning the dreaded bathroom, I snapped the chain of the necklace Dad had given me. I almost lost my key down the toilet. I would have to replace the chain, but in the meantime I hung it on a shorter one because not wearing it wasn't an option.

After I got organized, I decided to hunt some zombies to brush up on my shooting skills. I wouldn't be packing, obviously, but I still liked the idea of practice and it was while I killed the undead that my cell rang. Uncle Tim's name popped up on the screen. I paused my game and reached for it.

"Hey, Uncle Tim. How are you?"

"I should be asking you that. I wondered why I hadn't heard from you and then I saw the breaking news. That's an incredible collar for your brother."

"And justice for Dad."

He was silent for a minute. "Absolutely."

"How are you? How's the Senate race?"

"Busy, lots of schmoozing, but early polling is looking favorable."

"Congratulations."

"Thank you. Would you be free to join me for lunch?"

"I'd love to. Why don't you come here and I'll make us something."

"I'd like that."

"See you around one."

"I'll be there."

DAMIAN

"How good is this intel?"

"It's solid. Someone is following our digital footsteps. The team was able to reverse the search to pinpoint the IP address of the computer."

"And it was last active?"

"About a half an hour ago."

I swerved to miss taking off a car door then laid on the horn. Dumb fuck.

"You might want to switch to decaf."

I wasn't in the mood for Razor's shit. Thea was fucking bait and I didn't have her back. Cam was right. I was too invested. The guys on her were top rate. I had picked them out personally and still it fucking grated.

"She'll be fine. Your woman is a bit cutthroat. Seriously, man, you let her slip through your fingers and I'm snatching her up."

"Never going to fucking happen." I never had a home. I had one now.

"You're smarter than you look."

I jerked my head to him to see the fucker grinning. "Seriously, I'm happy for you. If I found me a woman like Thea, someone who actually tolerated my bullshit, I'd hold on and never let go."

Family, fucking hell I had one all along. "Talk to me about what the team found?"

"They're mirroring our search, it's like they're giving us a virtual middle finger, like they want us to find them."

"Or it's a trap."

"Or a call for help," he added.

"We'll know soon enough. We're here."

"What's the play?" Razor asked.

I didn't answer because my focus was on the man stepping from the shadows. "Fuck me."

"Who the hell is that?"

Guy Hartnett peered into the car. "Took you long enough."

THEA

The baked potato soup I whipped up had turned out perfectly. We were sitting in my kitchen. I had made sandwiches and soup. Uncle Tim wasn't eating, but he was nursing three fingers of scotch. Unusual for him, but he was running a Senate campaign. That had to be stressful.

"You look well, Thea. Your time away agreed with you."

More than he would know. I moved past that and studied his beloved face. He looked older since the last time I saw him.

"You look tired."

He lifted his glass and took a long sip. "I am. Campaigning is exhausting. It is definitely a younger man's game, but I've wanted the Senate for so long. When we were kids, I remember your father and I talking about what we wanted to be when we grew up. He always wanted to be a cop, was such a firm believer in right and wrong, black and white. I often straddle the line, but not your dad...incorruptible. Cam's the spitting image of him."

My soup was forgotten listening to Uncle Tim because there was an odd note in his voice. "Cam is like Dad. I think we both are."

"Yes of course." He ran his finger over the rim of his glass. "Your key is lovely."

Absently I touched it. "Thank you."

"I don't remember seeing that before."

"It's usually hidden under my clothes but I broke the chain."

"Ah. So can you tell me where you've been?"

How much could I share with him without impacting the sting on Guy? "The case Cam just closed on the dirty cops was originally Dad's case. There was a little trouble here for me connected to that case, enough that the men in my life wanted to ensconced me away somewhere safe."

"Smart men."

"Yeah. I'm proud of Cam. It wasn't easy what he did, but it was the right thing. I just know that Dad is smiling down on him."

"I've no doubt." He put his glass down. "I'm going to need your necklace."

So thrown from his odd request I said a bit bewildered. "What?"

"For almost three years I've been waiting, wondering. It's nerve racking."

The first pang of dread moved through me "Waited for what?"

"For my past to come back and haunt me."

Ice formed in my blood, but as the pieces started falling into place ice turned to red-hot rage. I all but snarled at him. "You?"

"It's hard defending criminals and sometimes it is even unethical, but to make a difference, to stand out, sometimes you have to do the unethical. Your dad never understood that."

It was Uncle Tim, not Uncle Guy. My dad's childhood friend was the one behind his death. I wanted to hurt him, rake my fingers down his face, but I held myself immobile. "Why did you do it?"

"It was his damn Boy Scout ways. He was digging and I encouraged him to stop, that no good could come from investigating his own. That it was career suicide, but he didn't listen. So black and white your father."

"Why did you really encourage him to back off?"

"Because if he dug deep enough he would have learned it wasn't just cops on the take."

The investigation into evidence tampering at the station, it had been Uncle Tim behind that. He didn't have a magical acquittal rating. He had been cheating. And then a thought turned me cold. Mrs. Cooke's attack. At my apartment that day, he had made a comment about my mail. I hadn't thought anything of it at the time, seeing him flip through my mail, but he wanted access to my mail at her place. "You had Dobbs doing your dirty work...Mrs. Cooke's attack and screwing with evidence. Did he also intimidate jurors at your command?"

"Cop logic runs in the family. Miguel is just a pawn. He is so hungry for money and power, he makes it all too easy for someone to pull his strings. Salvatore Federico realized that too, so he scratched my back and when I'm elected into the Senate, he will have a friend in Washington."

"So you had Dad killed?"

"He should have left it alone. I think he suspected at the end, I could tell when we talked there was a remoteness to him."

"And this?" I asked as I palmed my key.

"There's that lovely little box in your dad's study. You remember it."

His special box, I couldn't believe I hadn't made the connection. I'd seen him open it enough times through the years. "What's he got on you?"

"I wasn't sure he had anything on me, but when the case on

Dobbs started heating up I didn't want to take the chance. You were the executor of his will. If he left something, you would have found it."

Which was why he had been interested in my mail and when that didn't pan out. "You hired someone to come at me?"

"He would have been gentle unless you were uncooperative."

Gentle? The man put a knife to my back.

"The cops never showed up at my door. I actually thought it was all over until I saw that key just now around your neck—a key to the box that he kept all his important things in. I'm guessing he sent that to you right before he died. I thought he was getting wise to me, now I'm sure of it."

"You're an unimaginable bastard."

"And I'll be the next Senator for the state of New York."

DAMIAN

Guy took us to the IA base operations located a few blocks from where we picked him up. Anton was going to flip the fuck out when he learned Federico had played him.

"How long have you been working in Internal Affairs?"

"Since Edward shared his suspicions with me. He hadn't told me how deep into it he was, but after the shooting I contacted IA."

"So you played dirty?"

"And left a few breadcrumbs for Cam to find. I needed an in to get closer to Dobbs, but Dobbs is too stupid to pull this off on his own. He's motivated by greed, pure and simple, but he is not a logistical thinker, just the hired muscle. There's another player and recently I got some insight from the most unlikely source."

"We thought that player was you."

"I know."

"So who is this source?"

"Follow me."

There was a room at the end of a short hall and sitting at the table was an older man who looked tired and scared. Chris McKay.

"So you pulled him in."

"Yeah. He was getting reckless."

"So what's he got?"

"Timothy Gallagher."

Apprehension twisted in my gut and my body went cold. "Come again."

"McKay had been stalking him, following his every move."

"And you were following him while he followed Gallagher. What did you get?"

"Late night meetings."

"With who?"

"Salvatore Federico."

Cold turned into numb. "He knows Federico?"

Guy was barely holding on to his rage. "Yeah. We know Federico is linked to the dirty cops at the precinct, we know the dirty cops are linked to Edward's murder, and that fucking asshole Timothy Gallagher is the point where all the parts intersect...Miguel Dobbs was being played by two puppet masters."

That explained why Salvatore cut ties with Dobbs because evidence tampering was one thing, the murder of a cop was something else altogether. "Shit." I yanked out my phone. I called Thea, but her phone went to voice mail. I called Mic.

"Where is she?"

"Her apartment, her uncle arrived about a half an hour ago."

"Gallagher?"

"Yeah."

I had walked into firefights where I'd been outnumbered ten to one, dodged IEDs, been tortured even, but never had I felt the fear that crippled me in that moment knowing that Thea was even now with a killer, a man she trusted and loved.

"It's him."

Mic hissed over the line, "Fucking hell."

"I'm on my way. I want ears on her apartment now."

"Thea?" Guy grabbed his coat. "I'm coming with you."

"I've got Cam on the line," Razor said as we hauled ass out of the building, my discipline holding on by a thread as bloodlust consumed me. If he hurt her, even just one hair on her head, I'd kill him. Tear him apart, piece by piece…I would embrace the monster I had been called my whole life.

"Tell him we had the wrong fucking uncle."

Hold on, baby. I'm coming.

THEA

"What am I going to do with you? Getting whatever your father hid won't be enough. You're a loose end." Uncle Tim was pacing my apartment and I thought to make a break for it, but the callous, almost disinterested act he was putting on was just that, an act. He was alert and on edge and I didn't stand a chance at outrunning him.

Maybe if I could appeal to the man who I had looked up to my whole life, to my beloved uncle, it might snap him out of his homicidal ideas. "You've been such a huge part of my life. I have to believe we can find a way through this that doesn't end in more violence."

"Oh Thea, you're so idealistic. It's sweet and completely impractical. The good guy never finishes first. I love you, but we have to think of the greater good. When I become Senator I will have an impact on millions and millions of lives. I can't allow sentimentality to cloud my purpose."

I knew he was arrogant, had always believed he had a reason to be, I hadn't realized he was a narcissist. Sentimentality, the greater good…if we weren't talking about me I'd actually be laughing right now.

"You're my godfather."

"Yes and it will make me an even more likable candidate when I'm there to help your family through their grief."

The man was certifiable. How had we never known this? And I

thought I was good at reading people. "You're crazy."

True fear gripped me in that moment because I was dealing with someone who had long ago gone off the reservation. There would be no talking down or reasoning with him. My only play was to make an escape, but he was a man who had killed once already to keep the dream alive. Crazy and determined…a dangerous combination.

He reached for his phone. I should have known. He wouldn't do it himself; he'd bring someone in to do the dirty work. I couldn't believe I was actually listening to him make the call to place a hit on me. Where the hell was the goddamn cavalry? But no one was watching for Uncle Tim.

DAMIAN

"He's calling for a hit," Mic said. We'd just stepped into the surveillance van outside of Thea's building.

Anton was pacing, the man was barely keeping his shit together. "Son of a bitch. That motherfucker Federico lied to me." He reached for his phone.

It was smart of Federico to give up Hartnett to keep Gallagher protected because there was just enough truth in his lie to make it believable. On paper, Hartnett and Gallagher were very similar and with Hartnett playing dirty…yeah sending us in that direction was definitely smart.

"Lucien. Federico lied. You still got your guys on him? Yeah. He's calling in a marker. Yeah, take him out. I'll explain later. Thanks man."

Anton snapped his phone shut. "Lucien's got Federico's phones tapped and his place under surveillance. A precautionary measure given the chat we had with him. He'll take out the hit man Federico calls. But that fuck needs to go down too."

"We'll get him, but let's focus on Gallagher," Cam said.

"Razor, you're going in. Gallagher doesn't know you but Thea will know we're here."

"On it."

"We need to bring the cops in on this." Cam was thinking long term on nailing Tim, and he wasn't wrong, but my focus was getting Thea out of there.

"They come in now, they tip him off that we're on to him. You back a man like that into a corner and it doesn't end well," Guy said.

"I agree. Razor will secure the scene, I'll go in through the bedroom"

"We'll go through the bedroom." I knew that tone, Anton wasn't going to be swayed, I didn't argue. I like the odds better with him. "We go through, get Thea out and it's all over. The cops can then stroll in and make the collar."

"As soon as she's clear, you call." Cam was all cop right now.

"Done."

I reached for the door of the van, but Cam stopped me. "Protect her." There was the brother.

"With my life."

THEA

My heart dropped at the knock at the door. The man I had called uncle for as long as I could remember had planted himself in front of the door. He knew I was planning an escape and he wasn't going to let that happen. Bile rushed up my throat, fear making me sick to my stomach as the door was yanked open. For a few seconds I stared mutely convinced I wasn't seeing what I was seeing. Then he spoke. "You rang."

Razor walked into my apartment, stopped and gave me a blatant once over before he winked. "Didn't know there was a bonus to this job."

Tim moved fast, grabbing Razor by the collar. "Hands off. Understood?"

The expression that followed made Razor look like what he was pretending, a killer. "Tap her, but don't tap her. I get it."

"No guns. It has to look like an accident."

"Got it. That'll cost you extra."

"Just get it done. Tonight."

Tim turned to me. "Hired help is not what it used to be. I am so sorry it came to this. It's not personal."

"It feels fucking personal."

He walked over to me and snapped off the necklace from around my neck. "I'll get Rosalie and Cam through this, just like I did with your dad."

"You won't get away with this."

"I already have."

He started for the door, but stopped. "How did you get here so fast?"

My eyes flew to Razor who was as cool as ice, but Tim didn't wait for an answer and moved with surprising speed to haul me against him. A gun appeared, digging into my back."

"Your weapons on the table."

I brought my foot down hard on his before throwing my head back. He released me and I ran right before I heard the shot just as someone fell on top of me, taking me down in a bone-crushing hit. Another shot, then voices coming from down the hall. I tried to move, but whoever was on top of me wasn't moving. I thought it was Tim then realized it was probably Razor and he wasn't moving. The shuffling of feet, the weight at my back lifted and then I was being lifted and pressed against a chest. Cam.

"Razor."

"I'm here, babe."

"But, who was…" I pulled from Cam and turned to see Damian on the floor, Mic and someone I didn't recognize working on him. There was blood, so much blood.

"We need an ambulance right the fuck now."

My head spun right before everything went black.

Damian had taken a bullet intended for me, threw himself in the path of it to protect me. He had come out of surgery, but he had lost a lot of blood and had slipped into a coma. I sat at his bedside, his big hand in mine. I couldn't lose him. I couldn't live in a world without him. I pressed my face to his chest and prayed. Prayed for him to come back to me.

The box of letters that I had written to him sat on my lap. The doctors said he could hear me, that hearing my voice was important, so I sat in that hospital room and read the words my younger self had written, words that still rang true. And when I had read them all, I read them again.

It had been two days. Mom tried to get me to go home, but I didn't want Damian to wake and me not be there. The gang was in the waiting room. They took turns bringing food. I couldn't eat, hadn't in two days. I stayed right at his side, willing him to wake up.

"I'm putting snakes in your bed if you don't wake up—lots of snakes slithering around your legs and over your face. I'll even feed them right on your stomach. Don't test me, Damian. I'll do it."

He was so still except for the even rise and fall of his chest. "There was nothing in Dad's box to implicate Uncle Tim. His own guilt tripped him up. He had had Dad killed before he made the connection, but Dobbs is testifying against him, the recording of him hiring the hit on me, his attempt on you. He's going away for a long time, not even he can get himself out of it. And all his cases are being overturned. Jacob Hunter was re-arrested and is facing another trial." I stroked his arm and touched his face. "There *was* something in Dad's box and it was addressed to you. It was my grandmother's wedding ring. Daddy knew, I think he knew something was going to happen to him. He sent Cam his files and me the key. But Daddy's last gift to me wasn't the key, it was you." I dropped my head because the tears I had been trying so hard to hold back rolled down my cheeks. "You promised me a lifetime."

His hand moved in mine. My eyes flew to his face to see those pale eyes staring back. His voice was so soft but I heard every word, they burned themselves onto my heart. "We'll start with that."

Friends and family came in waves the day following Damian waking up, but now it was just the two of us and with the scare behind us, fear gave way to fury. He almost died and he was the one constantly telling me I did stupid things.

"What were you thinking?"

Even laid up in a hospital bed, the man looked formidable. In response to my question, he raised an eyebrow.

"Putting yourself in the path of a bullet. What the hell, Damian? What if he killed you?"

"Better me than you."

"No. It's not better, not at all."

"It's over, no point on harping."

"You're lying in a hospital bed with tubes and wires. I'll fucking harp."

"You would have been in a wooden box."

"You could have been."

"But I'm not.'"

"It was reckless."

"Come here."

"No."

He started to remove the wires from his arm. I ran to him. "What—"

Even recovering from major surgery the man could move, pulling me on top of him, pressing my body into his. "I've waited a long time for you and now that I finally have you I will move Heaven and Earth to keep you right where I've always wanted you, at my side. I will walk in the rain so you stay dry, I will forgo food so you can eat, I will take the pain so you won't feel any and I will absolutely step in front of danger to keep you safe."

Tears rolled down my cheeks and he wiped them away. "I've waited a long time for you too, so let's get an umbrella big enough for two, let's plant a garden so we always have food, let's share the pain because we have each other to seek comfort in and let's just avoid danger because living a life without you would be worse than death."

He touched my cheek and smiled. "You make some good points."

"Please smile more often."

He kissed me instead.

"You do realize you just spoke like a hundred words in a row. I think that's a record."

His hand moved down my back to my ass where he lightly swatted me. "Behave."

Everything below my waist throbbed. "That's not the way to encourage me to behave."

"When I get you home…"

"Where is home?" I loved New York, but I missed the cottage.

His answer settled happily in my chest. "Wherever you are."

EPILOGUE

It was loud and crowded. The smell of whiskey and rashers filled the tight space. Damian was right at my side, his arm around my waist, his fingers digging into my hip to keep me pressed tight against his side. His soft white shirt felt really nice against my overheated cheek.

Cam's voice carried over the other noises in the pub. "To Thea and Damian. Fucking finally."

"Cameron Edward Ahern. What kind of language is that to use on your sister's wedding day?"

Damian and I got married. He slipped my grandmother's ring onto my finger and promised to smile more, to laugh more. He promised to have my back when the zombie apocalypse came and would keep me stocked in coffee and sugar. And he promised to love me in this life and the next. I promised to not be reckless, to attempt to control my temper. I promised to never lose my sense of humor and to keep us stocked in cookies. And I promised to love him in this life and the next.

Mom was still on a rant, had been since learning of our plans for our wedding. "I still don't understand why we're having the reception at a bar."

Damian pulled me even closer. I glanced up to see him looking back. And then Damian Tate curled his spine and kissed his wife in front of everyone at McGinty's.

"He's running late, but he'll be here soon. He said not to wait."

"We'll wait. We only get together once a month, we'll all eat together."

Mrs. Cooke was sitting at the table in Mom's kitchen rolling out dough for cookies. She had made the move to Mom's permanent. I liked that they had each other, that Mom's house became the hub of the neighborhood and that every night of the week there were people coming and going. Damian bought Mrs. Cooke's house to set up HQ for his security firm, which was financially solvent because their ops had high price tags due to the complexity of them. And there was a need because his team was expanding. He kept her place exactly as she had it and she was able to visit whenever she wanted. She had started baking again. Confessed to us she had stopped because baking had been one of the ways she had shown her love to Mitchell and when he died it hurt too much. I understood that, boy did I understand that. But now that she was among her new family, she was whipping something up every other day.

Ryder strolled into the kitchen, Kimber right on her heels. "Table is set."

"Derrick and Uncle Guy are making drinks. Does anyone want one?"

"Martini for me," Mom said.

"A pink squirrel." Mrs. Cooke had a fondness for all the excessively sweet drinks, but I think she had more fun surprising us with her drink selections.

"Thea?"

"Nothing for me."

I got a look from both Ryder and Kimber, suspicion. I had news. At first I just suspected, but it was confirmed. I wouldn't share until I told Damian. I was a little nervous because though I knew he wanted kids, we hadn't discussed when. It was a little late now.

Anton entered from the back door. His sleeves were rolled up to his elbows. Cam came in right after him. "The firewood is stacked. You got the chimney cleaned, right?"

"Yes, Cam."

"If you run out of wood, let me know. I'll have more dropped off."

Mom rolled her eyes. "It's like I've never lived on my own before."

Anton unrolled his sleeves as he stepped up next to Mom and pressed a kiss on her cheek. "Not at all. It's just love, Rosalie."

Anton had been distracted since it all went down and I knew he had a score to settle with Federico. It scared me, that part of his life, but he had to do what he had to do and I just hoped I could help him when the time came, just like had helped me.

Mom's eyes turned bright. I had two brothers and she had three sons, but that list was growing. Razor, yoga man and Mic had been brought into the fold and with Damian's security team all moving closer to headquarters—Damian claimed it was logistically a good idea, but I knew it was because they were his family in a badass, mercenary kind of way—our makeshift family continued to grow.

Bullet came darting into the kitchen, Matthew right behind him. They both had recently resigned their commissions and were the newest members of Damian's team. As was his way, Bullet dropped on his butt right next to Mom and me, too disciplined to beg for food but ever hopeful.

"He's ridiculous. Six months out of the army and he has completely forgotten his manners," Matthew teased but there was nothing but love in his tone. "Are you still thinking about getting a puppy?" he asked me.

I adored Bullet. We never had pets growing up, but I wanted a dog...so did Damian. "Absolutely."

"When you're ready, we'll talk."

"I'm so ready."

"Alright. After dinner."

"Sounds good."

"I need to take this boy for a walk before dinner. We'll be back."

"Dinner will be ready in about a half an hour," Mom said.

"I'll come with you," Anton offered.

"Me too," Cam and Anton followed Matthew and Bullet outside.

We were just getting the food on the table when Damian arrived. The sight never grew old, watching him. He was still Damian, conserved his words, preferred the background to being the center of attention but I knew he loved me, as deeply and completely as a person could love. He had just reached my side when I grabbed his hand.

"I have to talk to you." He let me pull him out of the room and up to my old bedroom. I shut the door and leaned up against it. He had a wicked little grin on his face.

"Miss me?"

"You know I did, but that's not why I need to talk to you."

I never knew anyone could stand so perfectly still and yet I knew I had his undivided attention.

"We never talked details, but..."

"But what?"

"I'm pregnant."

He had no reaction, just stood there like a statue.

"I suspected, but I went to the doctor today to confirm it. Eight weeks. Baby will be born in May sometime."

Still nothing. I hadn't really been worried, but now I was beginning to.

"Damian?"

And then he was on me, had me pressed up against the door, the fingers of one hand pulled through my hair as his mouth claimed mine. He lifted my skirt, shifted my panties to the side and pulled his cock out, burying himself inside me like he was possessing as much of me as he could. And then he stilled, like he was committing the moment to memory.

"A baby," he whispered.

And I knew that was exactly what he was doing, marking the moment. My heart should have burst it was so full.

No words were needed, the moment deeply poignant and then he lifted my leg to get better penetration just as he rocked his hips. I linked my fingers at his neck and pulled him closer. We found our rhythm and when we came, it was together.

He rested his forehead on mine. "Thank you."

"You're happy?"

He shifted his hips and I bit my lower lip because damn he felt good. "What do you think?"

"We should probably get back. There are two detectives downstairs, they will easily deduce what we're doing up here."

"You're mine." He shifted his hips again. "I don't care if they figure it out."

His hips were picking up speed, hitting me in all the right spots that I didn't care anymore either. He never took his eyes off me as he slowly brought me to orgasm again, and watching him as he found his release, the moment or two when his body gave in, was my favorite because I saw right down to his soul and the depth of what he felt for me. He was beautiful, imperfect and mine.

may sometime

It felt as if I had just fallen asleep when I woke. I reached for Damian but the bed was empty. He stood next to Edie's crib and

Pilot, our German shepherd puppy, stood right next him; we had named our daughter Edie in honor of my dad. I climbed from bed and joined them, my arm coming around his waist as I looked down at our little girl.

"All I feel when I look at her is love, the kind of love I feel for you." He turned those eyes on me. "She's a piece of me."

I swallowed down the sob because I understood. I was his family, Anton, Cam and my mom, he had family, a big and loving one, but this beautiful little girl was a part of him.

His voice broke when he said, "Thank you."

ONE YEAR LATER
Deadwood, South Dakota

We had just landed and were running late. I called mom from the car to let her know we had arrived. She and Pilot were on a walk, he loved going to Grandma's. We had hoped to drop our bags at the cottage but there just wasn't time. Damian kept Amelia's cottage. Right after we got married, we returned to town for a visit. We had missed the reenactment, but it had been so good to get caught up with everyone and not have any drama hanging over our heads.

Damian and I discussed selling the place, but neither of us wanted to. We may not get to visit as often as we wanted, but we liked the idea of having a place when we did, her place.

Edie started clapping her hands in her car seat. She had wild brown hair like me, but she'd gotten Damian's eyes. She adored her daddy and her big, badass daddy adored her right back.

We reached Main Street to see a crowd had gathered at the end of it. Damian walked around the car and helped me from it, his hand lingering longer than needed, his eyes soaking me in like he had a tendency to do. He then freed Edie from her seat, tossed her in the air, which always had my heart stopping and her squealing in delight, before he settled her close to his heart. He reached for my hand and pulled us down the street.

Missy was the first to greet us then Maureen, Dinky and the

others moved in for hugs and kisses. Amelia's items were all back—the recipients of Amelia's things were appalled when they heard the story—and Janice was serving three to five years. We turned toward the bar and the sign that was not yet lit.

"Ready?" Missy asked.

The sign flickered on.

Amelia's

Mom had Edie and Pilot for the evening and having a night off Damian and I had spent it watching scary movies and making love on the sofa. It was late and I woke to find the apartment empty. I knew where he was, so I reached for a blanket and headed to the gym. I passed the table in the living room, then stopped and walked back to study the picture...one of Damian, Edie, Pilot and me. Dad's special box sat next to it and was filled with all the letters I had written to Damian, minus that first letter and the picture of me because he still carried them in his wallet. And just in front were his dog tags. It hadn't been my intention, but I loved the table because it represented the journey it took for Damian and me to get to where we were. I touched his dog tags, thankful that he was home and safe and then I walked down to the gym. He didn't have his late night sessions as often as he used to. The ghosts that haunted him were growing quieter and I liked to believe Edie and I were helping with that.

He was where he'd been that first time I'd seen him working the bag, and like then, he knew when I'd joined him. His back was bare, his devil moving as the muscles worked from his efforts. I moved right into him, wrapping my arms around his waist and pressing a kiss between his shoulder blades...right on the scar from the bullet he had taken for me. He turned and wrapped me in his arms as his chin dipped down, and for a few seconds we just looked our fill before he lifted me into his arms and carried me back upstairs. I had wished as a girl to know all about the quiet, reserved boy he had been, and I did now, I knew every part of his beautiful, complicated and damaged soul and I loved all of him. We reached our bedroom and Damian undressed us both before he pulled me down onto the bed. And to think I had once feared the silence. Words were so overrated.

The series continues with Anton Scalene...
Demon You Love
Winter 2017

OTHER TITLES BY LA....

COLLECTING THE PIECES

At fifteen I fell in love. His name was Jake Stephens and he took the abandoned, lonely girl I had been and made me whole. His love was a pure and unconditional love that made every day better than the last…a fairy tale of my very own.

But this story isn't about Jake. It's about Abel Madden; the man I meet after the fairy tale goes to hell. A cocky, arrogant man who says what he wants, does as he pleases, and makes no excuses for it. He irritates me—downright pisses me off at times—but he also brings me back to life.

My name is Sidney Ellis and this is my story of finding love twice—the first when I needed it most and the second when I never saw it coming.

BEAUTIFULLY DAMAGED

Burdened by a lifetime of horror and heartbreak, amateur fighter Trace Montgomery doesn't want to want the quiet beauty, Ember Walsh. His deep self-loathing keeps him from having any meaningful relationships, but Ember is an itch he can't scratch. The two push and pull, slowly crumbling their walls, seemingly brought together by fate, because the turmoil that haunts their pasts is interlinked in undeniable ways.

HIS LIGHT IN THE DARK

Mia Donati was my conscience when my own faltered and the light that led me home when I had lost my way. The girl who grew into the only woman I would ever love. A woman I had to let go, but when my past comes back to haunt me and I almost lose her, I'm ready to fight for her…fight to find a way back into her heart while keeping the demons from my past from finishing what they started.

ACKNOWLEDGMENTS

Thank you for reading Thea and Damian's story. I hope you enjoyed their journey. It takes so many people to get a book published, so I hope I don't forget anyone.

My Beta Beauties who read every variation of this story from the very first raw draft to the final version, thank you. Your input is invaluable and your friendship means everything...**Elsie, Markella, Devine, Dawn, Meredith, Tammy, Kimmy, Rosemarie, Yolanda, Sue, Ana Kristina, Andie, Raj, Michelle, Kellane, Amber, Donna, Sarah, Helena, Lauren** and **Audrey.**

Trish Bacher, Editor in Heels, this is the fourth book we've worked on together and I'm still amazed at your attention to detail.

Erica Smith for your artistry in building the ebook files.

Hang Le, I love this cover! It took us a while, but you nailed it. It so beautifully represents Damian and Thea. Thank you!

Melissa Stevens, you leave me in awe every time. The typeset and formatting for the paperback are amazing. And the devil tattoo you created is exactly what I envisioned. I can't wait for our next collaboration.

Kiki, Ruth, Amber and Sybil for your tireless work in promoting my books, thank you. You are the best and I adore you.

Kylie and the **Give Me Books** team for helping to get the word out on *Devil You Know*.

And finally thank you to the readers for taking a chance on my books.

ABOUT THE AUTHOR

To learn more about what's coming, follow L.A. Fiore...

https://www.facebook.com/l.a.fiore.publishing
https://www.facebook.com/groups/lafemmefabulousreaders
https://twitter.com/lafioreauthor
https://www.instagram.com/lafiore.publishing

Contact me through email at: lafiore.publishing@gmail.com
Or check out my website: www.lafiorepublishing.com

THE BEAUTIFULLY SERIES...

Beautifully Damaged
Beautifully Forgotten
Beautifully Decadent

THE HARRINGTON MAINE SERIES

Waiting for the One
Just Me

STANDALONES

His Light in the Dark
A Glimpse of the Dream
Always and Forever
Collecting the Pieces
Devil You Know
Elusive: Summer 2017
Demon You Love: Winter 2017

Made in the USA
Middletown, DE
04 April 2017